MICHAEL
DUFFY

THE TOWER

Michael Duffy reports for the *Sydney Morning Herald* on crime and other matters. Previously he wrote for Sydney's other newspaper, the *Daily Telegraph*. He has played in punk rock bands, written biographies of several Sydney characters, and is co-presenter of 'Counterpoint', Radio National's challenge to orthodox ideas. *The Tower* is his first novel.

MICHAEL DUFFY

THE TOWER

To Dorothy,

Michael Duffy

ALLEN&UNWIN

First published in 2009

Allen & Unwin
83 Alexander Street
Crows Nest NSW 2065
Australia
Phone: (61 2) 8425 0100
Fax: (61 2) 9906 2218
Email: info@allenandunwin.com
Web: www.allenandunwin.com

Cataloguing-in-Publication details are available
from the National Library of Australia
www.librariesaustralia.nla.gov.au

ISBN 978 1 74175 813 9

Set in 12/15 pt Granjon by Midland Typesetters, Australia
Printed and bound in Australia by Griffin Press

10 9 8 7 6 5 4 3 2 1

For Max Suich,
who brought me back to crime

The woman was falling close to the building, down the face of the enormous, unfinished skyscraper. She fell in silence, turning slowly, through the mist and light rain.

The police car far below was creeping up the inside lane next to The Tower. It was moving tentatively because it was night, and because of the rain. The woman landed on top of the vehicle with a loud crash, the force of the impact partially crushing the roof.

It took the two uniformed officers a while to get out of the car. When they did, one of them was sick in the gutter. His partner took a few steps backwards, her eyes fixed on the dead woman on the roof. She had obviously fallen from a very long way up.

SUNDAY

One

'Are you there yet?'

'Almost.'

He slipped under the blue and white tape and approached the constable with the clipboard. 'Senior Constable Nicholas Troy,' he said. 'Homicide.' He thrust his ID at the man, then continued talking into his mobile.

'I'll cancel tomorrow night?'

'Go by yourself,' he said. 'Get Aleisha to babysit.'

'You just want her at home by yourself.'

'Ha ha. We already bought the present. You should go.'

'Maybe.'

He reached the place and stopped. They'd already set up lights and you could see every detail. He'd been twelve years in the job, four in Homicide. But this was something new.

'I've got to go to work now,' he said, and disconnected.

In front of him was a police patrol car with a woman lying face down on its roof. There was something strange about the body, which seemed to have been compressed to some state between three dimensions and two. Crime scene officers and police were walking around the car, unusually quiet. Troy could see that they too were marvelling at the odds of the woman striking a moving car, let alone one of theirs.

And then there was the building.

The place was called The Tower and it was still a construction site. The project was massive in every way. When it had been conceived it was to be the tallest building in the world, although it had been overtaken by a skyscraper in Dubai recently. Occupying an entire city block, its progress through conception, planning and construction had been dogged by controversy. Colourful characters, a bankruptcy, allegations of corruption: the story of the place had grown as big as the structure.

He turned back to the body embedded in the car roof. The woman had long black hair and her skull had partially disintegrated. Blood covered the top of the car and some of the windows, especially the windscreen. The most disturbing aspect was the woman's limbs, which had snapped and hung over the sides of the roof at disturbing angles. A young security guard was standing next to Troy, staring. Suddenly he clasped a hand to his mouth and ran away.

Troy looked some more. The woman was wearing a very short black dress and it had ridden up so that her buttocks were visible. Her knickers were minimal and lacy, and for a moment Troy thought of Anna. The thought came to him and for a moment he couldn't do anything about it. He hadn't seen his wife in anything like that since before their son had been born eighteen months ago. He turned to a uniformed sergeant and asked, 'Shoes?'

No shoes had been found. No bag either. Nothing had come off the body, and the only jewellery the victim was wearing was a large bracelet on her left wrist. Troy moved around and examined the silver band set with glittering stones—fake, presumably. Anna liked jewellery, but he suspected she'd turn her nose up at something as gaudy as this.

He blinked and looked away, and saw McIver standing nearby. The sergeant hadn't shaved and was wearing a leather jacket over a black T-shirt and jeans. Troy wondered if he'd been drinking. The on-call team wasn't supposed to drink, but the sergeant did things his own way.

'You got here quickly,' Troy said.

'I was in The Rocks. Enjoying myself.'

They shook hands; the Homicide Squad handled murders all over the state, and McIver had been in Moree for the past few months.

'Anna's well?' the sergeant asked. 'And Matt?'

Troy nodded. McIver's third wife had left him last year, and as far as he knew there was no one else in his life to ask about. There were no children. He was wondering what to say when he heard a voice from behind.

'Filthy McIver.'

A guy in a suit had appeared. He was about fifty, and had a moustache, quite a good effort. You didn't see many of those anymore.

'Do I know you?' McIver said. The two men stared at each other and Troy watched patiently: the newcomer bloated and red-faced, McIver a bit younger, lean and tense. Finally McIver relented and said to Troy, 'Detective Sergeant Bruce Little, City Central.'

They shook hands.

Troy asked if they had a name for the victim, and Little said there was no identification on her. 'No room for any,' he said softly, looking at the half-naked body on the roof of the car. An inspector from City Central, Gina Harmer, was inside the building, he told them, organising a search. She was the local officer in charge of the scene.

Uniformed police had been arriving, pausing to look at the body before going into the building. Now crime scene officers began to erect a screen around the car, and one of them bumped into an onlooker.

'Let's clear the area,' McIver said loudly. 'I don't want anyone here who's not supposed to be here.'

The other people standing around ignored him.

'Some of the blokes want to have a look,' Little said. 'Anything to do with The Tower, big deal around here.'

'And when I say not anyone,' McIver said slowly, raising his voice, 'I mean no one.'

'Crime scene's not here,' Little protested. 'Up there.'

He gestured with his thumb.

McIver stared at him for so long without saying anything that Little looked at Troy for help. When none was offered, he turned to go.

'Are you and I going to have an argument?' McIver yelled.

People were paying attention now. Troy took a step towards him and stopped, unsure of what to do. It was always hard to know how pissed the sarge was when he'd been drinking. Right now he was swaying slightly, but Troy knew this mightn't mean much.

Little kept walking.

Here we go, Troy thought. Here we go.

But after a moment McIver seemed to forget Little.

'Anyone else here yet?' he asked Troy. 'What about Vella?'

Troy shook his head. Don Vella, the inspector in charge of the team, lived in Mount Annan, nearly an hour south-west of Sydney's CBD; he'd be some time yet.

McIver walked around to the other side of the car, keeping his big hands in his pockets, as he always did at a crime scene. Usually he was the most restless of men, and Troy guessed this was his way of restraining his imagination, forcing himself to do nothing except observe. McIver looked at the car and then raised his eyes to the top of the building. 'What are the chances?' Troy followed his gaze up; the skyscraper disappeared into the unseasonal mist after maybe ten storeys. It was clad in glass and stone as far as he could see, but he knew the upper section was still just a steel and concrete skeleton. Since the windows didn't open, the woman must have fallen from somewhere up there.

He wandered over to where Little was lighting a cigarette.

'You ever been up there?'

Little nodded. 'They show us around every few months, in case we get called in.'

'How could she have come off? I thought they had some sort of steel screen around all the floors where the walls haven't been finished.'

'Landing platforms, one on each floor until it's done. They stick out so the crane can unload stuff. Wall around them maybe so high.' He held a hand level with his waist. Then, 'Ought to do something about McIver. He's not in a fit state.'

'What?' said Troy, who'd been wondering if there were any platforms above the spot where the woman had landed.

Little's gaze shifted as McIver joined them.

'So what are we doing here?' Mac said. It was a reasonable question. Homicide dealt with murders, and there was no evidence this woman had been pushed. He yawned, but Troy knew he was not as bored as he seemed. If he really thought it was a suicide he would have left by now. Something in the situation had caught his attention.

Little took the cigarette out of his mouth. 'The problem is how she could have got in, just someone wanted to kill herself. This place has good security. Our super says it's likely she's brought in with a van.'

For some reason this seemed to annoy McIver. 'Ron's a bit of a thinker, is he?' He looked at Troy: 'Ron Siegert.'

'Point is,' said Little, 'makes it less likely she killed herself, if she was here doing something with other people. People like privacy to kill themselves. Maybe here on business.' He stabbed in the direction of the building with his cigarette. 'Maybe a prozzie, brought in for the guys working here tonight.'

Little sounded excited. Troy wondered how he'd made it to sergeant. But there were so many ways.

'And if she *was* killed,' Little continued, 'we were here within minutes. Could have blocked off the escape route of whoever done it. Only two ways out.' He pointed to the uniforms standing outside the pedestrian entrance to the building, and the one for vehicles just up the road. 'The killer might still be around.'

Troy looked at the lower storeys of The Tower. Like all construction sites in the city, it was surrounded by a high temporary wall. He pulled out a piece of gum and slowly unwrapped it.

'How many storeys is it?' he asked Little.

'One-twenty. But it's stepped in away from the road at forty on this side, so she must have come off there or lower.' The three men stared up into the dark. 'The glass goes up about twenty levels. So far.'

Troy grunted, thinking about the manpower they'd need to search a building this size.

Little's radio crackled and he turned away and had a brief conversation.

'Harmer says she'll be out soon,' he said, turning back. 'She's just sent up two search groups.'

McIver said, 'So where's the great man?'

'The super?'

'Himself.'

'Back at the station. That New Zealand game at the Football Stadium was called off because of the weather. He managed to get the uniforms before they were sent home.'

McIver walked away from them, back to the car, where he had a word with the crime scene officers. Troy was about to follow when Little said, 'Siegert calls The Tower a red ball, something he picked up in the States. Anything happens here is a media event, means it could get political. For him.'

'I remember there were some base jumpers,' Troy said, looking at Little's cigarette. He'd never smoked himself, but sometimes wished he had, to help fill in the time. A cop spent a lot of his life waiting around. Gum was all right but it wasn't the same.

Little nodded. 'Six guys got up to level forty and jumped off. Landed in Hyde Park. They got someone to film them and sold the footage around the world. That's when they brought in Siegert. The old super was put out to pasture.'

'Hardly his fault,' Troy said.

Security for The Tower was in the hands of a private company. He had seen a few of the guards wandering around in their dark grey uniforms.

'These days, never know whose fault anything is,' Little said, vaguely but with feeling.

McIver was coming back from the car, looking around. Looking bored.

'Keep an eye on these turnips,' he said to Troy, indicating the crime scene officers with a tilt of his chin.

'Where are you going?'

6

'See Harmer,' McIver said, and walked off in the direction of the entrance to the building site. After pausing to allow several uniformed officers to precede him, he disappeared inside.

Troy saw a GMO he recognised further up Norfolk Street, at the barrier. The medical officer gave his name to the uniform with the clipboard and approached the detectives. They spoke for a while and then Little went behind the screens with him. Troy stood by himself, feeling the cold move up through his shoes. He thought about calling Anna but she might still be putting Matt to bed. Their son had asthma, which seemed to mean a lot of work, what with the medication and cleaning the house. Much of this fell on Anna's shoulders, and he felt a bit guilty because he was often away on jobs. She didn't complain, but once the boy was asleep at night, she liked to have half an hour or so to herself. It was her way of coping. He looked at his watch and decided to give it more time.

Two

T his list of countries,' she said, 'what's it for?'

Sean Randall paused naked in the doorway, his half-erection not sure which way to go. Kristin was sitting on the side of the bed, bent over his wallet. God, she was white. Randall was Irish and he'd seen a lot of pale women, but not white like this, about as white as a person could be.

'You shouldn't go through my stuff,' he said.

There'd been a girl once, Moira he thought her name was, who'd help herself to a line if he left the room for even a minute. Nose on her like a vacuum cleaner, good healthy appetite. But he couldn't recall anyone going through his wallet before.

'I know,' she said, looking at him bold-eyed. Taking things between them to a new level. 'But I like to know about the men I spend time with.' Looking around the bedroom: 'It's not like you leave many clues.'

It was only a rented place. Nice big colour photo of the Taipei 101 tower on the cream wall. Stacks of *Wired* and *Fast Company* on the beige carpet. Big television in the corner, connected to the small digital video camera on its slender tripod. All their clothes scattered around, phones and shit on the bedside table.

'What's that rock?' she said, pointing to a chunk the size of a baby's head lying on the floor.

Randall smiled. They all asked that. 'Jack Taylor, my boss, went to Italy to select the marble for The Tower's lobby. You go to this huge quarry and look at all these huge lumps of the stuff, make your choice. When it turned up here six months later it was different—they'd substituted some flawed stuff for what Jack had picked. So he asked me to go over and sort it out.'

It was a good story. He'd flown over, selected some good stuff, huge rocks as high as he was, and signed his name on them with a big marker pen, then taken photographs of each rock. Attention to detail. Finally, just as he was leaving, he'd given the quarry sales manager an envelope. First-class return tickets for two to the Gold Coast, a week's accommodation at the Palazzo Versace.

'We got the right marble,' he said, and saw she was impressed, despite herself. This was good.

He felt his erection stiffening and came into the room and sat down, running his hand down her back as the give of the mattress pushed their thighs together.

'Come here,' he said.

Kristin turned and kissed him. Her lips were thin and her breasts small. In many ways she was not especially feminine, although her arse was big enough. But she was very determined, about everything, and he was enjoying that. His last girlfriend, if you could call her that, had tended to get emotional about things. Randall liked variety.

'So why are thirty-eight of the countries marked?'

He took her hand and put it on his thigh, feeling the small piece of paper drop between his legs. 'They're the ones I've been to. I want to visit every country on earth one day.'

She frowned in concentration and he waited patiently, working on her spine with his nails.

Eventually she shivered and said, 'I've been to thirty-two. How old are you?'

'Thirty-four.'

'Well, I'm only twenty-eight.'

They kissed for a while but then she stopped. 'You never told me you'd been to Iceland. Who do you know there?'

She was from Iceland, worked for the United Nations or some related NGO—she'd told him the first time they'd met but he hadn't taken much notice. He recalled her saying her organisation helped women who'd been trafficked for sex, and guessed she must be a player to get sent to Sydney, a far more pleasant posting than most places with trafficking problems. Randall liked players.

'I was flying from New York to Frankfurt one time and we had to land, some engine thing,' he said, licking her ear. 'Only an hour, we didn't even get off the plane.'

'So you're cheating,' she said.

'That's right.'

She put her arms around him and pushed him down on the bed, each of them a little excited now.

After a bit, she said, 'Is the camera on?'

'I thought you didn't like it.'

'I want it now. But don't get up.'

'It's okay,' he said, reaching out while she sat up, running her fingernails down his chest. He felt around on the bedside table, careful not to knock the open wrapper of coke, eventually locating what he was looking for. It had been difficult to find a camera with a remote control, and he'd wondered what other people used it for.

'Let's make a movie,' she said, coming down at him with her tongue out, her backside wiggling at the camera.

This, he thought, is going to be good.

But then the phone rang.

Three

McIver had been gone a while and Troy was starting to feel anxious. He was pretty sure the sarge was pissed. You were supposed to look out for fellow team members, but with McIver it was hard because he did like a drink. He thought about the last time they'd worked together, a domestic killing at Forbes. They'd been away for almost a month, which was not unusual. McIver had spent every evening with colleagues or acquaintances he made in town. Sometimes he would ask the motel where they were staying to provide a room so they could watch a DVD. He had a big collection, with lots of Westerns. Troy didn't like Westerns usually, but Mac's were pretty good. When it wasn't a film night, McIver would be at a pub or club, often with his guitar. He had a fine voice, and could play just about anything, though he had a particular liking for old American songs, blues and country. But always there was a bottle nearby.

Unsure what to do next, Troy headed over to the entrance to the construction site. When a security guard asked him his name, he produced his ID and went inside. In theory he should wait for instructions from McIver, who was his boss. But Mac didn't work like that. He decided to talk to the head of security.

The space—what would be the atrium of the building—was enormous, perhaps five storeys high, and well lit. Three portable offices were stacked at the far end. He had a word to one of the guards and was directed to an office. As he walked towards it, breathing the cold smell of concrete, someone called out to him. He turned and saw a short woman standing next to a man, both of them in uniform. The woman was about fifty with blonde hair. She would have been attractive once, he thought.

'Inspector Gina Harmer,' she said, extending her hand.

She had one of those looks that told you she was sizing you up, wanted you to know. As they shook hands her phone rang. She began a conversation about manpower and the guy next to her made notes on a clipboard he was holding. After a while, Troy continued on his way.

As he climbed the metal stairs he could hear raised voices inside. He opened a door with a sign saying SECURITY, and found two men standing by some sort of control panel. One, who looked Lebanese, was in a security guard's uniform. He appeared fit and alert, unlike some people in his line of work. The other was a tall guy in a suit, his head shaved, one of those stupid little clumps of hair just below his bottom lip. They stopped talking when Troy came in, and introduced themselves. Peter Bazzi was the shift manager for Tryon, the company that protected The Tower. Sean Randall was security manager for Warton Constructions.

'I just arrived,' he said with an Irish accent, coming over and clasping Troy's hand. 'Peter here called me at home. It's a terrible thing that's happened. Of course we'll give you our full cooperation.'

You will, Troy thought, as he wrote their names in his notebook.

He said, 'What were you arguing about just now?'

'It's your colleague. Peter let him go up unaccompanied. It's not company policy—we have liability issues.'

Troy looked at him more closely. Despite the annoyance the guy was showing, he had amiable eyes. Troy figured that, unlike many security managers, he was not ex-police.

'Do we know who the woman was?'

Randall's smile faded and he looked away from Troy.

Bazzi said, 'There's no record of a woman coming onto the site tonight.'

'I'll take that as a no?'

The guard looked anxious, almost distressed. He shrugged. 'At the moment we just don't know what's happened.'

No wonder the two men had been yelling at each other.

Troy looked out the window and saw the inspector still standing in the middle of the atrium, briefing another group of police. The search operation had been organised with impressive speed, especially for a Sunday night. He turned back to the various computer consoles. 'So where's Sergeant McIver?'

'There are two search groups up there,' Randall explained. 'One moving up the building and the other coming down from level forty, which is the highest point where she could have come off. Your sergeant said he was going to join the upper sweep, which had just reached level thirty-five. So Peter sends him up with one of our guards—you need a pass to operate the lift. But your sergeant tells the guard to stop at level thirty. The man protests but in the end does what he's told. McIver gets off and the guard comes back. This is making us nervous.'

Dealing with McIver tended to have that effect on people, Troy thought.

'If there is a killer up there,' Bazzi said, 'they could meet.'

That might be the killer's problem. McIver was armed and dangerous and under the influence. But he should be up there too, watching the sergeant's back.

'How long's he been gone?'

'Almost ten minutes now. I was just going to have a word with Inspector Harmer.'

Not a good idea, Troy thought. He said, 'I'll go up and get him back. Would that make you happier?'

Bazzi shook his head, but Randall looked at his watch. 'I'll come with you. You'll need someone to work the lift.'

Troy nodded. Despite the flavour-saver, the guy looked capable enough. Also, he didn't seem the type to make a fuss. Depending on the state they found McIver in, that could be important.

They clattered down the steel stairway and walked across the concrete floor towards the lifts—though only the two goods lifts were in use, according to Randall.

Troy said, 'Do you need a pass for the stairwells?'

It turned out that you didn't; in fact at the moment you didn't need a pass to get from a stairwell onto any of the floors. Randall went into a little speech about how security had to be a compromise between ideal standards and the requirements of construction. Troy found himself paying attention, despite the irrelevance of most of this. Randall was a natural talker, and it wasn't just the accent. He told Troy there were CCTV cameras trained on the lifts and the stair exits on the ground floor, which was how they knew the killer hadn't come down that way. 'If there is a killer,' he added.

'Is there a digital record of lift movements?'

'No,' said Randall, his amiability dropping a few notches. 'I wish there was. The system doesn't do that. It can do a lot. Turn a lift on and off. Make a pass inactive with the hit of a button. But there is no historical record.'

'So we don't know how the victim got up there?'

'No. But someone was watching the CCTV monitors here all the time from the moment we knew she'd fallen. So we're sure no one has come out of the lifts or the stairwells since she fell. There was no time. And this is the only way out.'

'Apart from the vehicle exit,' Troy said.

'Sure. But that's well guarded too, and we've checked the CCTV. Nothing.'

'We'll need the discs.'

'Harmer has them already.'

He continued to walk towards the lifts, but Troy stopped and pulled out his notebook to record the information he'd just been given. He'd always assumed construction sites were fairly simple places, but this didn't sound simple. While he was writing, Inspector Harmer left the group of uniforms nearby and came over to him.

'I don't want anyone up there until we've cleared the building,' she said.

She was very short. Whatever the lower height limit had been when she'd joined the force, she must have only just scraped in.

Troy said, 'I won't get in the way of your operation.'

'I believe your colleague's already up there?'

He nodded, and sensed from the look in her eyes that she knew it was McIver, knew something about him, and was not entirely happy. He often saw that look in the eyes of older cops.

'I can't spare anyone to go up with you at the moment,' she said. 'Give us half an hour, I'd appreciate it.'

The cop with the clipboard called out to Harmer, waving a mobile phone. She frowned at Troy and looked as though she was about to say more, but then the man called her again, urgency in his voice, and she walked away. Troy gave her a few seconds and then continued on his way to the lifts. If you were in McIver's team, you had to play by his logic. Fuzzy logic. If Harmer did know him, she'd realise this.

'Everything okay?' said Randall.

'Fine.'

The lift doors opened and they got in. The lift was big, with posters on the battered metal walls advertising safety regulations and a union finance company. As they ascended, Randall was quiet, staring at the flashing numbers above the door, biting his lip. He was wearing a bulky orange jacket now, and holding two hard hats. He handed one to Troy, and told him he had to put it on.

'OH and S,' he said.

Troy put it on, and thought about what he'd learned so far.

'It's Bazzi, isn't it?'

The Irishman's face was blank. 'What's Bazzi?'

'You record the name of everyone who comes onto the site?'

'If they're walking. And if it's a van, we check the driver's ID and record the rego number. Make sure it's supposed to be here.'

'Well,' Troy said, 'for a woman to be on the site with no record, the shift manager must be involved. It would take some arranging. I don't see how it could be done otherwise.'

Randall said nothing, his eyes still fixed on the flashing numbers. Then, as the lift stopped at level thirty: 'Until tonight, I had every reason to trust the fellow.'

The first thing Troy noticed when the doors opened was the wind. Randall had been zipping up his jacket in the lift, and now Troy knew why. Thirty storeys above the ground, no windows, the wind came straight at you, right through your clothes like you were being snap-frozen. The two men stepped out of the lift and the doors closed behind them. Apart from a light next to a stairwell nearby, the floor was in darkness. The temperature seemed to drop another few degrees.

Troy shivered. 'Sarge?' he called.

There was no answer, and the wind was so loud it was unlikely he'd be heard anyway. Taking out his mobile, he turned his back to the wind and dialled McIver's number. He put the phone to his ear but there was so much noise he could hardly make out the dial tone.

Randall had produced a powerful torch from somewhere. He turned it on and they walked around the floor, bare concrete with occasional piles of pipes and cable. They moved cautiously because of the darkness. Randall talked as they went. Maybe it was nerves, but he seemed to feel a compulsive need to explain everything they saw, yelling to make himself heard above the noise of the wind. Troy resisted the urge to tell him to shut up.

When they got to the edge of the floor Troy saw it was ringed with an impressive-looking steel fence broken at one point by a gap. This led onto the landing platform, which protruded a few metres from the side of the building. The wind was coming more strongly through the gap, and he felt it as he walked out and looked over the side. Far below he could see the enclosure that had been placed around the police car, illuminated by the lights inside so that it resembled a lampshade. He stepped back, the rain on his face, and looked around the desolate platform. Its base was made of iron plates, slick with water, and it would be easy to climb over the metal walls. Or be thrown. There were no shoes here, no coat or handbag. With some relief he went back onto the solid concrete, and they continued their search.

After they'd been around half the floor, with Randall yelling out comments, Troy suggested they split up. He wanted to send him back to the part they'd already covered, just to get the sound of him out of the way. But Randall said he thought they should stick together. He put out an arm as he said it, as though wanting to stop Troy from leaving him.

Troy called McIver's number again, and this time held it to his ear until it rang out. Bloody McIver, he thought. Should never have let him out of my sight. Then he heard something else—a cracking sound.

'That was a fucking gun!' said Randall.

Troy felt anxiety start to form in his stomach. 'Do you think the noise came from above or below?' he said, hurrying towards the stairwell.

'Below.' Randall sounded panicky.

Troy thought it had come from above, although with the wind you couldn't be sure. He wondered what McIver would have done, whether he would have gone up towards one group of searchers or down towards the other.

'Let's go up,' he decided.

Troy stepped into the stairwell cautiously. Randall almost pushed him inside and shut the door behind them. It was very bright.

'You keep the lights on all the time?'

Randall nodded jerkily. 'OH and S,' he muttered, as though this explained everything.

Troy stood for a few moments listening. There was no noise. He reached beneath his coat and pulled out his gun.

'Have you ever shot anyone with that?' Randall asked, looking at the pistol.

'I've never drawn it in my current position,' Troy said. 'Homicide's a safe job. Usually.'

'It's a Glock, isn't it?'

'It's a Glock.'

They climbed the stairs to the next level and he steeled himself and opened the door and stepped out. This floor was dark too, and at first glance seemed identical to the floor below, but Troy sensed a difference in the atmosphere. Reminding himself to breathe, trying not to hold his weapon too tightly, he whispered to Randall to turn off his torch and stay back. Instinctively, he began to walk towards the goods lifts. Just before he reached the corner, a figure came stumbling around it towards him. Troy raised his gun, but dropped his arm when he saw it was McIver, clasping his left shoulder and clearly on the point of collapse.

'Two of them at the lifts,' he gasped, opening his arms to Troy. 'One armed with a pistol. Mine.' For a moment the expression of pain on the sergeant's face was replaced by a scowl. Troy reached out and grabbed him beneath his leather jacket, taking his weight, seeing there was blood on his face. He could smell the alcohol on McIver's breath, and the stink of his sweat.

McIver sagged and put his good arm around Troy, and the two men clung to each other in an awkward embrace, the Glock in Troy's right hand now under the sergeant's left armpit, caught beneath his jacket. Troy was about to lower the sergeant to the ground when a man appeared.

The man took a step forwards and Troy saw that he was waving a gun.

'Give me your pass to the lifts,' he demanded.

An accent, possibly Indian. Troy peered at his face. Maybe Afghan or Pakistani.

'We're police officers. Let me put Sergeant McIver down, he's been shot,' Troy said, trying to keep his voice calm and level.

This seemed to upset the man. 'Just give me the pass,' he said, 'or I will shoot you.' He sounded agitated, and the hand holding the gun was shaking.

'Why don't you put the gun down?' Troy said. 'This man's a police officer and—'

'Is he dead?' the man cried.

'No, he's not dead.'

Despite his racing pulse, Troy found he was thinking quite clearly. The man sounded terrified. If he had killed the woman who'd come off the building, he might do anything to get away.

'I'll just put this man down so I can reach for the pass,' Troy said loudly and slowly. He wondered where Randall was, if he could hear. 'I can't reach it at the moment.'

As he spoke he felt McIver gathering himself, taking his own weight on the left side. Troy was able to adjust his right hand slightly.

'Throw me the pass right away or I'm going to shoot.' As the man brought his other arm up to steady his grip on the gun, Troy was certain the man was about to shoot them. He pulled the trigger of his own weapon, firing through the back of McIver's leather jacket.

The shot struck the man in the chest. He looked surprised but didn't fall. Troy fired again, and the man collapsed.

The wind was louder now, blowing across the floor, blowing right through him. Just like that, he thought. Just like that, I have killed a man. Never done that before. He wondered why he felt so calm. Slowly, he lowered McIver to the ground. He looked around but, as he'd expected, Randall was nowhere to be seen.

When he looked back at the man he'd shot, he saw that another man had darted from the shadows. He was kneeling on the ground next to the dead man, shaking him and calling out in evident distress. Troy sprang to his feet and pointed his gun at the newcomer. 'Police,' he yelled. 'Stand up and put your hands in the air.'

In the semi-darkness he could not see what had happened to the dead man's gun. On the ground, McIver groaned.

The kneeling man stood up slowly. There was something in one of his hands, but it looked too bulky to be a gun. Troy kept his own weapon trained on the man, telling himself not to press the trigger by mistake.

'Move slowly away from the body,' he yelled. 'Place any items in your hands on the ground, place your hands on your head.'

He knew he was making the right moves. They trained you for this, and now the training was kicking in.

But the man must have been to a different course. He took a few steps and then bolted into the shadows. Troy just stood there, trying to make out his footsteps. Then there was the sound of a door banging shut nearby; the man had doubled back around the core of the building. Now there were muffled shouts in the stairwell. Randall must have taken refuge there, and the man had run into him.

Then there was nothing except the noise of the wind. Dropping to one knee next to McIver, he took his coat off and rolled it up, putting it beneath the sergeant's head, fumbling in the gloom. McIver's eyes were closed and he appeared to have lost consciousness. He heard the stairwell door slam again, and just as he was rolling McIver onto his side a torch beam illuminated the sergeant's body. It was wavering and Troy yelled for Randall to keep it still.

'He took my pass,' Randall said. 'He hit me.'

He sounded distressed but Troy didn't look up. He used the light to examine McIver, wondering why he was unconscious when he'd been shot in the upper arm. There was a lot of blood on his head too—the hair at the back was warm and sticky—yet there was no sign of a gunshot wound there.

Randall pulled off his padded jacket and laid it over McIver's lower body to keep him warm. Now he was speaking into his radio, asking for Bazzi, talking to someone else, then to Harmer, reporting that McIver had been shot. Randall's teeth were chattering as he spoke, and Troy was shivering himself. The wind had picked up.

'Tell her he might have McIver's weapon, and tell her about your pass,' Troy called out. 'And get the torch over here.'

He needed to look at the man he'd shot, see if McIver's gun was gone, but at the moment it was more important to stay here, keep pressure on McIver's arm and make sure he didn't choke.

He felt angry. Not angry that McIver had got himself shot, or even angry at the man who had shot him, but angry that the sergeant was unconscious, that there might be something seriously wrong with him and that he didn't know what it was. That he was helpless to fix it.

Randall was holding the beam of light over them again, a little steadier now. Looking down at the orange coat over McIver's lower body, Troy saw there was blood on it that couldn't have come from the sergeant. He glanced up at Randall and for the first time noticed the blood on the other man's forehead.

'You okay?'

'The man had a pistol. I was trying to use the radio, it wasn't working in there and he came barging into the stairwell. He just belted me across the head. I wasn't ready for it.' He sounded almost apologetic.

'It's okay,' Troy said.

'I guess you guys get trained for this sort of thing.'

'We do,' Troy said, wondering if Randall was in shock. 'You're okay now. So the man had a gun?'

'Yes. He hit me with it.'

Troy told Randall to contact his base again and get them to tell Harmer the man definitely had a gun.

'I already did, like you told me to.' Randall was speaking very quickly.

'You told her he *might* have a weapon,' Troy explained. 'Now you tell her he's *definitely* got one.'

When Randall had finished speaking into his radio, he said to Troy, 'They'll be here any minute.'

'Was the man carrying anything else?'

'I think he had a handbag.'

It must be the victim's. They needed to tell Harmer this, too.

Troy wondered where the man with the gun might be by now. He might be downstairs in the atrium, trying to shoot his way out. It might be all over.

Randall straightened up suddenly. 'I've got to make a call.' He was fumbling in his pocket, looking anxious. 'I've got to ring my boss.'

'I think he'd know already.'

'No.'

Randall was turning to walk away.

'Wait,' Troy ordered. 'Call Bazzi. Ask him if he saw the lift come down.'

'Call Bazzi?' Randall said a little wildly as a lift door opened, blinding them with its light, and a small crowd of cops and paramedics rushed out. 'I can't. Harmer told me before. Bazzi's disappeared.'

Four

Twenty minutes later, back at ground level and out on the street, Troy watched as the ambulance with McIver inside left for Royal Prince Alfred. The sarge was still unconscious. One of the paramedics had told Troy the bullet that ripped open his arm had probably shocked him into tripping over, and he'd hit his head when he fell. This could sometimes lead to recurrent blackouts.

Don Vella had turned up with two more detectives, and they were up on level thirty-one. The head of the police media unit was around somewhere, and had told Troy not to speak to anyone. Not that he would: it was standard procedure to refuse to talk to the media unless you had the go-ahead from a senior officer. Sometimes police leaked information, but it was not something Troy had ever done.

Homicide Commander Helen Kelly had arrived at City Central and was talking to Ron Siegert. Other detectives would be going to the hospital to be with McIver. Having any officer down was a major event and Troy couldn't remember the last time a homicide detective had been shot. Kelly had said the same when they'd spoken briefly on the phone a few minutes earlier. Then, 'But if it had to be anyone, it was going to be Jon.' For a second Troy wondered who she was talking about, then realised Jon was McIver's first name. He hoped

23

he wasn't going into shock himself. Of course he was upset by what had happened, but the emotion seemed to be restricted to one part of his mind, a small part, and the rest of him seemed to be functioning normally.

Upstairs, after the medics had taken over from him, he'd searched the clothes of the man he'd shot. Probably he shouldn't have done this; physical evidence would need to swab him for gunshot residue. Kelly had said something about this on the phone. But with the shortage of officers and the speed things were going, he needed to do what he could, see if there was anything that might identify the man.

He couldn't look at the face. It was strange—him being a homicide cop it shouldn't bother him—but he hadn't wanted to see the man's face. The guy had no wallet, no ID, nothing at all. He'd explained this to Harmer when she arrived. She'd told him to go down to ground level and leave the investigation to other officers.

Now that he had nothing to do but wait, he was feeling odd. Not traumatised, nothing like that, but as though he were floating. He wondered if this was how it would be, or if it would all come down on him at some point.

His mind drifted back to his conversation with Kelly, who'd said, 'We're going to have to be very careful about all of this, you two being where you shouldn't, and then the shooting. Siegert's very unhappy. I suppose you went up to help McIver. I mean, Harmer told you not to, but I suppose you felt you had to help a fellow officer?'

'That's right,' he said, wondering where this was going; wondering if he should tell her what state McIver had been in, but knowing he wouldn't. He had felt the stirring of something. A different kind of danger.

Kelly said, 'Just be careful. I'd hate to see your career affected because of the sergeant.'

'What do you mean?' he said.

Until tonight he'd had few dealings with Kelly, and didn't know how to read her.

'I'm not saying there are any problems, Nick. I don't know enough about it yet. But when you make your statement, just think about what you're saying. All right?'

'Sure I will.'

'No, I mean *really* think.'

He knew he had to work this out for himself, but at the moment nothing much was coming. She had told him to wait at the scene until Internal Affairs arrived to interview him.

'Does this mean I'm off the investigation?' he said.

'Of course you are. Just keep an eye on things until I get there. You heard about this double stabbing at Bourke yesterday?' Troy had. It meant the squad—six months into a hiring freeze and already understaffed—was now desperately short of people.

Soon after she'd hung up, Anna called.

'You hungry?' she said.

'No.'

'Dry?'

'Yes.'

'Warm?'

'Of course.'

'You're lying.'

It was a ritual, based on some advice a sergeant had given him years ago: a cop should never be hungry, cold, wet or tired. She didn't ask if he was tired because she knew all about the rush he got at the start of the case, the rush that could keep him going without sleep for twenty-four hours or more.

'How's Matt?' he asked.

'He's good.'

'What you doing, watching TV?'

'Nothing on. I might have an early night.'

He thought about telling her what had happened, but if he did she'd stay up for him and he didn't want that. Not tonight. Things were not right between them, and sometimes it was easier to deal with stuff by himself. These days she slept on the couch in Matt's room, using his condition as an excuse. As though asthma was some life-threatening disease. In some ways for Troy that was better than having her in the room with him, there but not there. When he got home tonight he knew he'd just want to sleep, not be reminded of the state of his marriage.

He told her he had to go and disconnected, glad she wasn't watching television and didn't listen to the radio at night. News of the shooting would be all over the place by now.

Maybe he should have told the man he had a gun and would fire. There was no obligation for him to do this, but maybe he should have. Like maybe he should have been up there with McIver in the first place. He puzzled over this for a while, wondering if he could have handled it differently, come out of the situation with the guy alive. Nothing came to mind. He wondered if he was being too easy on himself, if his mind just didn't want to do that sort of hard work at the moment.

Troy stood in the drizzle for a while, staring up at the skyscraper. It was hard to avoid looking at it, yet when you did, your mind sort of froze, as if it was just too big to comprehend. There was one light on the edge of each storey, one above the other. The mist had gone and the column of dim lights extended up higher than before. Maybe he could see as far up as level forty, when the building stepped back, but he doubted it. The rain in his eyes made it hard to count the floors. Lowering his head, he became aware there were more people around, including lines of spectators at either end of the section of road that had been blocked off. Armoured men were getting out of the back of a big van—the on-call unit from the State Protection Group. About a hundred metres away, flashes were going off. He realised the cameras might be pointed at himself. The media had arrived. Of course.

Harmer came by, walking quickly, but stopped when she saw him. She put out a hand and touched him on the arm, asked him how he was.

'Jon will pull through,' she said.

'You've heard from the hospital?'

'No, but he's—' She stopped, as though suddenly aware of the difficulty of describing McIver. 'You know we just found shoes and a coat on level thirty-three?'

This was good. 'There you go,' he said. 'Mac's instincts are all right.'

'They were near the loading platform, so she could have done it herself.'

'You're getting it dusted?'

She nodded. 'It's pretty wet. Why was Sean Randall up there?'

'I asked him to take me.'

She looked unhappy. But all she said was, 'How did he hold up?'

Troy shrugged. 'Is he okay? At his job, I mean.'

'He's an engineer, no previous experience of security, but a quick learner. You need to go inside now, keep yourself intact.'

'Intact?'

'You're evidence.'

He looked down at his hands, covered in dirt and blood. McIver's blood. At that moment something felt like it wanted to burst out of his chest.

'You've closed down the site?'

'We're working on it,' she said. 'I'm trying to get the civilians out.' She turned to go. 'But I don't have enough officers yet. It's a nightmare.' All the same, she seemed to be enjoying herself immensely.

Troy went back to the screens around the car and into the enclosure, where the government contractor was asking Little if it was all right to bag the body. Crime scene had finished and gone upstairs. Little looked at Troy, who nodded.

The sergeant said, 'I suppose we need the autopsy as soon as?' He looked at the woman on top of the car. 'A face would be nice.'

'And I guess your constables would like their vehicle back.'

Several people sniggered and Little smiled. I can handle this, Troy thought. I am going to be okay.

He left the enclosure while the contractors got on with their job. The crowd at one of the barriers parted and a van reversed towards him. Troy saw Sean Randall wandering around, holding a big orange coat like the one he'd been wearing upstairs. He had a bandage around his head and looked distracted. When he saw Troy, his face lit up as though he'd found the missing piece to a puzzle. He came up and thrust out the coat.

Troy put it on and drew up the zip, and found himself shivering violently for almost a minute. When it was over, he felt warm again, and nodded his thanks to Randall, who was staring at him anxiously.

'Bazzi disappeared at eight thirty—just after we went upstairs,' the engineer said. 'As far as we can make out. Just walked out of the office and left the site.'

'His mobile?'

'Still on his desk.'

Thinking about the man who'd taken McIver's gun, Troy said, 'Did anyone see a lift come down after the guy took your pass?'

'When I called, Harmer was right next to the console. She and one of the guards saw it was coming down. It went to car park one.'

'So the guy with the gun's down there?' Troy said, pointing to the ground.

'Your colleagues are searching.'

Randall went back onto the site. Troy was about to follow when Little appeared, and said he'd been directed by Harmer to stay with him until Internal Affairs arrived. Because of the time of night, this might be a while.

'She wants you out of the rain,' Little said, looking dubiously at the coat Troy was now wearing. They began to walk and he said, 'Bloody McIver, eh? Man's had a charmed life.'

'I guess.'

'Anyone who could do that to Bobby Logan and survive, I mean, the guy's got balls.' Troy nodded, shifted his mind back to McIver. 'You know what I'm talking about?' Troy nodded again. Little looked unconvinced, but said no more as they walked across the road.

Troy did know about the Logan brothers, who were two of the city's most effective criminals. In the late eighties McIver had been a junior detective on an investigation that had locked up Bobby for ten years for manslaughter. McIver's evidence in court had been crucial and, from what Troy had heard, partly fabricated. That had been common in the old days, but it was harder to do now, and not Troy's thing. Cops had to make a decision about all that early on and stick to it, and Troy had made his.

'You think what he did was right?' he asked Little. It was nice to know where the people you worked with stood on these things. But the sergeant didn't seem to have heard him. He was preoccupied, working his cigarette hard to finish it before they got to the entrance.

Troy thought about the dead woman on top of the car, and the presence of the two Indians or Pakistanis. Their determination to escape, the fact one of them had the handbag, pointed to murder. Bazzi's flight confirmed he'd been involved somehow, maybe just by enabling access to the site. Because the body had struck the car, the police had arrived much sooner than the killers would have expected, possibly cutting off their planned means of escape. Bazzi had dithered for a while. Then he panicked and ran, which meant the killers had been stuck upstairs, presumably retreating from the police sweep until McIver had come upon them.

It seemed like a good working theory, and he went over it again, wondering if there might be any other explanation. Say the woman hadn't been pushed but had jumped. The Indians were up there for some other reason and came across the handbag, maybe next to the shoes and coat. They might have gone through it for money—but why would they have kept it? That suggested it had some significance, maybe there was something in it they needed. Something so big they couldn't just take it out and slip it into a pocket. Which meant not just credit cards and money. But what?

Little said, 'What was McIver doing up there by himself?'

'He works on instinct,' Troy said carefully. 'I'd say he was just trying to get a feel for what one of the floors was like with no one else on it.'

'A feel.'

'He's one of the best homicide cops we have. He would have joined the search a few minutes later. He just got unlucky.'

The thing was to minimise discussion of McIver's erratic behaviour, because eventually it would raise questions about whether he'd been drinking.

It was a typical McIver situation. Normally the sergeant thrived on confusion, or at least did better than most people. He'd once told Troy he'd discovered chaos theory before the scientists. But now, lying in hospital, probably facing an official reprimand, the odds had turned on him. If the two men up top had been cornered by the police search teams, they might have surrendered peacefully. No one else would have died and the killers—if that's who they were—would be undergoing interviews right now.

Returning to reality, Troy told Little what had happened when he'd found McIver. 'A big question is why the Indians needed a lift pass if they'd been able to go up in the lift earlier, with the woman.'

Little said, 'We found a pass on the floor on thirty-one. You didn't know?'

'No.'

'It had been stopped on the system. My guess is Bazzi gave them the pass to go up and then cancelled it for some reason. They must have chucked it when they found out it was stuffed.'

Troy thought about this. It fitted with the idea that Bazzi had been involved in providing access but not in the killing. He'd been told the woman had landed on the car outside, become upset and cancelled the pass while he thought about what to do. Wondered if he wanted to be an accessory to murder. Then the place was flooded with police and Randall arrived so he couldn't reverse the stop on the card even if he'd wanted to. McIver got shot, and he decided to vanish.

It wasn't strong enough to be a theory, but it was something for Troy's subconscious to work on. You didn't want to start to firm up ideas too early in an investigation, before you had enough facts. But you couldn't help wondering how the few pieces you had fitted together. It was a compulsion, even if at times it had to be resisted. It was why you were a detective.

He said, 'Is Randall any good?'

'As far as I know,' Little said. 'I dealt with him once when some stuff was being nicked. He seems pretty straight. Smart enough, for an engineer.'

Seeing Harmer's face through the window of the security office, Troy walked across the floor and climbed the steel stairs again, Little behind him. He opened the door and went into the crowded room. Randall was talking into a microphone on the desk. He nodded to Troy but it was Harmer who spoke.

'We've completed our search of the first forty storeys. The part of the building above that is sealed at the stairwells. We're now doing the area below ground, starting with the retail mall and the loading dock level, and working our way down the nine car park levels. The man with the gun is still down there somewhere.' She looked at Randall, who had finished with the microphone, and he nodded.

'He can't get out,' he said. 'You want to be very careful.'

There were building plans spread on the table next to him, and he began to examine them intently.

Harmer was flipping through her notebook, and after a bit she added, 'We've circulated Peter Bazzi as a person of interest. The locals are going to his house in Leichhardt.'

Troy nodded. Harmer might sound like a training manual, but she was doing well. The police response had unfolded like a minor military operation, and he knew this was quite an achievement in the circumstances.

'And now,' she said, 'I want you in the atrium—people you need to talk with will be here soon. If you disobey this time, I'll send you back to the fucking station.'

Most police swore; he swore a lot himself. It happened so much you tended not to notice it. But for some reason, coming from Harmer it grabbed his attention.

'Ma'am,' he said.

Little and he had just reached the door when there was a burst of excited chatter through several radios in the room. No one was paying attention to Troy anymore, so he stopped. He couldn't hear what was being said because of the static, but from Harmer's replies he gathered that the search team had found someone. In fact, they'd found more than one man—they'd found a number of people.

'Twenty of them,' Randall said. 'Did I hear you correctly?' He looked around in surprise and saw Troy. 'They've found a sort of camp down in car park nine. Beds and lights and stuff.' His voice had risen in disbelief. 'Men, they say they're workers. Indians, probably illegals.' There was excited talk in the room now. Randall shook his head slowly and Troy heard him say, to no one in particular, 'Holy shite. This is not possible.'

Troy led Little out of the office and they banged down the steel stairs. Feeling suddenly hot, he unzipped the heavy coat. Police and guards were standing around on the concrete floor below, talking in loud voices. News of the discovery must have spread already.

'I want to go down there,' Troy said.

Little stared at him, excitement fighting caution. It was not every day you had the chance to be part of something like this. 'Actually,' he said, 'I've got a pass. I did a job here, they never asked for it back—and I bet they forgot to cancel it.'

'So we know their security's pretty tight.'

Little shrugged and reached into his pocket. 'You want to go downstairs or not?'

He took them down to the retail floor, which was brightly lit and broader than the atrium above, although its ceiling was not nearly as high. 'This is where the bloke with the gun got off,' Little said. 'I thought you should see it before we go below.' Troy nodded and Little led him out. 'Upmarket food court in the middle here,' he said, pointing, as they crossed an expanse of concrete. 'There'll be eighty boutique stores too, around the perimeter.'

Troy followed him down a wide corridor lined with the shells of future shops. Some were already half fitted out, with shelves and internal wall lining. A few even had goods on the shelves, as though someone wanted to judge the effect. Little explained that the retail precinct was due to open in a month or two, before the top floors even had their windows fitted. The building's owners needed to start making some income as soon as they could. During the week, this level was crowded with shop designers and tradesmen.

As they walked, Troy asked who owned The Tower now.

'Some massive Hong Kong insurance company. They took it over when Tony Teresi went bust.'

Troy remembered. Teresi was the entrepreneur who'd devised The Tower and put the project together after a decade of planning and other difficulties. It had been a heroic effort but it had ruined him. He'd died of a heart attack soon after he sold up.

Little continued his quick tour of the floor. Troy knew the building had polarised opinion in the city, for all sorts of reasons. A city mayor had had to resign when it was found he'd taken secret campaign donations from Teresi, and other aspects of the planning process had been investigated by the Independent Commission Against Corruption. A community group had been formed to fight it. There were predictions it would take twenty years before it was fully leased.

Then there was the size of the thing, which many people thought out of proportion to the rest of the city. Anna hated it because of its bulk, and she was not alone. Troy hadn't formed a strong view either way, but he figured you either liked concrete or you didn't. Now, inside the thing for the first time, he found it hard not to be impressed by the will and energy embodied in the structure. It was like being inside a vast, multidimensional jigsaw puzzle.

He thought of the men below. 'How could people be living here without anyone knowing?'

'This place is like a small city,' Little said, taking them down another broad corridor. 'Hundreds of subcontractors, a thousand workers some days, a hundred and twenty floors above ground and eleven below. The car parks were finished over a year ago, but only the first six are being used. They park vans down there, store materials. All the major contractors have compounds where they keep their stuff. There's toilets, lunch rooms, lockers. But the bottom three levels are closed off.'

They came to a boarded-up opening in the wall, and Little explained it was the entrance to a subway that went under Elizabeth Street to Hyde Park. There was a door and Troy shook the handle. It was locked.

'There's one of these subways on each side,' Little said. 'This one, one at St James Station, two more to other buildings. But they're all boarded up like this.'

'Someone could get through if they had the key?'

'I looked into that when I was doing a robbery here last year. Stuff had gone missing from some of the compounds. The keys are secure, they're kept in safes off-site. And even if you got through this door,' he banged on the wood in front of them, 'you couldn't get through the other end, because that key belongs to someone else. In this case the City Council. And no one here has a copy.'

He walked back to the goods lift and took them down to the lowest car park. During the ride, Troy wondered if McIver had woken up yet. He should call the hospital.

When they got out of the lift, the first thing Troy noticed was that the ceiling was a lot lower again. A large number of people were standing about a hundred metres away, gathered around an opening in a wooden wall that closed off a section of the car park. The two detectives walked towards the crowd, and found a group of men sitting on the floor, guarded by a ring of excited police. Vella was there, and when he saw Troy he came over. There was no news of McIver, he said. As they spoke, Little drifted away, over to his colleagues. Troy asked what the other Homicide detectives were doing, and Vella said they were interviewing the security guards.

'I've got a few more coming, they'll be canvassing the area, getting CCTV and stuff. But tomorrow they all have to be somewhere else. Three of us are on a morning plane to Bourke.'

Troy grunted sympathetically. 'Where's Kelly?'

'Still at City Central. The man who runs the company that owns this place has turned up, he's trying to stop us closing down the site.' He shook his head and looked at his mobile, which was not picking up a signal. 'I don't rate his chances. I've got to get back up top.'

Harmer appeared through the door in the wall. 'Senior Constable

Troy. You decided to join us anyway.' She didn't sound too upset. 'So, which one's your man?'

Some of the uniformed cops stood aside and Troy took a few steps forward until he was only a metre away from the closest man on the floor. All of them were Indian or Pakistani.

'Curry munchers,' murmured Little, who had rejoined him.

Troy looked closely at the men, aware that he was being watched by all the cops standing around. The men on the ground were wearing cheap work clothes dirty with concrete dust. Their hair was matted with grime and the smell of stale sweat rose from them, like the odour of despair. Some were talking among themselves, while others were silent, dismay in their eyes. Their faces and bodies were grey where the harsh lights from the car park roof hit them, surrounded by deep shadows. There was something unreal about the scene.

'And this is Australia,' was Little's next piece of commentary. But it wasn't just Australia, Troy knew, it was the world. Little added, 'A few years back, the unions'd never allowed this sort of thing.'

Wishing the other detective wasn't standing so close to his shoulder, Troy nodded. The construction union was still powerful. One question was why they hadn't prevented what he was now looking at. Maybe it was unstoppable, he thought, looking at the hunched figures sitting there. Maybe no one could stop it.

Many of the men were staring at the ground and he walked among them, telling them to raise their heads so he could examine them. None of the faces meant anything. He walked around once more, but none of them seemed familiar.

'I realise this is not what you want to be told,' he said to Harmer, 'but he's not here.'

She stared at him. 'We've searched every level,' she said carefully, as if explaining something to a slow child. 'This is the bottom.' Troy shrugged. '*Would* you recognise him?' she said, searching for the right words. 'I mean—'

'My wife's Indian, I've travelled there,' he said. 'They don't all look the same to me. So yes, I'd recognise him.'

'Okay,' she said. 'I didn't mean to be offensive.'

'No.'

'These are Indians?'

'They're Pakistanis, I think.'

Harmer looked from Troy to the men on the ground.

'Shit,' she said at last.

He shrugged, feeling he'd let her down because he couldn't spot the man. Which was stupid.

Harmer pointed across the carpark. 'Why don't you have a look through there.'

Behind the wooden wall the air was stale. Troy stood near the entrance, looking at a mass of camp beds and personal belongings, primitive cooking and toilet arrangements. There were officers every-where, a camera flashing in one corner. A uniform came by with some documents in a plastic evidence bag. Other uniforms were searching through all the stuff on the floor. Troy realised they were looking for McIver's gun.

He walked around the space, staring at the suitcases on the ground, at the clothes and other belongings spilling out of them. Randall was standing there, looking blank. Troy realised he'd probably lose his job over this.

'No gun?' Troy said.

'No. Your colleagues searched the men. It could be anywhere.'

Little came up and said, 'Let's get out of this stink.'

He kicked a book that was lying on the ground and walked out.

Harmer took Little and Troy aside, away from the men on guard and all the police activity. 'They're not saying anything, but here's my best guess: they're illegals working for one of the contractors, who's been paying Bazzi to make it possible. There must be other guards in on it as well. We're familiar with the employment side of it, the use of illegals on city building sites. But the living arrangements here are a first.' She shook her head in a moment of bewilderment. 'Randall thinks the contractor who's pouring the concrete floors is the best bet as their employer.'

'It seems like a pretty elaborate set-up,' Troy said.

'This bloke is being paid on the basis of award wages plus overtime, which is pretty good. This is a huge job, so if he pays the illegals half the going rate, that leaves maybe a million dollars to be split between him and the smuggler who brought them to Australia.'

'Minus what they're paying Bazzi.'

Harmer nodded. 'I've just had a call from level thirty-one. Internal Affairs are here for you. You're sure you don't recognise the man you saw up there?'

Troy shook his head. Over the inspector's shoulder he saw a uniformed officer coming towards them, holding an object in an exhibit bag.

'Ma'am,' he said, pointing.

It was a gun. Troy took a step towards him but Harmer grabbed his sleeve.

'Level thirty-one,' she said. 'That's an order.'

Five

Upstairs, the floor had been transformed. There were screens blocking much of the wind, and bright lights illuminated the dead man on the ground and the area nearby, where McIver's blood stained the concrete. Crime scene officers were moving around methodically as they had moved in the enclosure down below, photographing and measuring, collecting evidence. Troy stood for a moment, taking it in, and shivered. He zipped up the coat and put his hands in his pockets. Almost immediately, two men appeared from the darkness. The senior one was Inspector Malcolm Ferris. Troy took his right hand from the pocket of the jacket and extended it to Ferris, who shook his head.

'We'll get you swabbed in a moment,' he said. 'Then you can clean up. We'll need your clothes, too.'

It took a moment to sink in. Troy realised he needed to flip the situation around: see himself as a suspect. That was what these men were doing.

As he finished running through his story for the first time, one of the lifts opened and Helen Kelly emerged. The commander was a tall woman with medium-length dark hair, and attractive. Some of the officers considered her glamorous, although standards were not all that high in the police force. But she dressed well and was thin. In fact, Troy didn't recognise her at first when she came out of the lift, because she was wearing one of Randall's bulky jackets. Now she came over to him and took him by the arm, her eyes full of concern. There was kindness there but calculation too: she wanted to know if he was going to fall to pieces. He told her he was all right, and he thought he was. His mood hadn't shifted at all since he'd last thought about it. Maybe this was as bad as it would get.

He hadn't had the chance to form a strong opinion of Kelly yet. She'd been with the squad only two months, coming over from Sex Crimes, which she'd run for several years. Married, early fifties, no children. McIver said she did everything by the book. In Troy's opinion this was not necessarily a failing, provided you knew the book backwards. He suspected she did.

The way she was talking to Ferris now, he could tell they'd met before. When they'd finished she came over and put a hand on his arm, said to Ferris, 'If I could just have a word with Nick, see how he is,' then led him away. When they were out of earshot she said, 'How are you? Really?'

'I'm okay.'

She looked at him. She had a nice smile that rarely made it to her eyes, but he didn't think she was insincere.

'It's a homicide?'

'Almost certain.'

She nodded briskly. 'I'm having trouble finding another sergeant. It's ridiculous, isn't it, that the police force should be short of homicide detectives?' It sounded like a conversation she'd been having with other people for a long time. 'I've got five people doing double shifts tonight, but tomorrow they all vanish.' She looked around. 'Rogers was supposed to be here,' she said, referring to the police commissioner. 'You haven't seen him?'

Troy shook his head. Kelly looked almost rattled, and this made him nervous. It was the job of senior officers to maintain unflinching enthusiasm, no matter how irrational this might be.

She went on, 'Have you heard of a man named Henry Wu?'

'No.'

The questions were starting to annoy him. He felt like telling her he'd been busy with other things.

'Runs Morning Star,' she said, 'who own this building. A very aggressive man, and well connected. Anyway, we've shut down the building site indefinitely.'

Of course they had. It was what you did. He said, 'I want to be on the investigation.'

'I can't permit that. I know you're anxious, this is personal, but there's procedure we need to follow.'

'It's not because of Mac—not only. I feel fine.'

She shook her head almost angrily. 'Sometimes it takes a while. After these good people have finished with you, go home and sleep. There'll be debriefing, counselling . . . I'll call you tomorrow.'

Don't be angry with me, he felt like saying, but she had turned her back on him and was talking to Ferris and his partner, who'd been waiting impatiently and only just out of earshot. Then she turned again and lowered her voice. 'You need to know something. Siegert at Central is gunning for you and McIver—he thinks you ruined the good reputation of The Tower, for which he feels responsible. He just told me the man you shot would be alive but for the reprehensible behaviour of my two officers.' Troy stared at her. 'It's going to be a media frenzy, and he's looking to distract attention from the illegals. There's concern about how this man Bazzi was allowed to get away.'

'That was hardly our fault.'

'Of course not. But it could be made to look like it. Do you see what I'm saying?'

Troy felt himself starting to sweat. He'd acted appropriately within the situations that had occurred, but Kelly was saying people might argue those situations should not have occurred. This was out of his league; it all came down to McIver. And Kelly was telling him something about that too, in the comments she'd made earlier on the phone. Troy was not used to politics, had rarely felt its breath on his cheek. But he knew it was out there, waiting for him like everyone else.

Kelly said, 'You and Mac don't share equal responsibility. He was the senior officer, disobeyed an instruction to come up here. You might want to consider that.' Troy's mind was blank now. He wanted to help McIver, but for the moment he didn't know what to do. Kelly said, 'You only went up to help him.' She was watching him closely, her lipstick glistening in the harsh arc light. 'Was he capable?'

'The sergeant was fine,' he said. 'He has my complete support.'

She pulled her lips back, and touched one with her tongue. 'That narrows your options.'

He nodded, dimly aware of what she was getting at, and said, 'So what happens now?'

'It goes to the commissioner. Once upon a time that wouldn't have happened, but these days . . .'

Troy knew what this was about, at least. Frank Rogers had been running the New South Wales police force for six months, and everyone knew how concerned he was about the media. Some said he didn't have much time for anything else.

'Siegert and I each try to be first to talk to Rogers in the morning,' said Kelly. 'He'll decide if you're to become a hero or a disgrace to the force.' He started to smile but realised she wasn't joking. She went on quickly, glancing behind her, 'Your statement will be the vital document.' She took his arm and started to guide him back to the two IA officers. Before they reached them she said in a low voice, 'Everyone knows Rogers is a genius at manipulating the media. But it's a two-way thing. They influence him too. What they print in the morning will be crucial.'

'Crucial?'

She nodded and turned away. He wanted to ask what she meant by that, but she was already shaking Ferris's hand, heading for the lifts.

The detectives took him over the scene, and he told his story again. He was thinking of it as a story now, a version of events that would strike different people in different ways. After he'd been swabbed for gunshot residue they took the lift down to ground level. They went in the officers' car down to City Central, not far away. The other two were silent during the drive through the dark and empty streets. They hadn't been exactly unfriendly, but it was clear they wanted to keep their distance. This disconcerted Troy, even though he knew it was how it had to be. He felt isolated. He had to make sure he was thinking for himself.

'Bloody City Central,' Ferris murmured as they circled the streets. Even at this time of night there were police cars everywhere. 'You ever worked here?'

'No,' said Troy.

'Don't. There's parking inside for six cars, and then you're on your own.'

Eventually they parked down on the side of the road that ran between the station and the Darling Harbour precinct opposite.

Inside the station a tall man in a suit was waiting for them. He was in his early fifties, like Kelly, and had silver hair and piercing, pale blue eyes.

Ferris looked from him to Troy and said, 'Superintendent Ron Siegert.'

The superintendent stared at Troy, making no effort to shake hands. 'We haven't met earlier because I've been here trying to clean up the mess Jon McIver and you created for us.' Troy had never seen anyone speak through clenched teeth before, but Siegert was coming close. When he said nothing, the superintendent went on, 'That man should not have died. I intend to see the right thing done here. There'll be no cover-up.'

His face was red with anger.

'We don't do cover-ups,' Ferris said tersely. 'Come on, we need to get Detective Troy's statement.'

Troy took a step forward and Siegert moved to block his way. He was close to Troy's face, trying to make a deal of staring down at him, although there was only four or five centimetres difference in their heights.

'I knew your father,' Siegert said.

Troy froze. His father had been dead for eighteen years. He'd been a cop too, although he'd left the force two years before he died. Troy didn't often come across anyone who'd met him.

Siegert said, 'We were detectives together. He was a good man. Jon McIver's not worth his bootlace.' The super turned on his heel and stormed off.

The IA detectives led him through corridors and up some stairs, and Troy thought about what Kelly had said to him about the media, trying to work out what she had left unsaid. Wondering if there was any message there. Anna sometimes went to services at an evangelical church called ChristLife, and when he'd gone with her last week there'd been a banner saying: WHAT WOULD JESUS DO? Now he asked himself: What would McIver do?

Slowly, an answer started to form.

'We're going to ERISP this,' Ferris said. 'Okay?'

Troy realised he had to think quickly now. A filmed recording of the interview was not what he needed. 'No way,' he said. 'Let's do a typed record of interview.'

'ERISP is standard.'

'It's what I've been advised.'

Ferris looked at him. Troy had chosen not to have a representative of the Police Association involved, and from IA's point of view this was good. They wouldn't want him to change his mind on this by pushing him too hard.

'If that's what you want,' Ferris said at last. 'But you know how it might look.'

'It's what I've been advised,' Troy said.

It was a nice phrase, and seemed to express some inner reality. As though there was indeed someone else inside him now, thinking more clearly than he was, telling him what to do.

Troy was shown to an area of the station where an old tracksuit and a pair of running shoes had been put on a chair. He changed into them slowly, retaining his wallet and keys. They'd already taken his weapon, back at The Tower. It was the absence of the gun rather than his suit that affected him most.

As they took his statement, it was typed up on a laptop. Troy kept things as simple as he could. At the end, the computer was spun around and Ferris told him to check what had been written.

Troy passed a hand over his eyes and yawned. 'I'm tired, can't see the screen properly. Can we print off a copy so I can read it on paper?'

'If you could just check this quickly we won't keep you,' said Ferris, pointing at the laptop.

'It's been a big night.'

'How 'bout I send you a copy to sign tomorrow.'

'No,' Troy said, forcing himself to keep it light. 'I want to take a signed copy with me now.'

Ferris smiled. 'To be honest, I'm not sure I can print this out here, I don't think my laptop is compatible with this system. I promise you'll have a copy tomorrow. I'll email it to you.'

What bullshit. Troy wanted to swear at the guy, but knew this was no time to be making enemies. 'I have the right to a signed copy of the record of interview. You told me that at the beginning.'

There was a pause and then Ferris stood up and took the laptop out of the interview room. His partner stared at Troy for a while. Then he pulled some papers out of his briefcase and began to study them. Troy could tell he wasn't reading.

When the IA men had gone, Troy took his copy of the signed statement and wandered around the station until he found a photocopier. There was no one about. He put the pages in the top and started to make two copies. When he was about halfway through, someone came down the corridor. It was Little.

'Still here?' he said.

Troy told him he was going home soon. They chatted about the investigation, but there had been no developments. The big news was that the man from level thirty-one seemed to have got away. All the car parks had been searched again, and there was no sign of him. The illegals were being interviewed, but all had denied any

44

knowledge of the two men from upstairs or the gun. Bazzi was not at his house.

The photocopier stopped and Troy removed the statement and the copies, trying to hide the text from Little without making it obvious. He shook the other detective's hand.

'Until we meet again,' Little murmured.

Outside, Troy made two calls and then wandered up Bathurst Street until he reached Hyde Park. There he stood under a tree for a while, looking up at The Tower. The rain had stopped and much of the building could be made out, soaring into the night sky. It was strangely beautiful, and he stood there for some time looking at it, populating it in his mind with all the people he knew worked there. A thousand, someone had said. He wondered if Kelly had found a sergeant to head the strike force. Eventually, after checking his watch, he walked down Elizabeth Street until he found a cab.

As they drove along Anzac Parade, Troy directed the driver to turn left into Lang Road and then into the Entertainment Quarter complex. He told him to stop down the end and got out and went over to a car parked next to the wall of the Fox film studio. A man was standing by the vehicle and they shook hands. The guy, a reporter from the *Daily Telegraph*, ran his eyes over Troy, pausing briefly at the ankles: the tracksuit trousers were about ten centimetres too short, and he wasn't wearing socks. Troy gave him a copy of the statement and then turned on his heel, brushing away questions. The reporter followed him down the road, pleading for more information about The Tower, but Troy ignored him. He got back into the cab and told the driver to return to Anzac Parade and turn left at Alison Road.

At the Shell service station he went into the shop and bought himself a bottle of orange juice. As he paid, he glanced outside at the parking spaces and saw a woman sitting in a car with the interior light on. He left the store and approached the car, and she got out.

They shook hands; her grip was firmer than that of the man he'd just met. She introduced herself as Sacha Powell of the *Sydney Morning Herald*, and he began to tell her about what had happened. He knew

McIver had spoken to her once or twice and he mentioned this, hoping there was some goodwill there. Her eyes lit up behind their glasses and he figured he was on the right track. For a moment he was tempted to lay out the political situation for her, describe Siegert's antagonism, the decision the commissioner would have to make in the morning. But he'd told himself as he was waiting in Hyde Park there was nothing to be gained by explaining all this—you didn't want to give these people any hint of your motives, it would make them suspicious. So now he stuck to the plan.

'Will Rogers support you?' she said.

He wondered if she'd heard anything, wondered why she thought Rogers might be an issue. But she was probably just fishing.

'Of course,' he said.

'He's a slippery bastard.'

'No comment.'

She smiled. 'Why are you giving me this?' She waved the pages at him. 'Tell me or I won't use it. I need context. Your media unit's not saying anything at all.'

He felt nervous—no, more angry than nervous—about playing games like this.

He said, 'Do you fucking want it or not?'

She put it behind her back and smiled again. He was beginning to dislike that smile. He wondered if anyone had ever told her it made her look like a shark.

'I have to go,' he said.

'I need more.'

He didn't think so.

For the rest of the drive home he felt a little wild, not sure of what he'd done. He recalled the feel of Powell's cool skin when they'd shaken hands and ran his own hand along his thigh, as if to clean it. The fabric was unfamiliar and he looked down, for a moment forgetting what had happened to his own clothes.

When he got home Anna was asleep in Matt's room. He looked at them both, then closed the door gently. He and she had had a good life together, once. They'd argued about it, when she first started sleeping in the other room, but not anymore. He wasn't sure which was worse, the arguing or the not arguing. Right now, though, he didn't really care. He went to bed and fell asleep immediately.

MONDAY

Six

Randall swung his Audi through the tunnels beneath the city and came up by the Automobile Club. He dropped down a gear and then opened up as he shot across Circular Quay, the bridge hanging high on his right. A minute later he was on it, zooming over its gentle rise in one of the few northbound lanes. They restricted them in the mornings, to allow for the flood of cars coming from the opposite direction into the city. There wasn't much sign of the flood yet: Henry Wu was an early starter.

At North Sydney, Randall turned off the freeway and made a hard right, then dived into the warren of streets that blanketed the peninsulas of Neutral Bay and Mosman. His flat was not too far away; after the business at The Tower last night, he'd gone back to Kristin's place in Edgecliff. The traffic running against him now, on the smaller roads, was heavier. He hoped to Christ he could finish with Henry quickly, get back onto the bridge before it clogged up. One of Randall's definitions of happiness was Driving Against the Traffic. You lived like he had, saw enough cities, and every extra hour you spent staring at someone else's tailpipe hurt.

But then, as Henry was presumably going to sack him, he wondered why he cared. When he'd called Wu last night to give him the news, he'd expected the fellow to be grateful for the heads-up. But it hadn't been like that at all, and later Randall realised it was the publicity: something like this could end up hurting a building's leasing potential. The Greens, the NIMBYs and all the other wackos were just waiting for the next scandal so they could escalate their criticisms of the project. For some people, the fight over The Tower had become a fight for the city's soul. They didn't realise the building was there now, and there was nothing they could do about it. If they kept on demonising the place and made it difficult for Morning Star to find tenants, the whole city would suffer. The Tower was that big.

As security manager, Randall saw he might be considered ultimately responsible for the presence of the illegals—no matter how unfairly. Plus, the police had shut down the building site. You could see that Henry would be upset about that too.

Randall actually worked for Warton Constructions, and Henry Wu was their client, but he was very hands-on. Jack Taylor, Randall's boss, called him the client from hell, but someone that big could come from anywhere he liked. Wu was obsessed with The Tower project— he'd even set up an office inside Morning Star to process invoices for materials. It was a highly unusual arrangement, apparently designed to introduce the company's Chinese accounting staff to the way the construction industry in the West worked. The set-up was cumbersome and the language problems diabolical, and some of Warton's managers had quit in frustration. They said Taylor should have refused Wu's demands, but Randall knew it was not that easy. Morning Star was a booming company across Asia and around the Pacific, and it had established a relationship with Warton. Maintaining that relationship was more important than the details of any one job, no matter how big.

He'd spoken with Taylor last night as well, mainly about the discovery of the illegals. Jack had been mightily pissed off, and said that Tryon, the security company, was out, but he but hadn't actually sacked Randall. Maybe he was leaving that job to the real boss. Maybe he was waiting until he found out just what had been going on in the basement of his building project. The problem was, Randall didn't know. He didn't have a fucking clue.

He pushed the car through a roundabout a little too fast, recovered as he came out, put his foot down, and then hit the brakes as a big four-wheel drive came out of nowhere, its snout appearing from the line of parked cars to his left. Luckily it stopped just in time, and he was able to swerve around it, narrowly avoiding a Jaguar coming the other way. As he cruised into the marina car park a few moments later, he told himself he'd done well, his heart rate unchanged despite the narrow escape. There was no doubt he was a cool driver. When he was in a car, everything seemed to come together for him. Not like last night on thirty-one. That bloody cop had been cool as ice—you could see he was a man without imagination. But he'd come through and handled it afterwards. Randall wished he was like that.

He had headed for the stairs when he saw the fellow with the gun, let himself in and huddled there, uncertain of what to do. The time had stretched out and after a bit he'd taken a few steps down towards thirty when the Indian had erupted through the door and jumped at him. He could have knocked the little guy over in mid-air—he hadn't seen he had a gun. He'd seen the handbag, though, maybe that was why he'd frozen. The handbag had surprised him. He'd been paralysed, couldn't move. It was just the way he was in physical situations. He'd never been good at fighting at school, although he'd usually been able to arrange things so it didn't come up.

The Indian's gun had come out of nowhere, smacked him on the head and he'd gone down, blood in his eyes, and the fellow had been clawing at his throat. At first he thought the man was going to strangle him, but it had been the pass he wanted, the pass hanging from a cord around his neck. When they'd got that sorted out—he'd reached up and yanked the thing off, thrown it down the stairs—the man had scampered off.

He walked through the almost empty car park towards the marina. Wu's car was there, a golden Mercedes. The Chinese loved their German automobiles. Henry lived in a huge house overlooking the harbour in

Mosman, somewhere near the zoo, but he liked to do private business on the big motor cruiser he had moored down here. Some days he'd sail it across the harbour to Rose Bay, get out and be taken into the city by limo. It was a roundabout way to get to work, but what's the point in living in Sydney, he'd said to Randall once, if you couldn't do things on the water?

So now, Randall thought, I'm going to be sacked on the water. It will be a first. I've been sacked before, but never on the water.

Randall pressed the buttons for Wu's boat. The gate had a keypad and speaker connected to all the vessels there, just like a security block of apartments. Wu's voice came crackling out, telling him to come out to the boat but wait before coming on board. The buzzer sounded and Randall pushed through the gate and walked down onto the pontoons, admiring the craft moored on both sides. One day, he thought. One day. He walked more slowly as he approached Wu's vessel. Henry was a mentor to him and in some ways he loved the man dearly. But he made him nervous.

Wu's boat was the biggest one there, a million dollars of fibreglass and steel lined with precious timbers and silk wall hangings. God knew how much greenhouse gas was produced by the huge engines that drove it through the water. It was so big it was ocean-capable. Wu had taken it up and down the coast, to Hobart and to the Whitsundays. The man was a modern-day explorer.

No, thought Randall, reaching the gangplank and taking a deep breath as he stopped and called out. That was the wrong word. Henry Wu was a conquistador, slashing his way through new worlds, seizing opportunities. And like anyone driven to extreme actions, he had his peculiarities. He was, to put it bluntly, fucking weird.

Henry was standing in the main cabin, coat off and wearing his captain's hat. Randall had made a joke about this. Once. There was another man with him, but even as Randall tried to make out his features he disappeared from sight. One time, over at Rose Bay, the positions had been reversed. Randall had been chatting with Wu when two other men arrived, Chinese guys in their dumb suits. Wu had taken him into another cabin, a big place with a large screen across one wall, and shut the door. Randall had stayed there for almost an hour, watching *The Sopranos*, until Wu had finished his business with the men. Randall had tried to open the door at one point, see if he could hear what was going on. The door had been locked. At first he'd experienced a mild sense of panic, but after a bit he realised the locked door was actually a good thing. Wu kept his life in separate boxes, and really, it was best not to know what was going on in the other ones.

Wu stepped out onto the broad rear deck and called Randall on board. He had this thing that played a piping noise, a recording from the British navy, and he'd played it for Randall the second time he'd been here, piping him on board. But not today.

There was no sign of the other man in the big room, the one with all the steering and navigation equipment. Wu led the way in and stood by the chart table, pointing to the day's editions of the *Herald* and the *Telegraph*. Randall, who hadn't seen the papers yet, stood next to Wu as he pointed at the front-page stories about The Tower. Wu was tall for a Chinese, although still shorter than Randall. But height wasn't the sort of thing to worry Henry. Right now he seemed calm, as far as Randall could establish, but that didn't mean a lot.

'Your phone's off,' Wu said.

He had hardly any accent, though he wasn't from Hong Kong originally. They said he'd come across as a refugee in the early eighties, done the long swim. The idea that Wu must have taught himself almost perfect English as an adult did not surprise Randall. Henry did everything well: he was not like other men. Randall had to call him Mr Wu in conversation, but he thought of him as Henry. He had to force himself sometimes, but it was worth it. It made the man seem more human.

'I was sleeping,' he said. 'It was a rough night.'

'So I can see,' said Wu, pouring coffee.

Randall tried to concentrate on the newspapers but he was thinking about the man who'd been here with Henry when he'd arrived, and who was now downstairs. The big man. Henry had always liked to have people around him, but it had become more consistent six months ago. Randall wondered if there was some sort of security threat, but it was not something he felt he could ask. He forced himself to read. The *Telegraph* story, like the one in the *Herald*, was mainly about the shootings on level thirty-one. The journalists were right on top of the detail. Both stories mentioned his own presence.

'Thanks,' he murmured, taking the coffee, and then: 'The pricks.'

Last night, Warton's PR woman had been assured by the police media unit that nothing beyond a bald account would be released until today. That would have given Warton and Morning Star time to dampen the whole thing down, or at least try to influence the story. And now this. There was a picture of the shot cop on the front page of both newspapers. Their websites would be pushing the story too, alerting readers from around the world to the latest disaster from The Tower.

'I talked to my police contact,' Wu said, staring at Randall. There was a cop he talked to, someone high up, although Randall didn't know who it was. Wu liked boasting about what he'd been told, and usually it was good stuff, but the source was always just 'my contact'. Maybe it was the commissioner. With Henry, anything was possible. 'This detail doesn't come from them—there's been a leak.' Wu touched the papers. 'These illegals. Did you know anything at all?'

'Nothing.'

'Nothing?'

Randall repeated his denial. He doubted it was enough to save his job. What he would like to know, before he left, was whether Wu had known. Peer over the edge of his own box for a moment and see what was happening in one of the others. There was no reason for Wu to have known anything, of course, except that money was involved.

'I'm sorry,' he said. 'I know it's a disaster. Bazzi had me completely duped.'

With Wu, you needed to admit your mistakes up front. It seemed to relax him. Once you did that, he could even be quite pleasant, in his own twisted way.

Wu said, 'I seem to recall you recommended him for the job.'

Randall nodded. 'He worked for the company that did our security before, seemed to know what was going on. Tryon handled him the wrong way.' He could feel the sweat running down his sides now, and wondered how long it would be before Henry could smell it. He said, 'I'm a fool.'

He'd never said that to another man before, and the words sounded strange. But with Henry, you did what you had to do.

Wu thought about this, looking out to the bay.

Then he said, 'I believe you.'

For a moment Randall wondered if Henry was trying to be funny. But Henry didn't do humour very often. He pointed at the closed door and said, 'That guy in there?', regretting it the moment the words were out. But he couldn't help it.

Wu looked around vaguely, smiled at Randall. 'He's not here for you. Don't worry, Sean.'

Wu put a hand on his arm and he tried not to flinch. *Why me?* he felt like saying, *Why would you have thought I meant that?* He shook his head to try to clear it. This was weird stuff, but lively too.

'Are you going to sack me?' he said.

Shit, he shouldn't have asked.

As if he hadn't heard him, Wu said, 'It's a rogue element.'

The way he spoke the words, Randall could tell the phrase had been used by his police contact. Wu rubbed the back of his hand across his jaw. 'In the circumstances, maybe not so bad. Those two idiots have distracted attention from the illegals.'

Randall blinked, realising the idiots were the two police, the victim and the hero. At least, the newspapers seemed to think Nicholas Troy was a hero.

'So that's good?'

'It could be worse.'

Randall felt a bit better. There'd been a pain in his stomach since he woke up this morning, but it was going away now.

He said, 'What do we know about the illegal workers?'

'You tell me,' Wu said, looking at him closely.

'Nothing.'

'There it is.'

Not giving him all that much.

'Okay.'

'It's not okay,' Wu said. 'We need to know what's going on with the police.' He stared at Randall. 'You make some friends. This man McIver, if he wakes up, send him a bottle of something expensive.'

'Right.'

'You need a contact in the investigation. In my experience, policemen can be lonely men.'

That wasn't Randall's experience, but he nodded politely. 'They're looking for friends?'

Wu smiled. He liked it when Randall picked up things quickly.

'Tell me if you need some money,' he said, and pointed at the bandage around Randall's head as though seeing it for the first time. 'You okay?'

It was over, Randall knew. Everything was all right again.

'More coffee would be good.'

'Let me see the bandage. Oh, poor Sean.'

Usually Wu was a prick, but occasionally he'd act as though Randall was the son he'd never had. It was strange, because Wu had two sons up the hill in his house. And Randall surely had a father, a builder and alcoholic back in Dungarvan. The last thing he wanted was to be adopted by Henry Wu. The man was stimulating and he was necessary, but Randall had always grasped the necessity of keeping a distance from him.

Wu gave him the coffee, which was lukewarm, and said, 'Have you got the new film?'

Randall reached into the inside pocket of his coat and pulled out a DVD in a flat plastic case. It showed one of his first sessions with Kristen. Wu put a hand underneath the map table, and he must have pressed something because a small part of the wooden wall behind him sprung open to reveal a white cavity, in which sat an identical DVD case. This was a trick Randall hadn't seen before. This case had the word

Bolivia handwritten on it, and Wu exchanged it for the one Randall was holding, putting Randall's inside the cavity and closing the door.

The man enjoyed his toys, Randall thought. Imagine having a craft like this, anything you wanted on it. Custom-made.

'She's from Iceland,' he said, pointing to the part of the wall now concealing the DVD.

'She knew you were filming her?'

'No.'

'I'm impressed you can fool them so often,' Wu said.

This was going better. 'We all have our talents.'

The first time they'd used the camera he'd told Kristin it was running only when the red light was on. She'd believed him. It was Henry who'd arranged to have the camera altered almost a year go, after he'd told him of the problem with the light.

'Did you know about Bazzi?' said Wu.

Randall shook his head. 'I believe he had at least one accomplice.'

He realised Henry hadn't even asked him for his account of last night. As though he knew about it already. As though Randall's account didn't matter.

'Another guard has gone too,' said Randall. 'Andrew Asaad.'

Wu nodded impatiently. 'We need to find these two men, find out what they were up to in my building. This girl.'

'You don't know who she was?'

Wu frowned. Randall had been told, the first time he went out east, that Chinese people didn't show emotion. Wu was the Chinese man he'd spent most time with, and it wasn't true of him.

'This is my main job, Sean,' he said, pointing vaguely at his briefcase on the floor. 'You know I have my little hobbies, but I wouldn't let them interfere in this.'

Randall didn't know much at all about Wu's hobbies. Not most of them, anyway. 'Fine,' he said quickly. In fact he placed little faith in Henry's denial, believing the fellow to be fundamentally dishonest. But that was not something you wanted him to know.

Wu said, 'What does Jamal say?'

59

Eman Jamal was the local manager of Tryon.

'Bazzi fooled him too. They've gone back over his records and there's no sign of anything wrong.' Randall cleared his throat. 'Jamal says they blew it on Asaad, though. Turns out the fellow's in a bikie gang, the Wolves. They missed it when they vetted him.'

'How long's he been there?'

'Six months.'

Wu grunted. 'He was brought in by Bazzi?'

Randall nodded.

Wu said, 'I hope Mr Jamal is improving his vetting procedures.'

'It's a pretty good company actually. Heads will roll.' Not a good choice of words.

Wu looked at him as though reading his thoughts. But all he said was, 'I want you to find Bazzi and Asaad.'

'The police will do that.'

'I want you to do it first, with the help of Mr Jamal. He will help?'

'He'll do what I tell him to.'

Wu nodded. 'It's a disaster, Sean, the attention this has drawn to The Tower. We're all very upset. You do understand that?'

'Yes.'

'Do you know what it means?'

'I guess it could affect your capacity to attract tenants who—'

'It means everything has changed. Lots of lives have changed forever, Sean. Yours too.'

Wu said no more, just stared at him. The man liked his dramas.

Randall shrugged, just wanting to get out of there, over the bridge and into the city.

Wu looked at the wheel. 'I'm sailing to work this morning,' he said. 'You want a lift?'

'I've got my car. Need to get to the site. Closing it down will cause chaos.' He looked at his watch: he should be there now.

Wu said, 'Tell Taylor to hold on. I'm meeting Superintendent Siegert and the head of the Homicide Squad shortly. The decision will be reversed.'

'You are joking?'

For a moment Wu looked offended, but then he smiled and gestured towards the open door that led onto the rear deck. Randall felt immensely relieved. Wu said, 'Happy hunting.'

'I'll see what I can find out from the cops.'

Wu smiled. 'You take care out there, Sean. Don't forget, the people in this town are descended from convicts. They're not honest people.'

'No.'

It was one of Henry's jokes.

'Not like you and me.'

Randall wasn't sure if he should laugh, he'd heard the line so many times now. But he did, instinctively, giving it all he had. For a moment he saw a flicker of pleasure on Henry's face.

As he walked out and across the gangplank, he knew he'd done the right thing. It was all going to work itself out.

Seven

The sea was like a washing machine for people, Troy thought. He would plunge into the surf, it would roll him around, and he would emerge clean and renewed. This was how he'd seen Maroubra Beach since moving there four years ago. His swimming had improved—he had a strong chest and good lung capacity—and before long he'd become an expert bodysurfer. Walking along the beach in cut-off jeans, with a tan in mid-summer, he felt as though he'd lived here all his life. But he always knew, when he went in, that the sea was in charge. Some people, the ones who were born here, could go through life without realising that. They were the ones who became champions.

He was catching a wave, gliding towards the beach with one arm outstretched, when Anna shook him. As he woke up he tried to pull his arm in, before realising he'd been dreaming. The clock on the bedside table showed it was almost seven, and for a moment he lay there, disoriented, not hearing what she was telling him. Then she was sitting on the bed, leaning down and pressing herself on him, and he could feel her tears on the side of his face.

'I love you,' she whispered.

He wondered if this might bring them back together.

'I love you too,' he said, her hair in his mouth. 'I didn't—'

She sat up and put a finger on his mouth, and just looked at him for a long time. Then she took the finger away and wiped her eyes.

'So you heard,' he said.

She stood up, her lovely face full of emotion, brushing the long dark hair back, the brown eyes warm in a way he hadn't seen for a long time.

'You're in the newspaper. Tracia brought it over.'

He recalled the two journalists, and wondered how they'd used what he'd given them. But that could wait. They'd taken his gun and he was on leave, so everything could wait. Pushing himself up, he took the mug of coffee Anna had left on the bedside table and sipped it. She was still standing there, looking at him as though he were something new.

'I'm on leave,' he said. 'Until further notice.'

Her face lit up and she asked him to tell her about the night before. He patted the bed beside him, wanting to feel her close to him again. She shook her head and said lightly that she had to go check on Matt. She left the room.

Troy sighed and stretched his arms, wondering how he felt. Not too bad, he decided, and swung his legs onto the floor. He sat for a while, longer than he realised, for when he looked at the bedside clock it was seven thirty.

After he'd showered he went into the lounge room and found Matt in his bouncinette, playing with his baby gym. Anna was in the kitchen, washing up. Troy sat down on the floor and talked to his son, running a finger over his soft cheeks. Matt gurgled back. Troy listened carefully, but there were no words he recognised. Matt was a late developer: he hadn't stood up yet, either. He took a tiny hand and pushed it gently against his own nose, breathing in the smell of it, so faint there was hardly anything there.

'How are you?' Anna was standing in the doorway, holding a copy of the *Herald*. She was wearing a white cotton jumper over green shorts, setting off her brown skin. When she went out she usually covered herself up: he remembered one of the joys of the first year of their marriage had been the sight of her skin at home, her legs and arms. It still gave him pleasure, although these days it made her nervous to see him looking at her like that.

He said he was fine, a bit shaken but better than he might have been.

'I'm so glad Vella has given you some time off.'

'Actually, it was Kelly. There's some procedure for this situation.'

When you've shot someone, he meant, but he didn't say it. He'd never been involved in a police shooting before, and he had little idea of what happened next. But Kelly would tell him today.

'Maybe we can go for a walk on the beach this morning,' she said. 'And the Dawsons tonight? I can call Aleisha.'

Aleisha was their babysitter, a pretty university student from around the corner. It was one of Anna's jokes that Troy secretly lusted after her. One of her less successful jokes, in his view.

'Is there any news about Mac?' he said. He wondered how he could have forgotten about the sergeant. Maybe he was more shaken than he knew.

'He's fine. He had concussion from falling over and hitting his head, but he'll live. They're operating on his arm this morning.'

He nodded, relieved. Anna was a nurse: if she said Mac was okay, he could believe her.

'It's in the paper?' he said.

'I heard it on the radio. It's a big story.'

Now she was crying, and he stood up and hugged her awkwardly, the newspaper caught between their bodies. He started to tell her about last night, but before he'd finished she'd grown tense. When the story was over, she detached herself from him.

'You could have been killed.'

As though it was his fault. But no, that was unfair. He wasn't thinking clearly.

'Once in twelve years,' he said. 'It won't happen again.'

'That's a promise?'

'I'll do my best.'

She smiled and looked away, thrust the crumpled newspaper at him.

'I couldn't believe it. Jon's on the front page. Your picture's inside.'

He took the newspaper and sat down. It was on the bottom half of the page, under the headline DOUBLE SHOOTING AT THE TOWER. He ran his eye over the story, then opened the paper and flicked to his photo on page four.

'You're famous,' Anna said, standing behind the chair and putting an arm around him, then taking it away again quickly. As though afraid of where all this emotion might lead them. He looked up at her and she smiled, then went back to the kitchen.

The pictures must have been obtained from the local newspaper in Dubbo, where he and McIver had worked on an investigation at an abattoir. It was the only time Troy had ever been photographed by the press, as far as he knew. He'd been coming out of the local police station and looked startled, his mouth half-open. The *Herald* story was okay, basically his statement to Internal Affairs—although this was not mentioned—fleshed out with a few meaningless comments from senior officers. The most senior one quoted, Assistant Commissioner Jane Blayney, said the detectives had acted bravely. Apparently she'd turned up at The Tower last night, although he hadn't seen her there.

'This is good,' he called out.

'Bravely' wasn't everything, but it was a start.

She came back in, wiping her hands with a small towel. 'You don't mind being a celebrity then?'

There was a smell in the room, and she crouched over Matt, checking his nappy. Troy stared at her bottom, the full curves as the shorts strained against her body. She was an attractive woman, slightly above average height, well-covered without being voluptuous. What a waste.

'It's not that,' he said, turning away. 'There's some politics. Jon shouldn't have been up there. I mean, he *really* shouldn't have. So a story like this, it helps.'

'There's no problem, is there?'

Anna was good at picking up situations, but the details of his job did not interest her. Now she was concentrating on Matt, not looking up at him but waiting for his answer.

'No problem at all.'

'You wonder where these journalists learn things,' she said. 'Maybe we could go up to Brisbane while you're on leave?'

Her parents lived there, and they hadn't seen them in a while.

'Perhaps,' he said. 'Kelly has to let me know the procedure.'

Anna stood up, murmuring to Matt, and took him out of the room without saying anything more.

The phone rang. It was his sister, Georgina, sounding worried, and excited too. He forced himself to repeat the night's events, give her some detail. Georgie was the only other family he had.

'The poor woman,' she said. 'Do you know who she was?'

It took him a moment to realise who she was talking about. With everything that had happened afterwards, he hadn't given any further thought to the woman who'd fallen onto the police car. He told his sister that, as far as he knew, there was no information at all.

She said, 'They say this Sergeant McIver shouldn't have been there, where you found him.'

'Who does?'

Georgie read aloud from the *Telegraph*. When she reached the end of the article, he decided it wasn't too bad. The journalist had somehow picked up the tension between Homicide and City Central, but it was in the story only obliquely.

'I'd better go,' he said, suddenly feeling restless.

'Call me,' she said quickly. 'You've got to talk to people at a time like this.'

'Sure.'

'I love you, Nick.'

His mobile was on the table and he turned it on, feeling a mild jolt of panic when he saw there were twenty-eight messages. Friends and colleagues, people from the church and the surf lifesaving club—it was good to be cared about, but right now he didn't want to talk to them.

The thing began to ring even as he looked at it, and he turned it off quickly.

Using the landline he rang Vella, but the inspector had his voicemail on. He called the office of the Homicide Squad at Parramatta, curious about the state of the investigation. Probably he should just let them get on with it, but he needed to do something, to have something to think about. They put him on to Ruth Moore, one of the squad's analysts, who'd been assigned to the investigation. She asked how he was and he told her, realising he would be having the same conversation with everyone he spoke to today. With Ruth it wasn't hard. She was a friendly young woman with long brown hair, tall and strong-featured. They got on well and he respected her work. In Dubbo they'd had a few good conversations, so good he'd taken to avoiding her towards the end of the investigation, when they were off-duty.

She told him the hospital said the bullet had glanced off the bone and played havoc with Mac's deltoid muscle, but with time he'd probably get most of the use of the arm back. Troy hoped so: you had to wonder how Mac would be if he couldn't play the guitar. The hospital also confirmed he'd received a minor head wound, probably from striking his skull when falling after he'd been shot. This had produced several blackouts.

He asked who'd be replacing McIver. Vella was still trying to find someone, Ruth said.

'You mean there's a death at The Tower and we still don't have an investigation?' he said slowly, not quite believing it.

'This staff freeze—'

'Rogers is crazy about the media. You'd think he'd make an exception in this case.'

'Maybe he will. Kelly's supposed to be seeing him this morning. Vella's been running it so far, but he has to go to Bourke.'

Troy didn't have much respect for Vella, who in his view was carried by McIver and another sergeant in the team. But he wasn't going to mention this to Ruth.

He said, 'Have we found the guy with the gun?'

'No. They searched the car parks again, then they went through the whole building. Nothing.'

They hadn't found Bazzi either, or another guard who had disappeared, Andrew Asaad. Their houses were under observation and there were plans to get warrants and conduct detailed searches. Time was moving on, Troy thought: twelve hours in and they had almost nothing. But it was not his business.

'Any prints on the landing platform on thirty-three?'

'Too wet.'

'Do we know who she was?'

'No.'

No one was happy when they didn't have an identity. It was not just that it made the investigation much harder, it was deeper than that. As though something fundamental was missing. Ruth told him they hadn't found the woman's bag either. He asked if there were any prints on the gun.

'Nawaz Khan, one of the illegals we found.' Troy stood up and ran a hand through his hair, wondering if Khan had been the man up top and he'd failed to recognise him. Ruth added, 'But there's no GSR. Not on him or any of them.'

'What about the man I shot?'

'Not on him either.'

Troy sat down heavily. It didn't make sense. In the circumstances of last night, it wouldn't have been possible for the man who'd shot McIver to wash off the gunshot residue before he was caught. Not if he was one of the men they had in custody. But it didn't seem possible that he'd escaped.

He said, 'What's Khan's story?'

'Nothing. He won't speak. The others are, but there's nothing useful from any of them.'

'He won't speak?'

'We don't know why, but he's not saying a word.'

Troy was silent for a moment, thinking about what she'd told him, picturing all the people he'd encountered last night and where they'd been in The Tower at different times. But it wasn't his business anymore, and at last he said, 'I'd better go.'

'You take care.'

She said it with feeling and he hung up and considered her, what she might be like if he got to know her better. But there was no way he would have an affair with someone at work; the complications would be unbearable. He'd once had a girlfriend at one of his early stations, a fellow constable, and after they broke up he'd had to apply for a transfer. He liked things to be uncomplicated. It was an ideal that was rarely achieved, he knew that. But it was his ideal.

Anyway, maybe Ruth wouldn't be so pleasant when you got to know her—people did change as you got closer to them. When he'd first met Anna, she'd been different. She'd been an Anglican, which had seemed strange to him because she was Indian. But she'd explained there were lots of Anglicans in India.

'There's lots of everything in India,' she'd said.

She'd been interesting to talk to. Something about her being Indian had grabbed his attention and held it, forcing him to concentrate on her as an individual, in a way he'd never been all that good at doing with previous girlfriends. There'd been lots, but he'd never lived with anyone for more than a few months; he didn't seem to have a talent for intimacy. Somehow, Anna had broken through to him and for a few years there it had been good. And then Matthew was born and everything had changed.

Don Vella called back. After they'd talked for a while he said, 'Kelly wants to know if you can come in and talk to some people. She's at City Central. Have another look at this bloke Khan.'

This was a surprise. Kelly must be really desperate for people. Vella didn't sound happy; he wouldn't approve of Troy returning to duty so soon. But Troy knew he wouldn't have said anything to Kelly, either.

'Has she talked to the commissioner yet?'

'I don't know. Can you do it? No need if you're not up to it, everyone will understand.'

'I'll be there,' Troy said.

He couldn't believe his luck. The prospect of an enforced holiday had been hanging over him like a jail sentence.

After putting on a suit he went to the kitchen, which looked out onto the backyard. The weather had turned warmer, and Anna was playing with Matt on a blanket she'd laid out beneath the mulberry tree. She was sitting with her legs folded effortlessly, lifting him up onto his rubbery legs, the two of them laughing. Troy grabbed an apple and turned away, suddenly feeling angry, leaving the kitchen before she looked up and saw him. If she did, she might come inside and ask what was wrong. He didn't really know, but guessed it was an after-effect of the night before. His emotions seemed to have been set adrift and his anger over the state of his marriage was surging through him with a new vigour.

'You act like there's a big problem, but there's no problem,' she'd said the last time they'd discussed it. She had postnatal depression and it would get better. She'd said the same thing before, in twenty different ways, said it was just a matter of time. But she'd been saying that for eighteen months, and refused to see anyone about it. He'd even made an appointment with a marriage counsellor at ChristLife, but she wouldn't go. That hurt him, that she couldn't see how important it was to him—to them.

The news came on the radio as he drove into the city and he heard a report of the previous night's events, based solidly on the story in the *Herald*. There was nothing about McIver being anywhere he shouldn't have been; the story expressed concern and even admiration for the police. He wondered if Rogers had made his decision yet. It might depend on what he thought of McIver. Troy had once heard that the two men had some sort of history. If Rogers wanted to get rid of Mac, here was an opportunity. Troy would be collateral damage. The commissioner had had a lot to say publicly about the standard of behaviour of police officers.

He switched off the radio and turned into Oxford Street, looking at the city's skyline ahead. The Tower reared up almost straight in front of him. The design was unpopular with architects because of the lack of originality. Essentially it was just a larger version of the Empire State Building, which apparently made both its appearance and its structure out of date. But the public seemed to approve of the design, whatever they might think of other aspects of the project. Maybe ordinary people liked having a bigger version of a famous building in their midst.

It was a clear day, the pollution washed out of the air by last night's rain, and the gleaming windows and light grey concrete were clear against the blue sky. The Tower looked even taller than it was because of its location: it was built away from the main cluster of buildings in the business district, which made it striking in photographs. Then he entered the grid of the CBD and lost sight of the building.

Parking around City Central was worse than Ferris had said last night—far worse. The police vehicles were almost on top of each other. He left his car far away and wandered back, down the lane that led to the front door. There was a big gold Mercedes there, almost blocking the road, with a large Chinese driver leaning against it, smoking. Way to go, Troy thought as he pushed the station door open.

Eight

The constable at the counter gave him directions to the super-intendent's office, and when he reached it he found Siegert, Kelly and a man Siegert introduced as Henry Wu, CEO of Morning Star. As Troy shook the guy's hand he could tell he'd interrupted an argument. They all looked at him impatiently. Siegert's face was flushed and his eyes were red; Troy guessed he hadn't slept last night.

'Mr Wu has asked us to reopen The Tower this morning, and I've been explaining why we can't do that,' Siegert said. He pointed to a copy of the *Herald* lying on his desk. 'Last night it was the site of what's probably a murder, plus another death, both of them the subjects of ongoing investigations that still need to establish all the facts.'

Troy wondered what facts still needed to be established about his own actions. But at least Siegert didn't seem to be as aggressive as he had been yesterday.

'We have almost a thousand workers up there,' Wu said. He went on to argue that if the place had been different, say a factory with that many workers, or a small town, the police would have cordoned off only those parts of interest to them. The same approach should be taken here. He spoke English very well and his voice carried an enormous amount of assurance. There was no anger in it, nothing to match the emotion still visible in Siegert's eyes.

'With respect, sir,' Troy said, 'we might close down the whole site if it was a factory. It all depends on the facts of the investigation. In this case we still don't have an identity for the victim and we're looking for one of her possessions. It might be somewhere on the building site.'

'The *construction* site,' Wu said impatiently, as though it was an important distinction. 'If the man with the handbag has escaped, presumably he's taken the bag with him?'

Siegert and Kelly looked at each other and then at Troy. There'd been nothing about the handbag in the paper.

Wu started to put his case again, and the others listened to him patiently. Kelly was being polite, and with the way she smiled and kept her eyes focused on him, Troy guessed the guy must have some clout. This went on for a few more minutes. The senior police would say a few words and then Wu would come back at them, still sounding completely confident that his view would prevail. Everyone seemed to be waiting for something. Troy wondered why Siegert didn't just throw him out. There was work to be done, and he wanted to know why he'd been called in.

The phone rang and Siegert snatched it up. He listened, grunting, and finally said something polite, his tone not entirely convincing. He replaced the phone heavily, as though it had just acquired a lot more weight.

'Blayney,' he said to Kelly. He turned to Wu. 'You can reopen the site at 11 am. Except for the encampment down in the car park, and the two crime scenes. But no cameras anywhere.' Looking at Troy now: 'Mr Wu is making a documentary about his building.'

Wu said, 'Actually, they approached us. They already have a distribution deal with over a dozen countries. There is considerable international interest in the Morning Star Tower.'

He stood up and looked at his watch. He had to flick his sleeve back to do so, and something about the gesture caused Siegert's face to redden again. But Kelly was fine, she was shaking Wu's hand and telling him to call them if he had any more problems. Wu pulled his hand from her grip, as though keen to leave the room. Siegert opened the door and said goodbye to Wu, who didn't even look at Troy.

Closing the door, Siegert looked at Kelly. 'This is all wrong,' he said angrily. 'And how did he know about the handbag?'

'It's The Tower, Ron,' she said. 'That does make things different.'

Siegert shook his head. 'I know that. But this is a murder, we don't have the victim's ID, we have a killer loose on the site. And then these illegals—'

'The killer's probably long gone.'

'We don't know that,' he said loudly. But his anger was not directed at Kelly, not really, although Troy knew there was something between them, something that was not being said, maybe because he was there. Recovering himself, Siegert stared at Kelly. 'This is not ideal, is it?'

She eyed him and then, as though the word hurt her, said, 'No.'

He smiled grimly. The admission seemed to make him feel better. Nodding slowly, he opened the door again to signal they should leave.

Kelly led Troy through the station, explaining that Vella had left earlier to prepare for his trip to Bourke. As they walked he realised she knew where she was going, which impressed him. Generally it took him a few days to find his way around a new place, his mind preoccupied by the early stages of an investigation. And this station had at least five levels.

'Wu must have good contacts,' he said.

'He had a point,' Kelly said over her shoulder. 'It could have gone either way.'

'Won't make our job any easier.'

'We just have to move on,' she said. 'I've got a sergeant, Brad Stone. He's from Fraud.'

'He's got homicide experience?'

'It's the best I could get.'

Troy was surprised. Things were bad in the squad, but he hadn't realised they were like this.

'You can't,' he said.

She found an empty room and went in, sat down and yawned. He realised she hadn't changed her clothes from last night, which meant she hadn't slept either. Still, she looked a lot better than Siegert had.

'He's a good detective,' she said gently, touching him on the arm for a moment. 'We have to do the best with what we've got.'

Putting a sergeant without specialist experience in charge of a homicide investigation was unprecedented, and he wondered why she wasn't admitting this.

'I could come back to work,' he said. 'Give him some advice.'

'You know I can't do that,' she said, but there was something in her tone that gave him hope.

'But I'm fine, really. Look,' he said, putting out his hand. 'No shaking.'

She smiled. 'Are you really okay?'

'Staying home will kill me. I want to be part of this.'

She seemed to be considering it, but then, with a certain reluctance, said no again. He argued with her some more, keeping it under control but forceful. After a bit he said, 'It's got to be a breach of some procedure to put a detective with no homicide experience in charge of this. Especially with The Tower involved. Compared with that, allowing me back to work is a small thing.'

He could see he'd touched a nerve. Finally she nodded her head.

'All right,' she said. 'As long as you're sure you're fine. But you'll still need to see the psychologist and do a stress shoot before you can have your gun back.'

Troy felt a surge of exultation. Anna would not be happy. But this was where he needed to be.

Kelly said, 'So, let's introduce you to Sergeant Stone.'

When they reached the office they'd been given, there were two people in it. One was Ruth Moore, unloading a big cardboard box, her skin flushed from the exertion. When she noticed Kelly and Troy she stood up and turned to the other person there, a big man who was sitting at a computer screen. He jumped to his feet with relief.

'Bloody e@gle.i,' he said. 'Never used it before.'

Kelly smiled tightly. E@gle.i was the system that recorded all the information gathered during an investigation. She said, 'Brad Stone, Nicholas Troy.'

Troy shook hands, wondering why Stone hadn't been at the meeting in Siegert's office. The sergeant had red hair and freckles, and a suit tight across the shoulders. He seemed physical and impatient, unlike any Fraud detective Troy had met.

'Welcome to Strike Force Tailwind,' Stone said.

'I need to go,' Kelly said. Then to Stone, 'I'm working on those bodies we talked about. My staff officer will call you.'

He nodded and Kelly smiled at Troy and Ruth, then walked quickly out of the room. She hadn't told Stone what Troy was doing there. It occurred to Troy that maybe he already knew. Kelly had known if he came in he would beg to be allowed to come back to work, and she had decided to say yes. She was very good.

Stone said, 'Try not to look so disappointed.'

'What?'

The big man was smiling broadly, making no attempt to hide his nervousness. 'I know you'd rather have one of your own in charge. But you Murderers seem to've run out of sergeants.'

Troy nodded. 'You've done homicide work before?'

Stone sat down and shifted in his seat. Troy wondered why he was so twitchy. 'I've been on loan interstate,' he said. 'Can't tell you the details, but it did involve homicide work.'

'It wasn't fraud?'

'There was a bit of everything.' Stone stared at him almost rudely. Then, softening, 'I'm hoping you'll play an important part in running this investigation.'

Troy thought it was a strange thing to say. 'I hope I will too. Who have we got?'

'Four so far,' Stone said. 'They're out at Villawood, reinterviewing the illegals.'

Villawood was the city's detention centre for people with no legal right to be in the country. Stone named the people who'd been allocated to them from Central and an adjacent station. It was crazy, Troy thought: he was the only experienced homicide detective there. And he was upset to hear one of the locals was Little.

'We don't want him,' he said. 'He's racist, I don't think he can deal impartially with Pakistanis.'

Stone stared at him. 'Any proof of this?'

'Just something he said.'

'What, one comment?'

'Yes.'

'I believe you have an Indian wife?' Troy wondered who'd told him that. 'Maybe you're a bit sensitive in this area. I wouldn't blame—'

'No, that's okay,' Troy said. 'Blame me all you like. I am sensitive in this area, and it's not just because my wife was born in India. I can't work with Little.'

He felt better having said it. Much better.

Stone, suddenly looking tired, scratched his chest. 'You're prepared to come off the investigation if necessary?'

'I'm saying you'll have to choose between us,' Troy said.

As soon as he spoke, he wondered where the words had come from. It was not like him.

Stone jumped to his feet again. 'Give me to the end of the day on this, okay?' Troy nodded and Stone made his way to the door. 'Come with me. I want you to look at someone.'

They went downstairs, and Stone explained that ballistics had confirmed McIver had been shot with his own gun, the one found in the car park. 'Our prime suspect is Nawaz Khan; he tried to wipe his prints off the gun but we got a few partials.'

Troy said, 'But there's no residue on him. And if Khan was the man upstairs, I would have recognised him. I saw all the illegals last night.'

'Have another look,' Stone said. 'You never know your luck. We got another one too, late last night. He'd been outside, visiting a doctor. One of the uniformed guys on the boundary spotted him in Norfolk Street. He was upset because he's got a brother among those we caught. He started emoting, and our blokes nabbed him.'

'Nice work.'

Stone grunted. 'One of his mates says this guy likes to go to a brothel in Darlinghurst, so we paid them a visit. Turns out he'd gone there after the doctor. Our people found a Thai girl who'd been trafficked.' He shook his head and smiled. 'The way we're going, this investigation will solve half the crimes in Sydney.'

Stone was scratching his chest again. He was not wearing a coat, and Troy saw that the holster beneath his arm was irritating him, as though he was unused to the feel of it. Yet it was an old holster, the edges of the leather rubbed smooth. Troy wondered why he was so uncomfortable with it.

They reached the custody section of the station and Stone had a word with the sergeant, who took them into the cell area and opened the hole in one of the doors. Stone gestured with his thumb and Troy peered in.

Khan was a lightly built man in his mid-thirties, wearing a paper smock and sitting on a bench staring at the wall. He ignored Troy.

'Recognise him?' Stone said as Troy straightened up.

'No. He's older than the man I saw last night.' Stone didn't seem too disappointed. Troy said, 'Did you ask the security manager, Sean Randall?'

'Not yet.' Stone peered in through the hole. 'Some of our colleagues gave Khan a hard time. That might have got things off on the wrong foot.'

He walked down the short corridor and indicated for Troy to look in another cell. The man sitting inside this one was big, with dark hair and sallow skin. He was reading a magazine and he too ignored Troy.

'Alex Sidorov,' said Stone. 'Australian-born, successful in the concrete business. Now we know why.' Troy raised his eyebrows. 'Uses illegal labour. Not a bad racket—a big site like The Tower, there's so much going on no one's going to bother you.' He indicated for the uniformed officer standing behind them to unlock the door, and stepped into the cell. Troy followed him in, and smelled expensive aftershave.

Sidorov closed the magazine, and Troy saw it was the *Economist*. 'Lives in Vaucluse,' said Stone, who was standing almost over the man on the bench. 'Done well for yourself, haven't you, Alex?' The man stared at both of them intently, as though this was personal. His cheeks and chin and nose, everything about him was big, slightly swollen. He was wearing a leisure suit in dusty pink, with white leather loafers on his feet. A smaller man might have worried about wearing such a feminine outfit, but Sidorov didn't look as though he paid much mind to what other people thought. Stone said, 'Alex isn't talking to us—not one word since we lifted him from the family mansion last night. His lawyer will tell him to talk eventually, and then we'll be able to go man to man. But right now, Alex is hiding behind his brief.' Stone was showing more emotion now, but Troy could see it was no good: Sidorov was feeding off it. After a while Sidorov grew bored and switched his gaze to Troy, but only for a moment. It slid away and he picked up the magazine again.

Stone turned around in the small room and almost pushed Troy out of the way as he left. When they were walking back to the office he said, 'That bloke's got the illegals terrified. I don't know what they're keeping from us.'

'Isn't it all over for them now? They'll be deported.'

'They'd be worrying about their families back home.'

'Sidorov brings them out?'

'No, someone else. Immigration are working on it. They think they have a lead on him: a Jakarta-based bloke named Jason. But that bastard back there is the reason Khan's not talking. I'm sure of it.'

Troy was having trouble following Stone. He seemed to operate in fits and starts. 'Well, maybe Khan's not important. There's no GSR on him—maybe he just found the gun.'

Stone scratched his head. 'The problem is, we don't have much else to go on. The security guards keep a record of whoever goes onto the site by foot and there's no woman on the list.' Troy thought this line of thinking was ridiculous. Given the massive security breach represented by the twenty-one illegals, there was no point in trusting anything the guards told them.

'On the other hand,' Stone continued, 'they only record the drivers' IDs and the numberplates of vehicles, and we've discovered there were about a dozen men working on level thirteen that night; they came in with two vans. Could have brought in a woman.'

'You've talked to them?'

'They say they know nothing about the woman. We're reinterviewing them later.' He stopped, and then said, 'I suppose it's possible. But they're tradesmen who were rushing to complete a late job by the end of the weekend. Two separate companies involved.'

Troy told him about Little's theory that the victim was a prostitute, and the sergeant shook his head. 'This stuff about whores and construction sites is an urban myth.' He seemed certain about this, more so than he'd been about anything else. 'I think she came in separately and on foot, which puts Bazzi in the frame, and this other guard, Andrew Asaad, who was manning the front gate.'

'What do we know about these guys?'

'Little talked to their boss, bloke named Eman Jamal. He reckons they're clean, but you know. Fucking security guards.'

Troy knew. 'What about Bazzi's house?'

'We've had it under surveillance but he hasn't showed. I'm off to get a search warrant for his place and Asaad's.'

Troy thought Stone had left it too long to search the houses, but all he said was, 'I should go see McIver.'

'I want you to attend the autopsy on the woman. It starts in half an hour.'

'McIver's a colleague and friend,' Troy said. 'It'll only take a few minutes.'

'I don't have the staff to spare you,' Stone said, rubbing his hands together.

'Just a few minutes. It's on the way.'

'No. You'll have to do it on your own time.'

Troy stood there, fists clenched. He didn't know how to handle this. Normally something would have come to him, but not today.

Stone said, 'You sure you don't want to take some time off?'

Troy took a deep breath and left the room.

Nine

The morgue was a low building on Parramatta Road, anonymous in a line of offices and antique centres. It ought to look more impressive, Troy had sometimes thought, given the weight of what went on inside. Death should be acknowledged rather than hidden away. But Sydney was a city in love with pleasure, where death always occurred off-stage.

When he reached the desk, he found Stone had got the time wrong and Fundis had already done the cut. He was told the professor was talking to some people and directed to wait outside his office. Eventually a weeping man and a stony-faced woman were shown out and led away by an assistant, and the secretary told Troy he could go in. Fundis, normally a cheerful man, was closing a file and looking sombre. He pushed it aside and greeted Troy, getting his smile underway again.

'You went ahead without an investigator present?' said Troy.

Fundis threw up his hands. 'I'm told it's a big priority, I'm ready to go, call this guy . . .' He looked around his desk and picked up a note. 'Stone, right? He doesn't answer his mobile, I leave a message. Call again, same result. I'm in court this afternoon, reckoned you needed it before then.'

Troy nodded. 'Sorry.'

'You okay?' said Fundis, leaning back in his chair and studying Troy with more attention than usual.

'I'm fine.'

'You're probably not. Lots of walks along the beach will help.'

'I run there,' said Troy.

'You should try walking sometime.'

Troy said nothing and Fundis looked at a piece of paper on his desk.

'Jane Doe, our twenty-third unknown for the year.'

'That's a lot.'

'They're not unknown for long,' said Fundis. 'Usually you people have a name by the time you get here.' He raised his eyebrows.

Troy shook his head, and asked how far the woman had fallen.

Fundis spread his hands. 'From descriptions in the literature I'd say a hundred metres. Twenty to thirty storeys, give or take.'

'That's quite a range.'

'It's not a precise science, especially where cars are involved. Someone survived a jump off the Eiffel Tower once because they landed on a car with windows that were just slightly open.' He smiled as though telling a good joke. 'The roof caved in at just the right rate to absorb enough of the impact.' Opening a folder, he slid a photo across the table, said, 'But not in this case.'

'Jesus,' Troy whispered. He could tell from the hair it was the woman's face, just a mashed and bloody pulp. 'Can you give us her dental history?'

'A bit.'

Fundis summarised the extensive damage to the woman's bones and internal organs, and then went through a list of other details: a healthy person in her late twenties; no food for at least eight hours before death; no sign of alcohol or drugs.

'Spermicide from a condom,' said Fundis. 'She'd had sex within eight hours before death.'

'Forced?'

'Vaginal bruising, so it was rough. There are flakes of skin beneath some of her fingernails, two broken fingernails.'

'Sounds like she was attacked.'

Fundis shook his head sadly, acknowledging Troy's hunger for information. 'Don't know. I can't say more than that, because of the state of her. The skin could have come from scratching someone at the height of ecstasy, if you know what I mean.' Troy nodded: he had his memories. 'And the nails could have been broken by the fall.'

Apart from that, her body told them nothing.

'Her clothes were classy,' Fundis said. 'Collette Dinnigan dress, expensive French underwear.' Troy took notes. The professor looked around then opened one of the drawers and removed a small plastic bag and pushed it across the desk. Troy picked it up, and saw it contained the chunky bracelet the woman had been wearing. Set into it were about twenty pieces of glass, each at least the size of a two-carat diamond. He put it in his pocket.

'You're not interested in that?' Fundis said.

'Isn't it a fake?'

'What if it's not?'

'Is Susie here?' Troy asked, recalling that one of the analysts here had some knowledge of jewellery.

'Conference in Edinburgh, then on holiday in Europe for two weeks. It's definitely worth an expert's opinion.'

Troy grunted. 'Anything else?'

'I think I might have a present for you.' The professor took another large colour photograph from the folder and gave it to Troy. It showed a picture of a dolphin jumping above a thin line of waves. Troy realised it was a tattoo on light brown skin, and there was the beginning of an undulation in the flesh where the waves were.

'Lower back?'

'More like upper buttocks,' Fundis said.

It might come in handy for identification. But there were lots of tattoos of dolphins out there.

Fundis was looked at his watch.

'Can I see the other one?' Troy said.

'The man you shot?'

Troy nodded.

'I'm just about to do him. You don't want to wait for your friends from Internal Affairs?'

'I'd like to see him now.'

'Is that a good idea?'

'It's not a bad idea,' Troy said.

He felt uncomfortable about not looking at the man's face last night. It was unfinished business. Fundis shrugged and called someone on his phone. They talked about number twenty-four and then began to chat about something else. Fundis nodded to Troy, who stood up. He knew where to go.

Downstairs, the attendant pulled out the long steel drawer and Troy looked into the face of a man who'd been in his mid-twenties. He had a light beard and thin features. He wore a grey jacket over a thin jumper and shirt, brown synthetic trousers. The clothes were clean, unlike those of the men they'd found down in the car park.

There were two bullet holes in the man's chest: one off to the side, the other almost in the middle. You were taught to fire twice, the idea being you corrected on the second shot. Troy wondered if this was what he'd done; he had no memory of seeing where the first shot had gone before firing the second.

The man looked intelligent, and Troy wondered why he'd wanted to kill them last night. How his life had reached that point. He straightened up, and became aware all his muscles were clenched. Stretching his shoulders, he stood aside and nodded to the attendant.

Back in his car, he called City Central and got on to Ruth. He asked her to check e@gle.i, to see if there was any reference to scratch marks on Nawaz Khan. She said there was no indication he'd even been examined. Troy banged the steering wheel gently and told her about the flakes of skin that had been found under the dead woman's fingernails.

'Is Stone there?' he said.

'He's at The Tower, talking to tradesmen.'

'Tradesmen?' He swore softly. 'Is everything okay in there?'

'It's chaos. I've got to go back to Parramatta to get more stuff. The sarge hasn't talked to anyone here about our requirements.'

Resisting the urge to discuss Stone, he commiserated and finished the call. He called Vella but got his voicemail; the inspector was probably on a plane.

He unwrapped a piece of gum and thought about the way things were going. The whole thing was a mess. For a moment he considered the possibility that he was overreacting, that he was still on edge from last night and wasn't thinking clearly. But it wasn't that. The investigation was out of control, and someone needed to be told. He called Homicide and asked to be put through to Kelly's mobile. He'd never called her like this before; he was too junior. And, there'd never been a need.

'What's the story with Stone?' he said.

'I saw the commissioner this morning,' she said. 'That stuff in the papers was good.'

'Stone doesn't know homicide, he—'

She was speaking quickly, her voice low as though afraid of being overheard. 'He still hasn't made his decision. There's a big push to blame McIver for what happened last night. The government's very concerned about The Tower.'

Troy didn't care about the politics anymore. He'd done his best last night. He had no more to give. 'Our analyst doesn't know what she's doing. There's been no autopsy of the guy I shot. Stone hasn't even searched the houses of the guards who let the woman into the building.'

He stopped. Normally he didn't complain, but these things had to be said. It was important the investigation function well, no matter who was in charge. They had to catch the man who'd killed the woman, it was what the job was about.

Kelly sounded surprised by his outburst, and not happy. 'Stone was presented to me this morning, out of the blue. Taking him and agreeing to make do with the resources we have was part of getting Rogers on side.'

'You mean a homicide investigation is being compromised—'

'Nick, pay attention. Your career is on the line here.'

He paused, thinking about where to go with this. 'I don't care. We just need to do good work.'

'You don't care?'

'Look—'

'No. Stop,' she said. 'You're not stupid, are you? You know how things work. We can't always have what we want.'

'But—'

'Just listen. This is a job, like any other job. Finish it as quickly as you can, do good work, and you can have a break. Has Vella told you about the conference?' Troy had no idea what she was talking about. 'I want you to go to a conference on DNA technology in Florida next April. It's being organised by the FBI, very important for us.'

He couldn't believe she was doing this. It was so blatant.

'That doesn't change anything with Stone,' he said.

'Give him a few days,' she snapped, letting some anger into her voice. 'If you can't do that, tell me now and I'll take you off the investigation.'

Troy took a deep breath, and told her that would not be necessary.

She said, 'You know you'll be one of our next sergeants, when the time comes. Don't blow it, Nick. Help me solve problems, don't create them. And another thing—drop the gum.'

He stopped chewing and said, 'What?'

'Is it some smoking substitute?'

'No.'

'It's okay for a general detective, but not a Homicide sergeant. Got it?'

She disconnected before he could think of an answer. One moment they'd been talking about Stone, the next about chewing gum. He guessed that was why she was a commander.

What would McIver do? This time, unlike last night, no answer came. But that was okay, he could think for himself.

He rang Danny Chu, another senior constable from Homicide who was working an investigation up in Taree.

'Well, well,' Chu said. 'Quick Draw Troy.'

'What?' Troy said.

'We get the papers up here, you know. I guess Mac was pissed as?'

Troy smiled but said nothing in case the phone was off. You heard too many stories of police phone calls that had been recorded by some investigative unit or other. He and Chu chatted, and finally they got to Stone. Chu had already heard the news, and wasn't happy.

'I thought Kelly promised internal promotions,' he said.

Troy told him about some of the things Stone had missed in the investigation so far. None of them was a disaster in itself, or would have been all that unusual in other parts of the police force, but in Homicide you just assumed the people around you would operate at a certain level of efficiency. He described Kelly's lack of concern.

'What would she even know?' said Chu.

Troy said he knew Chu had a mate in Fraud. He asked him to talk to the man about Brad Stone.

'Another thing,' Troy said, before ringing off. 'What do you think about gum?'

'Chewing gum?'

'Yes.'

'You chew gum.'

'I know.'

'You want an honest answer?'

'It's very important to me.'

'Well, it's not a great look.'

After the call, Troy drove the short distance to Missenden Road, stopped the car in a No Standing zone out the front of the hospital, and put the Police Vehicle card on the dash. He'd been here a year earlier on an investigation and thought he knew where ICU was, but his memory was out and it took him ten minutes to find McIver. There was a uniformed officer sitting in one of the chairs outside the room, and Troy showed her his ID. The woman smiled as though she knew him. He didn't recall meeting her before. Then he realised it must be the newspaper article: half the city now knew what he looked like.

She told him McIver had just come back from theatre and was still unconscious.

Troy sat down next to the bed and looked at Mac, who was breathing steadily. There was a big bandage around his left shoulder. He looked at peace, not his normal state at all, and Troy took his hand and pressed it. A nurse came in and he laid the hand down on the sheet and thought about last night, clutching McIver in that cold place high above the city. Then the shooting, as though he'd slipped through a hole in space, into a war zone. He'd acted quickly, wanting to save McIver and himself. He'd shot a man and killed him. Maybe going over it like this was some sort of nervous reaction. Maybe that was why he was feeling so angry. But then, he was an angry person, underneath. He kept it well under control and he was proud of that, but it was there. Maybe it was why he got on so well with McIver.

He wondered why none of Mac's ex-wives was there, and if he had any relatives. The sergeant was gregarious; it was strange to find him alone. There were two big baskets of flowers and Troy examined the cards: one was from the commissioner, the other from the police minister. He realised the arrangements were identical, and gave a snort of laughter. The uniform outside looked around the doorway and asked if everything was all right.

'Everything's normal,' Troy said. 'No visitors?'

'His parents were here but they've gone for a coffee. Others have been turning up. I've got orders to keep everyone out.'

Troy nodded and had a flashback to last night. There was something odd about it, something that had struck him as wrong at the time but which he'd forgotten. He had an excellent memory, so he found this annoying. As he left the ICU he puzzled over it, and at last it came to him. McIver was a cowboy—it was the word people often used to describe him. Cowboy. He was a lone ranger, a man on the edge of violence, ready for action. If any cop was able to deal with a confrontation, it was McIver.

But he hadn't. He'd had his gun taken from him by two unarmed men, and then he'd been shot with it. This was deeply unsettling. Troy realised he'd been worrying about himself too much this morning; Mac was going to have much more trouble getting over what had happened.

His phone rang. It was Ferris from Internal Affairs. He sounded upset, asked if Troy had shown his statement to anyone in the media. Troy told him he hadn't. The information in the press reports could have come from other sources, apart from one line in the *Telegraph* where the journalist hadn't changed the wording sufficiently. Troy wondered if Ferris would bring this up but he didn't, so he figured the sergeant was just going through the motions. The call ended and Troy allowed himself to relax a little. The media stunt seemed to be working out.

He knew he owed Anna a call, and was just about to dial her when the phone rang again. It was Sean Randall, wanting to apologise once more for running away last night.

Troy wished he wouldn't go on about it. He'd found himself liking the guy, and maybe there was even a sort of bond there from what they'd been through together. Georgie had told him he had to respond to what had happened as a human being and not as a policeman. Listen to his emotions. So instead of telling Randall to go away, he let him go on for a while. It was strangely soothing, but finally he had to interrupt.

'Don't worry about it. Let's have a drink some time.'

'I'll keep you to that,' said the engineer. 'And don't forget: anything you need to know about the building, I'm at the end of the line.'

As they disconnected, Troy realised he was comfortable with the other man's gratitude. He admired Randall for being able to throw massive towers up into the sky. Randall admired him for being able to deal with situations like last night. This was all good. But mainly it was what had happened to them; until McIver woke up, Randall was the only person who had any idea what it had been like up there. None of his friends could understand that.

Their messages were still in his phone, over thirty of them now. Anna had called, too, and he rang her back, apologising for leaving without telling her.

She sounded upset, but just said, 'You'll be home soon?'

'Soon. There's a few things they need to check.'

'Just come home soon,' she said, and hung up.

He hadn't dared tell her he was back on the investigation.

He'd stopped walking while he talked on the phone, and noticed he was in some sort of lobby with a prayer room nearby. Stepping inside he looked around and saw that it was empty and dim. There was a picture of a beach on one wall, and fresh flowers in a vase on a table that wasn't really an altar. Once he shut the door behind him it was quiet, and he sat down and closed his eyes for a few moments, letting things go, wanting to see what would be left if he just stopped moving for a while.

He found himself thinking about an old friend, a priest named Luke Carillo. He'd known him for a long time, longer than just about anyone. He'd been fourteen when his parents died, and because they'd had no living relatives, he and Georgie had been placed in foster homes. It hadn't worked out for Troy, who'd finally run away and spent a few years living rough. One afternoon he'd been walking along a street near Liverpool and came to a brick church with a wooden hall down the back. He'd stopped because he was tired; he'd taken some speed the night before and had only just woken up. From the hall came the sound of thumping, and he'd stood listening to it for a while. It was like someone was being whacked, the noise regular but not perfectly so, not machine-like. More like the beating of a heart.

He'd approached the hall, something he wouldn't have done if he hadn't been so dopey, and stood in the doorway, leaning against the frame, a kid whose whole life was before him and whose whole life was empty. He didn't eat properly, he didn't wash. There'd been personal hygiene issues he didn't like to think about, even now. From the doorway he'd seen Luke, a short man in his late middle age but still powerful, leaning into a punching bag while a scrawny Aboriginal kid paid it some serious attention. Luke turned and saw him standing in the doorway, but the kid had kept punching. After a while, Troy had taken a few steps into the hall. That was when things had started to improve for him. As though his life had stopped when his parents died and then, that evening in the hall, it had started again.

In the silence of the prayer room he took out his phone and rang Luke, who answered. This was a minor miracle: the priest kept his phone switched off when he was with people, and this meant it was hardly ever on, because he was the busiest person Troy knew. He had a church near Campbelltown now and, due to the shrinking number of priests, ran three parishes. The masses weren't so bad—no one came to mass anymore—but everyone who called themselves Catholic still expected a priest to marry or bury them, or baptise their children.

'Photos,' Luke had once said. 'That's what the Church has become—a photo opportunity.'

But he did what people wanted. He gave the sacraments, attended hospitals and nursing homes, helped at the local schools. There was so much to do.

'You been to confession lately?' Luke said on the phone.

His voice retained traces of Brooklyn; his mother had been a war bride, gone to the States in 1946, come home with her young son when the marriage went bad ten years later.

'No,' Troy said.

He told Luke about the shooting. Bless me, Father, for I have sinned, he thought. I have killed a man. But what he said aloud was more like the police statement.

'Sounds to me like you couldn't have acted otherwise.'

Luke's accent had actually thickened in the past few years, and Troy wondered if it had anything to do with the fact he had cancer. Not the cancer itself, of course, but the effects of it on his mind and character. He was in his late sixties, and until a few years back had seemed like a much younger man. Now he'd slowed down, sometimes seemed to lose track of things. It was the medication, he told Troy, though Anna said it might be the boxing, his brain might have been affected. Luke hadn't boxed in a long time, but maybe it caught up with you. His manner, the way he dealt with people, was changing. Little gaps and omissions of politeness you wouldn't notice if you hadn't known him before.

'I didn't warn him,' said Troy. 'We don't have to, but maybe if I had, he'd still be alive.'

'The guy was going to kill you, there was no time.'

Troy wasn't sure how much he cared about it. Maybe he'd just raised it because he thought Luke would be interested in the moral angle. Their relationship was deeper than this sort of conversation, but this was the sort of conversation they had.

He told Luke about the media business, and Internal Affairs.

'You need to trust your fellow man more,' Luke said.

Bullshit, Troy thought. Then the priest added, 'But not in this case.'

They laughed together, then the priest said, 'You okay?'

'I'm almost there.'

'It's Jon you should worry about.'

'I do.'

'I mean psychologically. I know a bloke or two's been shot. They're not the same afterwards.'

'What do you mean?'

'Just keep an eye on him.'

Troy could hear Luke's house phone ringing in the background. He knew only a few people had that number: the bishop, the local cops and the hospital. He didn't have it himself.

'Well—' he said, but Luke had already hung up without saying goodbye.

The squad sometimes used a jeweller in the CBD and Troy decided to get an opinion on the bracelet the victim had been wearing, since Fundis had been so insistent. He drove down Broadway into the city, heading for the Dymocks Building, where businesses such as small jewellers could still afford to rent premises. He deliberately didn't look up at The Tower on his right. Instead, he just stared at the people in the street, the mix of ethnic students around Railway Square, then the Chinese at the Haymarket and the increase of suits and high heels once he passed Bathurst. The variety of the city still moved him: almost a third of its people didn't speak English at home. This created situations that were interesting. He loved the texture of the streets, and knew it was important to keep up-to-date. Part of being a cop was sensing when things stood out, which required a strong feel for the background, for what was normal. It wasn't something you could learn in a hurry. You had to immerse yourself in the subject so it became part of you.

Troy believed that places mattered. Anna wanted to move to Brisbane, where her parents lived. They had had several conversations about this over the past six months. He felt a little betrayed—it was not something she'd ever mentioned before. It had only been discussions so far, not arguments. But he'd failed to convince her just how important his feeling for Sydney was to his work. She'd said he could learn another city, it wasn't all that different: people were people, wherever you went. This was not the way he saw it. He'd told her for him to work in Brisbane would be like expecting a lawyer to work as a doctor. That sounded clumsy, but at least it conveyed the impossibility of what she was proposing. She'd told him not to be ridiculous. 'If you don't want to move to Brisbane that's okay,' she said, 'but don't make out that it's on some other planet.'

Maybe they had been arguing after all.

He parked in a loading zone around the corner and took the lift to the jeweller's and got himself buzzed in. There was no one there except for an attractive woman in her late thirties. She had long hair dyed a strange colour, almost bronze, and was wearing a high-necked skivvy that clung to her. As though she'd stepped out of the seventies, he thought. She looked at him without saying anything, watching to see where his eyes would go. The skivvy was very tight.

'Can I help you?' she said.

Troy produced his ID and showed it to her.

She said, blankly, 'You're a cop.'

'That's it. Where's Bruno?'

'What sort of cop?'

'I'm with the Homicide Squad.'

Somewhere behind her eyes, shutters came down. He'd seen it before. Some people, when they heard what he did, just wanted him out of their lives as quickly as possible. Maybe they'd been touched by murder themselves. Maybe they were just healthy.

She told him her boss was out having coffee with a client, so he produced the bracelet and explained what he needed to know. Nodding seriously, she completed a receipt and held it out to him. He could smell the perfume she was wearing, something strong and full. There were no rings on her fingers and he wondered if this was a jeweller thing or if she wasn't married.

As he took the receipt he nodded at the bracelet. 'Seen anything like it before?'

She shook her head. 'Anything that ugly,' she said, 'it's probably very expensive.'

Ten

Soon after lunch, four detectives walked into the office. One of them was Little, who nodded at Troy and then introduced the others: two men and a woman, all young. Troy shook hands with Tom Ryan, Brian Bergman and Susan Conti. Four detectives was ridiculous; there should be double that number by now, more if they were serious.

'So we lost our crime scene?' said Little. 'Siegert reopened the building site?'

Troy nodded.

'What happened there?'

The others were staring at him. He said, 'You should ask Stone.'

'Do you know where he is?'

'Not at the moment.'

Troy could sense whatever authority he had slipping away.

'He called me a while ago to say he was getting the warrants,' said Little. 'He didn't tell you?'

Troy frowned. Stone should have been back by now.

'What about Ruth?' Little asked.

'Gone back to her office to get a computer and some other stuff.'

'Stone said he tried to call you but your phone was off.' Troy pulled out his mobile and checked the screen: it was still on. Little settled down in a chair with a sigh, as though he'd walked all the way from Villawood. 'There's more detectives coming tomorrow. We've got three plainclothes too. One's with Stone, the others are watching Bazzi's place.'

Troy nodded. This would give those here the chance to enter what they'd learned so far onto e@gle.i. Different detectives could use different levels: Troy had been given access to the whole system, and a check half an hour ago showed that a lot of things they knew weren't in there yet. He shook his head slowly: the phone call to Little was strange; maybe Stone was trying to freeze him out.

'It's a mess, isn't it?' said Little cheerfully. 'Stone said the local cops who're watching Andrew Asaad's place are stopping at five. That's all their super's prepared to give us.'

Troy frowned and looked at their faces. 'Let's have a talk, see what we know.'

'Do we tell you or do we wait for the sergeant? No point in going over it twice.'

'Believe me, we'll be going over it more than twice before we're finished,' Troy said softly. He saw he had their attention. 'Let's start at the top. Do you think this *was* a homicide?'

Little looked at the others. 'Well yes, because no note was found.'

'There's no note in over half of all suicides,' Troy said. 'But I think you're right. Those blokes who ran into us last night were keen to get away. And I'm thinking there must be some connection with the illegals. What did you learn at Villawood?'

'Basically we've got a good picture of the illegal labour side of it,' Little said. 'Immigration are very happy. It ties in with a visa racket they were investigating. But there's nothing for us there yet. The illegals are saying nothing, they say they don't recognise the bloke you shot, or the artist's pic of the one who got away.'

Troy had provided a description of the man who'd escaped while he'd been waiting for IA the night before.

'What about the gun?'

'None of the others saw Khan leave the car park. No one saw anyone else come in.'

'Did you get my message about scratch marks?'

Conti said, 'Nothing. He was examined, actually. It's just not on e@gle.i yet.'

He studied her while he thought about this. In her late twenties, she had dark hair and faintly olive skin. For some reason she reminded him of Helen Kelly. She was attractive too, although less assured than the superintendent. But they shared a keenness that they made no effort to hide. Most cops learned not to show this so obviously. He wondered if she was intelligent. Sometimes area commanders gave homicide teams their worst officers, glad to be rid of them for a while. It was something you had to work out as quickly as possible.

Bergman said, 'Khan's scared of something.'

Little snorted and said, 'Maybe us?'

'That's not what I picked up.'

'*Picked up?*' Little snorted. 'A policeman's shot with a weapon that's found later in a guy's possession, with his prints all over it. Of course he's scared.' Bergman turned red and looked away. Little said to Troy, 'We have to charge Khan now. Possession?'

Troy nodded. It meant he'd be taken out to Long Bay, so he'd be south of the CBD while the other illegals were way out west at Villawood. It seemed a geographic representation of the investigation's sprawl.

'What do they say about Bazzi?'

'Local Pakistanis looked after them ever since they arrived, brought their food down, accompanied at all times by Bazzi or Asaad. None of the other guards were involved, at least that they saw. They weren't treated that badly, taken out a few times.'

Bergman said, 'One of the men, Eli Qzar, says he has more information, wants to talk to the boss.'

'You told Stone?'

'I left a message. Haven't heard back.'

Bergman yawned, and Ryan pulled out his mobile and checked the screen.

'Let me tell you about the victim's body,' Troy said quickly, intent on shifting the mood.

He repeated what Fundis had told him, and waited to see what they'd make of it.

Little said, 'If we put the rough sex and the flakes of skin under the fingernails together with the missing bag, it sounds like possible rape and murder. That's assuming they had a condom with them. Do Pakistanis use protection?' He laughed.

Conti looked at him unsmilingly and said, 'Rapists do.'

Troy nodded. He pulled out the photograph of the tattoo on the woman's back. The others examined it and shook their heads.

'I personally know three girls who have dolphin tatts,' Bergman said.

Troy told them they now knew as much as he did. He wanted them to split up and go to Bazzi's and Asaad's places, talk to the neighbours, see if Asaad's family would speak to them. He would follow with the search warrants when they were ready.

'That means we get overtime?' Bergman said.

'Lots of overtime. Now get going.'

The others looked at each other.

'What about Sergeant Stone?' Bergman said. 'Isn't he in charge? Shouldn't we be telling him all this?'

'We don't have time.'

Little frowned and said, 'I'm not happy about the way this is being organised. We wasted the last few hours, ought to have been searching the guards' houses. It should be called Strike Force Headwind.'

Some of the others laughed but Troy just stared at him for a moment then said, 'So how the fuck do you think I feel?'

They left the room, but a minute later Little returned alone.

Troy, who was about to call Anna, put down the phone.

Little said, 'The sergeant told me you want me off the investigation, remarks I made about Indians. Realise what I said was particularly offensive because your wife is Indian. I want to apologise and ask to stay on. Stone said the decision is yours.' He paused. Troy saw there was perspiration on his face, and wondered how sincere all this was. 'I'm a team player. I wouldn't undermine the team by telling anyone, copies you made of your statement last night.' Little turned on his heel, pulling a pack of cigarettes from his pocket. He seemed nervous, but sure enough about what he was saying. 'Leave it with you,' he murmured as he went out the door.

As Troy sat there, wondering what to do, the phone rang. It was Danny Chu.

'My mate says Stone used to be in Newcastle; his last job there was with a strike force on some stick-ups. He moved to Fraud eighteen months ago but no one's ever seen him there. The rumour is, he was lent to the Victorians.'

'Lent?' There had to be more, but Chu's mate didn't know or wasn't saying. 'I'll call you,' Troy said.

He stared at his phone, daring it to ring. Someone came into the room and he looked up. It was Stone.

'Bloody thing's broken,' the sergeant said, taking out his mobile and dropping it on a desk. 'How'd you go?' He sat down heavily and gave a long sigh. 'Building sites,' he said. 'Good to get onto them, great to get away.' When Troy didn't answer, he said, 'You okay?'

'You've got the warrants?'

Stone banged his forehead. 'Knew I'd forgotten something.'

Troy thought about the briefing he now had to give Stone, about how long it would take to report everything he'd been told by the others only a few minutes ago. How much time they would all save with some coordination.

He said, 'Can I raise with you the possibility that this investigation is totally out of control?'

Stone pushed a finger into one ear and twisted it among the ginger hairs, squinting as though this required considerable effort.

'Are you sure you should be back at work?' he said at last, his tone still genial.

Troy said, 'Twenty hours into a murder and we haven't had a briefing. We don't even have a board on the wall for photos and stuff. Our analyst's disappeared. I've never been on an investigation like this.'

Stone opened his briefcase and threw two warrants on the desk. They were signed. He smiled, as though he'd just pulled off some terrific joke, and said, 'You need to relax a bit, take up a hobby.'

He stood up and took off his coat, then removed his shoulder holster. He looked around for somewhere to put it.

Troy said, 'What have you been doing for the past year? I know you haven't been in Fraud.'

Stone put the holster down on top of some files. 'They told me you were a good detective.' Suddenly he looked very tired. Sitting down again, he said, 'I can't tell you. You should keep it to yourself. Just say I come from Fraud.'

He didn't seem worried at all, he wasn't shifting around like someone who'd been caught out in a deception. He just seemed deeply weary. Troy thought about this, what he knew about Stone, putting the pieces together. Stone watched him, like a teacher waiting for a pupil to work out a calculation. A teacher who didn't care if the pupil got it right or not.

At last Troy said, 'You were undercover, weren't you?'

'Does it show?'

'What were you doing?'

Stone sighed. He opened a bottle of Coke he'd taken from his briefcase and took a long swallow. When it was down he said, 'There was this thing to do with the royal commission into the construction industry.'

'That was years ago.'

'There was unfinished business, and I got sent in to finish it.'

Tough guy, Troy thought. But you did have to be tough to go undercover. Tough or crazy.

'When it was done, they brought me back, but I'm not really a Fraud type of person. So here I am.'

Kelly should have told him, Troy thought. She should have trusted him. 'I guess you know building sites?'

'You got it.'

Troy had once been asked to do undercover work himself, but had refused. He knew it was not in him. There were qualities required, performance qualities he respected, that he himself just didn't have. But even if you could do it, you had to wonder what effect it would have on a man in the long run.

'And this is your reward?' he said, waving a hand around the room.

'It's a job,' Stone said. 'I've spent the last two months being debriefed, time off to calm down a bit. This is a job. Maybe a future.' He smiled. 'So long as you don't tell anyone.'

Troy nodded, looking at the big ginger man as though seeing him for the first time.

'This investigation is a mess,' he said. 'Do you want me to tell you what we should do about it?'

Stone burped. 'That would be just fine.'

Troy brought Stone up to date on what they now knew, including the possibility the victim had been raped before she was killed.

'We still don't know how she died,' Stone said.

'You still think it might be suicide?'

'You don't want to jump to conclusions, is all I'm saying.'

Troy shrugged impatiently. Stone did not interrupt again. When he'd finished talking, the sergeant sat for a while without saying anything, tapping his fingers on the desk and looking at him with a gentle smile. Troy wondered if he was supposed to say anything more, then realised this was how the other man thought, by pretending to be doing something else. He looked at Stone's large hands, the relaxed way he sat with his legs well apart. He could imagine him in a blue singlet and shorts, on a construction site. Pretending to be one thing while being another. Month after month. He wondered what Stone was being now, if you could ever come back fully after living undercover.

Finally, Stone spoke. 'This has been a bad start, but things will improve now. What I want you to do is run the investigation on a day-to-day basis. Full responsibility for the team and all outside people except Kelly.' He paused. 'And Siegert, don't talk to him unless you have to. You seem to excite the super. Any history there?'

'No,' Troy said. 'What are you going to do?'

'I'll try to get more resources. Go to meetings. Do some of the investigation. I understand building sites, I'll work with the plainclothes bloke I was with today.'

Troy didn't like the sound of this. He didn't want to be confined to the office. 'What did you do today?' he said.

'Interviewed the blokes who were working on level thirteen last night. Eliminated them from our inquiries. Toured the site with Sean Randall. Tried to interview Sidorov again, without any luck.' He looked at his watch. 'That sound okay?'

'I guess.'

'So, good luck with the searches.'

Troy was surprised. 'I thought I was stuck in the office?'

'I have to see Kelly.'

'We all meet at eight tomorrow for a briefing?'

'It's a deal. You've talked to Little about his attitude?'

Troy made a decision. 'Little is still on the team.'

Stone nodded. 'He's a good cop. If we lost him it might be a while before we got anyone else. Man's a shit, but you've got to think of stuff like that, operational requirements.' He sighed and for a moment his eyes went blank. 'If only we could match those skin scrapings to marks on a suspect, we might get more staff.'

Troy blinked at the idiocy of this. It occurred to him that although Stone had just promised to change, that didn't mean he could. Maybe he was no longer capable of functioning as a supervisor, or even as a competent detective.

'If we could do that match,' he pointed out slowly, 'we wouldn't need more people. We'd have the killer.'

Stone shrugged and stood up. He looked at his holster on the table for a moment, then opened his briefcase and stuffed it inside. Detectives were supposed to carry their weapon on their person at all times. He put a finger to his lips and smiled at Troy. 'Another of my secrets I'm sharing with you.' He grabbed his briefcase and went into the small office down the other end of the room, shutting the door behind him.

Troy picked up his phone and called Anna to tell her he'd be home late because he was back on the investigation.

'This is ridiculous,' she said. 'You've just shot someone. You can't go back to work. Helen Kelly's out of her mind. I'm going to have a word with her.'

'Don't do that.'

'You're not well. This morning you were clenching your hands, just sitting on the bed for half an hour doing nothing, staring at the wall. You need to see a psychologist.'

'Look—'

'You're the one's always telling me to see someone.'

He laughed, but she didn't. 'Well,' he said, 'if I do, will you?' There was no reply. 'Maybe I'm not a hundred per cent,' he said, trying to be honest, 'but I need something in my life right now, do you understand? I can't just sit around doing nothing.'

There was a pause and then she said, 'I'm sorry I can't be there for you, in that way.' She was crying. 'Not just yet. But it won't be this way forever.'

'I can't—' he began, about to say: *I can't wait any longer*, but she changed the subject, as she always did.

'People have been calling to see how you are. A few say they've left messages for you; Ralph really wants to talk.'

'I'll ring them,' he said. 'There just hasn't been time yet.'

'Talk to them, it'll do you good. That's what Georgie says.'

'You've talked to Georgina about this?'

'We're all worried about you, Nick. We love you.'

Words without actions, he thought, as he said goodbye and hung up. That was one half of his life. The other half was actions without words.

He saw he'd missed a call from the jeweller, and rang back.

'This bracelet,' Bruno said after they'd exchanged greetings. 'Austrian, 1930s.'

'What's it worth?'

The jeweller gave an exaggerated sigh. 'Always the money. No one appreciates beauty anymore.'

'If it's that good I'll buy one for my wife. How much?'

'You'd need a new job. I'd say a hundred thousand, if you could find another like it.'

'Wow.'

'It's an unusual piece,' said the jeweller. 'Who owns it?'

'I can't tell you that,' said Troy, and hung up.

But she hadn't been a prostitute.

He called the stations near the houses of Bazzi and Asaad and arranged for an inspector from each to attend the searches, as was required by law. The first one could not be there for an hour and a half, so there was no need to leave yet. He stood up and stretched. Stone had gone. Someone had brought in two big whiteboards, and he was seized by the need to start writing up the investigation, tape up the photo of the tattoo, organise his thoughts by representing them graphically. Needing a marker pen, he walked around the room, looking for the stationery cupboard. He found a box full of paper and envelopes and ordinary pens, but not what he was looking for.

Impatiently he left the room and stalked the corridors of the station, searching for a marker he could steal. The place was a maze. He turned a corner and almost ran into Gina Harmer. She stopped in front of him.

'Sergeant Stone spent two hours with the men installing the lifts up at stage two of The Tower today.'

She said it slowly, evaluating Troy's reaction to the unfolding sentence. At first he assumed she was talking about the men Stone said he'd interviewed on level thirteen. Then he recalled what Randall had told him about the design of the building.

'That's levels forty to one hundred?' he said.

She nodded. 'The men were very annoyed by the end of it. It's a long way from anywhere associated with the death of the woman.' When he didn't say anything, she asked, 'Am I missing something here?'

He shook his head uneasily. 'I'll try to find out what's going on.'

She shrugged and then smiled slightly. 'I have to go now. Shift briefing.'

She continued on down the corridor, leaving Troy pondering what she'd just told him. Levels forty to one hundred. It made no sense at all.

When he was back in the office, Kelly called him with the big news: Rogers had decided there would be no repercussions. 'Actually,' she said, 'Siegert didn't go in as hard as I'd expected this morning.' She sounded reluctant to be telling him this, as though she was only raising it because there was some mystery for which he was responsible. 'Is there any connection there, you and him?'

'No. He said he knew my father, they worked together.'

'Your father's a cop?' She sounded surprised.

'He was, a long time ago.'

'Rogers doesn't want you at the press conference. Sorry about that.'

She didn't sound sorry at all. Troy certainly wasn't.

He called Anna and told her the news. She asked when he'd be home and he said late.

'I suppose the Dawsons are off then?' she said.

'Yes. But you go.'

'Pete was looking forward to seeing you. You couldn't make it last time either.'

'Tell Pete someone's been killed,' he said.

He'd meant it as a light comment, but it didn't sound light at all.

She said, 'Someone's always been killed.'

Little called later, from outside Asaad's house in Punchbowl. They'd knocked on the door and talked to his wife, who was distraught and complained about the night before, when the cops had come trampling through the place looking for her husband.

'Says he's just a fifteen-bucks-an-hour security guard,' he said. 'But there's a Harley parked round the back.'

'She say who he rides with?'

'He's minding it for a friend. And no, we can't look in his wardrobe to see what's written on the back of his leather jacket.'

'The warrants are here,' Troy said. 'I'll go to Bazzi's place and then to you. After that, you and I go to Villawood to talk to the man who wants to make a deal.'

'Qzar,' Little said, overemphasising the pronunciation as though spitting something from his mouth.

Troy looked at the whiteboard. 'While you're sitting there, give Missing Persons another call.' He explained about the bracelet. 'Someone must have noticed she's gone, a woman that rich.'

'Unless it's stolen,' Little said. 'She might have had no idea what it was worth.'

Troy thought back to what the woman at the jeweller's had said. 'I doubt it,' he said slowly. 'It's not the sort of thing most people would like. You wouldn't wear it unless you were right into the style.'

'So we're looking for a wealthy party girl who liked dolphins and had unusual taste in jewellery.'

'That's about it,' Troy said. 'And was possibly involved in people smuggling and illegal labour hire practices.'

He disconnected. This was more complicated than any investigation he'd worked before. Usually the killer was family, friend or lover. And usually you had a pretty good idea who it was by now.

Eleven

Jack Taylor was a big man, about Randall's own size, with dark hair and pale skin that turned red easily. It was red now.

'Don't give me that, pal,' he yelled. Randall couldn't remember what he'd said to provoke this response. 'It's over for you at Warton. The best thing you can do is help us clean up the mess before you leave. Otherwise, you'll never work in this country again.'

'I'm expecting to hear from Jamal any minute.'

'It's four o'clock in the afternoon,' Taylor shouted. 'What's he been doing all day? They're sacked. You tell them from me, Tryon is out.'

'Who do we get to replace them?'

Taylor came up close, so close Randall could smell his breath. He had to stop himself from putting up an arm and pushing his boss away.

'You're our security expert,' Taylor said slowly, his voice heavy with sarcasm. 'You find us another company before you leave. And this time, pick someone who can tell the difference between their arse and their elbow.'

He left the room, banging the door behind him.

Randall flinched, and realised his head was throbbing. He wasn't handling this as well as he'd expected; there were too many variables. Wu and Taylor, talk about a servant of two masters.

And then there was Kristin. She'd rung him full of outrage, off on one of her emotional journeys. How could he not have known about the men living in his building? Did he have any idea what these people had been through? She went on and on about it, calling them *refugees*. Kristin liked her victims, spent her life on a high horse.

Normally he wasn't fussed, but this morning's phone call had been difficult. This particular high horse had come galloping into his life and was still there, stomping around. Kristin had said she was going to call Immigration, offer them her assistance. The idea of her helping anyone in a professional capacity was weird, he'd always thought of her in a strictly decorative capacity. He looked at his mobile and wondered if he should call her, what he would say. She'd sounded so angry she might leave him, and that was not what he wanted. As he considered the matter, the phone started to ring. It was Eman Jamal at last, waiting for him down below.

'Meet me outside,' Randall said, hoping Taylor wouldn't see the security chief.

In the street, the men shook hands and walked away from the offices.

'What's all the cloak and dagger?' said Jamal.

He was late thirties, a partner in Tryon. He and Randall had had a few good nights at a place Jamal had introduced him to in Potts Point. Pricey, but worth it.

'Taylor wants your head on a platter,' Randall said. 'I'm sorry.'

'Wants what?'

'Your head. It's a saying.'

'What's the platter got to do with it?'

Randall was sweating. He liked Jamal, but the fellow could be obtuse.

'He's going to sack Tryon.'

'You are joking. What about Wu, doesn't he have final say?'

Randall wondered how much he'd told Jamal about Henry. Not a lot, as far as he could remember. But he must have told him something, for him to bring Henry up now.

'It's a tricky situation. People are running for cover.'

Jamal stopped and put his hands together, his fingers laced, in front of his chest. Like a supplicant, Randall thought, but casual about it.

'So, Sean, what do I do?'

'You find Bazzi and Asaad, like I asked you to. Find them and you might save both of us.'

'What do you want them for?'

'We need to find out what the fuck was going on.'

'The police want them.'

'Of course.'

'That wouldn't be good.'

Randall put an arm across Jamal's shoulders. 'What are you telling me?'

'Asaad got two of his cousins into the company. We've just found they've been thieving from another client.'

'Jesus.'

'I've got it under control. But I don't want the cops getting their hands on Asaad. The pricks.'

Randall didn't know what to say. 'So . . .' he said.

'We're looking. Anything you can help me with?'

Last night Randall had told him he knew nothing about the illegals, and Jamal had said the same thing. Randall thought he believed him. He was believing him for the moment, anyway. You needed a few fixed points if you were going to navigate your way through a shit storm like this.

Jamal looked around, put a hand on the back of Randall's neck for a moment, and they started to walk again. As they walked he patted his stomach, and Randall realised he was searching for wires. It was ridiculous. He probably should be offended by this, but he just didn't have the time.

'You need to do some exercise, mate,' Jamal said. He looked around and lowered his voice. 'We went into Bazzi's place this morning. Early. Never guess what we found—ten grand hidden behind a panel in the bathroom.'

109

'The police missed it?'

'Cops hadn't been there yet. They had a car outside, but we got in the back. Someone knocked on the door after our blokes had been there for half an hour, they had to get out quick. They were almost finished, they'd been careful. No one will know we were there.'

'So he was into something?'

'Fucking oath. And too scared to go back and recover his dough.'

'He's probably left the country.'

'I'm looking into that.'

Randall had a thought. 'What have you done with the money?'

Jamal pulled a fat envelope from the inside pocket of his coat and thrust it at Randall, who took it automatically and then stopped walking.

'No,' he said, trying to give it back.

Jamal had his hands in the air, smiling. 'Mate, it needs a home. You don't get four grand for nothing every day. Don't wave it around on the street like that.'

Randall put it in a pocket, said, 'Four?'

'Two for the blokes who went in there. Four for me.'

'They probably found more than ten, kept some of it back.'

Jamal shrugged impatiently.

They walked a bit further. Randall thought about Wu and Taylor.

'We need something to give them,' he said.

'I don't reckon on seeing Bazzi again. The prick.'

'What about this other one, Asaad?'

'Couldn't get into his house, he's got family. But I got hopes for him. Man's your more typical criminal. Stupid.'

He'd been smart enough to get through Tryon's vetting process, Randall thought. But this was not the time to go into that.

Twelve

When Troy reached Bazzi's small house in Leichhardt, Ryan and Bergman were waiting outside with a uniformed inspector and a police cameraman. They all introduced themselves, and Troy asked where the locksmith was.

'He's just coming,' said Ryan. 'The neighbours say Bazzi keeps to himself, works long shifts, the occasional male visitor.'

'No wife or girlfriend?' Troy said, as he saw a small van come around the corner and drive slowly by, looking for a parking space.

'No. He goes to a gym almost every day, drives a Golf, which isn't anywhere around. We've put out an alert on it. No one here's seen Bazzi in over twenty-four hours.'

The locksmith came walking down the road carrying a toolbox. Troy sent Bergman around the back and waited impatiently while the man opened the front door. He stood back as the others went inside, and took out his notebook and recorded the time and the people involved in the search. The paperwork, he thought as he replaced the book in his pocket, always the paperwork. This was really what his job was like, the flavour of it. What had happened last night had been so unusual his memory of it was confused; sometimes when he recalled it there was a stab of terror, but other times it was as though he was thinking about a film he'd seen and already half forgotten. But the paperwork, that was real enough.

He went inside, and saw the semi was neat and painted in pale colours of sage green and faint brown.

'Trendy,' Ryan said nervously.

It was bare, but a quick tour convinced Troy this was a matter of personal taste, and not an indication Bazzi hadn't lived here all the time. The house contained plenty of food and clothes. The small second bedroom had an exercise bike in it and little else. When he returned to the lounge he found the inspector laughing over a magazine, looking around to make sure he wasn't being captured on video.

'Guy's a shirt-lifter,' he said to Troy, showing him a picture of two muscular men engaged in an intimate act. 'Magazines, DVDs too.'

Ryan called from the bathroom and Troy squeezed in. A wooden panel had been removed from the wall next to the toilet, and was leaning against the glass front of the shower stall.

'Like this when we came in,' Ryan said. 'He was in a hurry.'

Troy nodded. Bazzi must have come back last night before the police arrived. It would have taken only a few minutes to put the panel back on. Like leaving his mobile back at The Tower, it suggested Bazzi had panicked. He wondered what he'd been after.

Back in the lounge room, Bergman showed Troy some papers he'd found. 'Bank statements and pay slips but they don't seem to say much. Only five grand in his account. Nothing personal at all, no letters, diary, address book.'

'Computer?'

'Nothing except a manual for a laptop in the wardrobe.'

Ryan said, 'His toiletries are still here, shaving stuff and so on. I guess he had a cunning kit somewhere.'

Troy smiled. A cunning kit was the name given to the cash reserve some detectives carried on their persons for emergency situations, such as a night away from the wife.

'I think it was in the bathroom,' said Troy, wondering why Bazzi hadn't gathered his toiletries too. 'Is there a phone in the house?'

'No. Must have relied on his mobile.'

The inspector said, 'Seems like your bloke's shot through.'

Troy gave him a straight face, said, 'You reckon?'

On the way to Punchbowl, he called the hospital, using the hands-free facility for his phone. McIver was stable, but they weren't letting him use the phone yet.

'Thank you, God,' Troy said when he'd hung up.

Asaad's place was a fibro cottage that had been added to over the years and now contained a large family. There was a big yard, in contrast to the few square metres of sandstone paving at Bazzi's.

The search took a long time but it produced nothing much. There were the registration papers of the Harley in Asaad's name, a leather jacket with the word WOLVES across its back, and a few grams of ice and two thousand dollars in cash in a tin above a rafter in the garage. It looked like Asaad hadn't made it home on Sunday night. His wife and mother screamed at the police as they conducted the search, and Troy went outside to avoid a headache. He was writing in his notebook when Little joined him and fired up a cigarette.

'Bazzi was a Lebanese Muslim. Asaad's a Christian. Unusual for them to work together on something like this.'

'It's a great big melting pot,' Troy murmured, recalling the chorus from a song his mother had been fond of. It had been on an old cassette she'd had, the greatest hits of some long-gone year. 'And business is business.'

'You think the Wolves are in on this?'

In recent years the city's biker gangs had become more criminalised. With the exception of the Logan family, they were the closest thing Sydney had to a mafia. But still.

'Not their line, labour rackets,' he said. 'I'd guess Asaad was moonlighting.'

It was a short drive from Punchbowl to Villawood. Troy knew from previous visits that the European backpackers who overstayed their tourist visas were kept in a different part of the complex to the more serious illegals from Asia and the Middle East, often entire families without papers who could spend months behind the high mesh fences before being deported. The place was in the news from time to time, when human rights lawyers and migrant groups brought controversial cases to the attention of the media. Troy imagined Little had strong views on what went on here, but the sergeant was keeping them to himself as they walked across the gravel car park towards reception. It wasn't much of a place, Troy thought: cheap brick accommodation and lots of temporary admin buildings with air conditioners hanging off their windows.

They were met near the interview rooms by a fat Immigration official who introduced himself as Damien Cowen. After asking about McIver's condition, he said, 'There's been an incident with Qzar. He was beaten up in the bathroom late this afternoon.'

'You mean they're all being kept together?' Troy said with surprise.

Keeping his eyes on Troy, Cowen said, 'Qzar says he gave sensitive information to your colleagues this morning and asked to be put in protective custody. This request wasn't passed on.'

Little was shaking his head. 'That makes it sound like a deal. There was no deal.'

'Qzar says there was and you broke it. And you told the other illegals he'd given you certain information.'

'Ask your colleague, the bloke who did the interview with me,' Little said in disgust. He turned to Troy and said, 'This is bullshit.'

Troy stared at Little, who looked away, and said to Cowen, 'Is he okay?'

'Black eye. It wasn't much of a beating,' Cowen said, looking from one detective to the other. He didn't seem too worried. 'He's waiting for you in room three. I want to sit in on the interview.'

Qzar was a plump man of medium height, with a neat black moustache. Troy recognised him from the car park of The Tower the night before, but he looked different, washed and in clean clothes. The skin around his left eye was purple, and when he saw Little he scowled and started to complain about the day's events. His accent was thick, but Troy could make out what he was saying.

After introducing himself, Troy said, 'Who did this to you?'

'You think I'm stupid? You punish someone and my family back home will suffer.'

Troy listened as the man went on for a while. Occasionally he nodded. He had to establish a simple relationship. After a bit, he interrupted the flow of complaint again and said, 'I'm responsible for this investigation. Sergeant Little said you wanted to make a deal. I'm here to listen to what you have to say.'

'So you must be an inspector?'

'I'm the senior officer in the homicide investigation.'

This seemed to be good enough. Qzar said, 'The woman who fell from the building. That is very sad.'

'So what can you tell us?'

'What sort of deal are you authorised to make?'

'Deals like this are unusual,' Troy said slowly, aware that although the conversation was not being taped, Cowen was in the room. 'I'm going to have to talk to my superiors.'

'Then why am I talking to you at all? I told Sergeant Little I wanted to talk to the organ grinder, not the monkey.'

Troy felt the urge to smile but held it in. Qzar was upset now, almost jumping around in his seat, consumed by anger. It must be terrible to have all your dreams of a new life collapse in a moment, as had happened when the police came charging into the car park last night.

'Would you like some tea?' he said.

Qzar calmed down, said he would. Little took the order and went out to get it, knowing the drill. They needed to get the Pakistani feeling more in control of his circumstances.

Qzar said, 'I was sorry to hear about your colleague, the one who was shot.'

'He wasn't just a colleague,' Troy said gravely. 'He's a friend.'

'Is he well?'

'He's probably going to die,' Troy lied. 'So you understand we're pursuing this case with particular vigour.' Qzar nodded. 'Not that any of that excuses what happened to you this afternoon.'

'Thank you, sir.'

'But you understand my desire to find the man who shot my friend.'

As they waited for Little, Troy asked Qzar to tell him his story, and the man explained he was an engineer in his late twenties, married with two children, and his family lived in Islamabad. He had paid a businessman ten thousand dollars to get him to Australia and into a job. He had travelled by plane to Sumatra, where he'd been told the planned final leg, by air to Sydney, was no longer possible because the Australian government had just tightened up a particular regulation. So he'd been brought to Brisbane on a container ship and transported to Sydney in the back of a truck.

The job in The Tower was not what he'd been promised. The work was hard and dirty, and the hours long. But he'd received two letters from his family, sent via a friend in Sydney, to say the agreed wages had been transmitted to them regularly. Troy thought Qzar's experience was similar to that of many illegals, maybe better than most. Until last night.

'Which floors have you worked on?' he asked.

'We are on one-oh-five at the moment,' Qzar said proudly. 'I started on fifty.'

'You've done them all?'

'Of course not. The company has other employees we never see, we work on different floors.'

'Have you ever seen a woman up there?'

'Never, sir.'

Little returned with the tea and set the plastic cups on the table. Qzar added two sugars to his and sipped it, wrinkling his nose. Troy picked up his own cup to be sociable, and stared at the brown liquid dubiously.

'You're obviously an intelligent man,' he said, 'and a well-educated one too. Did you ever see anything on the building site you think might be relevant to the identity of the men who attacked Sergeant McIver?'

Qzar frowned and placed his cup on the table. He put his hands up to his forehead, giving the question the consideration it deserved. Overdoing it maybe just a bit. Troy put the cup to his lips and breathed in the steam.

'No,' Qzar said at last. 'This is my considered opinion.'

He sounded slightly regretful. Troy wondered what sort of a deal he was hoping to get, after an answer like that. Maybe he was just wasting their time.

'You've never seen them?'

'No.'

'What about the people smugglers, the men who transported you and brought you food?'

'They were different men.'

'Tell me about the man with the gun.'

Qzar brightened up. 'No, sir. First we have to make a deal.'

'Let's be clear about what you're offering. It is about Khan and the gun?'

'I need to be clear about what you are offering too, sir,' Qzar said, and went on at some length about his expectations in the matter.

Essentially, he wanted to be allowed to stay in Australia and bring his family here. As the man spoke, Troy had to stop himself from yawning. He could see this was going nowhere.

'If you help me,' he said, 'I will ask the government to approve your application.'

'Thank you, sir. But we are not children. So I must ask you for a piece of paper, something in writing, before I tell you of the very interesting thing I know.' He put a hand up to his left eye. 'This thing that is also very dangerous.'

'I can't do that,' Troy said. 'It's not how things are done in this country. But—'

'In that case, I think I need to see a lawyer.'

'I'm married to an Asian woman,' Troy said. 'I'm sympathetic to your plight and will do what I can. But I must have your inform-ation now.'

Qzar finished his tea and placed the cup carefully on the table. 'In that case, sir, I don't think we can do any business tonight.'

Little spoke for the first time. 'It's now or never.'

He said it roughly, and Qzar looked affronted, but Troy no longer minded. There was probably nothing to lose by becoming more aggressive now. Cowen, as if sensing the changing mood, also spoke. 'My department will fly you back to Pakistan as soon as possible, once we've confirmed your story. But you could also be charged with withholding information from the police here and put on trial. If convicted, you might spend time in an Australian jail. It could be a year or more before you see your family. If you cooperate, you'll be back with them as soon as possible.'

Qzar looked almost smug, as though he thought he had the upper hand. 'Thank you for your concern, sir,' he said, turning to face Cowen. 'But I have nothing to say to the police at this moment.'

Little was angry, Troy could tell. He could sense something coming from Cowen, too: a profound apathy, as though the man had long ago lost all faith in his fellow human beings. Little began to go over the ground again, his voice heavy with irritation, and Troy wondered about terminating the interview. His phone started to vibrate and he pulled it out, saw it was Stone. He stood up.

'Urgent call,' he said to Little. 'We through here?'

'Just about,' Little said through clenched teeth. 'You go out, we'll join you in a sec.'

Troy went outside and dialled his voicemail, walked along the corridor until he turned a corner and came to some sort of staff amenities area, empty now. He lifted his arms, up and down, trying to shift the tension that had built up in the small room. It wasn't just the room: there was something about Qzar that was irritating but impossible to describe. Perhaps nothing more than a cultural difference, the way he paused or hung his head. But still, it got to you.

Stone's message came on and Troy swore softly in the empty room. There was no news, just a request for Troy to call him when he was free. Troy called back but got the voicemail, left a few words and hung up, looked at his watch. It was time to get out of here.

When he opened the door to the interview room he was struck by noise: Qzar moaning and crying out, Little shouting in fury. The sergeant was on his feet on the far side of the table, shaking Qzar by the shoulders so that his head jerked back and forth, now stopping and slapping the back of his head. Cowen was observing this from his chair, his arms folded.

Troy closed the door, went round the table and grabbed Little from behind, pulling on his arms. The other man was strong; he tried to shake off Troy and then suddenly turned and shoved him heavily, catching him by surprise so that Troy took a step backwards and hit the wall.

'The fuck?' the sergeant yelled. 'We've tried it your way.'

He turned and slapped Qzar's head again. The Pakistani had been trying to get out of his chair, and the blow sent him sprawling. Troy thought the blow had been more for him than the man now on the floor.

Little stood over him, panting. Qzar looked up in terror, an arm half-raised, his eyes moving from Little's face to Troy's.

'He was just about to fucking tell us,' Little shouted in one last burst of rage.

There were tears in his eyes. Then he was in movement again, around the table away from Troy. He flung the door open, and left the room.

Shakily, Qzar got to his feet and took his seat again. 'I don't want any trouble,' he said quietly.

'Will you tell us now?' Troy said, thinking it was worth a try. Qzar put his head in his hands and started to weep.

Troy looked at Cowen, wondering if he should tell him what he thought of him. 'What have you got to say about this?'

Cowen considered the question for a while, as though it required a lot of thought. Then he shrugged. 'This is the strangest police investigation I've ever been involved with.'

Outside in the corridor, Little was standing with his fists clenched. He said, 'He was about to tell us more.'

'They're always just about to tell us.'

Little shook his head angrily. 'Forty-eight hours is what you blokes say, isn't it? If you don't solve a murder by then, you never will. So, look at the time.'

He stormed off down the corridor, turning after a few metres. 'You're too soft, you know?' he said loudly, coming back a few steps. 'Someone had to try something.' When Troy said nothing he added, 'You tried to get me off the case because of my attitude to Asians. What about yours?'

'This isn't about race,' Troy said, walking up to him. 'It's about you being a deadshit.'

Little shook his head sadly. 'Makes you nervous, does it, seeing these people in here?'

Troy pushed him hard against the wall, grabbed the front of his coat.

Little kept his hands down by his sides, said, 'Don't start something you can't finish.'

Troy pushed him again, then let him go.

Little, red and almost wheezing, said, 'Feel better now?'

Troy looked at his watch, needing to break the moment. It was just after seven. Little walked off but Troy stayed where he was, waiting for the emotion to subside. After a while it did. The vigilante approach was always an issue. On the whole he'd got by without being tempted. He didn't despise those who used it; certainly he wouldn't report Little, and if Qzar did he'd do his best to support the sergeant. He'd talked with Luke about this: the priest said you must never cross the line, it was hard to get back. Troy knew he never would, but he wasn't sure if this was for moral reasons, or just because he liked things to be clear.

Little was waiting for him in the reception area, and seemed to have calmed down too. He said nothing about their argument as they handed in the passes they'd been given earlier. There were several rows of empty plastic chairs in the waiting area, and a television up on the wall. Little stopped to look, and Troy realised Helen Kelly was on the screen: it was the evening news, and they were showing some of the commissioner's press conference. He heard his name. She was telling the camera about the shooting, saying the initial investigation had found Detective Senior Constable Nicholas Troy had acted responsibly, his own life and that of a wounded fellow officer being under threat as they pursued a number of murder suspects through a darkened building. The commissioner appeared on the screen and voiced the view that Troy had acted heroically.

Someone patted him on the back. It was Little, who was smiling.

'That's all right then,' he said.

As though this was all that mattered. And maybe it was. In terms of Troy's career, this was a big deal.

'I guess.'

It was still sinking in.

Little winked, said, 'The power of the press.'

Kelly came back on the screen and he watched her until the segment finished. She was smooth, the way her eyes sought out the viewers beyond the camera lens, as though she was talking to you directly.

'You should be there,' Little said.

Kelly looked in her element on the small screen, white blouse beneath a blue suit, standing next to the commissioner and looking serious and capable. He wondered how she did that. Lots of cops were serious and capable, but it didn't come across on television. For himself, he had no desire to deal with the media ever again. But still, he'd pulled it off. You had to enjoy success when it happened.

In the open air, Little lit a cigarette and they walked slowly back to their cars. It was chilly and Troy shivered, and realised he was sweating; some sort of reaction to what he'd just seen on television. His body had always been reliable, but today it was letting him down. He needed to sleep. Tomorrow he would be back to normal.

'I could break that prick in ten minutes,' said Little.

'Who?'

'Qzar. I reckon Cowen would have been up for it.'

'Dream on,' said Troy.

'No, I mean it. You can tell, the guy was terrified. Little tap on the eye like that and he's thinking he's been beaten up. Told me earlier he'd never done manual labour in his life before this.'

The point was, Troy told himself, there might be nothing there even if they did break Qzar. In any case, Villawood received constant visits from refugee advocates. If Qzar was ill-treated by the police, it would get out within days. McIver would have understood, so too would most of the detectives in Homicide. He thought about explaining all this to Little, but he was tired.

It was cold inside the car. While he waited for the engine to warm up, he listened to the two messages on his phone. One was from Stone, saying Troy had to attend the Police Centre the next day for a shooting test so he could get his gun back. It was standard procedure. Stone also said he wouldn't be able to make the eight o'clock briefing in the morning. There was no explanation and Troy felt a flash of rage. He banged the dashboard with a fist and took a few deep breaths, trying to get himself under control.

But the second message was something else entirely.

'Evening, Detective Troy. I've had a nice long sleep and now I'm raring to go. Get your arse in here as soon as possible. Don't forget—'

The message ended abruptly—as McIver's messages usually did.

Troy drove home as quickly as he could, exceeding the speed limits along the motorways, slowing down where he knew the speed cameras were. Enormous illuminated billboards flashed by with their promises. WORLD'S THINNEST CONDOM read one, beneath a picture of a naked couple in a tight embrace. WANT LONGER LASTING CENSORED? said another, accompanied by a toll-free phone number. The word CENSORED had once been SEX, but the advertiser had been forced to delete it after complaints.

The radio was on softly in the background but Troy wasn't listening; he was thinking about next morning's briefing, which he would have to do himself. Stone had said nothing about how the investigation should proceed over the next day, so Troy would have to work that out. He knew that team morale mattered a lot, and it was easy to lose sight of that among all the detail. He sketched out a plan, and thought about the speech he'd make in the morning. Then he rehearsed it, speaking the words in the car.

The house was quiet when he arrived home, but once he got into the hall he saw a light in the lounge room. Anna was asleep in an armchair, her legs curled up beneath a blanket. For a moment he watched her face, carved in shapes slightly different from those he'd seen in the women he'd grown up with. He still didn't know exactly what had happened when they'd met, but it had all been good; he'd fallen deeply in love for the only time in his life. And for two years, until Matt was born, things had been wonderful. Sometimes he wondered if they'd been so good that it couldn't last: there was some sort of limit, that was all you got.

He went into Matt's bedroom and leaned down to kiss his son, asleep in his cot. Troy saw he was clutching a new shoe, a tiny thing. He looked around the room for its partner and found an open box on the change table, with another shoe in it. Anna was always buying him stuff. Gently, Troy tugged the shoe from Matt's hands and placed it in the box, afraid he might choke on it. He left the room and went into the kitchen, where there was some food waiting for him in the oven. He sat down and ate it.

Afterwards, he went back to the lounge room, bent and kissed Anna on the forehead. She was awake in an instant, smiling but anxious.

'My goodness,' she said, getting up. 'What's the time?'

She spoke with an Australian accent but sometimes her phrasing was different. Her parents, Charles and Mary, spoke a slightly formal version of English, a bit like the man out at Villawood tonight. Her father could sound almost pompous. Having lived in Australia since she was twelve, Anna retained only traces of this. He'd loved that too, when they'd first met.

'My hero,' she said, touching his face and then moving away. 'Helen Kelly was on the news, and they showed a photo of you. I don't know why she let you go back to work.'

'I'm okay.'

123

'She should have given you time off.'

'So you didn't go to the Dawsons'?'

'Yes, we got home hours ago. You've had a long day.'

'It's always like this at the start,' he said, wondering if he should have something to drink.

'Why is it so important to you? What you do?'

He looked at her more closely. She'd never asked him this before. Maybe it had come up at the Dawsons'. There was concern in her eyes but also something else, as though she'd been working her way up to this question for a long time. And yet the answer was obvious. 'Because someone's been killed.'

'The victim will still be dead,' she said. 'You can't bring them back.'

'It's not about that.'

'So what *is* it about?' She stared into his weary eyes. 'I think it's about your parents. They never found who'd killed them, did they.'

Of course it was. He was surprised she'd never realised this before. But then, she'd never shown any interest before.

'That's it,' he said, and went into the kitchen.

He opened a beer and took it back to the lounge room. After a few mouthfuls he told her about Little and his racist remarks, and how he'd decided to keep him on the team anyway, for lack of other options. 'I keep thinking: what would McIver do?'

'You think about Jon too much.'

'He would have found a way. He's not one for compromises.'

'I wouldn't be so sure,' she said. 'He's spent a lot of his life pretending that he doesn't make compromises, all that cowboy stuff.'

'It seems to work for him.'

She shook her head. 'It's an act. How could he survive in the police force if he was really the Lone Ranger? Come on.'

She was right, of course. There was McIver the myth and McIver the operator.

'You're right,' he said.

'He's made compromises too, he's just better at hiding them.'

'Maybe.'

She seemed happy that he'd acknowledged her insight, and asked if he would call all the people who'd been in touch. Social obligations like that were important to her. He promised to do it tomorrow.

'Would you like me to call them?' she said. 'I could say you'll ring when you're up to it.'

He shook his head. He was up to it.

'Are you coming to bed?' he said. 'It'd be good to hold you. Just hold you.' He'd almost said it'd be good to hold someone. Anyone. The way he was feeling, it was that basic. There was fear in her eyes now, and he wondered what he could say. In the end he said, 'I need you.'

It was important. After what he'd been through last night, and the way things were between them, this was some kind of moment of truth. She must see that.

'Georgie says—' she began.

'I don't care what Georgie says. Will you sleep in our bed tonight?'

It came out more roughly than he'd intended, but he found he didn't care. She was turning away.

'I'd better sleep in Matt's room,' she said. 'He was a bit chesty this afternoon.'

She left the room hastily, without a backwards glance.

Always when he asked there would be some reason, as though each night apart was unique. All five hundred of them. But tonight had been different. To say no tonight, to just walk out on him like that, was really something.

He tried to stop thinking about it so he could get to sleep, but after he turned out the light he lay awake for a long time, staring into the darkness.

TUESDAY

Thirteen

He woke early, as he usually did in the first days of an investigation. Dawn was breaking as he got into the car, and he decided to go through Coogee and pick up a newspaper on the main road. Along Malabar Road the low orange sun half blinded him as he tried to make out the ocean between the houses. There was a queue in the newsagency, and as he waited he watched the other people, the way they handled their cash so differently. A middle-aged woman in shorts and a windcheater was counting hers almost obsessively, as though afraid she might not have exactly the right amount. A young man hadn't even bothered to take any money from his pocket, and held up the line when he was served while he searched for his wallet, finally extracting a fifty-dollar bill. Troy found detail fascinating, and was grateful he'd found a job where this was useful.

He drove past the racecourse at Randwick, where the jockeys were working the horses around the track. By seven he was in the city, breakfasting at his desk on coffee and a bacon-and-egg roll. He thought about the investigation, occasionally jumping up to make a change on one of the whiteboards. Later he would visit McIver, but for now the briefing was occupying all his attention.

After he'd been there half an hour, Don Vella rang from Bourke. He was in a car and reception was patchy, but Troy could make out a

129

string of comments about the investigation he was working. Then he yelled, 'How come you haven't put out the bracelet?'

'It's this guy Stone,' Troy said. Vella was right, last night's press conference would have been a good time to show the public a picture of the bracelet. And the dolphin tattoo. 'I was out at Villawood until late—I assumed he'd be on it.'

Assumed Stone would be running the investigation, like he was paid to do.

'Do you know anything about him?' Vella said.

'Not a lot. You?'

'Never heard of him. It's not good.'

Then the line dropped out. Troy looked at the phone in disgust. It was just like Vella—lots of comments and no solutions. But he was right: it wasn't good.

'Nick, how are you?'

He looked up and saw Helen Kelly, fresh-faced and wearing a charcoal pinstripe suit. She put her bag on a desk and told him she was on her way to an interagency conference in a city hotel. 'I thought Sergeant Stone might be here,' she said.

'He's decided to skip today's briefing.'

'You're okay to handle it?'

'I guess.'

Kelly didn't seem interested in Stone. She sat on the top of a desk, showing plenty of leg, and talked about last night's press conference. She had good legs, but he had no trouble keeping his eyes on her face because she was beaming, which was uncharacteristic. Maybe she really liked doing press conferences.

'I came to tell you IA are okay with what you did the other night,' she said. 'I'm very glad. You're a hero, Nick.'

He smiled. Other people had used that word already, but Kelly had waited until IA had cleared him.

'What happens next?' he said.

They talked about the stress shoot and the need to arrange a meeting with a psychologist. Then she smiled brightly. 'I want you to think seriously about this conference in Florida. You can get away from home?' He nodded; getting away from home would not be a problem. And he was feeling better about the conference. If that was the trade-off for working with Stone, why not take it? He'd never been to America.

She looked at her watch. 'I want to visit Jon McIver. He was out of it for most of yesterday and they were worried about his head, but it looks like it's okay—he'll be out of hospital in a day or two. He should rest for a few weeks but it's up to him, he might be feeling fine. We should persuade him to take some time off.' Like you persuaded me, Troy thought. Then, 'Vella told me about the bracelet. Can I see it?'

'It's at the jeweller's.'

'Still?'

'We were busy yesterday.'

'Make sure you get it today.'

He found a photograph and showed it to her. She examined it carefully. 'It's a nice piece. Probably bought overseas within the past twenty years. Before that, few Australians would have had the taste or the money. I don't think there would have been anything like this in the country before 1980.'

'You seem to know what you're talking about.'

'Well,' she grinned, 'we all need our hobbies. What's yours?'

He shook his head. He didn't feel the need, although lately he'd been thinking he'd like to learn a bit more about the city's history.

'You haven't released this to the media yet?' she said, waving the photo.

Don't look at me, he felt like telling her, but just said, 'We'll do it today.'

'I'd treat it as a matter of urgency. The tattoo as well.' She didn't sound too upset, which was strange. 'By the way,' she went on, 'Brad Stone told me about his arrangement with you. I appreciate that you're bearing so much of the organisational burden here. It won't be forgotten.'

This was it, Troy realised: the conversation Kelly wanted to have, the one that mattered to her this morning.

He said, 'Do you know where Sergeant Stone is?'

'He said something about talking to more of the workers at The Tower.'

Only a few minutes earlier she'd said she'd expected to find him here, in the office. Troy decided his first trip to America might have to wait.

'I didn't know that,' he said slowly, 'and I don't understand it.'

She smiled but it was an impatient smile. He wondered if she'd be smiling at all if he wasn't a hero. 'Brad told me he'd explained his situation to you.'

He said, 'You should have told me first. There's something not right about him.'

He had to be careful; if he protested too much, she might take him off the investigation. She slid off the desk, smoothing her skirt as she stood up.

'His life is at risk, he's helped put some very nasty crims in Victoria away. A decision was made at a higher level to keep his recent duties secret. We're not happy he told you, but I've assured them it won't go any further.'

'It won't,' Troy said. 'But other people can see something's wrong. He's not acting like a man running a homicide investigation.'

Her smile was warmer now. He wondered if she practised different expressions in front of a mirror.

'Well, you'll just have to reassure them, won't you? Don't forget he has a great knowledge of the construction industry, you can use that.'

'Isn't it a risk, to involve him in the same industry again?'

'There's not much crossover between Melbourne and Sydney. Look, it's what he wants. Brad's a brave man and he deserves to be looked after. Any of us would expect the same if we'd been through what he has.'

She looked at him to see how he was taking it. This was what leaders did: they kept telling their story, to see if you were still with them.

Finally he nodded.

A minute later she was out of the room. It would be easy to dislike Kelly, adopt the McIver position. But she was effective, Troy could see that. On the whole he liked her, suspected she might be the first female police commissioner one day. But there was a vast gap between them. She had a superior grasp of politics, and he realised she would never really respect him until he'd closed that gap, at least partly. Maybe he'd started on Sunday night, with how he'd dealt with the journalists.

His phone beeped and he saw there was a text message, from the man himself. Stone wrote: *Need put more pressure on illegals. Reinterview. Conti's dad was Bill.* Troy shook his head in wonder. 'Management by texting,' he murmured, and read the words again. The reference to Conti made no sense at all. As for the instruction regarding the illegals, he decided to ignore it. They'd wasted too much time at Villawood already.

Soon all the team members except Bergman arrived, along with two new detectives. Troy introduced everyone and began the briefing. Little asked where Stone was, and Troy said that he was working on obtaining more resources for the investigation. Bergman arrived five minutes late and took a seat at the back of the room, looking apologetic. Troy summarised the state of their knowledge. DNA samples had been obtained from everyone who'd been at The Tower that night, and were being compared with the skin scrapings from under the victim's finger-nails. He told them about the bracelet and dropped Kelly's name to emphasise its importance.

'The victim was probably rich,' he said, 'which makes it even more strange no one's reported her missing.' He'd rechecked with Missing Persons fifteen minutes ago. 'We really need to keep our minds open. We still have no idea what happened up there on Sunday night. Time is getting on.'

He looked at Little, who smiled and said, 'The clock is running.'

'We need to give the media the tattoo and the bracelet,' said Conti. 'We should have done that yesterday.'

Troy looked at her and nodded. But when he spoke, it was to allocate tasks among the officers.

Bergman and Ryan were to go over the reports that had been made by the uniformed officers from City Central who'd canvassed businesses in the streets around The Tower on Monday.

'I've read them and there's nothing there for us that I can see,' he said. 'Have another look and then revisit all the businesses facing The Tower on Norfolk Street. See if anyone was working on Sunday night.'

The others were to concentrate on the security guards.

'I'm going to interview McIver and see if he recognises any of the illegals,' he said. He ought to stay here and concentrate on the paperwork, but if Stone could break their agreement, so could he. And he wanted to see Mac.

The detectives stood up and prepared to leave the room, chatting and gathering what they needed. Troy saw David Johnson, one of the new detectives, bend over and say something to Conti, who turned away impatiently. You could tell there was something between them. He made a mental note to ask McIver what Stone had meant about Conti's father.

Fourteen

Randall had never been up here when the view was so good. The rain in the past week had washed all the shit out of the sky, and this morning he could see the Blue Mountains far to the west, and right down the coast to Wollongong. The glory of it still astounded him, that men like himself could build something like this, something that had never existed in nature. The daring of it, the achievement, gave life meaning. At university he'd had a girlfriend who'd been doing English literature, lovely big tits but obsessed by postmodernism. They broke up because she'd sneered at his friends. He'd had to explain that postmodernism was a fraud because it was never tested. There were no postmodern bridges or jumbo jets.

Level one-sixteen would contain Henry Wu's office when The Tower was finished. Henry came up to the floor a lot now, as though he couldn't wait. In fact, he liked to have meetings here with Randall. The man had a pass to the whole building and Randall knew he spent time wandering all over the place, talking to people. Sometimes Randall had come upon him in earnest conversation with a subbie, hunched over a plan or a piece of equipment. It wouldn't surprise him to see Wu one day with his coat off and a power tool in his hands.

Randall had never met a client like this before, and Henry himself hadn't been this way when they'd first met, during the construction of an eighty-storey tower in Shanghai. Back then he'd acted entirely normal, striding around during site inspections in his Zegna suit, surrounded by a group of lackeys in cheaper, darker clothes. Those appalling ties the Chinese wore. But here in Sydney, Wu had become more of a loner; removed from his context, he seemed to have changed. Or maybe it was just that here he had the freedom to express his true nature. All that weird stuff with the DVDs. But at least it gave them something in common.

Randall reached one-sixteen and wandered across the floor to Henry's corner, wondering why he'd been summoned today. Surely some revelation was at hand, possibly about his own future. The thought produced a twinge of discomfort in his stomach, and he rubbed it gently. There was no one here yet, so he walked a few steps and stared out at the view.

'Good morning, Sean.'

He spun around and saw Wu standing by the lifts, wearing a long, camel-coloured coat. It was cold up here, and Randall himself had on one of the padded jackets from the office down below.

'Cities always look best from towers,' Randall said; someone had said that to him once, and he wondered who it had been.

Wu nodded and said, 'They provide perspective.'

Christ. It had been Henry who'd said it to him. Get a grip, man, he said to himself. Get a frigging grip.

He waved—Henry didn't like shaking hands—and followed him across the floor to the place where his office would be. It looked out on the harbour and also down on the main part of the CBD to the north. Randall tried to see the bridge, but there was only a partial view over the top of the other city towers. Wu had had them set up a desk and a few chairs here, looking ridiculous on a dusty Persian rug laid out on the concrete. The two men sat down and Wu talked for a few minutes about his plans for his office, exactly how he wanted the lighting and the way he intended to decorate the place. The walls were to be made of some of the most expensive wood in the world.

He'd shown Randall the plans on a previous visit, and explained how the inside of the room was being built in China. It would be flown down and installed in a few months, when the floor was ready for the fit-out.

Noticing a piece of dirt on his sleeve, Wu brushed it off carefully. 'I'm doing an interview this morning with the documentary people,' he said. 'They want to talk to me here. What do you advise?'

'I thought the police had banned them.'

'They think they have. But this place is so big, no one really knows what goes on here. Almost no one.'

Randall looked around and shrugged. 'Nice view,' he offered. 'If they can get it on camera.'

Wu pointed to a place in the air several metres away, and said, 'I'm going to put that golden Buddha we have at home in the alcove just there. I paid a hundred and twenty-seven thousand for it at Sotheby's in New York. You've seen it in our house.'

Randall grunted. He'd never been anywhere near Wu's house, but he knew Wu was being polite in suggesting he had. Still, it irritated him the way Wu mixed details of his private life up in professional conversations like this. As if anyone cared. It must be a demonstration of the man's power—he could bore you and you just sat there and looked interested.

He realised with a start that Wu had noticed his lapse of attention and had stopped talking. The pain shot through his stomach.

'So, Sean,' Wu said. 'We're here to talk about your job.'

Randall nodded, keeping his eyes on Wu now like you'd keep them on a dangerous animal. The man certainly had some European blood in him, his face was more elongated than most Chinese, something about the cheekbones. But only just. Sometimes, in different light or from another angle, you couldn't spot it at all.

Suddenly the face creased in a smile. 'You've found out where this Asaad is?'

Wondering what this had to do with his job, Randall shook his head. He'd passed on Jamal's information yesterday, about Bazzi's disappearance, and the possibility that Asaad would be easier to find. 'Jamal's people are working on it.'

'Mr Smith thinks it's taking them a long time.'

'Who?'

Wu shifted his gaze and Randall turned his head and started. A man was standing two metres away, hands in the pockets of a dark blue coat, smiling at him.

'Jesus. You gave me a shock.' He wondered if anyone else was on the floor.

'Why don't you come and join us,' Wu said, pointing to a chair.

Mr Smith sat down, keeping his hands in his pockets. He was Chinese too, but a lot bigger than Henry. 'Mr Smith works in our accounting office.'

'Is that right?'

'Now, we need to know about this guard.'

Randall explained what Jamal had told him about Bazzi's house, leaving out the money that had been found there. Ten thousand bucks would mean nothing to Wu.

He was still talking when Wu interrupted. 'Bazzi's almost certainly gone, he seems to be a resourceful individual. Let's focus on Asaad.'

Randall said Jamal was going to call him when he found where Asaad was hiding.

'Call him now,' Wu said, 'so that Mr Smith's trip up here hasn't been wasted.'

Randall wondered what was going on here. But he knew Henry wouldn't appreciate him asking. And he didn't like the next thing he had to say. 'There's a problem. Jamal says if he finds Asaad he's obliged to tell the police. He won't tell us unless you promise not to sack Tryon.'

Randall had made this up. He was hoping to get Henry to put some pressure on Taylor so Jamal wouldn't lose his contract.

Henry took it more calmly than he'd expected. 'Tryon are fools, Sean, not like us. You know that.'

Randall shrugged. 'It's what he says.'

'I don't even employ Tryon. But maybe we can work something out.'

'Do you think so?'

'Of course.'

Randall wasn't up to this bullshit. It was too cold and he hadn't had breakfast. And driving across the bridge this morning, he'd realised how serious this was becoming, wondered what Wu might do. How far he was prepared to go. It was another of the things he didn't like thinking about, but now he ought to, and it made him scared.

Wu said, 'You're hot, Sean?'

Randall put a hand up to his cheek and felt sweat. He tried to ignore the eyes of the man in the blue coat as he pulled out his phone and called Jamal. When Jamal's phone began to ring, he said, not looking at Wu, 'What will you do with Asaad?'

He said it softly and Wu asked him to speak up.

Randall shook his head, regretting that he'd spoken.

'It's not your concern, Sean,' Wu said. 'All you have to do is say the address. If we should happen to overhear you, well . . .?'

Jamal answered the phone and Randall asked after Asaad. After a bit he said, 'Give me the address.' Jamal recited it and Randall said, 'That's not good enough. I need it now. Call me the moment you have it.' Randall disconnected while Jamal was still talking, said to Wu, 'He hasn't got it yet.'

'What about the deal, if he tells us instead of the police he keeps his contract?'

'We already talked about it. He's assuming we have a deal.'

Wu stared at him for a moment then nodded. I'm a good liar, Randall thought. I should never forget that. Generally he only lied reactively, at least where work was concerned, but maybe he should make more of his talent. You have to play to your strengths.

Mr Smith stood up, bowed slightly to Wu and walked off to the lifts, ignoring Randall. He was a big bastard. What was scary was the way he and Wu seemed to communicate without speaking.

'He's disappointed,' Wu said.

A disappointed fucking accountant, Randall thought, wondering what he was going to do next. On the phone, Jamal had said he really ought to inform the police of Asaad's whereabouts.

It was the thing about lies, they could be hard work.

He unzipped the top of his jacket. There was no doubt he was sweating a lot, and the pain had returned to his gut. Maybe it was hunger. He wondered if giving Asaad's address to Wu would be some sort of crime. But he had no idea that Henry was going to harm him. Absolutely no reason to expect that would happen.

'We need to talk about the man running the police investigation,' Wu said. 'Sergeant Stone.'

'I met him yesterday on level seventy-two, talking to a plumbing contractor.'

Wu frowned. 'Did you ask him what he was doing?'

'He said he couldn't tell me. He said the investigation has thrown up leads in several directions.'

'Stay away from Stone,' said Wu. 'My police contact tells me he's been brought up from Melbourne; they're using this as an opportunity to look into something else here.'

Shit, Randall thought. Shit. 'What?'

'My contact is still finding out. The New South Wales police force is a complicated organism. Did you know it's one of the largest in the world?'

'Yes.'

'Fifteen thousand officers, multiple sources of power, lots of secrecy, conflicting agendas.' It was like Henry was doing a PowerPoint presentation. Randall looked around, half expecting to see other people standing there. But he was alone, the lecture was for him.

Wu said, 'We think it's to do with corruption in the union. It could even go back to the royal commission into the building industry.'

'That was years ago.'

'Is Warton paying anyone in the union?'

'Only the normal stuff. It's a pretty clean site, for Sydney.'

Wu scowled. 'There's a political angle. I'll find out soon and let you know. But as a matter of urgency, we need to get closer to the investigation. I raised this before.'

'I've suggested to Nicholas Troy we have a drink together,' Randall said.

Henry nodded.

Sensing that there was nothing more to be said, Randall stood up; one of the things Henry liked was people who knew when a meeting was over without being told. As he walked towards the lifts the pain in his gut reached up and grabbed his chest, making it harder to breathe. He wondered if he should see a doctor.

Fifteen

At the hospital, Troy remembered the way to the ICU. When he reached it there was no cop sitting in the corridor. Inside, he couldn't see McIver, and felt a brief moment of panic. He inquired at the nurses' station and was told the sergeant had recovered so well he'd been moved to a room in a normal ward.

'He's under the name of Williams,' said the nurse, an Irish woman with freckles and a nice smile.

'Williams?'

'He hasn't got a guard anymore. I suppose they thought a new name was cheaper.'

He eventually found the room. McIver was alone, standing in pyjamas over by the window, one arm in a sling, the other connected to a drip attached to a mobile stand. He was talking into his mobile and turned around when Troy came in, gestured to a chair by the bed. Troy put his backpack down and stood watching. McIver scowled at the phone and disconnected. Troy thought he looked thinner.

'I saw a bloke acting oddly down there,' McIver said.

'How odd?'

'He was sticking a piece of metal down the side of a car window.'

'That's odd.'

'So I call security, it takes four minutes to reach someone and then three more for them to get a bloke there. Talk about response time.'

He walked slowly across to the bed, dragging the mobile stand, and lay down.

'You're looking well,' Troy said.

'I'm terrified,' McIver said. 'Hospitals are dangerous places.'

He launched into a rant that involved lots of stories about people who'd died due to the incompetence of medical staff. There were statistics too, pieces of information he'd remembered from newspapers. Troy smiled. It was a familiar McIver tirade, a sign of recovery.

He looked around the room, at the flowers and cards, and an unopened basket of fruit covered in clear cellophane. A pile of women's magazines sat on the chair, and he moved them so he could sit down. A woman must have been here—maybe his second wife, the one who still talked to him. Or maybe someone else. McIver was the most sociable man Troy had ever met. It was one of the reasons his marriages failed, Mac said, because he could never stay at home for long.

Troy asked, 'IA been here?'

McIver scratched his unshaven cheek. 'They turned up when I was out of it, efficient as always.'

'The statement I gave them—'

'Kelly gave me a copy this morning.'

Troy smiled. 'She's good.'

McIver shrugged and winced. 'She's under a lot of pressure,' he said. 'Worried about taking you back so soon, but says she has no choice; Rogers refused to give her any more people except this Stone character. The word is that Blayney doesn't like Kelly, doesn't like ambitious women.'

'But Blayney *is*—'

'Exactly. So, tell me about Bradley Stone.'

Troy shook his head and opened his backpack. He pulled out his laptop, and soon McIver was peering at pictures of the men found in the car park of The Tower. As he looked, he said quietly, 'I believe thanks are due.'

'Don't mention it.'

'I won't, again.' McIver looked at the pictures once more. 'Nope,' he said. 'Not there.'

Troy pulled out a photograph and laid it next to the computer.

McIver said, 'He's the one you shot?'

'Yes.'

'He wasn't the one who shot me. My shooter must have given the gun to this one. So my one got away. I don't see him anywhere here.'

Troy pointed to the picture of Khan on the screen, and made it bigger. 'Are you sure it's not him?'

McIver studied it carefully. 'I'm sure. They jumped me as I came around a corner. I had my gun out but it was so bloody dark I didn't see them until they grabbed me. They were pretty keen and got the weapon away from me. When I tried to get it back, one of them popped me. We'd moved about a bit. There must have been some light, because I saw both their faces.'

McIver was looking pale, as though the memory was hurting him. Troy typed his statement into the laptop, asking him to describe the clothes of the man who'd shot him.

'Plain blue bomber jacket, zipped up, grey trousers and joggers.'

'Reckon he knew how to use a gun?'

'I have no idea. He was close, pointed it and pulled the trigger. It bloody hurt.'

Troy decided not to put this in the statement.

'Go on,' he said.

'I tripped and slid down to the floor. One of them comes and starts searching me, I'm trying to fight him off. Feeling a bit strange. Have you ever been shot?'

'Keep going,' Troy said.

'The other one's looking at the lift buttons, but they know that without a pass they can't get a lift to come up there. They're talking to each other, once they realise I don't have a pass, deeply pissed off. Suddenly they're gone, I'm alone. I'm freezing. Maybe I blacked out for a few seconds—I think I did. I try to use my phone, get up and stagger around. I have no idea what I'm doing by that point. And then I meet you and we do our little dance.'

When the interview was over, McIver asked about the state of the investigation. Troy gave him a summary. When he'd finished, McIver just grunted. He was slumped against the pillows now, as though exhausted.

Troy said, 'Who's Bill Conti?'

McIver opened his eyes. 'He was my boss for a while, years ago. Very clever bloke. Have you met him?'

'He had a reputation?'

'Got caught up in some stuff in the early eighties, when it was hard not to. Bad luck, definitely not the sort of thing you need. They kept the reins on him afterwards.'

'Stuff?'

'He fell off the perch in the end. Had a pretty wife as I recall.'

'Has a pretty daughter, too.'

Troy went over to the window, pulled out his phone. He called Stone and, miraculously, got through to him.

The sergeant sounded upset. 'I thought you were going to stay in the office.'

'We needed Mac to look at the pictures this morning,' Troy said. 'It's a priority.'

'The others are out at Villawood?'

Troy told Stone what they were doing, and the sergeant swore. When he'd finished he asked about McIver. As Troy explained Mac's response to the photos, he looked at the sergeant on the bed. He had opened one of the manila folders Troy had brought, and was staring at the photos of the victim.

Stone said to Troy, 'We need to go back over what we know. Confirm there were only twenty-one men living down there. We've been assuming that, but what if there were more? What if your two were part of that mob?'

Troy rubbed his forehead, finding it hard to believe Stone had not had this checked before. He said, 'That's a good idea.'

'Mind you, the men we caught all say there were only twenty-one,' said Stone. 'And the man you shot was dressed differently.'

'They could be lying.' It was something a detective learned early: everyone lies.

'Get onto Little,' said Stone. 'Check the bedding, see how many toothbrushes we got.'

'Okay.'

'And another thing. I've had some trouble getting around the site. Go and see that bloke Randall, will you? Tell him what we're doing. We need him on side.'

'I thought you were doing that sort of thing.'

'Just fucking do it, will you? Why does everything with you have to be so hard?'

He disconnected and Troy pulled out a piece of gum, slowly put it in his mouth.

McIver said, 'Haven't got much to go on, have you? No victim ID, no suspect, almost no physical evidence. I hope this Sergeant Brad Stone is good.'

'I hope so too.'

'Is he good?'

Troy gave this question the attention it deserved. Then he sat down and described Sergeant Brad Stone.

When he'd finished, McIver shook his head.

'For her to compromise a murder investigation like this—' Troy began, but McIver interrupted.

'She'll be doing someone a favour. The situation she's in, she might not have any alternative.'

Troy didn't care about the politics. 'You once said Kelly doesn't have an appreciation of homicide.'

McIver stared at him, but Troy could see he was thinking of something else entirely.

The sergeant said, 'You've got to give Stone some leeway. Maybe he is acting strangely, but who knows what he's been through? It must be like coming back from a war.'

Troy said, 'He has my complete sympathy. But if he's so fragile, why's he running a homicide investigation? Kelly's not stupid.'

'You're going round in circles,' McIver said impatiently. 'Our lot are probably doing a favour for the feds or the Victorians. Kelly says she'll play her part, she gets locked in, and then this investigation comes out of nowhere, she hasn't got enough staff to give her the options she'd like. It's bullshit but it happens.'

Troy realised Kelly must have told McIver much of this when she saw him earlier. Got him on side.

'This is speculation on your part?' he said.

'The reason hierarchies were invented was because one person can't know everything,' McIver said. 'There's just too much to know. We specialise in murder, Kelly specialises in politics. She's done okay by us these last few days.'

Troy said, 'She was prepared to cut you loose if it came to it.'

'You don't know that.'

'I do.'

McIver stared at him intently, as though listening to his own heart-beat. For a while, nothing was said. 'Well, well,' he murmured at last. 'You're sure?'

'Yes.'

'I told you it was dangerous to go into hospital.' With a shrug he took a few magazines from the top of the dresser next to the bed and began flicking through them one by one.

Troy thought about Kelly and Stone. He didn't want to believe what McIver was saying, but perhaps that was only because of the limits of his own experience.

McIver said. 'Pass me that *Dolly*, will you?'

Troy saw that when he'd cleared the chair he'd dropped one of the magazines on the floor. He bent down and retrieved it. McIver snatched the magazine and began to go through it, stopping about halfway. He opened the manila folder on the bed and peered at one of the photos inside, then smiled widely and held up the magazine.

'*"Tattoos of the rich and famous"*,' he said, reading a headline. He held up the magazine. 'Recognise anything?'

There was a double-page spread of photos of tattoos on celebrities' bodies. One was of a young woman, taken from behind. She was wearing low-cut jeans and appeared to be pulling on a shirt at the beach. The tattoo just above the jeans was clearly visible: a dolphin, jumping out of the water.

'*"Margot Teresi"*,' McIver read out loud, '*"Australia's fifth-richest woman. Seen displaying her dolphin at Tamarama Beach."*'

Troy grabbed the magazine and read the words for himself.

'Margot Teresi,' he said slowly, savouring the name.

'Do you think she was any relation to Tony Teresi?'

It was a game McIver liked to play.

'The bloke who started The Tower?' said Troy.

'Yeah.'

'Probably not.'

McIver lay back, his good arm behind his head.

'Kelly wants me to take a few weeks to recuperate,' he said. 'But I figure on being back soon.' His face brightened and he smiled broadly. 'Let's face it, without me, you're all helpless.'

Sixteen

The project office of Warton Constructions was on Norfolk Street, above a branch of Westpac Bank. Troy had come to see what more Sean Randall could tell them about The Tower's security arrangements. Randall greeted Troy in the lobby on the second floor, where two men in bright green polo shirts were waiting in plastic chairs. There was no bandage around Randall's head today, and his wound appeared much less serious than it had the other night. He took Troy through to his office and led him over to a large window with a view of one of the lowest floors of The Tower. In the street below Troy could see two television crews, filming the entrance to the building site. He looked up, taking in the decorative stonework and the tinted glass.

'Inspiring view,' he said, as Randall showed him to some easy chairs and a secretary took his order for coffee. He wasn't just being polite.

'I try not to look at it too much,' Randall said. He had a leg over the side of the chair and looked comfortable and competent. Different from the other night. 'It's kind of frustrating. I'm an engineer, I like building things. But if you want to become a senior project manager with Warton, you have to do a few years at everything. Like security.'

He scratched the little beard beneath his lower lip. 'At the moment, I can't say I'm enjoying it.'

He smiled and Troy liked his honesty. Despite the sentiment Randall had just expressed, there was still a certain sense of ease about him. Troy had noticed this before in people whose careers brought them into contact with inanimate objects a lot.

'The job was going okay until now?'

Randall nodded. 'The most exciting event I've had was the base jumpers. I thought I might get the sack then, but it worked out all right.' He studied Troy for a moment, as though wondering whether to be frank, and then plunged in. 'We were actually pretty unhappy with the security company we had at the time. It belonged to Tony Teresi, the first owner of the project.'

Troy took care not to react at the mention of the name. He'd told Stone about McIver's possible identification of the victim, and they'd decided to keep the information to themselves for the moment. 'Couldn't you sack them after Teresi sold the project?' he said.

'We were locked into a contract. The base-jumping incident breached their performance agreement and gave us cause to terminate, which was good. Fortunately for me, I was the one who spotted that.'

He smiled, as though the memory was still a happy one.

'So then you hired the new company?'

'Tryon Security. They've been fine. Until now.' Randall shook his head. 'I actually got Bazzi the job with them—he'd been with the old lot and he was the only manager there who saw what was going on. It's weird to think he's betrayed me like this. You got any word on him?'

'He's disappeared. Asaad too.'

'You think they've left the country?'

'It's possible. Tryon would have done background checks before they took them on?'

Randall nodded and sighed. 'That guy in the *Herald* this morning, saying how could we have had twenty people living in the building without knowing about it. They've got no idea of the scale of this place.'

Troy nodded. 'Bazzi was given a promotion when he first came on board at Tryon, but they dropped him back after a few months. He came to see me about it, said there was no reason. Maybe he got upset and went on the take.'

Troy had his notebook out. 'Did they ever check the floors down below? The empty ones?'

'Once a month. We're not stupid, but you have to rely on your own people. This thing with Bazzi, it's—it's like one of those moles in the secret service, isn't it? Very hard to spot unless you're looking.'

Troy saw where this was going. 'Don't tell me—'

'Bazzi did the lower car park checks the last two months.'

'Alone?'

'With Asaad.'

There was a knock on the door and the secretary reappeared with a tray. She put cups of coffee on the low table between the two men. Troy couldn't help looking at her as she bent over, her red skirt tightening.

After she'd left the room Randall laughed. 'Like what you see?'

'She's all yours?'

'We had a thing. But there's too many beautiful women in this city to stop at one.'

'I'm married,' Troy said. His voice sounded a little strained even to his own ears.

'I was married too. Everyone should do it once.' Randall laughed. 'If I'd been prepared to be unfaithful, I might still be married.'

'You reckon?'

'Maybe. Funny how things turn out.' He'd put both his feet on the floor and was leaning forward.

Troy said, 'Tell me about Teresi's security company.'

'His daughter ran it, actually.'

Troy concentrated on his coffee. 'His daughter?' he said.

'Margot. Attractive brunette, mid-twenties. I had some meetings with her when we were trying to change the contract. She wanted more money. I said it's not about money—we're paying you plenty—it's about performance.'

'What was she like to deal with?' Troy said, trying to keep the interest out of his voice.

'Tough, but not really effective. She had all her old man's aggro, but the shrewdness wasn't there. I heard she wasn't all that interested in the family business, but Tony insisted. I got the impression she just came into work a few hours a day and yelled at people.'

Troy didn't want to linger on Margot Teresi in case Randall noticed his curiosity, but he must have stayed with it a second too long, for just as he was about to change the subject, Randall straightened up. His eyes lit up and Troy saw he'd got it.

'My God,' said the engineer. 'It's her, isn't it?'

Troy's heart sunk. 'Why would you say that?'

'Jesus Christ.'

'Did you see the body last night?'

Randall shook his head. Inwardly cursing himself, Troy said it might be Margot Teresi, it was one of the possibilities they were looking into. 'Don't tell anyone,' he said. 'We haven't confirmed it. Haven't done the death message yet.'

'The what?'

'We haven't talked to her family.'

Randall nodded, looking at Troy with keen eyes. 'Hell of a job you've got, isn't it?'

Before Troy could answer, Randall's gaze slid off to the wall and the energy suddenly left him. It was as though some transforming revelation had struck him. Sinking into his chair again, he whispered, 'I've had it.'

'What?'

'Margot Teresi. I mean, the poor woman—but Jesus, the publicity's going to be huge. Morning Star will need to show they're responding. Sacking me will be part of that. It's the way it goes.'

Troy felt a twinge of pity. 'Won't Warton just move you to another job?'

'Morning Star are their biggest client, and they're hard bastards. I'm out.' Randall was running a hand slowly over his shaved head. His face had gone red, but was now returning to its normal colour. He shrugged. 'I always wanted to see more of the world,' he said in a voice suddenly hoarse with self-pity. 'This could be my opportunity.'

Troy laughed. 'Tell me about Tony Teresi.'

In a moment Randall was alert again. 'A very interesting bloke, like one of those big entrepreneurs of the eighties, but with a difference. He wasn't just a money juggler, he wanted to build productive businesses. Pretty good at it, too.'

'He worked in America, didn't he?'

'Spent a decade or two in the gaming industry; must have done well because when he came back here in the nineties he owned two casinos, in Las Vegas and Macau. Came back because his wife was dying of cancer. She wasn't that old, wanted to be near her parents. So, the casinos are still churning out cash but he can't break into that industry here, it's too tight. Tony looks around, buys some coalmines up and down the east coast, bit like a hobby, and then becomes interested in how the coal gets to the ports. Before long he's out of coal and big in the railway business. Very big.'

'I thought the railways are owned by government.'

'Government owns the tracks but they sold off the freight services that run on them. A lot of the buyers lost their shirts in the confusion that followed, paid too much, the winner's curse. Tony comes in as a second-generation player and cleans up. The commodity boom gets bigger and he keeps making money. He did other stuff too, but basically it was coal and casinos.' He paused.

'So what happened?'

'Tony's wife dies and he takes it bad, really bad. Starts thinking about mortality, leaving some monument. I only know what I read, I never met the bloke, but that's when he started work on his idea for the tallest building in the world, here in Sydney. The Olympics were coming up and there was a feeling this city could do anything. It was going to be called Elena Tower—that was the name of his wife.'

Troy nodded, remembering more of the story himself now. The new owners had changed the name to Morning Star Tower, but it hadn't caught on.

Randall went on, 'It takes him five or six years to buy an entire block, fifteen separate properties. It's on the fringe of the CBD but, even so, incredibly difficult. No one thought you could own a whole block in this city anymore. A massive achievement.'

'He paid too much though, didn't he?'

Randall explained how The Tower had become an obsession. Teresi became impatient and started paying up to fifty per cent more than he should have. The finances became precarious. The Empire State Building design was picked because it had been his wife's favourite building, but it created all sorts of problems for a building of this size.

'But couldn't he afford his folly?' said Troy.

'He just kept paying too much for everything. He wanted the greatest new building in the world—a monument to Elena, like a modern Taj Mahal.'

Randall stood up, walked over to the window and, craning his neck, looked upwards. 'For me he was a hero. When I was at university, people used to look down on engineers—the arts crowd said we had no imagination. But you need imagination to create something like this out of nothing.' He waved a hand and turned back. 'What have they got to put up against this? There's no Picasso anymore, no James Joyce. But we can build things like The Tower that we've never built before.' He sat down and Troy wondered what this was all about. 'Anyway, Tony had been spending all the profits from his other businesses on The Tower. Then the coal boom dipped and there was a problem with the casino in Macau. Suddenly Tony was going backwards. Morning Star had been a twenty-five per cent owner from the start, and had an option clause in the contract, so they got the rest cheap. People say Tony lost several hundred million by the time he got out. But even so,' Randall pointed out the window, 'there it stands.'

'What happened to Tony?'

'Basically, he lost the lot. The shareholders sacked him at the AGM two years ago, and a week later he died of a heart attack.'

'How many children?'

'Just one. She got some bits and pieces. Not all that much, but I doubt she struggled.' He shook his head. 'Still,' he said, 'poor Margot.'

Troy was anxious to be off to visit Margot Teresi's place, wherever it might be—Ruth was getting the details—but he wanted to learn as much as he could from Randall first.

'Are Morning Star good to work for?'

'Their local manager is Henry Wu. Born in China but got out to Hong Kong years ago. They're tough people but they're spending big.' He swivelled in his chair and pointed again at the facade of The Tower. 'The pattern work on those granite slabs goes up for the first forty storeys. I mean, who's going to see it? But for them it's important to be able to say it's there. Have you been to Asia?'

'Once.' He had been to India on his honeymoon.

'Different ways of thinking. Morning Star are looking to dominate the insurance industry in the Asia-Pacific region within ten years, so there's a lot of symbolism here. They've added about fifty million dollars to the detail and upgraded materials—you should see some of the stuff they're bringing in.' He explained how normally with a new office building, the tenants would be expected to do the fit-out of the entire floor. But Morning Star were doing the area around the lifts on each floor themselves, with particularly fine timber work. 'We're using beautiful tropical timber. They get the marquetry done in China and fly it down in sections. Huge quantities of some of the best stuff available anywhere in the world.'

'They must have a lot of money to spare.'

Randall shrugged. 'They're the modern equivalents of the companies that built the big New York skyscrapers in the twenties and thirties. And they know it. Symbolism matters to them. They like the way The Tower's the same as the Empire State Building—but bigger.'

Troy said, 'Any thoughts on why Margot would have been there on Sunday?'

'None.'

'How easy would it have been for her to get in?'

'Once you assume Bazzi's involvement, it becomes pretty straight-forward, with Asaad involved too. She might have known Bazzi from

155

the old company. He could have arranged the shift so there were no other guards near the front entrance at a certain time. She walks in. Asaad's on the gate, he doesn't note her on the list.'

'Sergeant Little tells me your CCTV camera at the pedestrian entrance was disabled for the period we're interested in?'

'Yep, another reason why it must have been that entrance. As shift manager, Bazzi had the key and the password; he must have switched off the camera. The other one, at the vehicle entrance, was left on. It doesn't show anything.'

Troy nodded. He knew all this already—the police had viewed copies of all the CCTV footage—but it was useful to see just how far Randall had conducted his own inquiries. He closed his notebook and stood up, said he'd be going. Randall, getting to his feet more slowly, looked suddenly serious.

'Your boss, Sergeant Stone,' he said. 'He asked for a pass for all the lifts in the building, which we thought a bit strange, but we gave it to him. Turns out he's been going all over the place, as high up as level ninety-two. What's that all about?'

'I'm sure he'll let me know what lines of inquiry he's pursuing later today,' Troy said.

He started to walk towards the door but Randall didn't follow him. Instead, he called across the room, 'Stone interviewed me yesterday, but he didn't seem all that interested. You're the one running this inquiry, aren't you?'

'Now, why would you think that?' Troy said.

'It's pretty obvious. With all due respect to the sergeant.'

The door in front of him opened and Randall's secretary appeared. She smiled at Troy and he smiled back.

'Angel, this is Detective Nicholas Troy. I think we'll be seeing a lot more of him.'

'That's good,' she said.

Troy smiled some more and turned to say goodbye to Randall, who was crossing the room now, his hand out. He seemed distracted and Troy guessed he was thinking about his future.

'Thanks again for the other night,' the engineer said. 'Let's catch up for that drink when you've got the time.'

They shook hands. Randall had a good firm grip. Troy liked the man. It was good to meet someone about his own age, at his own level, tackling similar sorts of career problems; discovering the world was more complicated than he'd realised.

'We'll do that,' he said.

Downstairs, Troy stood on the footpath, taking in the busy, sunlit street, so different from Sunday night. The television crews he'd seen earlier had left, and two trucks were waiting to drive into the building's vehicle entrance. The people walking by were looking at The Tower with particular interest. There'd be a lot more interest when the victim's name was made known. Remembering he was short of cash, he went to the ATM outside the bank, where he made a withdrawal. As he waited he noticed the sign saying customers might be filmed while making a transaction. He looked for the camera and estimated from the angle of its lens that it would have no coverage of the other side of the road. Still, there was a possibility Margot Teresi had walked along this footpath, or even used the machine. As far as he knew, no one had checked.

He went into the bank and asked to speak to the manager. Some of the tellers were staring at him, presumably on account of the photo in the newspaper. It was not an enjoyable sensation: as a detective, he was used to looking at others. If you became the object of attention yourself, usually it meant you had failed.

A man a little older than himself, wearing a short-sleeved white shirt and a name tag that identified him as Alan Wainwright, came out of a door beside the tellers' counter and shook his hand. They went into a plain office with no windows. Troy explained his request, and Wainwright opened a top drawer and took out two DVDs in slim plastic cases, which he put on the desk. He pushed one across to Troy.

'I called our security director yesterday to ask if I should contact the police and offer these,' he said, his voice a little strained with the

157

excitement of it all. 'He hasn't got back to me, but it's company policy to hand over CCTV footage if and when the police ask for it, so it's all yours.'

Troy nodded his thanks and slipped the case into a coat pocket.

He looked at the remaining DVD, wondering what it was. 'Can I have that too?'

'You'll have to tell me what it is you want,' said Wainwright.

This is stupid, Troy thought. But the manager was completely serious. Troy leaned back in his chair and thought about what he'd seen since he came into the bank. It came to him after a few moments.

'There's a camera in the banking chamber,' he said. Actually, he didn't recall seeing it, but there must have been one.

Wainwright nodded and pushed the second DVD across the desk.

The manager said, 'It has a not-bad view across the street. It's amazing what they can pick up these days.'

Troy went still, and told himself to keep breathing. 'I don't suppose you keep it on at nights?'

'We keep it on all the time.'

Troy stood up and shook the guy's hand. As he left the bank he cursed Ryan and Bergman, who had canvassed businesses along the street. They'd missed the cameras altogether. Sometimes, he thought, it was a wonder any crime got solved at all.

Seventeen

Randall had never been in this part of the city before, way out west. He'd had no idea a place like this existed in Sydney. A few minutes earlier he'd passed a strip of shops, all with bars on their windows and doors, one a burned-out shell. Men were sitting on the gutter drinking from bottles in brown paper bags, staring at him with dead eyes. This was badlands territory. Randall paid attention to the sound of the hire car's engine, hoping it wouldn't break down.

It was early afternoon and he was looking for the address Jamal had given him, Asaad's cousin's place, in a suburb he'd never heard of called Hebersham. His thought was to warn Asaad to leave the city. Get out and far away; name like that, he must have contacts abroad. If it was the money, Randall could help: he had the cash Jamal had given him—it was Asaad's anyway. Of course Asaad ought to be in a police cell, answering questions about his involvement in the death of Margot Teresi. But that wasn't going to happen, because of the damage that might do to Jamal. Still, Asaad certainly didn't deserve to fall into the hands of Henry Wu. Not that Randall had any idea of what that might mean for the fellow. But it was not something he wanted on his conscience.

You had to wonder if Henry had had anything to do with Margot Teresi. Randall tried not to wonder about it, because to wonder was not pleasant, but it kept coming back into his mind. When he hadn't known who the victim was, a link between Henry and the dead woman had never occurred to him. Even now he had no idea what that link might be. But Margot Teresi was a coincidence, and the way Henry had been going on, it made you think. And yet, even if he was capable of killing someone, which Randall didn't believe he was, Henry wouldn't be so stupid as to do it on the site. He kept coming back to that. The fellow might have a capacity for violence, maybe even reckless violence. But he was not stupid.

Randall needed to look in the directory; he was lost again. Maybe he wasn't in Hebersham anymore. As far as he could work out there was a clump of half a dozen suburbs that ran in and out of each other, all the same place really, sharing a postcode the way he bet the women here shared the men. Lots of uncut grass, makeshift curtains, even its own design feature, this weird little copper-coloured peak on top of the roofs of many of the houses, as if some architect had decided to badge them as public housing. And the people, he thought. There weren't too many on the streets—they wouldn't be great walkers out here—but the young women he'd seen had been fat, pushing strollers, trapped. Randall felt trapped himself.

He pulled over to the side of the road, making sure there were no people around. Earlier, he'd ended up in a cul-de-sac, no warning, no No Through Road sign—he'd just come to the end of the road and had to reverse, do a three-point turn. Two guys standing around the open bonnet of a red car had stared at him. They were wearing T-shirts, one had just a blue singlet on. And serious tatts, not small and stylish but running down their big arms like skin diseases. One man had started to walk towards Randall and as he came closer you could see what he was holding was not some tool but a bottle of beer. The fellow had moved slowly, his face expressionless. Randall had completed his turn and got out of there before the need for conversation arose.

Jumping at shadows, he thought, now leaning back against the headrest but keeping his eyes open, flicking his gaze at the rear view every few seconds. A big white car came slowly down the street and the pain flooded into Randall's stomach as it went past, his hand up to the side of his face. He'd seen the car before, when he was coming through Mount Druitt. Or a car like it. Big white Commodore, the car of officialdom. An area like this it could be Social Security, Housing, Health. A parole officer, council engineer, truancy. Big white cars keeping welfare-world in line. The car kept moving, turned the corner up ahead, and disappeared, unlike the pain in his gut.

'I've had enough,' he murmured, and pulled out his mobile and a piece of paper.

He called the doctor whose name Angela had got for him, some GP with an office near The Tower. They couldn't see him that afternoon, so he made an appointment for tomorrow. At least, he thought it was tomorrow, realised when they'd hung up he just had a date but didn't know what today was. Should write it down somewhere. He took out a handkerchief and mopped his brow while he examined the street directory. Kept thinking about Henry Wu.

In Shanghai, Randall had fucked up big-time. On an evening when he should have been supervising a concrete pour on level forty-nine, he'd been at home humping a Chinese girl he'd met a few days before. Most Chinese women he didn't find all that attractive, flat faces and flat chests; they probably didn't find him attractive either. Live and let live. But this one was from some ethnic group to the west, and she was something else. As if she wasn't meant to be here but defiant with it, holding herself high and back. He could still remember her vividly.

But in China it wasn't easy and you had to take opportunities when they occurred. Which is why he'd been screwing the woman during working hours when back at the site the big hose up on forty-nine had wriggled its way loose and thrashed around for a bit until they got the flow stopped. By then three men had been knocked into space. Jesus. It was a typical Chinese situation, of course. Randall had checked the metal bracket securing the pipe mid-afternoon and everything had been fine, but someone had stolen it and replaced it with old rope between then and when the liquid concrete started to come thrusting up the pipe from way below. A long pipe, lots of pressure. Lucky it had only been three men.

Warton had paid their families well, ten years' wages each. There were plenty of workers in China would have lined up for a deal like that. But still. The cops had got onto it quickly, come banging on the door of his place while the girl was still there, surprisingly rude. They were rude, the Chinese, generally in small ways. Peripheral rudeness. But up front they tended towards a more neutral position, and the ones Randall dealt with had mostly mastered the art of hiding their dislike of Westerners. Like, build us a skyscraper and here's your money, thank you very much. See you in a few years in Vancouver. Or Paris. Or Sydney. But these cops had been something else.

Henry had saved him. Turned up in person at the police station two hours later, two long hours, and arranged his release. He was Morning Star's construction manager for Asia back then, Hong Kong-based but fortunately in Shanghai that afternoon. Henry got him out, no charges, and Randall at first thought this is the way it goes—a crazy town, shit happens, no one wants it to become a place Westerners won't want to work. Not yet, anyway. So life returns to how it was.

But it hadn't. His boss at Warton, a beefy Aussie named Jensen, had driven him to the airport the next day and told him his time in China was finished. Jensen had always seemed a decent guy, liked a drink, but straight, just wanted to do his job.

'I can take it from here,' Randall had said as they approached the chaos of Shanghai International.

Jensen swung towards the car park and told Randall he had to see him onto the plane. That was the deal. Randall felt mildly flattered to be the subject of a deal. Important Western engineer handled delicately. Nice story to have on the CV. The unofficial one, not the one he'd have to drag out now in the search for another job.

'I've always wanted to ask you,' Jensen said. 'Randall's not an Irish name, is it?'

He said it as if he were really interested, as if the question had been bothering him. So Randall told him the tale, half shouting as they made their way through the crowded airport building, him not knowing which airline it was, not even which flight they were dumping him on. He told Jensen how his mother had been working as a chambermaid in London in the 1970s, innocent Irish girl seduced by a local tradesman doing some work in the hotel. Familiar story. But then, a surprise happy ending: Ben had married Kaitlin and returned with her to Dungarvan, fitted in quite well. He was a drinker for a start. Said he'd never felt at home anywhere until he moved to Ireland.

'Here we are,' Jensen said.

A queue in front of the United counter.

'Where am I going?'

Jensen put down Randall's second bag and looked at him, moment of truth. Now he'd learn they weren't going to pay him anything, he'd never work in this industry again, rhubarb rhubarb.

'If I had my way,' Jensen began, and Randall felt a little kick of hope somewhere in his chest.

If I had my way was good. The moment you said that you were admitting you'd lost. Jensen explained that if he had his way, Warton would sack Randall because he'd just killed three men. Even though there were aspects of the accident that made him uneasy, Randall was still to blame. This was sounding good, Randall thought, wishing he could fast-forward Jensen. They had reached the counter.

'But Henry Wu thinks you deserve a second chance,' Jensen said.

Randall blinked. The guy who'd got him out of the police station yesterday? Couldn't say he knew Wu, just one of a dozen Morning Star executives he'd met over the past year.

'Where we go today?' said the woman behind the counter.

'Houston,' said Jensen, pulling out Randall's passport and putting it on the counter. Randall wondered how they'd got him into the States so quickly, but he guessed there were ways and means.

'You'll be met,' Jensen said, presenting Randall with a sealed envelope. 'The Southern Building, a nice project. Things could still work out for you in Warton, mate. You just need to sort out your priorities.'

'Thank you,' said Randall, not quite believing this. Houston. Globalisation: don't you just fucking love it.

Jensen put out his hand and Randall took it, tightening his grip.

'I won't tell anyone what happened yesterday,' Jensen said. 'I believe in second chances. Read the Bible, mate, join a local church over there. With His help, you can get through this.'

There had been tears in Randall's eyes. Sweet Jesus, it's never over till it's over.

He put the car into gear and drove off, seeing from a sign that he was in Dharruk and working his way through the short roads over to Hebersham, looking for street names: Mackellar, that would take him into Richardson and Timms. The roads were short and winding, redolent of a discredited planning fashion Randall had seen around the world, the Radburn model. He had an interest in residential building; it had started with observing his father.

After moving to Ireland, Ben had set up as a builder in the early eighties. It had been touch and go for a long time—the drinking didn't help—but at some stage he'd accepted some acres outside Cork as payment for a debt. Real wasteland it had been, Randall could still remember his parents arguing over it. But ten years later, Ireland was booming and the land was worth fifty times what it had been. Ben had somehow fallen in with an honest partner and they'd developed it themselves, turned it into a light industrial estate. Most of Ben's development projects since then had ended in one form of disappointment or other, but the estate kept pumping out rental income, so none of that really mattered. He drove a Jaguar and was respected in the rolling hills south of Dublin as a cunning businessman, at least by those who didn't know any better. Which was most people.

You can be lucky.

It was Randall's ambition to get into housing himself one day. His father had given him the bug, and also many lessons in how not to do things. For years Randall had resented this, resented having a dad who was such a flop, even if most of the world didn't know it. But lately he'd seen that you can learn from other people's failures as well as their successes. All those master classes on his father's sites during university holidays.

He approached a T-intersection and saw a white car shoot across the top of the street. He couldn't tell if it was the same one as before. He slowed down, glad he'd gone to the trouble of getting a hire car just in case he was followed. Not that he had reason to think he would be.

Henry had turned up in Houston just once, for a very pleasant night out. It was a bit tense to begin with; Henry had put some money into an oil exploration project and been out there that day, turned out it was a dry hole. They'd had a few drinks and Randall had ended up telling Henry of his dreams—you have to talk about something. To his surprise, the man had been interested and they'd talked for hours. The opportunities around Houston, lots of raw lumber in the air. Randall had a plan, reckoned to start with some stick-built stuff, get into bricks down the line.

'I'm going to be pretty liquid in a year's time,' Henry said, 'there'll be a few million looking for a home. I like the idea of Texas.' He gave Randall to understand this was his own money, nothing to do with Morning Star. Made Randall sit up. Henry Wu, serious player.

'But first,' Henry said, 'I'd appreciate it if you'd help me out with an exciting project. You know Sydney?' Sure I know Sydney. 'Well, that's where it is.' Randall had thought, fuck Sydney. Not part of the plan.

'I'd have to ask Warton,' he said.

'Leave Warton to me,' Henry said. 'You want another bottle of this chablis? It's very good.'

Randall realised he'd drunk most of the bottle himself, and said no. Something told him even then that with Henry he had to be on his best behaviour.

And yet. And yet. There'd been talk that night, about the woman he'd been with that time in Shanghai, when the accident had happened. Henry had wanted to know about the woman. It had emerged that

Henry liked to talk about these things. That was how he'd got into providing him with the DVDs, later, when he came to Sydney.

Not long after he'd settled here, Henry had taken him to his club. Chinese place, amazingly pretty waitresses in skimpy clothes, but nothing sordid. Lot of class, lot of money. They'd talked about sex some more, and things had developed from that. Henry had asked him to do a favour or two in other matters as well, irregular stuff but no danger to himself, interesting to see the guy was into a lot of action. A blind eye to some people coming and going at The Tower, copies of certain invoices. Henry had expressed his gratitude and asked if there was anything he could do for Randall, who said Sydney was fine but he was a bit bored, didn't feel he'd really *connected* yet.

'Connected?' Henry said, asking Randall to explain. And Randall had been so bored that he had.

Two days later, this Chinese guy turns up at Randall's office with a small and beautifully wrapped box, size of a cigarette pack, present from a friend. Inside, coke. Lovely stuff, lots of it. And on a scrap of paper, a phone number. He'd called, thinking it was Henry's mobile, he should say thanks, astonished that the guy knew how to get this sort of stuff and was prepared to share with Randall. The phone was answered by someone with an accent, said his name was Gregor and he'd been asked to take care of Randall, give him good gear for a good price. After that, Sydney had started to make sense for Randall. There were a lot of girls out there who liked getting high. Knew how to express their appreciation.

Pushing Henry from his mind, he turned the car down Richardson and into Timms, slowed as he looked for numbers. There were some cars parked along the way and he could see a yard with grass high as a country field in a rainy season. Next to it an unloved brick house, rags hanging in the windows, one of those dumb peaks on the roof. It was the one, the number Jamal had given him. Slow the car down and park, it's show time. Save the man from the wrath of Henry Wu. I'm a good man at heart and I want my conscience to be clean.

Except there were bikes. Big, serious American machines. Oh shit. Randall's heart was pounding as he cruised past, picking up speed and counting the motorcycles in the carport up by the house. There were at least four, maybe more, but the carport was obscured now by a big black Ford parked outside. Tinted windows and big wheels and mufflers, a real cop-magnet. Say what you like about the criminal classes, at least they're predictable.

He hung right into the crescent and drove away. Walking into a house of bikies was not part of the agenda. They might trounce him, take the car. He'd read that bikie gangs had resources; they might note the number of the rental vehicle, track him down later.

He was shaking, feeling queasy as he deep-breathed the aroma of the air freshener inside the car. Just keep the capsule going, Sean. Keep it steady and back on track to the city, you've done your best, but Asaad has his tough mates to protect him from Henry Wu. They deserve each other. Get back to the rental precinct in Kings Cross, back into the Audi, nice clean smell of leather. Forget all this.

Fuck it, he thought. I tried.

Eighteen

At the office, Ruth gave Troy a piece of paper with Margot Teresi's phone number and address. She lived at the Horizon, a well-known apartment block close to the CBD. He thanked her, explained that Margot Teresi might be the victim. 'You know who she is?'

'The celebrity. She went out with Damon Blake but they broke up.' Seeing Troy's blank face she added, 'The singer.'

'Party girl?'

'She gets into the mags, drives a Porsche, different man each year.'

'Who is it now?'

Ruth shrugged. 'It's hard to keep up. I could check.'

Troy sat down and called the number. After a while a woman answered. 'Margot Teresi?' he said.

'Not here. Leave a message.'

The woman sounded as though she'd just woken up. Troy looked at the time on his screen: it was eleven o'clock.

'It's the police.'

'Oh God. Not the car again.'

Troy identified himself. 'Do you know how I can get in touch with Ms Teresi?'

'I think she's up the river.'

'Is there a phone number?'

The woman answered wearily. 'No. And it's out of mobile range.'

He said he needed to come and have a talk. In response to a further question, the woman said her name was Jenny Finch. She didn't sound enthusiastic about the prospect of the police calling by. But she didn't sound worried either. She asked for half an hour so she could have a shower.

Troy wondered if a rich young woman with an apparently active social life could disappear for two days without anyone knowing. He wondered what river the woman on the phone had been referring to, and what it had to do with anything. But after a decade in the police force, he knew the world was full of strangeness and mystery that usually signified nothing.

The Horizon was a slender white tower, very tall, and dominated the skyline of Darlinghurst just as The Tower dominated its end of the CBD. Troy made his way to Teresi's place on level nineteen. He was by himself, because there'd been no one to come with him and this was too important to wait. The door was opened by a thin woman in her early thirties, wearing a white T-shirt and black jeans. Her skin was pale and unhealthy, like tissue paper.

'Welcome to the Horizon,' she said in a low voice after he'd shown her his badge. 'I assume you haven't been here before?'

'No,' he said, wondering if this was supposed to be offensive.

'What do you think of it?'

'It's very white, isn't it?'

Actually, as he'd seen when he came in, the outside walls were a light beige. But from a distance the building looked pure white, and that was how he still thought of it.

'Less is more,' the woman said, pausing as though this was somehow significant.

He nodded politely.

'Won't you come in?'

She showed him into the lounge room and through to an oddly shaped balcony, which thrust you out into the sky. It was where the view was best. He didn't know why she was showing it to him, but he had a look anyway.

Below him, Woolloomooloo spread down the hill to the silver harbour. He could see all the way out to the Heads and up the North Shore. To the left was The Tower, big even from this distance, protruding above all the buildings around it. Bending his neck he looked down to the street. It was a long way, and he quickly straightened up.

'I'd never make a mountain climber,' he said to the woman, who was standing behind him patiently, as though the view had long ceased to impress her. She had her arms wrapped tightly around her chest.

They went back inside and she showed him to a couch, sitting in a large armchair herself. Jenny Finch seemed to be a troubled soul. Her eyes were vacant and didn't meet his gaze. Despite what she'd said on the phone about taking a shower, her hair was dry and looked brittle. He wondered if she knew anything about Teresi's death, or if something else was wrong with her.

'Do you live here?' he said.

She nodded with her whole body, rocking in the chair, but said nothing.

'Tell me about the place at the river,' he said.

Margot had a house on the Hawkesbury above Brooklyn, where she'd sometimes go for days without telling anyone.

'Not even you?' he said.

'Margy says she doesn't want to feel tied down. It's tedious when people ring up wanting her all the time.' She paused, as though speaking required a great deal of her available energy. 'Some nights, after she's been to a club or something, she just gets into her car and keeps driving.'

'What happens when she gets to Brooklyn?'

'She's got this boat. You know, a tinnie.'

'She uses the boat in the dark?'

'I don't know, maybe she sleeps in the car. The seats go back.'

Troy wondered where the car was now. 'So she stays at the house by herself?'

'Usually. She says it gives her time to think.'

'What does she think about?'

The woman frowned at Troy as though the question was stupid. Maybe it was.

At last she said, 'Everything. There's so much to think about, don't you agree?'

Troy stared at her. 'Is she up there now?'

'If her car's not in the garage. Have you looked?'

'How could I look?'

'Aren't you a cop?'

Troy took two photographs out of a pocket and laid one of them on the coffee table. It showed the bracelet, and he asked Jenny if she recognised it.

'It was Elena's,' she said with a catch in her voice. 'Ghastly, isn't it?'

He put down the other photograph, of the dolphin tattoo, wondering if Jenny Finch had even heard about the death at The Tower. There were no newspapers in the room and he couldn't see a television screen. She stared at the dolphin.

'That's Margot,' she said at last.

'I'm afraid,' he said slowly, 'we think something might have happened to her.'

The woman raised her legs and clasped her knees, and rocked back in her chair. She began to cough, a dry, rasping sound. When it didn't stop, Troy went to the kitchen to fetch a glass of water. He gave it to Jenny who drank it and stopped coughing. Tears were running down her cheeks, attracting the light, bringing life to the sallow skin. This was the worst part of his job.

'It was The Tower, wasn't it?' she said after a while. 'She was the one.'

'We think so.'

'Oh God,' she whispered. 'I can't do it.'

'Do what?'

'Identify the body,' she sobbed. 'Please don't ask me. I just can't. It would make me sick. I need to keep the nutrition in me, it's very important.'

Behind her head a transparent white curtain across the open door to the balcony was flapping gently in the breeze. He thought about telling her that an identification was out of the question. But he wanted to keep her fear alive, keep a little pressure on so she'd give him some names. It was one of the first things they told you as a detective: keep information to yourself unless there's a reason to share it. Sometimes, it's all you've got.

It didn't always work, but it did now. Jenny was eager to please and told him about Margot's friends.

'Damon Blake?'

'Last year's model. Ben Wilson came after him and then . . . I don't know. There's an older guy who's rung a few times these past weeks, I don't know his name.' The hands holding the glass of water were shaking. 'Please don't make me do it. I won't.'

'Tell me about the new man.'

'She'd go into her room when he rang. She didn't always do that before, but this was like some big secret.' Her voice had dropped to a whisper.

'So, you're Margot's flatmate?'

Jenny nodded. 'I had a bad run, and Margy took me in. We rub along.'

'When did you last see her?'

'Sunday afternoon. Then I went for a walk to Paddington. I like the shops there, although it's never been the same since they opened the new Westfield—'

'When did you get home?'

She thought for a while, as though it was a difficult question. 'At seven. Margy said she was going out at six. I think, sometimes, it's best not to be here when she's going out.'

'Why's that?'

'She took a long time to get dressed, she'd put on music and dance around the place, she was happy. I'd rather go out.' She looked sadly at a painting on the wall; it was large, mottled grey with a few black scuff marks. 'Margy had nice things. She wanted me to go clubbing with her more often, but, you know . . .'

'A Collette Dinnigan black cocktail dress,' Troy said gently. 'Did she have one of those?'

Jenny started to sob again. She was so thin Troy wondered how her body would take the physical effects of grief.

After taking down details of the dinner party Margot had planned to attend that night, he said, 'Who's her next of kin?'

'No one. The others are all dead.'

'If it is Margot, if she died at The Tower, would that surprise you? I mean, that she was there?'

Jenny slowly stopped crying and thought about this. Troy waited patiently.

'She was a very obsessive girl, she got that from Tony. Lately she'd started to brood a lot about how The Tower had destroyed his reputation. She could get quite upset about it. I'd never seen her obsess about something like this before.' She shook her head rapidly as though to clear it. 'She thought he'd been badly done by. She once took me up there.' She looked at Troy anxiously. 'I won't get into trouble, will I?'

'No,' he said. 'I'll need to get a written statement from you later, but you won't get into trouble.'

'At a police station?'

'We'll see. Do you know the name of Margot's dentist?'

Jenny put a hand over her eyes. 'Oh my God.' She sat quite still for half a minute, then: 'I went there once, it was in Edgecliff. I don't know the name.'

'In the building over the station?'

'Level five,' she said. 'Or three.'

'What time did you go to The Tower with Margot?'

'She always went up at night. We took a taxi, a man met us at the gate and took us up in the lift. I didn't want to go but she told me I had to see it, as a member of the family. It was incredibly dirty.'

'Dirty?'

'Dust, you know. Concrete and stuff.'

'What did Margot say while you were there?'

173

'It was all about how Tony's business associates had driven him bankrupt. She became really passionate, not like Margy at all.'

'She was a calm person?'

'No way.' Jenny tried to laugh. It was an unpleasant, barking sound. 'She used to get angry a lot. But that was just her way. This thing about The Tower was a lot deeper, it only came up in the last year. Maybe less.'

'Would you say she was depressed?'

Jenny shook her head fiercely. 'She's not the one who was depressed. She was . . . energised.'

'Did you ever hear her talk about the business with her father to anyone else?'

'Once a journalist came here. She had some documents and thought they were really important. He didn't agree. She was pretty upset.'

Troy wanted to ask her more about everything, but it would have to wait until he got her back to the station. For the moment he was after the broad view. 'Do you remember anything about the man who took you up The Tower?'

When she described the man, it sounded like Bazzi.

Jenny was crying a lot now, working a box of tissues on the coffee table. 'It was just that I was family,' she said. 'Margy wanted me to know Uncle Tony was a genius, he'd built this mountain in the sky.'

'So you're Margot's cousin?'

'Why else would I be here?'

He said, 'Did the man take part in the conversation when you were up there?'

She shook her head. 'He had this pass to the lifts, it was like he was an employee. You could tell they'd met before.'

'How many lifts did you go up in?'

Jenny frowned, trying to remember. 'Three I think. When we reached the top she showed me this giant metal box they have up there.'

He looked at her, wondering if she was making this up. The metal box in the mountain in the sky.

For a while he didn't say anything more, not sure whether to go on or get her down to the station now for a formal interview. She was a gold mine, and it made him nervous that he was here without a partner, that there was no tape running. But there was something wrong with her and you had to think about the emotional effects of taking her to the station. Some detectives wouldn't worry; they thought if you could just get someone onto your territory, you were ahead. But it wasn't always like that.

Jenny was curled up, her arms clasping her knees again, crying rhythmically now, as though on a familiar path. It was better than the barking sound. Suddenly she stopped and blurted out, 'Oh God. I'll get all her stuff, won't I?'

'Did she have much?'

Jenny nodded emphatically. 'Shares, bank accounts, companies, accountants. This is a nightmare.'

'Do you have family, anyone you could call?'

'I could call my mum.'

He stood up. 'Why don't you do that? I'm just going to have a look in Margot's room. Where is it?' She pointed to one of the doors leading off the lounge, and he opened it and went into the room beyond. Glad to get away from her for a moment.

The room was an elaborate home office. Against one wall stood a big antique walnut desk with curved legs and an inlaid leather top. There was a row of timber filing cabinets too. He wandered around, opening drawers. In one he found a small plastic container with the words SPARE KEYS embossed on it. Inside were keys with tags marked FLAT, RIVER and CAR. Poor security but convenient, he thought, as he pocketed them. He flicked through a pile of opened letters and statements from financial institutions on the desk. From the names he came across, it seemed Margot Teresi had been involved with a number of companies. His guess from looking quickly through the pile was that her affairs were up-to-date, but after a few minutes he realised they were so complicated he'd have to get a forensic accountant to go through the place and give him a summary. They'd need to get into the computer standing on a small table next to the desk, which he discovered was protected by a password.

He found two things though: her latest Optus phone account, which also went into his pocket, and an advice that her car was due for its annual registration payment. He noted the plate number in his notebook.

A planner on the wall showed regular meetings of various kinds at least once every second week, through to the end of the financial year. But there was no sign of a diary or address book anywhere in the office. The wastepaper basket on the floor was empty. On an impulse he pulled out his mobile and Margot's phone bill, and dialled her phone. He got the answering service message: her voice was confident, slightly impatient, as though she had a lot to do. A lot to live for.

The room had another door. It led to Margot's bedroom, where there was a big sleigh bed made from some honey-coloured wood and piled high with a doona and lots of pillows. There was a row of built-ins across the back wall. Troy opened them and saw they were full of an astonishing quantity of clothes and shoes. Margot seemed to have owned at least four dresses identical to the one she'd been wearing when she died, although they were made by different designers. No wonder it had taken her so long to get dressed for a night out. Against another wall were two large Georgian chests of drawers, crammed with underwear, belts, scarves, folded knitwear, and dozens of other items. Troy opened a few drawers and checked their contents unenthusiastically. He wished he had a partner to share the search, preferably a woman.

There was an ensuite and he had a quick look through the cupboards. There was no medication there, apart from some headache tablets. The signs were that Margot had been a healthy young woman. The rubbish bin on the floor was empty.

He went back into the bedroom and opened yet another door, and found himself back in the lounge. Jenny Finch was sitting where he'd left her, staring at the curtain flapping in the breeze.

'Rung your mum?' he said.

'Yep,' she said, sounding a bit brighter now. 'She's coming over. My dad, too. I've still got both my parents. Aren't I lucky?'

He nodded, grateful for the change in her mood.

'I'll be fine if you have to go now.'

'That's good. Do you know if Margot had an address book and a diary?'

'She had both, matching tan covers. But they'd be in her bag, she always took them with her.'

'Even when she was out socialising?'

'They weren't that big, and she always took a bag with her. With that dress, it would have been the Prada.'

'I'm sorry?'

'A simple black bag with a long strap.'

He nodded and turned to go back to the bedroom.

'One thing,' she said.

He stopped. 'What is it?'

'It's just, on Sunday when I was going out, I saw someone I recognised coming towards the building. He didn't see me.' Troy waited patiently. 'It was Damon.'

'Damon Blake?'

She nodded vigorously. 'They got on really well, until the argument.'

'When did they break up?'

'Six months ago.'

'And then there was Ben Wilson?'

'The magazines got that all wrong.' She lowered her voice as though confiding important information. 'Ben and Margot were never serious.'

'Had Margot seen Damon since they split up?'

'He rang a lot, at the start. But she wouldn't have anything to do with him. She found out he'd been seeing someone else, it was why they split. They both took it badly, but Margot was determined, you know.'

'Did he keep ringing?'

'No. I was a bit surprised to see him outside, but then I thought, there are lots of people in this building.'

'You don't know that he came in here?'

'No. I didn't say that. You ask a lot of questions.'

'Just one more for now. What does he look like?'

'Pretty average build but well put together. He moves nicely. Long black hair. Good cheekbones.' She thought about what she'd said, and added, 'He has great bones.'

Troy went back into the bedroom, closing the door and taking out his mobile. He got onto Stone straight away, resisted the temptation to ask him what he was doing, and explained what he'd found.

'This is all good,' Stone said. He told Troy he'd get someone over to Edgecliff to obtain the dental records, and arrange for a full search of the apartment. They needed access to Margot's email account and internet search history as soon as possible.

'Now, get back here and bring the woman with you.'

Troy asked if anyone had gone through the bank CCTV footage.

'How would I know? You're supposed to be organising all this.'

Stone sounded as impatient as Troy felt. The investigation was moving at last, but it was still a mess.

He disconnected and looked around the room, still on a high from the good work he'd done so far that day. A fuller search wouldn't hurt. Gritting his teeth, he got on with the job.

After a quarter of an hour, having found nothing of interest, he went back out to the lounge. Jenny wasn't there so he knocked on another door and when there was no reply went in. It must be her bedroom: the curtains were closed and the place smelled faintly musty. He wandered through the rest of the flat, but there was no sign of her or her keys. He wished he'd told her to stay put, although it might have made no difference.

He found a piece of paper in the office and wrote a quick note, asking Jenny to call him, put it with his card next to the phone, then had one last look around the room. The curtain was still flapping so he closed the door in case a strong wind blew up. Then he let himself out into the corridor and made his way to the lifts. He felt in his pocket for a piece of gum, but he'd forgotten to load up this morning. A lift arrived and there were two women inside, kissing. They stopped and stared at him as he entered and stood facing the door, his back to them. On the way down, one of them giggled. He could really have done with some gum.

When he emerged from the building's front door, he remembered what Kelly had said that morning and pulled out his phone to call Bruno about retrieving the bracelet. There was a police car parked on the road just outside, and he wondered if Stone had sent it. Two uniformed officers were climbing out, not demonstrating any obvious enthusiasm, and he identified himself to them. They were from Kings Cross, not Central.

'Jumper,' said the senior one. 'Must be the season for it.'

Troy paused in his dialling and said, 'What do you mean?'

'Two days ago one came off The Tower. And now here.'

Troy grunted and walked quickly to his car, thinking about what he had to do when he got back to the office. It was only when he was in the car, punching numbers into the mobile, that he realised what had just happened. He put the phone down.

For a while he just sat there, his mind blank.

That night he said to Anna, 'I killed a woman today. By not thinking clearly.'

Matt was asleep in his room and the two of them had eaten together. Troy had drunk some beer, not a lot, but more than he usually did. Now, their plates empty, he told her about Jenny Finch and the terrible thing she'd done when he'd been just a few metres away. It made him angry that he'd had no idea she was going to do it, that she'd given no warning. People lived in high buildings with balconies all the time, didn't they?

He tried to picture her face, but all he could remember clearly was her white skin. He remembered a line from the Bible. And I looked, and behold a pale horse: and his name that sat on him was Death. Father Luke was keen on the further reaches of the Bible, more so than most Catholic priests. At one stage, in his early twenties, Troy had done a Bible class with him for several months. Thinking back, he couldn't imagine why. But a lot of it had stuck, he had a good memory.

Anna stretched out her arm and put a hand on his wrist. Said, 'Some families attract death.'

She liked to generalise about such things. Maybe it was even true. When he didn't say anything, she took away her hand and added, 'It's not your fault.'

'Stone thinks it is.' The sergeant had been furious and was going to talk to Vella about it. Troy had told him there'd been no one else to take, the investigation was still understaffed. Stone had said that was no excuse.

'Maybe it was my fault—I was too impatient,' Troy said, turning his hand to take Anna's.

'I blame Helen Kelly,' she said. 'You shouldn't be back at work.'

She didn't seem to care about Jenny Finch. He knew she was not unkind, just scared of anything that might lead towards intimacy.

Standing up, he came around behind her and put his hands on her shoulders, feeling them tense up as he did so.

'What are you afraid of?' he said softly.

She stood up, half turning, and he knew she wanted to get away from him.

'I don't want to have this stupid conversation again,' she said, pulling away.

'No, I really want to know. Why are you so tense when you're with me? Can't we just—'

Then she said something that surprised him.

'I don't know how Matt and you would manage if something happened to me.'

She was crying now, and he felt them being drawn back into a familiar place. A dead end. He sighed, his emotional energy exhausted. A woman had died today. Really died.

'Don't worry, love,' he said. 'I can do his bottle and change his nappies. We'd survive. I'm not completely helpless.'

She was looking alarmed. 'It's not that. I sometimes wonder if you'd want to look after him. If you'd keep him at all.'

He was shocked. This was more than just an attempt to change the subject. 'Why?' he said. 'Why do you feel that way?'

'I don't know. I do not know.'

'It's crazy talk.'

'No it's not. It's what I feel. I have to deal with him every day. The medicine, his breathing, the doctor—'

'It's only asthma.'

'You don't know what it's like.'

'I look after him a lot.'

He did, too, on his days off. He did more than many men would do.

'You're strong,' she said.

He was sick of being strong.

'This doesn't have to destroy us,' he said. 'Why don't we see a counsellor? You need to talk about this with someone if you won't talk about it to me.'

'We're talking now.'

We're talking, he thought, but we're not saying anything.

'This is crazy stuff, about Matt and me. Will you talk to someone, maybe Georgie?'

'I'm all right,' she said, standing. 'I just need more time.'

'Will you stay with me tonight?'

She shook her head impatiently and went out the door. It occurred to him that he might stop loving her one day. Maybe he already had. The thought scared him, and he pushed it away. Needing some warmth, he reached for his mobile and turned it on, thinking to call some of the people who'd left messages with him, have some conversations. But the message bank was empty. That was strange, he thought, wondering what had happened. He must have deleted them by mistake. Suddenly he felt very weary. What he needed was a good night's sleep.

Nineteen

Randall was at mass in the church in George Street near the Haymarket, counting the congregation. Twenty-eight lost souls like himself, six o'clock on a weekday evening and nothing better to do than come to mass. Most of them were middle-aged but there was a young woman, he bet she was Irish, over to the left, curly black hair and creamy skin, a bit solid but with kindness in her face. She'd looked at him when he'd come in late, taking his place and crossing himself. Father, Son and Holy Spirit. He was an irregular attendant at church, but had dropped in here a few months ago because he was early for an appointment in the vicinity. The priest that day had been Irish. For the previous five years that wouldn't have done anything for him; most times he would have avoided the Irish if he had the choice. But on that particular evening the man's voice had calmed him, taken him back to the safety of his childhood.

Maybe he'd felt like this because the priest was quite old, like the priests of his childhood. Actually, Randall had lived in Sydney ten years ago, for three months, as a backpacker. There'd been a fellow from Donegal in the church at Bondi, called himself the chaplain to the Irish community. Meaning he listened to the blathering of a lot of homesick drunks. Randall hadn't been going to church then, but he'd met the

182

man briefly at some party. He'd been young and keen, not like a real priest at all. The old priest was here again tonight, and he was the real thing, big red nose to prove it.

The rest of the congregation kneeled, and Randall was left standing for a moment before he followed suit. He wasn't paying attention to the mass at all. That was okay. He'd been to some classical music concerts in Houston, a Canadian girl he'd been seeing was cultural. They'd been good occasions to think, just as mass was; he bet lots of people used them for that purpose. Like plays, except that with plays women expected you to talk about them afterwards.

Henry had called that afternoon. Randall had driven back to the city carefully, saw he hadn't been followed, changed cars in William Street and had gone back to work. Clean desk, dealt with a few messages, and then, bang, it was Henry on the mobile. He'd been expecting it, of course. But still.

He told Henry that Jamal was still looking for Asaad. Jesus. He needed to have a word with Jamal. At the moment he couldn't see how he was going to handle Henry. It wasn't just this business of the address; there was a darkness around the fellow that couldn't be ignored forever. This Margot Teresi business had shaken everything up.

Henry said, 'You need to talk to the detectives more. This man Troy, build up a relationship.'

'I'm trying.'

'You're failing.'

'I talked to him not long ago. The dead woman is Margot Teresi.'

'You should have called me immediately.'

'I was just about to. Aren't you interested?'

Sometimes, conversations with Henry reminded him of his brief marriage. Recriminations loaded with assumptions.

Henry didn't seem interested at all. He said, 'Make him like you. One man in the right place is all you need.'

The problem with Henry was he always wanted more. And for what? Sometimes, Randall wondered if the Houston deal would ever happen. But that was separate, and of course it would happen, because

183

he could make Henry a lot of American money. That would still be there after this matter had blown over.

'He's a happily married suburbs guy,' Randall said.

'Think about him,' said Henry. 'Every conversation you've had with him. Every expression on his face. Think. Every man wants something.'

He'd hung up without saying goodbye. Randall's wife used to do that too.

The mass was almost over. Kristin had called this afternoon, wanting to meet him tonight. Wanting to talk about the illegals. He knew he couldn't stand it, had given her some excuse. There was something new about her since this business had started, as though she'd assumed some sort of authority. Over everything, him included. That was what she did, in her job, just waited until a situation came along where she actually knew something, and suddenly her job turned her from a nobody into someone people had to listen to for a few weeks. She was even involved in The Tower investigation in a minor way; he'd told her some details and she'd got her NGO involved. It was giving the immigration department information the United Nations had on trafficking women from Thailand. The way she went on about it when she'd called him, you'd think she'd actually gathered the facts herself.

The priest was finishing up now, everyone crossed themselves and turned to pick up their bags and coats, head back out to the cold world. Randall moved slowly, one of the last to leave.

Outside he almost bumped into the girl. She had freckles; he hadn't seen them in the dim church. Freckles hadn't attracted him in a long time, but for some reason they did now.

'Excuse me for asking,' he said. 'You're not Helen Walsh's sister from Rathmines?'

'Indeed I'm not.'

She was Siobhán Casey from Galway.

He asked if she fancied a drink over at Scruffy Murphy's, and she took a step back.

'I'm over Ireland for the moment,' she said, looking him up and down. 'That's a nasty scratch on your head.'

'I was pistol-whipped.'

She considered this. 'I know another place down the road.'

'That's all right then.'

'So what happened?'

'Let me buy you a martini. It's a long story.'

They were in bed at his place later that night, after their cocktails, after dinner, after everything. He'd used the last of his supply to keep it exciting, needed to call Gregor and get a delivery, maybe at work tomorrow.

He hadn't bothered turning the camera on. The girl was all right, she put in a lot of effort, almost too much, there was sweat between her breasts, under her arms. Usually women would comment on the amount Randall sweated. First they'd tell him how little hair he had, and Siobhán had done that earlier; not like an Irishman at all, she'd said. But in the sweat area she was giving him some competition and he'd needed a few lines to get his mind off that. She'd clicked into party mood, he had a bottle of Stoli going on the bedside table and now she had a swig, sitting up in bed. She lit two cigarettes, handed him one.

'God, that was good,' she said. 'Wasn't that truly good?'

'Fantastic,' he said, reaching for his mobile.

She looked from it to him. 'Jesus,' she said. 'I don't believe this.'

Trying to take it from him playfully, but he wasn't in the mood. He turned around and sat on the side of the bed with his legs apart, his Johnson flopping down on the sheets as he rang Gregor's number. Wondered where the fellow was—this was the second time today he hadn't answered. Man was in a service industry, for Christ's sake.

She came around the bed, her cigarette gone, and kneeled down in front of him, flicking her hair back. There were freckles on her breasts too. 'We need to get this show on the road again,' she said.

He could see she wasn't naturally like this; the coke was making her frolicsome. That was what it was for.

The mobile rang and he stared at it in surprise.

'Randall?'

It was Eman Jamal, saying he'd just had a visit from Henry Wu.

Randall wasn't sure he'd heard correctly.

'It's eleven o'clock,' he said, panic running like electricity over the surface of his naked body. Pushing the girl's head away.

'How the fuck he knows where I live? Had this big bloke with him. Really big. I didn't know whether to ring you.'

'I'm glad you did.'

'He never told me not to.'

Wu had insisted on being told Asaad's address, and in the end Jamal had given it to him.

'Why'd you do that?'

'He's a scary guy, mate, you know his rep.'

'I've heard stuff,' Randall said, putting a hand on the girl's shoulder, trying to push her away, but she wouldn't go. 'You think he's, ah, violent? Potentially?'

'Mate, you've said it yourself.'

Jamal blathered on, sounding eager to please. Randall realised he must have done a deal with Wu, given him Asaad's address in return for keeping his company's contract with The Tower. Cutting out the middle man. Which meant Henry didn't trust him anymore.

'Did he mention me?'

'No mate.'

'Did he ask you where you got Asaad's address?'

'I told him I'd only just got it from my people. Said I was about to ring you. Don't worry, I didn't drop you in it.'

What bullshit.

'Cheers, buddy.'

'You take care.'

Randall disconnected. This is it, he thought. The time when I find out what Henry Wu is capable of. The sweat was running down his sides now, so much of it he could feel the trickle of moisture. He looked out into the hallway, over towards the front door. Feeling scared again, it was eating away at him.

186

'This is no good,' the girl said, straightening up and doing the thing with her hair again. Her voice was slurred. 'Percy doesn't want to come out to play.'

He slapped her on the side of the face and she fell backwards and lay still on the carpet. He got up and stood over her, noticed her body was almost the same colour as the beige carpet. She looked serious and her cheek was red, but she wasn't crying.

Looking up at him, she said, 'I think it's time for me to go home.'

WEDNESDAY

Twenty

There was a colour photograph of Margot Teresi on the whiteboard now. Troy looked at it as Little fidgetted and Stone ran over the state of the investigation with them. Stone had already told him that he was taking back control of the day-to-day management of the investigation. Troy had been relieved; maybe his complaint to Kelly had had some effect. He was still second in charge of the investigation, but now he could get out of the office more.

In other parts of the room, detectives worked the phones, putting together a picture of Margot's life by calling every number listed in her phone records. On the board, Margot was still alive, rich, vivacious. Other pictures were up there too, including an artist's image of the man who'd shot McIver, almost certainly a Pakistani.

'Obviously having a victim ID is good,' Stone said, 'but we still don't know an awful lot. We're hoping the details of Margot's life will lead us to an explanation of what happened. I'm seeing Ben Wilson; Nick and Conti are visiting this singer. We're still chasing Jenny's parents.'

Troy wasn't paying much attention. Stone had an annoying habit of repeating himself, going over the known state of the investigation out loud, as though afraid he'd forget it otherwise. This contributed to the sense of things going around in circles, even when they weren't.

He looked at his watch. He'd talked to Damon Blake's agent yesterday evening, and learned the singer was in Brisbane, due back this morning. They had an appointment in his apartment later.

They'd discovered Bazzi had a bank account in a business name, and had been receiving three hundred dollars a week from a company owned by Margot Teresi. He'd withdrawn two hundred dollars every month, presumably to pay Asaad. Ten thousand dollars in cash had been withdrawn the morning after Bazzi disappeared. In Melbourne.

Little said, 'What about the payments Sidorov must have been making to Bazzi?'

'No sign of them yet,' Stone said. 'Bazzi's gone cold on us. He could have had an escape plan. I've got Melbourne airport checking their cameras in case he flew out under another name. We've discovered Tryon missed Asaad's connection to the Wolves. The Gangs Squad are talking to people, trying to find where they might be hiding him.'

'We'll never find him.'

'You never know. If he was working on the side, not cutting his brothers in on some action, they mightn't be happy with him.'

Moving on, Stone explained that a thorough search of Margot Teresi's apartment had revealed nothing, except that she'd been obsessed by The Tower. There were hundreds of pages of photocopied newspaper stories and documents relating to it. Her Porsche was in the garage down below, as Jenny Finch had said it might be. Other police had visited the house on the river and found it empty. The investigation would now start to interview all of Margot's friends and anyone else she'd seen recently.

Troy had some thoughts on this, and was about to voice them when Stone turned to Little and said, 'Tell us about the illegals.'

'Can we talk about the victim a bit more?' said Troy.

Stone frowned. 'Later,' he said. 'We need to push on. I want to know where we're at with these people.'

It seemed to be another of his habits: jumping around mentally.

Little explained the illegals were being held in individual cells now, unable to talk to each other. Ruth had drawn up a timeline for each man, showing what he said he'd been doing for the whole of the evening on which Margot Teresi died. They'd been cross-checked, and today would be followed up with new interviews.

The illegals claimed they'd been exhausted, on Sunday night as every night, after working a twelve-hour day. They'd cooked and prayed, in some cases written letters or read for a while. It was possible to go for a walk in the car park, outside the area where they lived. It was also possible to use the stairwell to go to other floors, but Bazzi had caught two of them exploring the retail level a few weeks earlier and got violent.

'The retail floor's being fitted out, the level of activity's increasing,' Little explained. 'He didn't want them wandering around.'

'The poor bastards must have been desperate for a bit of space,' said Troy.

'They were moved to other accommodation for a weekend's break once a month, some sort of boarding house in Campsie. It's a pigsty, but they were free to come and go. Visit the Opera House. Several visited the Thai prozzie we caught in Darlinghurst, Sally Tanuchit. Some of them have friends here. This seems to have been a well-run operation, where pretty much everyone benefited.'

'Are we sure there were only twenty-one living there?' said Stone.

'We checked the stuff we picked up there. There were only twenty-one beds.'

Stone was looking at a spreadsheet. 'Putting what we know together, we can't account for Khan's whereabouts for about half an hour that night, between eight fifteen and eight forty-five.'

Little said, 'One bloke reckons Khan was a bit of a wanderer, he went upstairs some nights. Actually, the bloke wondered if he was a bit embarrassed about using the toilet in the camp, went off to have a piss in private.'

'The time's right,' said Stone. 'If they'd met on the retail level, the shooter could have given Khan the gun and kept going.' Wherever it was he'd gone. 'Let's try Khan again this afternoon. We'll have another go at Sidorov too.'

'What about the construction company?' said Troy. 'Reckon they knew this was going on?'

Stone shook his head. 'Taylor swears blind he had no idea, and I believe him. There was nothing in it for them.'

'Still, they don't look good.'

'Stupidity's not a crime.' Stone rubbed his forehead as though he had a headache. 'You can see what might have happened. Margot was in the building pursuing this weird obsession her cousin told us about. She accidentally sees something she shouldn't have, some indication of the illegals. She's killed to keep her quiet. It was a big operation, a great deal of money involved, some nasty people.'

'It was idiotic to kill her on-site,' Troy said.

Stone shrugged. 'She turned up in the middle of something, posed an immediate threat, someone panicked.'

It was a theory, Troy thought. 'Why would Bazzi have let her onto the site, given he knew about the illegals?'

'The place is huge. You've got your twenty-one workers tucked away right down in a car park, it's night-time. You wouldn't think there was much chance of her crossing paths with them.'

No you wouldn't. Troy thought Stone's theory possible, though unlikely. But for the moment he couldn't think of a better one.

Later in the morning, when most of the detectives had gone out, Stone emerged from his office and told Troy he had to go to Parramatta to see Kelly and the media officer, to decide when to announce that the victim was Margot Teresi. They also had to get pictures of the shooter and his dead colleague out to the media.

Troy said, 'Do you have to go to Parramatta to do this? It's a five-minute phone conversation.'

'Kelly wants me out there.'

'Just say no.'

'There are other things she wants to discuss.' Suddenly Stone's voice was angry. 'After the way you handled Jenny Finch yesterday, you have no credibility as a critic of my management style. You need to reflect on that. Make sure you take Conti with you to see Blake. Do you think you can do that?'

Troy felt himself turning red. After Stone left the room, he sat staring at his computer screen for the next five minutes. Finally, he started to read through the new notes and witness statements on e@gle.i. They were building a picture of Margot's life, her activities in the days before she died. There were no breakthroughs, no startling anomalies jumping out of the pile of information, but the investigation was acquiring a shape and substance. There was something there for his subconscious to work on.

The most important new information was the report on the CCTV he'd obtained from the bank, which had been viewed by Conti and Johnson. They'd compiled a list of everyone going in and out of The Tower on Sunday evening. It showed Margot entering alone at 6 pm, an hour before she landed on the roof of the police car. Troy wondered what she'd been doing for that hour. From what Jenny Finch had told him, he assumed Margot had treated the visits almost ceremonially, perhaps as a way of honouring her parents. Maybe she'd gone up to an empty floor and just sat there.

He looked again at the list of people who'd entered the building that night. There hadn't been much happening after the security guards changed shift at 4 pm, until just after 7 pm when Margot landed and the police activity began. The notes indicated that two of the people seen entering on the CCTV had not had their names recorded on the guard's list. One was Margot Teresi. The other was a man who'd come in at 6.05 pm. Conti and Johnson had called him Mr A, and there was a note saying they'd shown his picture to Inspector Harmer and several of the guards. No one could identify him.

Troy examined the photograph carefully. It showed a tall man, probably in his early sixties, although you couldn't see most of his face. He seemed to be bald on top, but it might be the way the light was falling in the photo. He didn't look like a construction worker. Troy picked up the phone and called Randall. The engineer answered immediately.

'You're still employed?' Troy said.

'For the moment. You too?'

'Sure.' He wondered what Randall meant, then figured he must have given away more about his frustration with Stone than he remembered. 'Can I show you some photos?'

He explained what he wanted, and Randall said he could visit the police station anytime. Troy looked at his watch and asked him to call by later in the morning. It was time to pay a visit to Damon Blake.

The singer lived at the massive old finger wharf that jutted out into a bay next to the Botanic Gardens. When they arrived, Conti leapt out of the car while Troy stayed seated, reaching into his pocket for a piece of gum. His hand was on it when he recalled what Kelly had said about the chewie. He looked at Conti, standing eagerly on the footpath. She dressed well, didn't smoke, didn't chew. You had to think about these things. He took his hand out of his pocket, empty.

'This is where my grandparents landed,' she said as they walked inside the big building. Back in the nineties the wharf had been renovated with enormous effort. Now, like so many of the city's old buildings, it housed an upmarket hotel, as well as a complex of expensive restaurants and apartments. All traces of history seemed to have been purged.

The door of Damon's apartment was opened by a young woman of considerable beauty. Troy was torn between looking at her and the striking view of the city skyline over her shoulder. The woman said her name was Donna, and took them into a vast lounge room. She was tall and blonde and curvaceous, and had long red fingernails. She moved slowly, demonstrating a profound lack of interest in the two detectives.

The room was big and there were sliding glass doors along one side, looking out on a large balcony and then towards the Gardens and the tops of the city's towers over the trees. In the foreground, large white boats sat motionless in the sunshine. Conti looked at Troy and raised her eyebrows.

Donna called out and a man appeared immediately. In contrast to his girlfriend, Blake was keen and focused, beaming his personality at Troy and then Conti, as they turned away from the view. He was in his late twenties, average height and build, handsome but not overly so when his face was in repose. What made him different, Troy realised as he watched Blake working on Conti, was the way he moved. He moved like a dancer, and there was an extraordinary assurance there that insisted you look at him. Troy couldn't see how it worked, but the effect was undeniable.

'I'm afraid we have some bad news,' Troy said. 'It's about Margot Teresi. She died on Sunday night.'

Blake staggered backwards. He stared at them as though he couldn't quite believe what he'd heard. It was almost cartoonish, yet Troy suspected it was sincere enough.

'Was it in the car?' Blake said.

'I'm sorry?'

'She drives like a maniac.'

Donna, who seemed to have been brought out of herself by the news, said, 'They're from the *Homicide* Squad, Damon. Poor Margot.'

Conti said, 'You knew her?'

'Sure, we were all mates.'

Conti opened her mouth but closed it again. She looked at Troy, who related what they knew about Margot's death. He took it slowly, watching the singer's response. Blake seemed to be in shock.

'We need to ask you both a few questions,' he said gently.

Blake stared at him as though he didn't understand the words.

'I'm sorry to have to do this right now,' Troy went on, 'but you might be able to help us work out what happened.'

Blake nodded, and Conti murmured something to Donna and the two women went out of the room.

'When did you last see her?' Troy said as Blake sat down.

The singer was trembling and upset, and Troy realised he was nervous himself: the interview with Jenny Finch came back to him, his failure, and his legs went weak. He looked around, sunk down onto a sofa.

Blake shook his head. 'We saw her last week.' He named a club that Troy had heard of but never visited. 'We didn't talk, just nodded. We went out together for a year or so, but that finished six months ago.'

'Why did it finish?'

'She finished it. Margot did.'

There were tears in his eyes now.

'Did you still see her socially?'

'Sure. We were at a dinner party about ten days ago, at Miranda Edwards'.'

Troy recognised the name. They'd discovered from their work on the phone records that Edwards had been Margot's best friend; Johnson and Bergman were interviewing her that morning.

Damon added, 'We had a good talk, Margot seemed fine. She and Donna get on, it's all very civilised.'

'You visited her apartment on Sunday afternoon?'

'Miranda's?'

'Margot's.'

The singer looked steadily at Troy, not lifting a hand to the tears running down his cheeks, and shook his head. 'No.'

'Someone saw you in the street outside.'

Blake rubbed his cheek. He hadn't shaved and there were a few pimples around his mouth. Troy wondered how he dealt with that when he was performing. There must be some kind of makeup. Or maybe the pimples weren't usually there.

Blake said, 'I go for long walks around the city. The street recharges me, you know? Sometimes I walk by Margot's place.'

'Did you argue when you split up?'

'Sure. But it's like, I haven't been dumped in a long time. It probably did me good.'

He gave a smile of patently false modesty. Troy stared at him and wondered how it must be, to have a life where every conversation was like giving an interview to a magazine. The question was whether there was anything else there, or if this was what Blake was. Troy suspected there was more, and he talked gently for another five minutes, trying to find a crack, but Blake stuck to his story and there were no inconsistencies.

Troy said, 'Do you think Margot was happy?'

'Very much so. She was one of the most centred people I know.'

'Centred?'

'Women are much stronger than men, don't you think?'

'Her parents died not that long ago.'

Blake nodded. 'That was before I knew her. I think the way she dealt with that was part of who she was. It made her strong.'

He looked at the doorway through which Conti had taken Donna, as though comparing his two girlfriends. As though inviting Troy to explore that avenue.

Troy said, 'Did she ever talk about her father and The Tower?'

'Not much. She'd put that behind her.'

'Did she ever visit The Tower?'

'No.' Blake's face expressed puzzlement. 'Why would she?'

'Her cousin told us she did.'

'I wouldn't believe anything Jenny tells you.'

When Conti had finished with Donna, the detectives said goodbye and left.

In the car, Conti asked how it had gone. Troy thought it had gone well enough; no one had jumped off a balcony. But he didn't say that.

'I wouldn't say he's all that easy to read. How was Donna?'

'Smarter than she looks.'

'She looks pretty smart to me.'

Conti gazed at him with round eyes but there was no humour there: she was a serious kind of woman. Finally she said, 'They saw quite a bit of Margot; there don't seem to have been many hard feelings.'

'Why did Blake and Margot split up?'

'She dumped him, but it was no big drama apparently. She never stuck with anyone for more than a year.'

'Like a sort of policy?'

'I got the impression Blake's the same, one for moving on.' She stopped for a moment and looked away. Then: 'Donna said they all had dinner together not long ago.'

'At Miranda Edwards'.'

'Margot seemed happy, her normal self. Donna says she was a beautiful person.'

He looked out at the traffic. The council was tearing up part of the road, and they'd been stuck for five minutes.

'Call Johnson,' he said. 'See what they got from the best friend.'

He listened while Conti rang the other detective. When she'd finished she said, 'Edwards says Margot was deeply depressed. At the dinner party ten days ago she hardly said a word. Donna was very hostile towards her. Miranda says she only invited both women because Damon insisted. She doesn't think he understands women very well.'

Troy nodded. This was better.

'She says after he dumped Margot she was upset, there was still a lot of emotion there.'

'The beautiful people have been lying to us.'

'You going to turn the car around?'

He thought about what they'd just learned and asked Conti to call Ruth to find out who had done the follow-up search of Margot's apartment. By the time she found out, the traffic had freed up and they were almost back at the station. The detectives had been Ryan and Bergman.

Troy pulled up outside Central.

'You can't park here,' she protested.

'We're not staying. Go get the keys to Margot's place.'

They found what they were looking for at the Horizon almost straight away. Troy led the way into the kitchen and opened a sheet of newspaper on the large table there. He pulled on some gloves and located a big rubbish bin inside a cupboard, and tipped its contents onto the paper. Conti looked at him.

'They already did this,' she said. 'I saw the list. It's just tissues and stuff.'

There were no food scraps there, just what looked like the contents of the bin from the bathroom. Someone must have transferred rubbish from one bin to the other. He spread out the tissues and the cotton buds, a toilet roll and a few empty packaging boxes. One of the clumps of tissue was bigger than the rest, and he gently prised it apart. Inside was a used condom.

Troy thought about Bergman. He'd have to have a word to Stone about getting rid of him. Or maybe this was unfair, maybe it was Ryan who'd missed the condom. But he didn't think so. Being a cop meant making snap judgements about people that were usually right.

When they got back to the station, Randall was waiting for them. Troy experienced a surge of affection on seeing the engineer that took him by surprise. For a moment his emotions were all over the place, and he had a vivid memory of Sunday night. He'd assumed its effects would gradually fade, but it didn't seem to be happening yet. Conti left them and Troy took Randall down the corridor to the screening room, and ran the part of the Westpac CCTV footage that showed Mr A walking along Norfolk Street, his head bare, looking down at the footpath.

'Recognise him?'

'No.'

Troy told Randall that the guy was not mentioned on Asaad's list, and played the film again. It was definitely a man not wanting his face to be seen. When he got to the entrance he glanced up and down the street before disappearing inside.

'Like a man ducking into a brothel,' Randall said.

The comparison hadn't occurred to Troy, who grinned.

Randall leaned back in his chair and smiled. 'Come on,' he said. 'Don't say policemen never stray.'

'I'm sure it's been known.'

'No need for some. That's a very attractive detective you've got working with you.'

'I'm a married man,' Troy said, still smiling. He found Randall uncomplicated to talk to. The way he reduced everything to sex.

'I'll swap her for my secretary. We could double date.' The engineer rubbed his hands together.

'You can dream,' Troy said. He shook his head and, forcing himself to concentrate, said, 'How likely is it Asaad would have made a mistake and left two people off his list?'

'He'd have been sacked if his company ever found out. It's one of their performance criteria in the contract.' Randall laughed. 'I'm still learning about security, but contract management is something I do know.'

Troy fast-forwarded the CCTV to 6.40 pm and slowed it down a bit. At 6.45 pm they saw Mr A exit the building. It was harder to make him out now, it was darker. You could see his face a little, as he walked down the footpath, but he kept his chin tucked down and the image was poor. Troy knew there was almost nothing to be done by way of enhancing the picture.

'There goes the answer to our questions,' he said as Mr A walked out of sight.

Randall stood up. 'Any news on Bazzi or Asaad?'

He seemed very interested in the details of the investigation. But then, he was a security manager.

'Our inquiries are continuing.'

Randall smiled. 'Feel like that drink I owe you tonight?'

Troy was tempted. He had the feeling Randall would be a good companion for a relaxing evening, which was something he could do with. These days, being at home was harder work than being at work. But there was no time. He needed to write up what he'd just learned, tell everyone who needed to know.

As they walked towards the front of the station, Randall said, 'Do you like your job?'

Troy did, but he'd learned not to admit it. You told people you loved that kind of work and they avoided you. Or asked you why.

'It's okay.'

'Have you got any leads at the moment?'

'Not really.' He wouldn't tell Randall anyway. Unfortunately there was nothing much to hide, from Randall or anyone else. 'It would be sweet to have an identity for Mr A. Or even a clear picture. We'll show what we have to the rest of the guards who were there that night, then give it to the media.'

'You don't sound full of optimism.'

Troy shrugged. If Mr A wanted to talk to the police, he would have done it by now.

Back in the office, he asked Conti if there was any word on Blake. The singer hadn't been at home when they'd gone back to his flat after the discovery at the Horizon. Troy had asked two of the plainclothes officers attached to the investigation to find him and bring him in. This time it would be a serious conversation.

Conti hadn't heard anything, but told him they'd had a call from Long Bay: Nawaz Khan, the man whose prints had been found on McIver's gun, wanted to talk. It was exciting news and she remained by his desk, moving from foot to foot. Troy looked around and saw that all the sergeants were out of the office. It was a perfect excuse to get away. Even Stone would agree this was urgent.

'Let's go,' he said.

Half an hour later they took their seats in an interview room at the jail. Khan had a certain strength to him; he had none of Qzar's nervousness and despair.

Troy asked him what he wanted.

'I am a computer programmer,' Khan said. 'I do not shoot policemen.'

'I'm sorry?'

'You have charged me with possession of a gun.' He turned his hands palm-up and looked at them. They were calloused and cracked. 'At home I have four servants. No one in my family has ever laid concrete before.'

Conti said, 'You've refused to tell us anything about the gun, and we're now considering charging you with attempted murder.'

Khan didn't even look at her. Maybe he realised the idea was absurd. Or maybe he just didn't like dealing with women in positions of authority. He said, 'How many days is it since you arrested me?'

'We picked you up Sunday night. It's now late Wednesday morning. I'm sure you can work out how long that is.'

Ignoring her, Khan said to Troy, 'I want a deal.'

203

'What sort of deal?'

'The sort where you give me what I want and I give you what you want.'

Here we go again, Troy thought. 'What do you want?'

'There was a one-day cricket match in Karachi yesterday. Pakistan against the West Indies. If you tell me the result, I will tell you about the gun.'

Troy scratched his head. Why now? he wondered. 'That's the deal?'

Khan nodded gravely.

Troy said, 'So tell me about the gun.'

'No. I want to know the result first.'

Troy didn't know. With all the activity of the past days, he was out of touch. 'We'll have to go and find out.'

'No,' Conti said.

Khan was smiling now, enjoying the slight confusion among his captors.

She said, 'Narrow victory to the Windies.'

Khan scowled and looked at her briefly. 'You're sure?'

'Yes. We can get the score for you later.'

Khan ran one of his hands along the edge of the table, looking at his fingers when he'd finished as though testing for dust. Maybe that's what you did when you had servants.

'I'm disappointed, naturally,' Khan said. 'Our national team has been improving lately. And then there was Jenkins' groin injury.' He shook his head theatrically.

Troy said, 'The deal.'

Khan said nothing for a moment, as though gathering his thoughts. Then he began to speak.

'I sometimes went up to the retail level of the building and wandered around; I found it refreshing to be by myself for a change. I was up there on Sunday night, and I saw the gun on the ground in one of the shops. I thought such a thing might be useful to protect myself, so I took it.'

'Did you see anyone else there?'

'No.'

'Why did you think you might need to protect yourself?'

'It was just a precaution. The people who brought us here seemed to be treating us squarely. But I suspect they are men of violence, and I wondered what would happen when the time came for them to give us the false papers we had paid for.'

'So you thought you'd arm yourself?' Conti said.

'I thought having some protection would not be a bad thing.'

Troy said, 'Didn't you wonder why the gun was just lying there?'

'I thought one of the guards might have dropped it.' He shrugged. 'I did not think about it much, to tell you the truth. In my country, there are many guns.'

They talked about it some more, Conti going in hard so that Khan was forced to look at her, Troy holding back and considering his story. He was consistent, and however strange it might be, his story of finding the gun fitted in with what else they knew.

Conti said, 'Why are you only telling us this now?'

Troy could tell she was beaten, at least for the moment.

Khan said, 'When you caught us it was a great blow. My future, my savings have all gone. I needed time to adjust to this change in my life at the psychological level.'

'So you withheld information from a murder investigation?'

'I'm sorry.'

'Did you see anyone else down there?'

'I've told you before, I saw no one.'

Troy asked him about Bazzi and Asaad, and Khan said he knew both of them by sight.

'You saw one of them that night, didn't you?'

Khan shook his head, almost with contempt. It was the wrong question.

Troy said, 'You saw another man, the one with the gun. He killed a woman by throwing her off the building. You can help yourself by telling the truth.'

Khan closed his eyes. 'I saw no one.' Pause. 'Maybe I should have spoken to you earlier.'

There was something else there and Troy wondered how to get it. He said quietly, 'Is there anything you can help us with?'

For a while the other man considered this. Then he said, 'I can tell you how they gained access to the building. Would that be useful?'

Conti looked at Troy, who kept staring at Khan, not sure if he'd heard correctly. 'That would be appreciated.'

Khan opened his eyes. 'One night when I was on the retail level looking at the shops, I saw two men come in through a door in the wall.'

'Did they see you?'

'No. It was a long way, I couldn't see them clearly, but they were Pakistanis. The security guard Bazzi let them in. They were carrying big bags, and they took them over to the goods lift and put them down, and then they walked back to the door. Bazzi was talking to one of the men, and when they'd finished he shook his hand. The other man he ignored. When they'd gone through the doorway he closed it and locked it. Then he went back to the lift and I went back down the emergency stairs.'

'Was Bazzi there when you got back?'

'I ran down, I didn't want him to notice that I was gone. When I arrived, some of my friends were carrying the bags over to our kitchen. That was how the food always arrived—Bazzi would bring it down in the lift.'

'Did you tell anyone what you'd seen?'

Khan shook his head. 'If Bazzi had found out that I'd seen, I don't know what he would have done.'

Conti asked for more details, and Khan described the exact location of the door. It was the entrance to the tunnel that ran under Elizabeth Street to Hyde Park. They went over what he'd seen several times.

At last Khan said, 'This has been helpful?'

'When did this occur?' snapped Conti.

'About a fortnight ago.'

'I can't believe—'

'Yes,' said Troy. 'It is helpful.'

Twenty-one

Randall left the police station and looked at his watch. Christ, his doctor's appointment was for five minutes ago. He ran through the streets, dodging other pedestrians. He felt so good today he wondered why he was bothering; he didn't need a doctor at all. He was there before long, hardly panting at all as he announced himself to the receptionist.

She consulted her book, and looked up at him with gloomy triumph. 'You're a day early, Mr Randall.'

'That can't be.'

She showed him the page. 'It's written here. I talked to you myself. But if it's something urgent, maybe I can squeeze you in later today?'

'It's nothing,' he said, turning to go.

Just memory loss.

Back on the street he walked more slowly, allowing people to pass him. When he'd lived in Sydney last time, he'd thought of it vaguely as one big leisure camp. But since he'd been back he'd been impressed, slightly appalled, by how hard everyone worked. It had got him down, the neat busyness of the place. Still, the whole world was going this way. He took a deep breath, trying to get up to speed again. Bite the bullet. Call the man. He pulled out his phone and dialled.

'Mr Wu.' He increased his pace, the effort blunting the panic now expanding inside his chest. 'I have some news. I talked to Troy at City Central—we're becoming great mates. An unknown man went into the building soon after Margot Teresi on Sunday night. Came out around the time she died. The police think he might be involved in her death.'

'They have a photo?'

'Not a good one. They're releasing it tonight.'

'You have a copy for me?'

'Ah, no.'

Why was Henry never happy? It was a fucking police station, you couldn't just take whatever you wanted.

'So you're giving me a heads-up, as they say. Of what, seven hours?'

What, he wondered, was Henry's problem?

'I've just been with Detective Troy. It's all they've got.'

'You think he'd tell you everything?'

'I believe I've won his confidence.'

Randall walked fifty metres while waiting for Henry to speak again. People passed by, brushing his coat, absurdly unaware of the importance of these seconds. After Jamal's call last night, Randall felt his future was in the balance. Again. The pain was back in his gut. Then a beep indicating a missed call. A quick look. Gregor. Thank God.

'Nothing on Asaad?' said Wu at last.

'Jamal told me he gave you the address last night.'

'You knew nothing before that?' He didn't sound angry, but that didn't mean anything. 'I need an answer, Sean.'

Tricky call. Jamal couldn't be trusted anymore. Time for the truth.

'He told me earlier and I went out there myself—I was going to take care of it. But there were too many bikies at the house. I thought I'd go back today.'

'I wouldn't do that.'

'I want to help.'

'I mean, I wouldn't do that because it's too late.'

Randall stopped walking and stood with his back to a shop window, letting all the other pedestrians pass. He wondered what Henry had done to Asaad. Probably got him to a safe place, somewhere he wouldn't talk. But why? Not his business. It would be difficult to deal with Henry if he allowed himself to dwell too much on what he might be capable of. And he had to stay friendly with Henry because the man was going to finance the business in Houston. This was the logic of the situation.

'Are you still there, Sean?'

'Always, Mr Wu. You know that.'

He was babbling.

'You lied to me, Sean. I'm considering cutting all connections with you.' Pause. 'Do you know what that signifies?'

Why did he do this to himself?

'No, Mr Wu,' he begged. 'Please.'

The pain was stabbing just behind his navel.

Wu said, 'I told you this woman's death had changed everything. I think you've had trouble believing that.'

'I believe it now.'

'I'm going to tell you how you can redeem yourself. But I need an expression of faith before we can go on. I want you to promise to do whatever I ask you.'

It was a big ask. But of course, there was no alternative. So he told Henry he would do whatever he wanted.

He realised how bad this would look to an outsider, some third party eavesdropping on his life. The indignity and sorrow of this moment. But fuck them. You needed to know every step on the path he'd taken to understand how he had reached this place. He'd never wanted to be this vulnerable, but fate had brought him here.

'Stay away from Stone,' said Wu. His voice had returned to its warm tone, the one that made Randall feel good. 'Stone is no good for us. But I have another idea. Do you have a pen with you?'

After the phone call had finished Randall started to walk again, trying not to think about what Henry had said to him, concentrating on the street. On the city. He realised he hated the place. Sydney was a place stripped of history and uncertainty, pain and poetry. No one here gave a fuck about what had happened yesterday. In Dublin it was all around you. He used to find it stifling, but now, having experienced its opposite, he regretted that lost nourishment.

As he walked, people in good clothes passed quickly and with purpose, on their way to money-making.

'What rough beast,' he said to them, 'slouches towards Bethlehem to be born?'

Theatrical but necessary. Sometimes you need to assert who you are, and if that's a stage Irishman in the new world, so be it. But now a fellow had stopped and was asking him a question, saying, 'I'm sorry?' Must have heard the words.

'Talking to myself,' Randall said.

The man walked off, looking slightly annoyed.

What the fuck would these people know about words? I can talk, Randall said to himself. *I can talk*.

Twenty-two

After returning from Long Bay, Troy called McIver, who was keen to discuss the investigation. Khan's information about the tunnel was at the front of Troy's mind, and they discussed this in some detail. 'They would have needed a key to the door at the park end,' he said. 'That's owned by the city council. It's hard to see how anyone could have got a copy.'

'Very funny.'

'We talked to the council on Monday. Their keys are kept under strict security.'

It had been a proper check too, not one involving Bergman. But now it would be done again, and this time they would find they had been lied to.

'You might find the handbag down there,' McIver said. 'If not, search the park.' Troy nodded. It was unlikely an item like that would still be there, but stranger things had happened. McIver said, 'This concrete bloke's the key, you break him yet?'

Troy told how Stone had had several more goes at Alex Sidorov, who'd now been charged with employing illegal labour. The businessman hadn't said a word. 'He's got a top brief and there's no reason for him to say anything.'

'You need to drive a wedge between him and the people smuggler. Jason.'

The people smugglers were still a mystery. They'd raided the house in Campsie where the illegals had sometimes been taken, and found no one there. It was a rented building, and all the details on the lease form had proved to be false. Between them, the illegals had been able to describe two of Jason's employees. One might have been called Izhar. They had police artist's pictures, but they were not high quality. But these men were definitely not the two whom Troy and McIver had encountered.

McIver said, 'We'd be thinking our two might be employees as well?'

'Unless they weren't,' Troy said. 'They might have been relatives or friends of the illegals, who'd come for a look around.'

McIver asked what the forensic accountants had learned about Margot, and Troy said, 'She sold the last of her father's companies a year ago. Left with about three million in shares and bonds, and another half a million she'd put into a fashion start-up. Plus the two properties and the Porsche.'

'And that makes her the fifth-richest woman in the country?'

'You don't want to believe everything you read. She probably was at one point. Briefly.' Troy explained about Margot's obsession with her father's reputation, her belief he'd been ripped off. 'We've tracked down the journalist she'd talked to at the *Financial Review*, Paddy Brewer. He says there's nothing there. Tony Teresi lost a lot of money, but it was all in line with the contract he had with *Morning Star*. Margot showed Brewer a copy. Tony conceded a bit too much to the Chinese. But he desperately needed a second investor, had to give away more than he liked.'

'So when things started to go bad, he was vulnerable.'

'Brewer says this is hardly unusual. Teresi was a tough businessman, he'd done the same sort of thing to others. When Brewer put that to Margot, she got very upset, threw him out.'

After a pause, McIver said, 'I wonder why she got so obsessed by this. She must have known the business world, the way things work.'

'Both parents dying like that,' Troy said. 'It would knock you around.'

When he heard about Mr A, McIver grew excited, demanding to know all the details. Troy sensed how frustrated he was to be stuck in hospital.

'We'll put his blurred photo out to the media,' he said. 'But it really is too poor for anyone to identify him.'

'It might prompt his conscience.'

'Come on!'

'Unless,' McIver said, 'he was involved in killing her.'

After the call ended, Troy sat still, looking at a wall, holding the phone to his ear so no one would interrupt him. Often after a conversation with McIver things came to him. Talking to the sergeant could open up areas of his mind previously closed. McIver had observed this and once noted it would be helpful if it could occur during the conversations rather than after them.

Now for some reason he was thinking of Matt, recalling the last time he'd seen him, asleep in his cot. It was often this way during an investigation; he wouldn't see his son for long periods and would start to think about him more during the day. He remembered taking the small shoe from between his hands and replacing it in its box. It had been necessary to tug to get the shoe out of Matt's grip, and he'd laid it gently on the tissue paper in the box. Now he placed the phone on his desk and forced himself to concentrate on that action. That scene. What was its link to the investigation?

He logged onto e@gle.i and searched for the investigator note concerning the detailed search of The Tower that Harmer had organised on Monday. For fifteen minutes he read through it. The search had not begun until midday. Finally he picked up the phone and called Randall.

'You've decided to have that drink?' the engineer said when he came on the line. 'Any news on Mr A?'

Troy said he was ringing about something else. He asked Randall to remember their walk through the retail level on Sunday night.

213

'A couple of shops had items in them,' Troy said. 'You said the people doing the fit-outs put stuff on the shelves to get an idea of how it's going to look.'

'Sure.'

'One of the shops had a few handbags in it. I saw boxes on the floor too, the boxes the bags had come in.'

'I'll take your word for it.'

'They weren't there when we did the detailed search on Monday.' He'd learned this from the note.

'Well,' Randall said slowly, 'I guess the interior designer had finished with them and took them out in the morning. The site was reopened at eleven.'

Troy grabbed a handful of hair and tugged gently at his scalp.

'I need to talk to the people who own the stores.'

'Don't want much, do you?'

Troy didn't think Randall was too upset by the request, though. He had the impression the engineer enjoyed his brushes with the police investigation. Maybe he was as attracted to Troy for the moment as Troy was to him. They were like two war veterans in search of comprehension.

It was three o'clock, the point in the shift when time spent at a desk begins to draw out. The dangerous period, when some cops take a junk-food hit to keep going. Troy was back from his debrief with the psychologist. It had seemed pretty routine; the man had said he'd be in touch in a few days.

He thought about calling Anna. Once it had been easy to talk to her, almost anything had provided material for endless conversation. Today the energy was not there. He went out of the room to the kitchen to get a cup of coffee. People looked at him as he went, two stopped to introduce themselves and talk about the investigation. When he reached the kitchen, a uniformed sergeant was getting something from the fridge. He closed the door and turned around, holding a container of yoghurt, and blinked when he saw Troy.

'I used to work with Jon McIver,' he said. He was a heavy, red-faced man. 'The man's a complete prick. How is he?'

'The sergeant's recovering from his near-death experience,' Troy said, looking around the room for the coffee. 'The two of you didn't get on?'

The man was almost angry. 'The Perry case. You know about that?' Troy nodded. 'I don't believe that sort of thing is ever justified.'

Troy had never discussed Perry with McIver, but from what he'd heard it had involved an attempt to fit up a very unpleasant individual. Unlike the Logan trial, this one had gone wrong. 'Can I tell Mac who was inquiring after his health?'

'The name's Ian Ralston, but he'd only think I wanted to know if he was dead yet. Spare cups under the sink.'

Ralston opened his yoghurt and took it out of the room, and Troy made himself some coffee. While he was stirring it, his mobile rang. It was Luke. They chatted for a while, and the priest asked after Anna. A few months earlier, Troy had visited Luke and tried to talk about the problems he was having with his wife. It was the first time he'd spoken of them to anyone, and he'd been expecting some sort of sympathy.

'Do you go to mass every week?' the old man had said.

This is not about going to mass, Troy told him. I want to know what to do if this never ends, if we are never man and wife again. You should pray, Luke said. Pray to God for His help. I have prayed, Troy replied. I pray often. I drop into churches when I pass them during the day. 'You must be patient,' said Luke.

Once upon a time, his friend would have expressed more concern. But now Luke was drawing in on himself, falling back on the dogma that had sustained him for over fifty years. What was being jettisoned was humanity. Troy found this hard: old people were supposed to be wise.

Now he said into the phone, 'Is the chemo working?'

'Too early to tell. When I heard you'd almost taken a bullet there, it put my own woes in perspective.'

'That was just a minute's excitement. There's no comparison.'

'You have to permit an old fellow his perverse logic.'

'I'll come out as soon as I can. When this investigation is over.'

'I want to see Taylor fight Mundine next month. Will you take me?'

'Sure.'

The archbishop had offered Luke retirement when he'd turned sixty-five, but he'd refused. It would have meant closing his church because there were no longer enough priests to go around.

'You're doing God's work too, Troy,' Luke said, coughing.

He hadn't been preachy before. Troy could hear his voice fading and thanked him for ringing, then ended the call.

He sipped his coffee and wondered why, if he was doing God's work here, God wasn't more grateful. The relationship with God was rather like his relationship with Anna. Mainly one-way. But he didn't have to persist with either. He could end them both whenever he liked.

A uniform appeared and said Damon Blake was down below. He had a lawyer with him.

'That was quick,' said Troy.

'Called him from the car. His solicitor was here before we were.'

In the interview room, it was obvious that Blake was contrite and apologetic, even before he opened his mouth. It was something about the way he was sitting, another performance. Troy realised that if Blake told them the truth at any point it would be in the nature of a random event. Everything he said would need to be checked.

Troy said, 'I'd like to go over the events of Sunday afternoon with you again. You say you went for a walk but didn't go into the Horizon or see—'

'My client's recollection has changed,' said the lawyer. 'He was confused this morning, upset by grief, but now he's had a chance to go over that day and clarify things in his own mind.'

'I believe our officers found him in the underwear department of David Jones.'

The lawyer shrugged, as though he found the comment unworthy. Maybe it was.

'I did go up to Margot's apartment,' said Blake. 'And I had sex with her.'

'Did you use a condom?' Troy said.

'Sure.'

'Is there a reason you didn't tell us this before?'

The lawyer started to say something but Blake cut him off. 'It was Donna. If she knew I'd seen Margot again, she'd leave me. I meant to tell you but I couldn't, not with her there in the next room.'

'I think that's enough,' the lawyer said to Blake. Then, to Troy, 'I note that Damon volunteered this information without any pressure from yourselves.'

Troy switched his gaze from Blake to the lawyer, wondering if he could afford to dislike him. But it would involve effort, and there just wasn't the time.

'You said Margot was happy when you had dinner with her the week before,' he said to Blake. 'Do you want to change that too?'

'I'm sorry?'

'We have other witnesses who say she was moody that night.'

Again Blake's face changed, as he did a bad act of someone trying to remember something.

'I'm sorry I lied. She *was* moody.'

'Donna lied too. She said Margot was happy.'

'Donna wouldn't have a clue. She's not observant that way.'

He stopped and then said, 'But Margot was pretty fired up on Sunday, I can tell you that for sure.'

'Oh yes?'

'And it wasn't just the sex.'

Troy said, 'What do you mean, exactly, by fired up?'

'She was feisty, full of energy.'

'Can you be more specific?'

'She was Margot.'

Stone had been expected back by early afternoon, but there was no sign of him. He called at four, and said they'd be announcing Margot Teresi's death that evening and issuing an appeal for Mr A to come forward. Troy told him about Damon Blake, and the sergeant grunted.

'So she wasn't raped.'

'No.'

'That's something.' He paused. 'Even I've heard of Damon Blake. The media on this is going to be huge. They're already going crazy out at Parramatta.'

Troy wasn't interested in the media. He said, 'The tunnel is interesting.'

'The what?'

Stone didn't yet know about what Khan had told them. When Troy told him, he was angry.

'I can't believe someone didn't tell me this,' he said, so loudly that Troy had to hold the phone away from his ear.

'I thought someone would have told you.'

'That's you. It's your responsibility to coordinate. What the fuck have you been doing?'

'It's been busy here. I'm telling you now.'

'What if Kelly found out about it? What sort of a goose does that make me look?'

He went on for several minutes, and brought Jenny Finch's death into it too, as another example of Troy's poor judgement. Eventually he calmed down.

'I won't be coming back to the office today,' he said. 'Any other surprises for me?'

'No. Where are you?'

'I'm at The Tower, talking to the air-con people.'

The air-con people. There was so much Troy wanted to say that he didn't trust himself to speak. He hung up in silence.

Most of the detectives dropped in around the end of the day. There were now a dozen people working on the investigation. Troy called Conti, who was at the town hall talking to the security manager about access to the keys related to public parks. He confirmed they'd found no handbag in the tunnel and went downstairs with Johnson to ask Siegert for help in searching Hyde Park the next day.

The superintendent seemed withdrawn, and Troy saw he had the day's newspapers in a pile on a table by the wall, opened at the stories about The Tower. Troy brought him up to date and the superintendent groaned.

'You don't know for a fact the shooter escaped through the tunnel?'

'It seems likely. We think he'd used the tunnel before.'

Siegert sighed again and looked down at some papers on his desk. He said the morning's relief would conduct the search with Johnson.

'Thank you, sir,' said Troy.

Siegert turned a page and did not look up at them. The burdens of command.

By seven, everyone else had gone, and Troy was wondering what had happened about the shop owners at The Tower. He was about to ring Randall when the man himself walked into the room, followed by Harmer. He was looking pleased and carrying a big paper bag. Troy was hungry, and for a moment hoped it might be a takeaway.

'A present for you,' Randall said, walking over to his desk.

Out came a black bag with a long strap.

Harmer smiled. 'Christmas is early this year.'

As Troy opened a drawer in his desk and took out some latex gloves, Randall said, 'A carpenter working on the store came in on Monday morning and put everything on the shelves into a bag, just like the owner had asked him to. An employee picked it up and took it out later in the morning, and it's been sitting in her boot ever since.'

Troy opened the handbag and removed a large wallet.

'Margot Teresi's?' said Harmer.

There were credit and charge cards in Margot's name, but nothing else. He up-ended the handbag but there wasn't much there: a key ring and a small pack of tissues fell out, some throat lozenges and a few receipts.

'At least we've got the bag,' Harmer said. She sounded unusually excited for a woman with her experience, but this investigation was having that effect on people. Media attention could change the way you saw a case.

'It's not much,' he pointed out.

'What do you want?' Randall said.

'A diary would be nice. And her address book.'

'I suppose you were hoping for a lead on Mr A, her phone?'

'We don't need the physical phone, we go through her records,' Harmer explained. She seemed to trust Randall.

Troy said, 'Mr A doesn't seem to be anyone Margot called that we can identify. But one number she'd rung a lot is a mobile that was purchased under a false ID.'

'Could be her drug dealer,' said Randall.

'We'll follow up all possibilities,' Troy said a little abruptly. 'Thanks for finding this. It's a help.'

'We're here to help,' Randall said. 'All you need to do is ask.'

'There's something else,' Harmer said, glancing briefly at Randall then back to Troy. 'Sergeant Stone is still at The Tower. He seems to have interviewed a lot of the workers on the site. People are wondering why.'

'People?' said Troy.

'We have a good relationship with Warton Constructions. They're not happy.'

'I'm sure the sergeant has his reasons.'

'This is serious,' Randall said. 'Let me make it official. He's asking questions and speaking to people totally unrelated to the investigation. For a while it was just irritating, but now the union has expressed its concern to my boss. I've been given a day to sort it out. He's asking questions that some blokes say concern industrial relations. But it's not just that. He had a strange conversation with one of the structural engineers this morning. Insisted he keep it confidential.'

Troy looked at both of them, trying to hide his unease. 'What about?'

'About shift rosters. From last month.'

Shift rosters.

'I'll look into it.'

Shift rosters.

Harmer nodded goodnight to them both and left the room.

Randall stretched and yawned. 'Feel like a bite?'

'Sure.' He felt too excited to go home, and wanted the chance to find out more about Teresi and The Tower. 'Is there anything more you want to tell me about Stone on a formal basis?'

'No. The union don't muck around. They've been pretty good on this job, and we don't want to put that at risk.'

Troy called Anna and told her he'd be home late. As he spoke, he remembered the emptiness of their conversation last night. But she sounded cheerful, even perky, rattling on about what she'd done that day and her plans for the weekend. It was the way she was most of the time they were together, as though there was nothing wrong between them. He'd never seen it before, but he realised now that this was the worst thing about his marriage, this lie. If he and Anna fought more, at least talked about it, there would be more honesty. But on top of the problems they had, he was expected to put up with this pretence that everything was okay. And he had, he'd gone along with the lie.

He hung up, and Randall said, 'Are you all right?'

'Let's eat.'

'You're sure you're okay? No problem getting the night off?'

'No problem at all. Where will we go?'

'There's a place I know, a club. Some of the Morning Star people go there and they've made me a temporary member.'

Troy told him he had to make a call first and went out into the corridor. He rang Stone and got his voicemail, left a message about the union complaint. When he hung up he looked at his phone angrily, thinking back over what Harmer and Randall had told him. If Stone reacted to the message he'd just left in his normal manner, nothing would happen. That meant the union might walk off the site tomorrow. If the police were blamed, the repercussions would be enormous.

Reluctantly, he dialled Kelly's number, hating Stone for leaving him with no choice. Kelly answered and started to explain the arrangements for the imminent press conference, as though that was what he must have called about. At last she said she had to go as she was being called by the media officer. Quickly Troy explained about the union, but she didn't want to know. She sounded uninterested, unsympathetic, impatient.

'I'll call you back after the conference,' he said.

'That won't be necessary. These things happen, Nick, and we sort them out. In this case, you sort them out.'

'But Stone's the OIC—'

'You want to go to Florida, I expect you to be able to handle something like this.' As though he'd already been bought and repriced. *Maybe I don't want to go to Florida*, he was about to say, but she had already said goodbye and hung up.

This was new, to be dismissed by her quite so thoroughly. He couldn't understand why she'd done it.

He went back into the office and found Randall waiting for him.

'Are you ready?'

Troy nodded, realising it would be good to have a long talk with Randall. If he was going to sort out this union business as Kelly wanted, he would need the engineer's help.

Twenty-three

They left the station and walked until they reached the arcades beneath one of the city's latest and most expensive developments, the International Centre. As they went, Randall said, 'I've been having nightmares.'

'You should see someone.'

'What about you?'

'I had my debrief today.'

'You reckon they can fix you up in one session?'

Troy looked to see if he was joking, but the man seemed genuinely worried. 'I don't know,' he said, more gently now. 'The guy suggested I do some more exercise. You ever done any boxing?'

He bunched his fists and did a few jabs as they walked, looking at Randall for a response.

Randall laughed uncertainly. 'I didn't know people still boxed.'

Troy explained how he'd once fought as an amateur.

'You look too intelligent for that,' Randall said.

It was about testosterone, not intelligence. Troy explained how boxing had helped when he was younger.

'Why didn't you keep it up?'

'I joined the police force.'

The police had been the beginning of a new life. He recalled his training at the academy in Goulburn, how he'd taken to it so intensely that he'd stopped thinking about his life to that point. The past had become irrelevant, the rubble on which something better had been erected. He hadn't thought about it in a long while.

They waited to cross George Street, watching the crowd all around them.

'You like this city?' Randall said.

Troy had never felt like he had any choice, he saw Sydney as the world. It was a limitation, he knew, but not one that worried him.

'Sure,' he said. 'What about you?'

'It's a fine place,' the engineer said. 'A fine place.'

He led them to a modest doorway with a sign on a small brass plate in English and Chinese lettering. The English version read FORTUNE CLUB. They climbed the red-carpeted stairs inside and came to a wood-panelled lobby where a tall Eurasian woman greeted them from behind a glass counter. She was in her forties and beautiful, and as they reached her a door to the right opened and a Thai woman appeared. She was much younger and also beautiful, and like the older woman wore a long silk dress with bare shoulders and plunging neckline. Troy wondered what sort of club it was.

Randall told the women they had a booking and a moment later they were shown through another door into a big, noisy restaurant. As they made their way between the tables, Troy saw that most of the diners were older Chinese men, usually in large groups and with a fair scattering of women he took to be their wives. He adjusted his idea of what was going on here. The waitresses were all extraordinarily attractive, dressed like the woman who was leading them to their table, but otherwise it looked like a normal restaurant.

When they were seated, the woman took their orders for beers and Randall smiled. 'Are we happy?'

'What's not to be happy about?' Troy said, looking around.

Not all of the waitresses were Asian. A young Scandinavian woman was serving lobster at a table nearby.

'I thought this might help your education in things Chinese,' Randall said. Then, wriggling his body slightly, 'Aren't these chairs comfortable?'

Troy wondered if he was being serious. The chairs were padded and had gilt arms, but they were hardly worthy of mention. Yet Randall had closed his eyes and looked incredibly relaxed, as though for a moment he was experiencing the height of luxury. Then he came back, eyes wide open and laughing again, saying something about the need to chill out. Troy nodded. Maybe Randall was, as Anna put it, a man who listened to his body.

Their beers came, along with menus almost as padded as the chairs, and the waitress said someone would be along to take their orders shortly.

Randall drank half his glass in one swallow. 'The point of this place,' he said, 'is for men like Henry Wu to be waited on by the most gorgeous women. These men are seriously wealthy, they're gradually taking over the world, and this is part of it for them. It's not about sex. It's about power.'

Troy watched a Mexican woman whose body was composed entirely of curves glide by with a tray of drinks.

'Sex,' he said, 'comes into it.'

'Strangely not,' Randall said. 'It's very important that this not be a knocking shop. The girls get paid a great deal to be waitresses, and if they get caught with customers out of hours they're sacked.'

'You know a lot about it.'

'Henry is an interesting man; he's behind this. I worked with him in China for a while. The money sloshing around up there is unbelievable. Once you've been to some of the nightclubs in Shanghai, this place doesn't look so unusual.' He shrugged and finished his beer quickly. As soon as he put the glass on the table, a waitress appeared to remove it.

'Henry explained this place to me when he signed me up,' he said. 'He knows I like women. The Chinese are pretty pragmatic about that sort of thing, but you have to obey the rules.' He ordered some more beers, and when the waitress had gone said, 'What about Indian women?'

'I wouldn't know,' Troy said.

'Not much action lately?'

'My wife's had postnatal depression.' Troy grimaced. It was not the sort of thing he wanted to share with other people. But something about Randall, this place, was relaxing him. Maybe it was the padded chair. He felt better now than he had in a long time. Maybe he'd been keeping things bottled up for too long.

If Randall was surprised by what Troy had said, he didn't show it. 'Bad luck,' he said, looking at the menu. 'What are you going to have?'

In the end Troy let Randall order for both of them. He seemed to care about his food, and obviously knew his way around a Chinese menu. For the next hour, as they worked their way through a banquet and two bottles of wine, Randall did most of the talking, telling Troy how he'd worked for Warton in Shanghai, one of thousands of Western architects and engineers across Asia. As he spoke, Troy found himself warming to the man. He mightn't appreciate boxing, but beneath the easy manner there was earnestness and ambition and curiosity, all qualities Troy valued. He asked why he'd become an engineer, and Randall told him about his father.

'What about you?'

Troy explained how his parents had died.

'Were you in the car?' Randall asked.

'No.'

He remembered the two uniformed police who'd come to the front door and told his grandmother, remembered her collapsing on the floor.

Randall said, 'Fourteen would be a hard time to lose both your parents.'

Troy looked away. Sometimes it seemed as though his whole life had been a response to the searing pain of that separation. But of course, most of the time he didn't think about it.

His grandmother had looked after them for a few months, but she'd been afflicted by premature senility. Georgie had recognised it first but said nothing. The penny didn't drop for Troy until the day he found her purse in the kettle.

'I was a handful,' he said. 'Didn't help gran at all. Georgina, my sister, was very angry at me for a long time.'

They'd been made wards of the state, and Georgie had blamed him for that. After a few months in a boys' home in Liverpool, where he'd been in fights almost every day, he'd been fostered by a big family in Guildford. Catholics, but not happy people. Troy had never been sure why they'd taken him in. The father was an electrician with a government department. Georgie had gone to a solicitor and his wife in Killara, on the other side of the city geographically and socially. They hadn't seen much of each other after that.

'The guy at Guildford used to get drunk about once a week,' he recalled. 'Really hammered. After I'd been there a year he was laying into his wife one night—this woman was a saint—I subdued him with a frying pan.'

'Subdued?'

Troy shrugged. 'It was only aluminium.'

'Still, you're a strong bloke.'

'I wasn't so big then, but I had to do something pretty drastic. It knocked him out.'

He could recall the awkward weight of the pan, how hard it had been to wield. He'd used more force than he'd intended.

'That's why I got into boxing,' he said. If you've got that anger in you, Troy thought, you need to learn how to control it. He really should take up boxing again.

'He didn't tell the cops about the assault?'

'Wouldn't have done his reputation with his mates much good.' Troy smiled at the memory. 'I was lucky, over the next few years I did a lot of stuff I shouldn't have. Picked up a few times, but never charged.'

It was just as well, or he'd never have got into the police.

'Hard times?'

'Not really.'

After the frying pan incident, he'd lived on the streets. Actually, it had been in a shed at the back of an old railway yard. In those days, western Sydney was full of recently closed industrial sites. The authorities had come looking for him, but a month later he'd turned fifteen, and never saw them again. There'd been a government payment for homeless kids in those days; they'd called it the running-away-from-home allowance. At the time it had seemed a bearable sort of existence.

The hard thing had been losing his parents. Sometimes, gathered around a bong with other homeless kids, in the shed or some squat, he'd look at them, go over the little he knew of their backgrounds. Most had come from single-parent homes, some had been abused. They had parents who were drug addicts and crims. He felt like saying, *There's been a mistake. I shouldn't be here*. But he hadn't known who to say it to.

'Street kid,' Randall said, sounding impressed.

This was why Troy rarely talked about those times.

'It was what I did,' he said. 'Not who I am.'

He'd tried God. Never went to church, but sometimes, at night, lying there in a sort of loft at the top of the shed, feeling scared and clutching his mother's rosary beads, he would pray. He got into speed and dope, nicked things to make it possible. On balance he felt God had looked after him. A few years later he'd met Luke, and gradually the priest had turned him around. He'd got a job, gone to TAFE to finish his schooling and achieved a reasonable pass.

'I wanted to be a priest for a bit,' he said. Most people were surprised at this, but Randall just nodded. Troy recalled him saying earlier he was a Catholic too. It was something else they had in common. 'I was all for it, but one day Luke told me I was only doing it to please him. He said I wasn't cut out for that, but still needed a family. It was either the army or the police.'

'Why the cops?'

'Luke said it was like the priesthood. Having an unhappy past could be a help.'

'So this is why you're so self-controlled.' Randall added quickly, 'I'm not saying you're a loner, but you're independent, aren't you?'

He was going deep too quickly. But Troy was in the mood. He finished his wine and waited impatiently as a waitress refilled his glass. 'I guess. After something like that, both parents at once, you don't want to take any chances.'

It was a long time since he'd talked about himself, and he remembered now how useful it could be. Some things do not exist until they are said. Things can die unless they're said again.

He was feeling good. And it wasn't just the wine.

Randall's attention had been distracted by something behind Troy. 'Don't turn around,' he said, 'but Henry Wu is over there.'

From the corner of his eye Troy saw two Chinese men in expensive suits approaching them. They'd eaten already and were on their way out. One of them, the taller one, stopped a few times to speak briefly with other diners. Troy recognised him as the man he'd seen in Siegert's office on the first day of the investigation, arguing to have the site kept open. He saw that the men Wu was talking to made an effort to rise, but he would indicate by a hand on their shoulder that this was not necessary. They seemed deeply grateful for this.

The sight made Troy uneasy. In his life he'd had almost no dealings with wealthy people. He mistrusted them, but knew they were probably no better or worse than most. But the way the man was weaving his way across the room made his skin crawl. He looked at Randall and saw he was staring at Wu. The Irishman was slightly flushed, maybe from all the wine they'd drunk.

Wu cleared a nearby table and walked over to theirs, as if he'd been heading for them all along. As Randall stood up, Troy caught a glimpse of his face just before he composed himself. He looked nervous, not himself. Then he was beaming, introducing his client to Troy, who got up and extended his hand. Keeping his hands by his side, Wu bowed slightly, showing no sign that they had met before.

'You're enjoying your meal?' Wu smiled at Troy, bestowing his amiability as though it was precious.

Troy pushed hard against his resentment, wondering what it meant that Wu had allowed them to stand up.

'Please, sit down and enjoy your meal in peace. I thank you for your work in the Morning Star Tower.'

Then he was gone, and Troy noticed people at nearby tables staring at Randall and himself.

'The royal progress,' he said.

'Something like that,' Randall agreed. There was sweat on his brow. 'He's an important man in a big company. Morning Star has done very well ever since the PRC got Hong Kong back. A lot of joint ventures on the mainland with the army people, huge expansion throughout Asia, Africa.'

'They're in business with the Red Army?' Troy said.

'Half the big companies in China involve the army,' Randall said. 'You should go there one day. It's a wild place.'

A slender waitress clad from ankle to wrist in silver lamé arrived with a tray and placed a bottle of Möet and two frosted glasses on the table, explaining they were a gift from Mr Wu. She opened the bottle with a pop and a big smile, while Randall regarded the performance appreciatively. Troy kept his eyes off the woman. The way he was feeling tonight, he might leap up and hurl himself on her. Not really, but he was feeling strange. It was a long time since he'd drunk so much, and it was affecting him differently from how he remembered. But then, the emotions the alcohol was working on were new: the shooting on Sunday night had hit him harder than he'd been prepared to acknowledge. Certain things had been brought to the surface.

He told himself he shouldn't have any more to drink, and then he was picking up the champagne glass and the thought disappeared.

'It looks like your job's safe,' he said after his first mouthful. 'They can't be going to sack you if they're giving you the good stuff.'

'The champagne's for you,' Randall said, pinching his little beard. 'You're the one in the papers. To be honest, it won't do me any harm to be seen here with you.'

Randall was using him but at least he was open about it. Part of his charm.

'I have to pay for this,' Troy said. 'I can't accept gifts from people involved in an investigation.'

'You might not be able to afford it.'

'I can't afford *not* to pay. So, your travel plans are back on hold?'

'I want to stay on.' Randall leaned across the table, full of energy. 'They're terrified someone will use the opening of The Tower next year for a terrorist attack. The tallest building in the West. Every TV network in the world will be there. It'd be quite a coup for al-Qaeda or their Asian franchise. Coordinating security for that would look very good on the CV.'

As long as nothing happened, Troy thought. 'You're basically a happy man, aren't you?'

Randall smiled. 'In China right now, Australians and Irishmen are building cities from scratch in paddy fields. And making their fortunes in the process.' He gestured around the restaurant with the hand holding his champagne glass, so vigorously that some of it spilled. 'We pass this way but once. I want to be part of it.'

Randall put his glass down and excused himself. Troy watched as he made his way across the room, a big, confident man, stopping at one point to say hello to someone, straightening up when a waitress interrupted them with some hot plates, putting a hand briefly on her shoulder as he said goodbye to the diners and moved on. The performance reminded him a little of Henry Wu, men at sea on the oceans of the new world, in search of adventure. And I am just a cop, he thought, still in the city where I was born.

So, be a cop. He thought about what he should ask Randall when he came back. Take advantage of the opportunity to learn some more about The Tower. Part of him didn't care, he was having such a pleasant evening, but there was work to be done. Facts to be checked.

When Randall returned, he told him about Jenny Finch, and the big metal box she'd claimed to have seen at the top of The Tower. 'Could she have imagined it?'

Randall shook his head. 'It's a tuned mass damper. Six hundred tonnes of steel right at the top of the building. It can be made to rock slowly using an oil hydraulic system. It stops the building from swaying.' Troy raised his eyebrows. 'Tall buildings are slightly flexible and they sway; even ones a lot smaller can move several metres each way in a strong wind. In The Tower, once we get all the windows on and the wind resistance increases, that would be a big problem. People inside would notice, on the top floors they might even get seasick. A damper stops that.'

'My God.'

So Jenny Finch had been there after all.

'Skyscrapers are wonderful things,' Randall said. His eyes lit up and Troy realised this was one of the things he dreamed about at night. 'My favourite part is actually the other end, the substructure. Once we finish digging the big hole into that beautiful Sydney sandstone, we lay concrete pads on it and then construct something called a grillage. Are you with me, Nicholas?' They were well into the Moet by now, and Troy nodded, leaving Jenny Finch behind. 'Layers of horizontal steel beams. On top of that there's a cast-iron plate, and the columns rest on that. Some of them go up five hundred and eighty metres.'

'I'm impressed.'

'It's all to do with mathematics.'

And lack of imagination, Troy thought. No matter what the maths told him, he knew he could never have the confidence to design something like that, and believe it would stay up. It just wasn't in his nature. He worried about things. He liked worrying about things.

'Burj Dubai is over two and a half thousand feet. Then there's us. The next biggest is the Taipei 101 in Taiwan,' Randall said. 'That's sixteen-seventy feet. The Twin Towers were one thousand, three hundred and sixty feet.'

'You're not a worrier, are you, Sean?'

Randall laughed and lifted his glass to admire the tiny bubbles. He looked around the room. 'So, do you like it here?'

'I could die happy now.'

'We'll stay a bit longer. No rush to get home?'

Troy didn't want to go home at all. 'No,' he said. 'What about you? Have you got somewhere to go, a girlfriend?'

Randall leaned back in his chair and shook his head. Then he leaned forward again. 'Can I tell you a secret? In confidence between ourselves.'

'You surely can.'

'At the moment, I pay for it.'

'For sex?'

Troy was aware of the occasional colleague who went to brothels, mainly when they were away on a job. But he'd never talked about it with anyone, not like this. He liked the way Randall was perfectly open about it.

'The thing with my secretary ended last month,' Randall said. 'I just haven't had time to find anyone else, and then, with this business on Sunday at The Tower . . . I've got strong needs. If they're not fulfilled, my work suffers.'

Like he was talking about going to the gym.

'You should get married again.'

'You're not a walking endorsement for that advice. I saw the way you looked at Angela.'

Troy laughed uncertainly.

'Don't worry, she took it as a compliment. Asked if she should ring you. A hero like you, you deserve the best.'

Troy counted to three slowly and shook his head. 'The thing is,' he began, not sure if he wanted to say any more. But he did, of course. 'There's a woman at work.' He thought about Ruth. There was something there, but he hadn't let himself think about it before. And he wasn't going to think about her now. 'I'm not up for any complications at the moment.'

'My point exactly,' Randall said enthusiastically. 'I've found this great company, they employ students, immigrants, in their own flats. Attractive girls. I pay a bit more but they're pleasant, they make an effort. So I pay my three hundred, and an hour later I'm a happy man and my IQ has returned to its usual level and I can do my job again.'

'I'm not sure if affects me so badly,' Troy said.

But you had to wonder.

'Well, abstinence affects me,' Randall said with feeling, examining one of the dessert menus that had just been placed on the table. 'If you don't do anything about it, you start giving off that air of desperation, and no woman will look at you. It becomes self-perpetuating.'

Troy wondered if what Randall had said about Angela was right, and if other women had noticed too. He'd never felt particularly needy before he met Anna.

'You've given this a bit of thought,' he said.

'My philosophy is, you get the basics right, satisfy your physical urges, and then you can soar. For me, sex is like going to the toilet. I plan to go places. You can't go places if you're always busting for a leak.' He looked at Troy, saw the disbelief on his face, and laughed. 'Have you ever paid for it?'

Troy shook his head, too far into the conversation now to pull out. Not that he wanted to. 'I've thought of it sometimes, there's sense in what you've said. I'm just not sure . . .'

Randall nodded, as though this was all clear.

Troy said, 'I wouldn't know how to arrange it. I mean, not properly.'

'But you've thought about it.'

'Well, the way things are . . .'

He stopped. He wanted to talk about it, but he still didn't know Randall all that well. Maybe that was why he felt he could talk about it. But things seemed to be moving too quickly. Jesus, he was no good at this. And he'd had far too much to drink. Best to stop here.

Randall seemed to sense that he'd gone too far.

'How's the investigation going?' he asked.

Troy gave him a brief summary. He said more than he normally would, but he was glad of the change of subject.

'Two Immigration investigators came by today,' Randall said. 'They wanted information about every worker on site. Seemed disappointed when I gave them a list of a hundred contractors and wished them good luck. They also asked about Sidorov and his workers. Seems they're after the people smuggler, but Sidorov isn't giving them anything.'

Troy nodded. Liaison with Immigration had thrown up a few problems. It had taken Stone almost two days to sort out the necessary arrangements, and the flow of information between the two organisations was still poor. Troy told Randall this, and explained a few of his problems with Stone. He didn't say much, but Randall seemed to get the picture, and asked about the sergeant's background.

'He's a transfer from interstate,' Troy said vaguely.

There was only so much he should say, and anyway he was still thinking about what they'd been discussing before.

'He doesn't seem to know much.'

'He's okay.'

Randall looked at him, held his eyes. 'You're really running this investigation, aren't you?'

'I guess.'

He half regretted the words as soon as they'd left his mouth. Normally he was not boastful. He was about to withdraw what he'd said, but it was too late. Anyway, it was a dinner, not a press conference. And Randall was not a modest man himself: he would understand. To a point, you had to enter into the way other people saw the world.

He said, 'I'm not sure I can keep him away from the union.'

'You've talked to your boss?' While Troy was wondering what he could say, Randall went on, 'I'll raise it with Siegert in the morning. We get on.'

Troy was relieved. 'That'd be good.'

'Leave it to me.'

Problem solved.

Randall looked at his watch. 'Time I was going. I have urges that demand satisfaction, even if you don't.'

Troy was surprised, it was only just after ten. He felt a sense of panic at the thought he would soon be alone again. The alcohol had put him into a good place, and he didn't want to leave it. Did not want to be sent back into the cold world.

'One more drink?'

'Afraid not,' Randall said. 'Things to do.'

Troy was almost angry. 'Needs to fill?'

'I'm only human. Not like some people.'

Realised the anger was for himself. He was no good with surprises, with change. Always he had this need to try to keep control of things. It was a weakness.

A waitress delivered the bill, in response to some signal from Randall that Troy had missed. Troy pulled out his wallet and Randall put up his hand.

'This is on me,' said the engineer.

'How much is it?'

'I'm not going to let you pay.'

'You don't understand.'

Troy pulled out a hundred dollars and threw it on the table. He looked at the notes sadly, but if he didn't pay for his share of the meal he'd have to enter it in the police gift register. And there was no way he wanted to have a conversation with McIver about why he'd had dinner with Randall. He tore off a corner and gave it to Troy.

'Here's the number of the people I use. Very discreet, you should pay in cash.' He put up a hand as Troy opened his mouth. 'Just take it, I don't care what you do with it. But you've got to do something. You can't go on like this. It'll drive you mad.'

Twenty-four

After he'd left Troy and been to see Gregor, Randall met Jamal in a hotel in Double Bay. He'd already divided the stuff into two small packages and passed one to Jamal. It was a good deal for Randall; Gregor gave him such a good price that the extra he charged Jamal almost covered his own half too. He'd upped the order a while back and Gregor hadn't said anything. One of the advantages of being in with Henry Wu.

'It's just coke,' he said softly, leaning over and talking right next to Jamal's ear. 'I mean, Jesus, it's not like we're taking the serious stuff. Crack or ice. People who do that, they've got real problems.'

Jamal giggled, ordered two more Stellas. The man was toasted, could hardly sit on his chair. It's what I do when I run out of the powder, he'd said to Randall on the phone earlier. I start to drink, and that's not good for me. He giggled some more and Randall smiled fondly. A man with appetites like this you could work with. That was something he'd learned from Henry.

'Man you buy from,' Jamal said. 'Heard something about him. Gregor, right?'

'Russian dude.'

'A guy was killed the other day—in Westmead?'

237

'I read about it.'

'They're saying, what they're saying is, he owed Gregor and couldn't pay up.'

Randall's head jerked up. He said, 'I always pay cash up front.'

Jamal examined Randall carefully. 'All I'm saying is—this guy's with Wu, right?'

Randall must have boasted about it to Jamal. He couldn't remember, but it was the sort of thing he did. He moved a hand. 'He's just a fellow Wu knows.'

Jamal spoke slowly, trying to keep the drink out of his voice. 'Henry Wu. The chief fucking executive officer of one of the biggest insurance companies in Asia.'

'Only the Australian branch.'

'Man knows a drug dealer.' More of the steady gaze.

Randall looked away, not knowing where to start. If you knew Henry like I know Henry.

'He's, um . . .' It was only flashes. The deaths in Shanghai, what was going down with Troy, he could never speak of those. But he wanted to share something with Jamal, his old buddy who'd got into bed with Henry yesterday, cutting out Randall to give him Asaad's location. The prick. Now he wanted to share something of who Henry Wu was, give Eman Jamal a little fright. He thought about the DVDs he provided for Henry, but that was too much. Information like that, you let it out and it might come back one day to hurt you.

Then an incident appeared from the clutter of his memory. He was not sure at first if it was something he'd dreamed, but as he started to speak it came together and he knew it was true. It had really happened.

'Henry rings me one day,' he said, 'six months ago, asks if I'd do a favour for a friend, inspect a factory this fellow's thinking of buying. Tempe, Arncliffe, we go down and there's a few German motors and Chinese in suits, we do a walk-through. They ask me about structure, I tell them it looks good.'

He could recall the day brightly now, how before long he'd realised it was about Henry. As they'd walked through the empty factory the other guys had watched Henry all the time. They'd been scared of him. After the inspection, he'd said he'd really need to spend some more time there and they'd thanked him and left, just one of them staying behind, some sort of employee named Chen, while Randall pulled on his overalls and spent another hour crawling around the foundations, scattering pigeons up in the roof. Big old machines, clutter everywhere, it was a place where they'd made cardboard boxes, printed them too; one room was stacked with large tins of ink.

It was a warm day and he'd been by himself, wandering around this factory. In the back he'd found a room with concrete walls and on one of them was a large red stain, splattering the wall, with drips down to the floor. It must be ink, he thought, someone must have spilled some red ink. Feeling dizzy—it was a hot concrete room with one of those old industrial windows with chicken wire embedded in its yellowish glass—Randall had walked across to the window, not that you could open it, of course, and then he'd seen the tooth. Lying on the concrete, maybe three metres from the stain.

He'd left the room then, not wanting Chen to find him in there. Not that Chen could give a shit; he was still leaning against the Merc in the sun, still smoking, when Randall finished his inspection.

'We good to go?' he said.

Randall nodded, pulled off the overalls, found his clothes beneath were soaked in sweat. Wondered why they'd let him see the blood in the back room. Decided it was an oversight. Important never to mention it.

'The factory burned down two weeks later,' he said to Jamal.

Henry had called and said his friends had intended to have a formal building inspection, as Randall had urged, but hadn't got around to it before the fire.

'Oh well,' Randall had said politely.

'They bought the building anyway, a quick decision had to be made. Based on your generous action in looking over it.'

'Right.'

'The insurance company might need to have a word. If you'd be so kind.'

An assessor had visited Randall the next day to confirm it had been a solid building.

'What company was he from?' said Jamal.

'Not Morning Star.'

Jamal finished the Stella and put the bottle carefully on the table. 'So it didn't matter about the blood.'

'The blood?' Randall was confused. 'The blood was *there*, buddy.'

'I know it was there. But it's not there anymore.'

'This guy told me the building belonged to a company owned by Henry Wu. Nothing to do with Morning Star. His own corporate entity.'

'The Chinese are like that. Business, personal. It's all mixed up.'

'No kidding.'

Jamal shrugged, looked around the bar. 'I'm just saying.'

So there it was. If it hadn't been for the blood, Randall would have forgotten the whole thing.

'Did Wu get the payout?' Jamal said.

'I have no idea.'

'Why do you think he let you see it? The blood.'

'He didn't.'

'Come on!'

'Seriously,' Randall said.

He'd thought about it a lot, and he was certain it had been an accident. It was one of the things that worried him about Henry, that he was not just crazy but sloppy too. Like all the stuff with the DVDs. As though at some level he didn't give a shit.

Still, it had worked for him so far.

'He's a strange man,' he said.

'You're not wrong,' Jamal said, standing up. 'I've got to go. You good?'

Randall said he was just fine, and watched as Jamal crossed the room, a simple man lacking the complexity of spirit needed to understand Henry Wu. Like the cop, Troy—he was simple too. But Randall was complex, Henry respected that. He recalled a night at the casino with Henry, they'd spent an hour or two in the high-roller room Henry

240

frequented. Afterwards, he told his driver to take them somewhere else. He'd asked Randall politely if he had some time to spare and Randall had said yes, thinking maybe they were off to a high-class brothel. He'd been wondering about Henry for a long time. If he actually did it.

They'd driven south towards the airport along Southern Cross Drive, not a promising direction but Randall had faith in Henry's resourcefulness. Before they reached the airport they swung left, though, and headed along the northern rim of Botany Bay, an empty freeway with abandoned container trailers along the side of the road. Randall had grown nervous, he didn't like quiet and lonely places, but then they turned down a road and into the port area, all bright lights and security guards and moving trucks. Henry had the man stop outside a chain-link fence and he'd just sat there and watched a ship being unloaded at one of the docks. Over the five-container stacks on the vast tarmac you could just see two big blue cranes, picking up containers and bringing them off the ship, replacing them with others from the wharf. The ship was called *Ocean Pearl*. In the foreground, enormous gantries were running silently up and down, moving containers around the storage area.

'They're very fast,' Randall said, impressed by the scale of the thing and the energy being expended. At this time of night, too.

Wu nodded. 'Less than twenty-four hours' turnaround these days. The wealth of the east, coming to this barbarian land.'

Randall knew Henry was quite serious: he had a big streak of sentimentality inside. Maybe that was why they got on so well.

'What sort of stuff?' he said.

'Everything,' Henry murmured. 'Thousands of containers come into this country every week. Customs checks less than one per cent.'

Oh shit, Randall thought.

'I love this country.'

He looked at Henry and nodded. I don't want to know about this, he thought. But if I do, it's cool. He needs to know that.

The other man smiled and said, 'Time you were in bed.'

'Simple pleasures,' Randall said. 'You know me.'

Henry liked that. But as he said something to the driver, he kept his eye on Randall. The car moved off and Henry patted his knee and started to talk about their future business partnership in Houston. It was what he did when he wanted to be pleasant, but he was serious about it too, he'd obviously given it a lot of thought.

Randall hoped that counted for something.

Twenty-five

Outside the restaurant, after Randall had said goodnight, Troy turned and began to walk back in the general direction of the police station. He moved slowly, not wanting to go home, reminding himself there was nothing there for him now. Actually, that was not true. There were reasons to go. But the reasons not to go had stacked up until there were just as many of them, so the two piles of reasons were in serious competition for the first time. The awkward conversation he'd just had with Randall made this clear. The meal he'd just finished, this moment, seemed real, the rest of his life like an old dream. In the real moment he felt liberated, as though his emotions had been anaesthetised for a long time, and now he was waking up. The shooting had disrupted his life, but it was a disruption he needed. An opportunity to move forward.

He walked through an arcade beneath a big building and stopped before a newsagency. In its large window were posters showing the covers of twelve women's magazines. Each of them was dominated by the picture of a model, a singer or an actress. On ten of them the woman was showing a great deal of cleavage. Troy studied them closely, wondering why the women who bought these magazines were so attracted to the sight of other women's breasts. Presumably this must be the case, or

243

else there'd be different pictures on the covers. He thought about which of the women on the posters he'd be with tonight, if he could choose.

In one of his conversations with Luke, the priest had said of him, quoting the Bible, that he was not given to wine, no striker, not greedy of filthy lucre, but patient, not a brawler, not covetous. I have been patient, Troy thought. Maybe for too long.

He reached into his pocket for a piece of chewing gum, wanting to get the after-taste of the meal out of his mouth. But there was no gum there. *My gum days are over*, he said to himself, and this seemed to be significant, although in his present state he couldn't see how and had no desire to think it through. His fingers closed on the scrap of paper Randall had given him. He walked another few blocks and stopped. If he did not call the number, the thought of it would nag at him for days, sapping his energy, putting him back under. He had no desire to go there again, to go back into the hole where he now saw he'd been living. For better or worse, he'd been shown the way out. By Sean Randall, a man who seemed to know a bit about this sort of thing.

The woman on the phone was friendly, had a nice voice, quoting him prices that seemed high but he had nothing to compare them with. Randall was an expert, he could trust the man's judgement. He told her what he wanted and she said she'd call him back. Troy went to an ATM and took out some money. He walked slowly along the footpath, away from the station now. Looking up at the narrow band of stars above, waiting for something to happen. The woman rang back in five minutes, and gave him a name, Tanya, and the address of an apartment in Sussex Street.

It was an anonymous block of apartments; there were hundreds like it around the city and its suburbs. Troy had climbed their stairs and taken their lifts many times. On level four he walked down the empty corridor, realising the anonymity helped. You'd think something like this ought to be personal, and that paying for it would take away all the meaning and all the pleasure. But of course that was rubbish, this was simply about a physical desire shared by millions. As he pressed the buzzer next to the door whose number he'd been given, he told himself he was just doing something thousands of men did every day.

The door opened and a young woman looked out at him. She was Malaysian, wearing a very short red dress. When she smiled she looked friendly and Troy felt something inside of him give. Until that point, he'd been prepared to walk away.

She said, 'Won't you come inside?'

Just over an hour later, Troy caught the lift down from the woman's flat. He felt exhausted, as though he was about to fall over. The pleasure had been intense, and he wanted to cherish it, so that later, tomorrow, he would not regret what he had just done. He knew that from here on it was up to him what effect it had on his life. It had been necessary, he told himself, and it had been good. Very good. Raw, heart-thumping sex. What he needed.

When he got to the ground floor the concierge he'd talked to on the way up was standing near the glass door, looking at some sort of altercation occurring out front. He was hopping from one foot to the other. Troy reluctantly became alert as he reached the man. On the footpath outside, two youths were badgering a much older man, pushing him up against a pillar. Unlike his assailants, the old man looked Chinese, and was plainly terrified. As Troy watched, one of the youths reached behind the man, feeling for his wallet. Life goes on, Troy thought.

He pushed the button on the wall that opened the doors and went outside. 'I'm a police officer,' he yelled, pulling out his wallet and holding out his badge. 'Up against the wall.'

The two youths turned, there was that moment when everything stopped, and then they made him as a cop and took off down the street. Normal life resumed. Their victim was leaning against the pillar, breathing heavily and pressing a hand to his chest. Troy pulled out his phone and turned it on.

'Are you all right, sir?' he said.

He went up to the man and put his arm around him, looking into dark and wary eyes in a lined face. The concierge joined them and began to talk to the man in Mandarin. They obviously knew each other, and Troy took his arm away. He looked at his phone, undecided, suddenly realising he'd rather not put in a call. This was in City Central's area.

'It's all right, officer,' said the old man. 'I'm lucky you were here. They didn't get my wallet.'

'Did you know those men?'

'No. I'll be fine.'

The man seemed as nervous of Troy as he'd been of his assailants.

'Would you like me to call the police, or an ambulance?'

'Really no.' Going through the door now, into the building. 'Thank you again.'

'What's your name?'

The concierge said, 'Mr Foo. I look after him now.'

The doors closed and they were gone, shuffling towards the lifts behind the counter. He let them go. Sometimes, you just had to accept your luck.

When he got to bed that night, Troy did not dream.

THURSDAY

Twenty-six

He was woken at seven by Anna leaning down to put a cup of coffee on the bedside table. She straightened, folding her arms around her dressing-gown. Wrinkling her nose she said, 'What did you get up to last night?'

She must be able to smell the alcohol on him. He could smell it himself, yet he felt surprisingly well. He began to tell her a bit about Randall, but already she was backing towards the door.

'Matt's in his high chair.'

She had opened the curtains before waking him, and he sat up and sipped the coffee, looking at the blue sky outside. It had continued to grow warmer since the weekend. He thought back over what he'd just tried to say to Anna, wondering if it would do. The art of lying well was to keep it simple and mix it up with the truth. He knew this from observing many masters of the art, and many more who were not so masterful.

On the way home last night there'd been no sense of guilt. There was none this morning, either, even as he thought back over what happened. The woman had offered him a drink as she led the way into the lounge room, and before he'd finished saying no the dress had been off and she'd been standing close to him. She had some sort of frilly knickers on but nothing else. Her breasts were heavy but slightly flat.

It wasn't that she was beautiful or passionate, but she'd wanted to please him and this had been more than enough. Beforehand, he hadn't been sure how he'd react, the first time with another woman in years. But it had been just fine. As he took off his clothes, with help from her, he'd realised that Randall had been right. We pass this way but once. What we don't do today will remain undone forever.

Hearing Matt gurgling in the kitchen, he put down the empty coffee mug and went to have a shower. He knew that what we do today remains done forever too. But the guilt he'd feared he might feel wasn't there. He felt content, at peace for the first time in ages. As he towelled himself dry he thought how good it was to have met Randall. He'd been on the way to becoming seriously depressed, but he'd been shown it didn't have to be like that.

In the kitchen, Anna was encouraging Matt to use a spoon to feed himself some cereal. He was throwing it around the room. Troy pretended to duck and the boy laughed.

'He likes seeing you,' Anna said. 'He's always happy when you come into the room.'

Turning his back, he poured himself some more coffee.

'I made you some fruit, it's in the fridge.'

He made a face and she slapped him playfully. He smiled, finding he could look into her eyes this morning just like any other. You spent years wondering if you could lie, and all along you were a natural.

He sat down next to Matt and began to feed him. While he wielded the spoon he told her about Sean Randall and how he was on the verge of being sacked, turning him into a good story. He rambled on, answering her questions about the investigation, leaving out the gore, realising as he went that he'd always lied to her in this way, cutting and pasting his work stories so as not to shock her. In the early days of their marriage he'd found out what she wanted to hear and what she didn't, and had adjusted his conversation ever since. He'd been lying to her for years, practising for this moment without realising it.

After they'd finished with Randall she got onto the subject of all the people who'd tried to get in touch with him. She'd even started a list: friends from the area, fellow clubbies from lifesaving, two members of his football team.

'Let me call them back for you,' she said.

She had his phone and he took it from her, as gently as he could.

'I'll call them today.'

'I looked on your phone but I couldn't find any messages.'

'I, ah, deleted them by mistake.'

'Nick!' She was shocked. 'Are you all right?'

Never better. 'Tell you what. I won't go in this morning. I'll stay here and call people. I'll let Stone take the briefing.'

'Were you supposed to?'

'Yeah.'

Here was a chance to get his priorities right. Talk to his friends, avoid those who had it in for him. It was a beautiful idea, the sort of thing McIver might do. He'd tried to explain things to Kelly and she'd rebuffed him. So let's take things a step further, push back.

Anna said, 'Don't get into trouble.'

'If they don't pay me to be the boss, I'm not going to do his job,' he said, liking the way this sounded.

'Not doing the sergeant's job is one thing,' she said, as she expertly cleaned half of Matt's face with one swipe of a damp cloth, 'but you have to turn up to work. Don't give them reason to discipline you.'

'If I go in, Stone will be at the building site and I'll just end up doing the briefing again.'

'So go somewhere else. Why don't you visit Jon in hospital?'

'I'm not supposed to see him during work hours.'

'At least it would be work-related. Good to stay in touch with Jon, too. My father says every boy needs a teacher.'

Troy smiled. 'I'm not a boy.'

'He says most men grow up much later than they think.'

She undid Matt's straps and lifted him from his seat, then looked at Troy.

'What?' he said.

'You seem happy. You haven't been like this for a long time. I think your night out did you good.'

In the car he called Stone and got his voicemail. He left a message saying he wouldn't be in for the briefing. You had to cover yourself to some extent.

At the hospital he was surprised to see McIver sitting on the edge of his bed with his trousers on, working his way into a long-sleeved shirt. Troy put the plastic bag of grapes he'd bought on the bed.

McIver looked at it. 'You've got to be kidding.'

'They're symbolic.'

He tried to help the sergeant with his shirt.

McIver said, 'You'd make a terrible girl. I thought you'd been banned from seeing me. Have you been sacked?'

'Not yet. I'll go fetch a nurse.'

'Don't bother,' McIver said, grimacing as he forced his arm out of its sling and into the sleeve. 'I'm not supposed to be leaving.'

'Then why are you?'

'A doctor mate was in here last night, he says I'm making a good recovery. The only reason they're keeping me in is because one in a thousand people in my situation has a relapse, and they don't want me to sue them if I'm the unlucky one.'

Troy looked at him dubiously. 'You're sure about this?'

'Believe me, I can almost use the arm again. How do you think I got my trousers on?' He started doing up his buttons, clumsily. 'The greatest risk now is infection, hospitals are full of it. That's why I'm leaving.'

McIver had briefly studied mathematics at university many years ago, and was a keen student of risk analysis. This gave him some unusual opinions, but Troy knew there was no point in challenging them.

'Where's your bag?' he said.

'I'm travelling light. If you'd just turf the fresh fruit out of that plastic, you can empty the top drawer into it. Then we're out of here. Do you reckon it's too early for a drink?'

'I'd say so.'

McIver grabbed the get-well cards that were sitting on the windowsill and pushed them clumsily into the bag. His left arm didn't seem to be working at all well, but he was cheerful. He said, 'The thing I've learned about alcohol in the bloodstream these past few days, your body doesn't top it up automatically.'

'Is that right?'

'You have to do it yourself.'

As they passed the nurses' station, the sergeant said, 'Jon McIver releasing himself on his own recognisance.'

The nurse frowned. 'You're still at risk and I want you back in your bed immediately.' Looking at Troy she said, 'You're a bad man for helping him.'

McIver said, 'Detective Troy is helping me escape so we can catch some *really* bad men.'

'I'll have to report this, you know.'

There was probably a law against helping someone leave hospital, but Troy didn't care. He looked at the clock behind the nurse, and saw the morning briefing would be well underway by now. His mobile was turned off.

As they walked to Troy's car, McIver said, 'Have you noticed how nurses like cops?'

'The younger ones do,' Troy agreed, thinking of Anna. 'Then they grow up.'

But the sergeant was not listening, he was off on one of his riffs. Getting out of hospital had lifted his spirits. 'They like order, and we maintain order. And people who like order think about threats to it a lot. So do we. Basically, we're both anxious types of people who need reassurance.'

Troy grunted. He didn't see this in Anna and himself.

McIver said, 'The one back there, did you notice the name on her tag?'

It had been Sue Ann, but Troy wasn't going to say so.

'She must be twenty years younger than you,' he said.

'I've been thinking lately I need a younger woman. They can be more forgiving.'

'Not necessarily.'

McIver frowned as they left the hospital, as though the matter was of considerable importance. 'You have to choose carefully, too.'

When they reached the car, Troy said he'd take him home.

'It's all right,' the sergeant said. 'I'll come into the city with you.'

They got into the vehicle and Troy started the engine. It had been a good day so far, but you couldn't expect it to last forever.

He said, 'You're not well enough to go to work.'

'Just take me to your leader, and leave the rest to me.'

They set off, and Troy concentrated on finding his way through the heavy traffic. McIver had his eyes closed and was looking pale.

As Troy drove, he told McIver about Damon Blake. The singer had scratch marks on his upper back, and his DNA had been taken to compare with the skin scrapings found beneath Margot's fingernails. Then there was the union complaint about Stone. And the handbag.

'So you didn't have to search for it after all,' said McIver.

Troy realised he'd forgotten to cancel the morning's search of the park after Randall had brought the bag in last night. He felt a pang of guilt. If he'd gone in for the briefing, he would have realised and been able to stop it then. Now it was too late.

They drove in silence. Eventually McIver opened his eyes and looked around. 'This is not the way to the city.' He didn't sound angry, just interested. But it was a dangerous kind of interest.

'I'm taking you home,' Troy said. 'What you do then is up to you.'

'I hope we're not about to have a serious disagreement, Constable.'

We have to at some point, Troy thought. 'You're still a sick man, and I'm taking you home. If I brought you into work they'd sack me.'

'I hope you don't mind me pointing this out, but you don't seem to be firing on all cylinders yourself.'

'I'm taking you home.'

'If you do that, *I'll* sack you.'

'You can't sack me.'

'Wanna make a bet?'

As they drove to Gladesville, McIver abused him, without pause and expertly. It was done with a light touch and only gradually did Troy realise McIver was quite serious. He also realised he didn't care. Today he felt different about things: better.

McIver said they would never work together again and reflected sourly on Troy's lack of loyalty. For a while Troy shut him out, but then he listened, thinking he might learn something. He said a few things himself, but it was just like throwing petrol on a fire. McIver was more angry than he'd expected. Maybe he should have taken him to work, but it was too late now.

Finally they reached Gladesville. Troy stopped and they both fell silent for a moment.

'This is your last chance,' McIver said, his eyes glinting with fury. 'I'd say you're in enough trouble as it is.'

For a moment, Troy wavered. But then he wondered what McIver would have done in this situation when he'd been thirty-two.

'Get out of the car, Sarge,' he said quietly. 'We've both got things to do.'

He got back onto Victoria Road and was soon stuck in traffic, so he checked his phone messages. There were several: one from Randall saying what a good time he'd had last night, one from Georgie, and others from acquaintances interstate who'd only just heard about the incident on the weekend. There was nothing from Stone. As the traffic ground its way east, he called a few of them, using the hands-free phone.

After his third conversation the phone rang. It was Randall.

'Big night?' he said.

'Pretty good, thanks. It was an interesting place.'

'I mean afterwards. Did you call that number?'

'No,' Troy said, examining the car up ahead. 'I didn't.'

'You can tell me.'

'Maybe some other night.'

'You looked to me like a man in no mood to go home.'

He wondered for a moment if Randall knew, the way he was going on. But he couldn't.

'What about yourself? Did you call the magic number?'

After a pause, Randall laughed. 'If you're not going to show me yours, I'm not going to show you mine.'

They talked some more, agreed to have lunch soon. Hung up.

It took forty minutes to get back to the office. When he arrived, he parked and got out of the car, wondering what sort of reception he was going to get from Stone. If he was there. He let his anger about the investigation rise up, washing away any sense of guilt for his own behaviour over the past few days. A young woman came around the corner from the street, brown and wearing a blue singlet and Adidas track pants. She was moving gracefully but seemed preoccupied. It was Susan Conti.

'Nick,' she said when she saw him.

She'd been to a gym not far away, and he told her about his own exercise, the running and swimming. They slowed down, and stopped before they reached the door.

They discussed the investigation and she described her interview with the Thai prostitute who worked at the brothel where one of the Pakistanis had gone on Sunday night. Immigration and someone from a United Nations agency had been there too, and Conti was fired up with details of sex trafficking.

'This woman paid fifteen thousand dollars to the trafficker to come here. Now she has to work it off.'

'Like the men,' he said, thinking of the illegals.

She bridled. 'It's different. They're not working as prostitutes.'

She sounded disappointed in him. If only she knew, he thought. He asked about the morning's briefing.

'The sergeant didn't seem on top of things, exactly. He seems like a good bloke, but he's not a natural organiser.'

Her brown eyes were flashing.

'Oh well.'

'He's not what we expected. I've heard a lot about your blokes, elite squad and all that.'

Don't get me started, he thought. But with his own failure to call off the search for the handbag, he could hardly criticise Stone.

She said, 'I'd always thought I wanted to work in Homicide one day. But you're not a happy family, are you?'

He decided to change the subject. 'It's a hell of a building, isn't it? The Tower.'

Here too Conti had her own opinion. 'My brother's an engineer. He says it's a stupid design, because the structure takes up too much of the floor space.'

'I would have thought the Empire State Building was a good model?'

'The ratios all change because it's so much bigger. There's an engineer called Baker my brother worked with in Seoul, he invented something called the buttressed core. Like a centre with three fins sticking out. Most of the really big new towers use it.'

She was talkative when she got going.

'Don't tell Sean Randall,' he said.

'I think he'd know. This is a good one for him to be sitting out as an engineer.'

'It's not going to win any awards for design?' Troy said.

Conti shook her head. 'Not for security, either.'

Maybe she had a sense of humour after all.

They went into the police station.

'Any luck with the tunnel?' he said.

'We know someone at the council must have given them the key. We just can't prove it. Yet.' She pushed open the door to the women's change rooms and went inside.

The office was busy, with half a dozen detectives at work on the phones. Troy looked through the glass panel at the front of Stone's office and saw him there, talking to a woman whose face he couldn't see, but who might be Kelly.

'G'day, Nick.'

He turned around. It was Danny Chu, sitting at a spare desk and peering at the computer screen. He stood up and they shook hands.

'Back from Taree?'

Chu nodded. 'We made an arrest. I was looking forward to a break, but the super brought me in this morning.'

'We could do with some help. You're looking good.'

Chu was a balding man of medium height, with an easy air to him. He looked as unlike the common idea of the tough detective as it was possible to be, and Troy knew just how effectively he could make this work for him.

'You know someone's making a doco about The Tower?' Chu said.

'I believe so.'

'They talk to you?'

Troy looked at him carefully. 'You are kidding.'

'I've got a friend in the industry. Apparently, Siegert spoke with them. Before all this happened.'

'On camera?'

Chu nodded. 'The word is Rogers wanted him to. So he said some nice things. Nothing too effusive, but he was pleasant about the project.' Chu snorted with laughter. He was one for the gossip.

Troy said, 'Rogers wouldn't be too happy about that now.'

'I've heard they might be calling the doco *The Tower of Babel*.'

'Don't even joke about it.'

Troy glanced around the room, trying to catch Ruth's eye. He wanted to know if they'd had any response to last night's media appeal. But she was hunched over her desk, not looking at him.

He called out, 'Anything on Mr A?'

Someone said, 'Eighteen calls, all of them useless.'

It was disappointing. He started to tell Chu about Mr A. As he was talking, Stone emerged from his office and crossed the room. He was staring at Troy, his expression blank.

'Morning,' he said. 'The superintendent would like a word. Now.'

Troy saw that Chu was staring at the floor.

When he got to the office, Kelly had moved to the far side of the desk, to Stone's chair, and she told him to close the door. She was wearing a brown jacket today with traces of gold in it, but it was her skin that held his gaze. She was still attractive but he couldn't help comparing her with the woman he'd been with last night, seeing the creases in Kelly's throat and the wrinkles around her eyes. One day he would be old too; you really did have to seize the moment. He looked into Kelly's eyes and saw they were glinting: she was more real than the other woman, more dangerous.

'How are you, Nick?'

'Okay.'

'You're not really, are you?'

'I'm just fine,' he said, trying to keep his voice steady.

'Your wife has left two messages for me complaining about bringing you back to work.'

Jeez, he thought. 'I'm sorry about that, but this morning she said—'

'It's not appropriate behaviour, Nick.'

'Have you talked to her?'

'Of course not.' She went on about it, using the term *appropriate behaviour* again, as though it meant anything. At first Troy felt angry with Anna, but soon he saw it was not his wife he was upset with but Kelly. There was a kind of love in Anna's actions. He was about to defend her when Kelly abruptly moved on.

'You've complained to me about Sergeant Stone's running of this investigation. Your phone call to me yesterday was concerning. I know you've expressed similar views to him. I came in this morning to the briefing, to see how things were for myself. Imagine my surprise when I found you hadn't even turned up.'

'Ma'am—'

Her voice became formal. 'I've considered this, and decided your complaints are unreasonable and indicate that you're having ongoing problems working with Sergeant Stone. This has led to problems with your own performance, problems I haven't seen in your work before.'

He stood staring at her, trying to grasp the significance of what she was saying.

'Your failure to reinterview the illegal immigrants on Tuesday as Stone requested, your failure take someone with you to interview Jennifer Finch, the unnecessary search for the handbag you arranged for this morning—which Sergeant Stone called off, fortunately.' Most of the details were right, but the way she was putting them together it sounded as though she were describing someone else, some idiot. She went on, 'I believe this is threatening the effectiveness of the investigation into Margot Teresi's death. This morning, as a senior member of the team, you should have attended the briefing here. Instead, you visited McIver after Stone specifically directed you not to do that during work hours.' She waved a bit of paper at him. Troy could see Stone's signature on it. 'You don't deny you did this?'

'No, but—'

'I might say that direction was given on my instructions, although there was no need for you to know that at the time. Sergeant Stone was your superior officer.'

'Ma'am,' he began, 'the union—', but she went on, speaking over the top of him.

'As a result of all this, I'm removing you from the investigation. You have the rest of the day to brief your replacement, Danny Chu. You'll report to Parramatta tomorrow.'

For a moment he couldn't speak. He wondered why she was overreacting like this. There was a roaring in his head, and then it struck him. Bloody McIver. He'd said he'd do something, and he hadn't been joking. He'd talked to Kelly on the phone, while Troy had been driving in from Gladesville. Otherwise, she wouldn't even know they'd met that morning. This was bad. The loss of whatever he'd had with Mac was even more painful than being taken off the investigation.

Kelly said, 'Nick, this is not a reprimand. It's partly my fault, I shouldn't have brought you back to work so soon.' She rubbed her cheek. 'Tell your wife that, will you? Tell her I'm sorry I didn't call, but I've been so busy.'

'I'll tell her.'

'She must be quite a woman, the second message was feisty.'

Troy nodded, incapable of speech.

'Do you have anything to say at this point?'

He had a lot to say, but he wasn't sure how rational he'd be right now. He was proud of Anna. It occurred to him that Kelly might be right, that he hadn't been acting normally, but the thought was obliterated by a flash of anger at McIver. Shaking his head, he left the room.

As he made his way to his desk, Little called out, waving some papers in his direction.

Troy said, 'I've just been taken off the investigation.'

All around him, people stopped working for a moment. There was silence, everyone aware of Kelly still in the office. Gradually the sounds of their efforts resumed. Life went on.

'Why's that?' said Little.

Troy shrugged. The anger was building, he could feel it pressing on his chest. Maybe he would pay McIver a visit later on, have it out with him. 'I don't want to talk about it. Not now.'

He opened the top drawer of his desk and took out the few personal items there, putting them into his backpack. Little was talking to Chu nearby, but he found it hard to concentrate on what they were saying. The thought that he would have nothing more to do with finding Margot Teresi's killer was distressing. This was the most important investigation he'd ever been involved in. It seemed to him, absurdly, that there ought to be some regulation to prevent Kelly taking him off it. But there wasn't, of course.

Chu said, 'Can we go through this from the beginning? Maybe go out and have a coffee?'

Troy hardly heard him. He turned to Little. 'You were going to speak to Jenny Finch's doctor. Did that happen?'

'She'd been in and out of the Sydney Clinic for years.' Little looked at Chu and then back at Troy. 'Tried to kill herself three times before. Her doctor thought moving in with Margot was good at first, but lately he wasn't so sure.'

261

'Why was that?' Troy said, lifting the backpack onto his shoulder.

'Didn't like Margot's obsession with The Tower. Made him wonder if she was such a good influence on her cousin.'

'Well, I'm off,' Troy said, putting out his hand.

Little shook it. 'I'm sorry about this.'

Chu was upset.

'Little can tell you all about it,' Troy said. 'I'm not in the mood.'

But he didn't feel as bad as he might have.

He realised this was because of the woman he'd been with last night. It was something no one could take away from him.

Twenty-seven

Troy parked his car at the south end of Coogee Beach, and walked out to the headland. The spray was breaking on Wedding Cake Island. He made his way along the boardwalk, knowing he was on the brink of self-pity and determined to stay away from it, but not sure what to do. Boxing might be good, he'd been thinking about it lately, and maybe it was time to go back; he could help out at one of the police youth clubs, maybe. That was assuming kids still boxed. Even when he'd started, it had been kind of old-fashioned.

His phone rang and he saw that it was Randall. The engineer said he'd talked to Siegert about Stone and the union. The super was going to have a word. Troy listened without interest, and said, 'I've been taken off the investigation.'

Randall exploded with sympathy. He felt Troy's pain. For five minutes he went on, squeezing the emotional juice from what had happened. This was pleasant, but at last Troy had had enough. He said goodbye, anxious to be on the move, thinking he might drive down to the nearest youth club and see what was going on.

'No,' Randall said. 'We can fix this.' There was a note of seriousness in his voice, something Troy hadn't heard before. Still, there was no point in going on about it.

'I'll call you in a few days. We should have a drink.'

'Wait,' said Randall. 'Did you do anything about the union complaints about Stone?'

Troy described how this had contributed to his downfall.

Randall said, 'I haven't told you everything I know about this.'

'What?'

'This is completely off the record. Stone worked undercover for a long time on a construction site in Melbourne.' He paused and Troy said nothing. 'You don't seem too surprised.'

'I'm thinking about it,' Troy said.

'There's more. Stone is still involved in investigating the union. Up here now.'

Troy, who had been walking while he spoke, stopped and leaned one arm on a wooden railing, looking down at the waves breaking at the foot of the cliff. His heart seemed to be pounding in time with the surf.

'I don't understand,' he said.

Randall explained that the construction industry in New South Wales, riddled with corruption and violence from time immemorial, had wanted a police investigation like the one in Victoria. Something thorough, an undercover job. But the government refused to allow it, claiming the union wasn't as bad up here. The industry knew the real reason was that the union was a major financial backer of the government. Enter the federal government, keen to see the union exposed because of the damage it was doing the national economy. The result was a lot of tension in federal and state law enforcement circles. When Margot Teresi came off The Tower and McIver was shot, someone had had the idea of bringing Stone up to Sydney and inserting him in the investigation.

'There's a federal election next year,' Troy said when Randall had finished.

'You've got it.'

Troy didn't want to believe it. Kelly and her superiors had their faults, but the idea they'd use a homicide investigation for political purposes was too much. Apart from the moral angle, they'd be worried about the risk of exposure. He turned around, leaning back into the railing, seeing two women with prams walk past. Ordinary life goes on, and behind it, this craziness. But no, it wasn't possible.

'It's a murder investigation,' he said. 'They wouldn't compromise that. One of the killers shot a cop.'

'Stop and think,' Randall said. 'There are people out there with different agendas to yours.'

I don't have an agenda, Troy thought. 'Kelly would not do this,' he said slowly, but already there was doubt in his mind.

'It's a favour for someone important,' Randall said. 'I could tell you who that is and just what she hopes to get out of it. I won't. But I've been told.'

No. 'She wouldn't compromise a homicide inquiry.'

'It wasn't meant to do that. It was supposed to be a little side deal. The idea was that Stone would have access to the whole site in his role as a murder investigator, go anywhere, talk to anyone. It was a very specific industrial issue they were interested in, involving one incident, one industrial officer they were out to get. It was only supposed to take him a day or two.'

Troy said, his voice almost breaking, 'But how could he possibly run a murder investigation too?'

Randall sounded impatient. 'He wasn't supposed to do it for more than a few days. He actually got what he wanted on the first day, that should have been the end of it. But then he told his bosses he was on the trail of something bigger, he just needed another day or two. Like idiots they said yes, and then he just went feral. There's something wrong with the guy, the way I hear it, and Kelly and the feds are very anxious about him. Imagine what will happen—'

'You knew, didn't you?'

'It was a good idea. It just got stuffed up in the execution.'

'You bastard,' Troy said, his voice low. 'You knew.'

'Labour problems here are a nightmare,' Randall said quickly. 'The cost of a tall building is eight per cent more than it should be. The state government doesn't want to know about it because the industry is one of its biggest—'

Troy turned off his phone. For a moment he considered hurling it into the sea far below, but instead he stuffed it in the pocket of his jacket. One of the reasons for being the sort of person he was, dedicated to his work but not particularly ambitious, was that you didn't have to be part of this sort of obscenity. But it found you in the end.

He began to walk back to his car, wondering what to do. Who to tell. McIver was out of his life now. Danny Chu was no good, not confrontational enough. It would take him a few days to become impatient with Stone, and even then he wouldn't make waves. Essentially this was about Kelly, and she was a powerful woman. He didn't know what he could do about her.

He stopped on a patch of rock overlooking the sea and breathed in the ocean air. The problem, the one he found he did still care about, was that the investigation had hit two dead ends as far as finding out the identity of the shooter. Assuming Sidorov stayed quiet and Conti couldn't break anyone at the council, they wouldn't find Margot's killer, not if Stone remained in charge. He would insist Chu stayed in the office, and Chu would do as he was told. The investigation would continue to limp on as it had, but they had no new lines of investigation. Unless they had a break, in a few weeks there would be a meeting at which Kelly, under pressure from the commanders who had lent detectives to Tailwind, would review the lack of progress and decide to reduce the number of staff. Troy knew from experience that this would be the beginning of the end. And it was not acceptable, it was not how the death of Margot Teresi should finish up, as an unsolved murder. One that had led to two other deaths. A homicide investigation deserved integrity and determination. The living owed a debt to the dead.

As he began to walk again, he sought relief in thoughts about the previous night. The woman had had smooth black hair and skin the colour of weak coffee, and when she'd removed her dress there'd been a certain playful knowingness in her expression that had come as a pleasant surprise. As if it was more than a commercial transaction. This had been a lie, of course, but she'd lied well. From then on his memory was hazy, almost erased by the physical intensity of the experience. Bits of it came back now. There'd been a large mirror on one of the doors of the built-in wardrobe opposite the bed. She'd used it skilfully, allowing him glimpses of what they were doing. After a while he hadn't looked.

'Contemplating your fate?'

Troy turned around. He'd reached the park and McIver was standing just a few metres away, his hair tousled by the wind that had sprung up.

'How'd you find me?'

There were other things he wanted to say to McIver, but for the moment he couldn't remember what they were. There was so much to be angry about.

'I called Anna. She hadn't heard you'd been taken off the investigation, so I told her. She said you sometimes come here when you want to think.'

Troy was irritated. 'She doesn't know that.'

McIver came and stood next to him on the grass, awkwardly zipping up his leather jacket, with the left arm in its sling inside. He was swaying slightly and Troy didn't think it was the wind.

'You spoke to Kelly,' he said.

'I did.'

McIver was closer now, and Troy could smell the alcohol mixed with other smells, such as aftershave. He wondered if his father had had a distinctive smell, if he did himself. It needed a child's nose to really tell. When Matt was older he'd have to ask him.

'She's taken me off the investigation.'

'She told me.'

'This is bad.'

'I agree.'

He looked at McIver. 'I thought we had some sort of friendship.'

'You should listen to your feelings.'

'I won't forget this.'

McIver stuck his hands in his pockets and turned his back to the wind. 'I'm picking up a vibe here. You think I did this, don't you?'

'You told me you'd make me pay. Outside your house this morning.'

'Like this?'

'Kelly knew I'd seen you. A few hours later, I was taken off the investigation.'

McIver shook his head sorrowfully. 'You should know I wouldn't do this.'

Troy's chest seemed to expand. 'No?'

'No.'

Troy believed McIver, and it felt as though something had been set free. The anger seemed to flow out of him, into the ground. For a moment he said nothing. Then: 'I'm sorry.'

'You're getting paranoid,' McIver said, smiling. 'Still, a man with all your enemies, it's understandable.'

'Kelly told you about Stone and me?'

'Doesn't make much sense, removing you.'

'Do you know what's going on?'

'Haven't a clue,' McIver said. 'I've got my own problems. When I got home I found I'd been burgled. The pricks took my Les Paul acoustic, most of my DVDs too.' Troy knew his movie collection had been large and much-loved. 'The strange thing is, they left all the Clint Eastwood ones. Why do you think they did that?' Troy took a deep breath and McIver added, 'There's no need to answer.' He cleared his throat. 'After the locals had been, I called Kelly to tell her I was ready to come back to work.'

'She let you?'

'She's desperate. Blayney is still screwing her on staffing, with Rogers' support. It's almost like they want her to fail. She told me the news about you, so here I am. But I know nothing.'

Troy was momentarily disappointed. McIver had always known something, always had a clue. But now he was the one with the clue. Randall had given it to him only half an hour ago.

'Let's go for a walk,' he said. 'I've got something to tell you.'

*

The walk didn't last long. Troy explained what Randall had told him, and the news seemed to depress McIver. When they reached the Palace Hotel at the other end of the beach, he said he was tired and needed something to eat. They went inside and ordered some lunch. A song was playing loudly through speakers behind the bar. It was rougher than Troy usually liked, but catchy. He'd heard it before and tapped his fingers on the bar.

'"Water and Wine" by the Saints,' said McIver. 'A top ten hit.'

'You follow the top ten?'

'Not usually. But a Saints' song is different.'

Troy had vaguely heard of the band. 'It's been a while,' he said.

The lyrics were difficult to hear, but he'd made out the word 'crime' twice.

McIver said, 'With those drive-bys down south last month, it seems to have caught the public mood.'

The sergeant was looking pale. Troy told him he should go home.

'Soon,' McIver said. 'But tomorrow I come back to work. I'll make some calls tonight, see what's going on. Basically, Kelly's a dangerous woman because she's fighting for her own survival.'

Troy turned on his phone and checked for messages. He'd had it switched off since he'd left the station. Sacha Powell had called from the *Herald*. Wondering what she wanted, he told McIver.

'That's quick,' the sergeant said. 'Nice bit of work with the press on Sunday night, by the way. But I wouldn't make a habit of it.'

'You think I told her I'm off the investigation?'

'I'm just saying—'

'I didn't.'

'Well, someone must have.' McIver smiled. 'It wasn't me.'

Troy deleted the message. There were a few others but none were important. Kelly had not called to say she'd changed her mind.

'The media on this is driving them half-crazy,' McIver said. 'With The Tower on the front page almost every day, this documentary coming up, the government's going insane. They want results, closure. All we've given them is more bodies. Another drink?'

269

They had another. McIver was emotional, and got into an argument with two English backpackers, who made a loud remark about convicts. He stood up, swaying, and the English backed off.

'They're right, though,' he said when he'd sat down again. 'This is a convict city.'

He seemed invigorated by the exchange.

'That was a long time ago.'

McIver snorted. 'We're an army of occupation. Never be anything more.'

'Come on—'

'S'why we have to stick together.'

'Cops?'

'Cops who've been through stuff like us. Up there last Sunday night.' He looked at Troy almost pleadingly, with eyes that were moist. There was a tipping point in his emotions when he was drinking, but they'd reached it much earlier than usual. 'Mate,' he said, 'ask me anything you want. You and me. Anything.'

Here we go, thought Troy, wondering if Mac was on painkillers.

'You must wonder, I see you looking at me sometimes, wondering.'

'I don't know what you're talking about.'

McIver waved a hand dismissively, almost knocking over his glass. 'A good detective like yourself. A good man.' Again he waved his hand. 'So ask anything you like about me.'

It was a sincere request, Troy could see. He had no idea what had prompted it, but he knew McIver was serious. The sergeant was pissed, sweating and tired. But something was on offer here, and couldn't be refused.

'The Perry case,' he said.

'Good pick.' McIver paused and thought about it. 'So you've heard about that?'

'It's part of the mythology.'

'I see. And you want to hear the details?'

'As you're offering.'

McIver nodded: a deal was a deal. 'There was a chapter of the Wolves at Guildford, same as your mate Asaad, when I was on general duties at

Parramatta, long time ago. This biker called Perry was selling drugs to single mums and forcing them on the game when they couldn't pay. He liked the single mums.' As he spoke, McIver seemed to come more alive; the memories were feeding him. 'This fucked up their lives and one killed herself and her kids and I got—I got . . . Want another beer?'

Troy shook his head and McIver gestured to the barman, who looked dubiously at Troy but started to fill a glass.

'Louise Daly her name was. You remember some and not others.'

McIver stopped talking and frowned at a backpacker who'd been trying to listen in. The man moved away. 'So my sergeant and me, we fitted the prick up with a serious drugs charge. This girl called Jasmine, she came to us for help, showed us what Perry'd done to her. Man was a complete animal, said she'd testify, support our story. So we thought we were very clever. It went to court and then Jasmine turned on us. Some of the Wolves had paid her a visit.'

'Didn't you have her in witness protection?'

'Of course. She got bored, got out the back one night and left her baby with the bored officer who was supposed to be guarding her. Called a friend and they met at a pub. She came back to the house later, said she was sorry. We only found out down the line some of the Wolves had turned up at the pub with the friend.' McIver looked pained by the recollection.

Troy said, 'Her change of heart only became clear in court?'

Mac nodded. 'There she was in the box, fitting us up, saying she'd seen me plant the gear.'

'The jury wouldn't believe it, surely?'

McIver looked closely at Troy, who smiled. Reassured, he said, 'Created doubt, that's all it takes. But then Perry disappeared, and that was the end of that.'

'Disappeared?'

McIver waved a hand airily. 'He moved to New Zealand.'

'Who scared him off?'

'Mates in the Armed Holdup Squad.' He finished the beer and rubbed his face. 'They had a word.'

It must have been quite a word, Troy thought. He felt like another beer, but he had to drive. McIver was slipping off his stool. Troy took his good arm, and slowly the two of them walked out of the bar. On the footpath outside, McIver stopped and looked at Troy. 'Would you have done it?'

'Different times.'

'What if it happened now? Your choice, to do or not.'

'No other options?' Troy said, looking out towards the sea, not wanting to have this conversation. The old Armed Holdup Squad had been notorious for the corruption of some of its members.

'No other options,' McIver said.

Troy took a deep breath. 'No,' he said.

McIver grinned as though he'd said something funny. He held out his hand for Troy to shake.

'The other shoulder's hurting like buggery,' he said. 'I hate this sling.'

'A sling's okay.'

'No. It makes you look like an invalid. It's like a sign of vulner—' He seemed to have trouble with the word. 'You know.'

They walked towards the taxi rank. McIver looked in the direction of the sea, breathing in its smell. 'You still do Nippers?'

When Troy moved to Maroubra, he'd joined the surf club and trained to become a volunteer lifesaver. Each summer now, he spent some of his weekends on patrol at the beach, and taught kids on Sunday mornings.

'Sure.'

'Some men would rather lie in.'

Troy looked at all the people swarming around them. People like him. He knew he needed them. The meaning of his life came from the fellow-feeling they gave him, and which he had for them. He recalled something from the Bible. Faith without works is dead.

McIver shook his head. 'We'll have to see which way it goes,' he said vaguely. Then, coming alert again, 'You and me, we have something. Don't deny me again.'

There were tears in his eyes. At first Troy couldn't believe it. McIver was crying. Awkwardly he put out an arm and held him stiffly.

'I didn't even know what was happening before it was over,' McIver said. 'Then woke up two days later and thought I'd had a bad dream. But now this. Few times a day. It's not the alcohol.'

He spoke with great effort, as though he'd prepared these exact words. Then he pulled away from Troy and reached blindly for the door of the taxi.

Troy drove to the police youth club in Daceyville and found someone there to talk to, ended up staying quite a while. They gave him a tour of the place, and by the time he'd finished the day was almost over. When he finally reached home he found Anna in the kitchen, cooking dinner. She turned and gave him a hug, expressed concern at what had happened. He ran a hand down her back, closing his eyes, resisting the urge to compare the feel of her with the woman from last night. She pulled out of his embrace, and said she had to get the food in the oven. He told her about his day, and as he spoke she nodded, frowning in concentration at a recipe book propped up on the bench. The conversation was running down and after a bit he just stopped and she didn't seem to notice.

He went into the lounge room to sit on the floor and play with Matt. Later she came in and asked if it was all right for her to go out after dinner to a Bible study group at ChristLife. He said it was fine.

'Liz and Mark asked us over for a barbeque on Saturday,' she said. 'I said I wasn't sure, but now you'll be here I'll say yes. And the Duttons are coming on Sunday.'

He nodded. At Homicide, when you weren't busy working on an investigation, the weekends were free. Life had to go on. The dead owed that to the living.

He stayed up for a while after Anna came home, thinking about the events of the day, not feeling tired. Finally, after eleven, he decided it was time to try to sleep and went to have a last look at Matt. The door to the bedroom was closed, which was not unusual. Anna had started closing it a week or two ago. But when he went to open it, he discovered it was locked too. A rush of fury went through him and he had to restrain himself from yelling at her to open it. Still, after last night he had no right to be angry with her anymore. Suddenly feeling very tired, he stumbled off to sleep alone in the big bed.

Twenty-eight

Randall didn't know how it had happened, but they were arguing. He hadn't known Kristin long enough to have a major argument with her, so it seemed all wrong. But her strange behaviour demanded confrontation. Going through his wallet had been a joke, almost. But not this.

'I didn't give you a key to my place so you could go in and search it,' he said, trying to remember why he had given it to her, someone he'd only known for a few weeks. It was the way she talked to him, the way she put things: she'd made it seem natural.

'What have you got to hide?'

'It's not that.' She'd turned up at his flat that night, an hour before they'd arranged to meet, well before he'd got home, and gone through his stuff. 'You haven't even given me a key to your place.'

'What's in the cabinet in your room? It has a most solid lock.'

They'd gone over this already. He'd told her the cupboard contained travel documents, plans and mementos of past jobs. One locked cupboard in his entire apartment, for Christ's sake.

'And that disgusting book.'

'There's nothing wrong with it.'

'I read some of it. I found it obscene. Everyone knows it's obscene.'

He put some spatchcock in his mouth so he wouldn't have to speak, and stared at her. Apart from being pale, her skin was incredibly smooth. He didn't know if that was an Icelandic thing, but it was almost like plastic. Her features were nothing special, her mouth rarely smiled, but he was still entranced by her skin, especially where it stretched over her cheeks, from the jawline to the bones beneath her eyes.

And then her hair, a colour somewhere between blonde and white. In many ways she was ordinary, even disappointing, but these two qualities, skin and hair, were so extreme they made her a type, and Randall had long been fascinated by types.

'And what a title,' she said. '*Atlas Shrugged*. Pompous capitalist crap.'

'Ayn Rand had a lot of good ideas.'

'She was a libertarian bitch, and an appalling novelist. I'm distressed that you can enjoy that muck. You do enjoy it?'

'I do. The businessman as hero. You think what you do is important, and so do I.'

Kristin stood up, furious, and threw her napkin down onto the plate. It hit her wineglass, which teetered. Randall put out a hand and steadied it. Things like that mattered, objective reality: stopping a glass from falling. She stormed away from the table, almost running into a waitress carrying a stack of plates. Randall watched the apologetic dance and then Kristin was gone, but only to the toilets, not the front door.

Still, this was better than talking about the illegals, which had occupied the first part of the meal. He checked his phone to see if Troy had rung, but there was no message. That afternoon Wu had called, told him Troy had taken the bait, told him never to tell anyone about the number he'd given the cop the night before. For a few hours, Randall had ignored the implications, just like he'd been ignoring them ever since Wu gave him the number yesterday. But they sunk in. He realised Troy might work it out and come after him, full of anger. He was a very physical fellow, although these past few days he'd hardly been acting impressively. Last night at the restaurant he'd been all over the place. Randall felt a small glow of pride at the thought that he'd come out of Sunday night in better shape than Troy. And Henry was happy with him again, because of how he'd handled the detective. It was as though he'd had a disease and it had been passed on.

Margot Teresi's name had been released to the media, so now the whole world knew she was the victim and was talking about it. Jack Taylor hadn't said a word. They'd been in meetings together twice that day, and Taylor had said nothing, he'd treated Randall the same as normal. It looked like his job was safe. Thanks to Henry.

The problem was, as he sat there waiting for Kristin to come back, Randall found he didn't feel good about Troy. He didn't know precisely what it was he'd done, but he had a strong feeling it might be painful. Troy was a decent sort of fellow doing an important job for poor pay. He didn't deserve to get Randall's germs. I have not always been a good man, Randall thought, but my crimes have usually been victimless, or at least done to strangers. This is different. But then, Troy is such a decent fellow, he might not blame me. He might blame himself.

Kristin came back from the toilets, all bouncy as she flopped into her chair, complete mood transformation. He'd given her some stuff earlier in the evening, in the bar where they'd met, and she must have done a line or two in the ladies' just now. He hoped the waitress wouldn't notice, but she probably would. They needed to go, and he shovelled the last of the wild rice on his plate into his mouth. Kristin seemed to have lost interest in her food, and looked around for someone to bring them the bill.

Kristin reached out and put a hand on his wrist. He liked the way her skin was so pale it made his look dark. He was fair himself, and usually with women it worked the other way round.

'This Thai girl, Sally,' she said, and he nodded, recalling the prostitute picked up by the cops on Sunday.

'Immigration were very enthusiastic at first,' she said, 'but it's gone wrong. They say there's not enough evidence for them to charge anyone with sex trafficking.'

'Didn't the papers say she had some huge debt she could never pay off?' He'd read that she only came here because they'd told her she'd be a dancer. But then, she would say that.

'I know.' Kristin grasped his wrist more firmly. 'It's terrible. Can you imagine? Forced prostitution.'

A waiter turned up with the bill at last, and Randall gave him his card. Kristin put hers on the tray too; she always insisted on paying her share.

'So it's a question of evidence?'

'It's a question of police determination. They've backed off, it's all too hard.' She stood up, face flushed, realised the cards hadn't been brought back yet, and sat down.

'What can you do?' he said.

'One of the detectives, Susan Conti, was really keen to pursue it,' she said. 'But now the police have been taken off Sally's case.'

'Is this Conti any good?'

'She's sympathetic. But has no power.'

Their cards came back and Kristin stood up. 'Now let's go and fuck.'

Jesus. 'I went to the doctor today about a pain in my stomach. She gave me some medication that has a side effect. It interferes with my libido.'

'It's the cocaine,' she said, so loudly that a woman at the next table looked over. 'You need to ease off.'

'No it's not. I have this pain.'

'In your stomach?'

'That's right.'

He stood up and took his briefcase, and they walked out of the restaurant.

'What is this medication called?'

What the doctor had recommended, until the tests could be run, was something called Mylanta. Off the shelf. He had a big bottle in his bag, and if Kristin thought the medication was in there, she'd grab it and do a search. Right now she was very frisky.

'I don't remember,' he said. 'It's back at the office.'

'I think there must be some mistake. Tomorrow, you tell me the name.'

Outside the restaurant, Randall said, 'Tonight, do you mind if we just sleep?'

Some girls would have thought this rather sweet, but Kristin didn't look happy. He knew she had strong needs and took them very seriously.

'I think I'll go home to my place then,' she said. 'I'm a healthy woman. In bed with you, I might be too frustrated.'

'Well—' he said.

'I think it's best.'

She stuck her arm out, and a passing taxi pulled over. He could see she was furious.

'How about we go away together for the weekend? I'll pick you up at five on Friday.'

'That's tomorrow. Where will we go?'

He had no idea. 'Somewhere nice. A surprise for you.'

'Okay.' She kissed him hard on the lips. 'But tomorrow, I want to know the name of your medication.'

He watched the taxi pull off. She was so efficient, he thought, at just about everything. She hadn't encountered messiness yet, and would probably make sure she avoided it for life. He wondered where they would go tomorrow night. Leave the mobile at home. Somewhere far away from Troy.

FRIDAY

Twenty-nine

Troy woke early, just before dawn. Matt started to grizzle so he went to the boy's bedroom and found the door was now unlocked. Anna must have got up during the night. She was still asleep on the couch, and he changed and dressed Matt as quietly as he could. Then he took him out to the kitchen and prepared some hot water to warm the bottle of formula standing ready in the fridge. Anna had stopped breastfeeding a few months ago. While the bottle stood in the water, he took Matt into the main bedroom and propped him up on some pillows on the bed while he changed into jeans and a warm top. The baby looked at him earnestly as he got dressed and began to cry. Troy put on a little pantomime act, held his finger to his lips, tried to look concerned. The baby stopped crying and furrowed his brow, apparently in concentration. As he returned to the kitchen, Matt held in the crook of his left arm, he continued this one-sided dialogue.

When they left the house it was light, and there was more than a trace of heat in the air. Troy pushed the stroller down in the direction of the beach. It would be two months before the water was warm enough for most people to swim, but from now on the sand and the broad pathway above it would attract more and more people in daily rehearsals for summer.

Troy steered the stroller around a long stretch of pavement covered in broken glass. Unusually for a beachside suburb, Maroubra had lots of public housing. Anna had a friend who was a midwife and made home visits in the area. If she went to one of the blocks, it was procedure to notify the local police as she went in. If they hadn't heard from her within half an hour, a car would be sent around immediately. Despite this, the suburb was now an expensive place to buy a house, although the new owners coexisted uneasily with the welfare population. Someone at the surf club had suggested this was why so many of the new houses looked like concrete fortresses.

When they reached the beachfront, Troy turned right and pushed the stroller towards the Malabar headland, a vast area of grass and trees that contained a riding school and several rifle ranges. On its far side there was a sewage treatment works and then, a little further on, the site of a former hospital recently turned into housing for the wealthy, and then the large and still very current Long Bay jail. It was an unusual combination of elements for the coast, which elsewhere consisted largely of houses, beaches and national parks. Troy liked it.

It was only by accident that he lived here and not inland. Four years ago, a solicitor had called to say someone had left him and Georgina a house. It turned out their mother had an uncle they'd never heard of, a single man who'd lost touch with her decades before she died. Now he had died too. Georgina and Troy had met the solicitor at the house, a small, dark-brick place built in the 1940s. They'd walked through it and Troy had liked the bare, grassy backyard and the way the sunlight came in through the windows, making patches on the old carpet. It seemed peaceful, and reminded him of the house they'd lived in before their parents' deaths. It reminded him of a time when he had been a different person.

'His name was Wal Barton,' said the solicitor. 'He said to apologise to you, and left you all his possessions. Which means the house and contents.'

'Apologise for what?' said Georgina.

'He didn't say.'

Troy said, 'When's the funeral?'

'It was last week. He didn't want you to be told until now.' The solicitor thought about what he was going to say next. 'There were no mourners.'

After they'd finished at the house, Troy and Georgina had gone to a cafe near the beach. She told him she didn't want her share: the house was his. When he protested, she described her husband's earnings and career prospects. 'We don't need any more money,' she said, putting a hand on his arm.

He knew it was not just that. It was about the different lives they'd been handed after their parents died. He said he'd think about it.

At the time, he'd just started seeing Anna. She was a nurse and they'd met when he was at Westmead interviewing an assault victim. Things between them grew serious, and the house at Maroubra became part of it; suddenly he could see a future for himself and her, there. A family, for heaven's sake. Him. It was a future he'd never imagined, but which he found he desperately wanted. So he'd called Georgina and said he accepted her gift.

Much later, Anna had pointed out their lucky financial situation meant he could walk away from his job any time he liked. He could afford to take a few months off and do nothing. At the time he'd wondered why she'd said this, but she hadn't mentioned it again. Money wouldn't have been a problem in their lives even if they'd had a mortgage. He could always find work in the private-security sector, earning much more than he did now. Like Ralph Dutton, who was coming over on Sunday with his family. He'd left the police a while back, and these days he lived like a king.

But that was not for him. Troy knew that being a homicide detective was his vocation. No matter what Helen Kelly might be doing to the squad, it was the only place he wanted to be.

When they reached the car park at the southern end of the beach, Troy took Matt from his stroller and walked through the trees and across the sand to the rock pools. Troy crouched to look into a few of the pools but they were bare, long since stripped of anything edible by the city's expanding population, with its varied range of culinary desires. He held Matt tightly, breathing in the baby smell of his hair.

'We're fifty years too late, mate,' he murmured, looking into the rock pool.

He stood up and walked back slowly across the sand, feeling the sun warming his back, basking in a contentment he had not had in a long time. He resisted the temptation to hug Matt again; sometimes he held him so close the boy had trouble breathing.

There was a sign saying DANGEROUS RIP: SWIMMING PROHIBITED. He stood in front of it for a while, watching twenty surfers in their wetsuits paddling on the swell. It wasn't a good day for it, and after a bit Matt began to grizzle, so he turned back to the road. He put the boy in the stroller and soon he was fast asleep.

When they reached the shops he decided to go into a cafe. Often Matt would wake up when the motion of the stroller stopped, but when Troy parked it next to a table and sat down, he continued to sleep. Troy ordered a flat white and reached for a copy of the *Telegraph* on a nearby table, trying to make as little noise as he could. The main story was about a leadership struggle in the federal government, something Troy had stopped paying attention to long ago. The other item on the front page, concerning the murder of a South Korean student in a flat in Pyrmont, occupied his attention as the coffee came and he began to sip it. Maybe he'd be assigned to the investigation. Then he turned the page and saw a photograph of himself. The one from Dubbo. He blinked and checked the date of the newspaper, thinking it might be from Monday. But it wasn't, and he should have known this because there was a photograph of Margot Teresi next to his own. On Monday they hadn't known the victim's identity.

TERESI MURDER INQUIRY IN CHOAS, ran the headline.

Police Commissioner Frank Rogers has rejected claims the investigation into the death of heiress Margot Teresi has been compromised by a political agenda. Informed sources claim inquiry chief Detective Sergeant Brad Stone has been using interviews with workers at The Tower, where

Teresi died on Sunday night, to gather information on the activities of union organisers.

Matt began to cry but Troy read on. The article described Stone as 'a Victorian detective formerly attached to the royal commission into the construction industry'. It reported that Detective Senior Constable Nicholas Troy, Stone's deputy, had been stood down from Strike Force Tailwind yesterday. The official reason was his need to recover from the shooting incident at The Tower, but an anonymous source claimed the real reason was that Troy had expressed concerns the political agenda was compromising the homicide investigation. As Troy was the only experienced homicide officer on the team, the source said this would affect its chances of finding Teresi's killer.

Troy rocked the stroller. When this didn't work he picked up Matt and cuddled him until he stopped crying.

The police minister had denied all knowledge of Stone's activities and said he would be looking into the claims today. An official from the Police Association was quoted as saying, 'The idea that a homicide investigation might be hampered by the federal government's political agenda is deeply disturbing. We'll be seeking more information and considering our response.'

Hear, hear, thought Troy, bending down to kiss Matt gently on the forehead.

Henry Wu, of Morning Star Australia, said he had no knowledge of a covert police operation at The Tower. He pointed out that the state government, a supporter of the union movement, would be unlikely to condone such an action.

Troy put Matt back in the stroller and stood up, wondering who had leaked the story. Kelly might think it was him, but he didn't care. All he felt was relief in having the thing out in the open.

Later that morning, driving to Parramatta, Troy turned on the radio. It was ABC local, and the presenter was asking her guest the secret of his success. Troy didn't recognise the man's voice, so he didn't know what he was successful at. The guest paused for thought and then said, 'Empathy. I guess I was just fortunate enough to learn how to empathise with my fellow human beings.'

Troy changed stations. On the next one a man was describing the great sex he'd had during an affair with a famous actor's wife. Troy switched again, found a station where the host was abusing a politician, and left it on. The radio was a reminder of what awaited him when he was not involved in an investigation.

When he reached work, McIver was there already, talking on the phone. His face was a little pale against the dark blue shirt he was wearing, adorned with a black tie beneath the sling, but otherwise he looked well, much better than the previous day. His expression was animated as he listened to what the person on the other end of the line was saying.

Troy looked around the office, spotting copies of the *Telegraph* on some desks, catching a few of his colleagues glancing at him. One of them smiled, but stopped when he saw Kelly standing in the doorway.

'Nicholas, my office, please,' she said. 'You too, Jon.'

She turned and disappeared down the corridor.

McIver got off the phone and stood up. Troy saw he was wearing black trousers with pointed boots.

'You,' he said, 'should not be back at work.'

'Can't keep an old warrior down, mate,' McIver whispered as they followed Kelly. 'It's all about keeping your immune system happy, did you know that?'

Troy had no idea what he was talking about. He was glad that in this, at least, things were returning to normal.

Kelly's office was several times the size of the one where they had had their conversation the previous day. It was largely bare, as though the space was unnecessary except to proclaim her status. Even the desk was clear, unlike almost all the others in the squad. On a shelf behind the superintendent sat a pile of newspapers and a photograph of herself with a man in evening clothes, taken at some event. Presumably this was her husband. Troy wondered why it was positioned where Kelly herself couldn't see it.

'Shut the door and take a seat,' she said.

'Any news on the Korean girl?' McIver asked cheerily.

Kelly blinked as though uncertain at first what he was talking about. Then she pointed at the two chairs on the other side of her desk. When the two detectives were seated she paused, staring at Troy, in silence. He stared back, trying to see if he could detect any sign of her ruthlessness in her eyes. Of course he couldn't. If hard people carried a sign of their true nature in their faces, others would avoid them. It was one of the disappointments of life, the fact that destructive people were so often charming and intelligent.

At last she spoke. 'Did you talk to the *Telegraph*?'

'No, ma'am.'

More staring.

'Whoever did, a brave officer's life has been put at risk.'

Not to mention several careers, Troy thought, realising the implications the revelation might have for Kelly herself. The government wouldn't be happy. Or the commissioner—it was possible he hadn't known about the covert operation either.

McIver crossed his legs. 'If it's any help, ma'am,' he said, 'Senior Constable Troy doesn't have a reputation as a leaker—unlike one or two of our colleagues, who shall remain nameless. In my experience he's a self-contained man who deals with problems in a professional manner.'

Troy's ears burned a little. McIver's manner was so casual you could forget he was an operator too.

Kelly nodded as though she wanted to believe him. Maybe she did. 'There's been a change of plan,' she said, looking at both of them. 'Stone's been moved on, for his own protection. Mac will replace him; he assures me he's well enough for light duties. Normally I wouldn't have either of you back at work, but with this murder at Pyrmont . . .' She looked at her watch. 'Frankly, we're desperate. And you,' looking at Troy, 'are back on the investigation.' She stopped.

Troy felt a surge of relief, but he said nothing, expecting more from her. She owed it to them to explain this change of mind—to explain the claims made in the newspaper article. But in the end, the effort seemed too much for her.

'You can go,' she said angrily.

It was not like her, he thought. Not like her to leave anything out. She might be manipulative, but she was good at it and didn't like to cause unnecessary distress.

'Can we keep China,' McIver said, 'to make up for this?' He wiggled his left arm.

Kelly frowned, seemed about to say something nasty, then nodded impatiently. 'We need a result here. Stone did well. But we need a result.'

As they left the room, Troy thought she looked unhappy.

Back at his desk, McIver smiled broadly. 'I don't know what you did to her, mate, but she didn't enjoy it. That *Tele* article gave them both barrels.'

'Wasn't me. I thought it must have been you.'

'Not I. Which leaves . . .? Apart from the rest of Strike Force Tailwind, all of Kelly's competitors in the climb up the greasy pole.'

'Nice about Chu,' Troy said. 'He's a good operator.'

'He's also a poof.'

Troy stared at McIver, not catching the significance of the observation, just enjoying the fact they were working together again.

'And this is a good thing?'

McIver smiled. 'Couldn't be better. Bazzi's gay too. He's been missing for four days now; we need to dig deeper, get China out into the bathhouses, nightclubs. Whatever.'

Chu lived a quiet life in a Newtown terrace with the man who'd been his partner for five years. McIver knew a lot, but it was possible he did not know this.

On the other hand, it was possible he did.

When he got back to City Central an hour later, Troy called Randall and told him he was back on the investigation. He'd been thinking about who might have leaked to the *Telegraph*.

The engineer sounded happy. 'Had a word to someone at the paper, did you?'

'It wasn't me.'

'You don't need to be shy,' Randall said. 'I won't tell anyone.'

'It was you, wasn't it?'

'Don't be ridiculous.'

'Well, thanks,' said Troy.

'If it was me,' Randall said, 'I'd say you're welcome.'

That night, Anna went out to her book club and Troy looked after Matt. They played for a long time. The boy had been pulling himself up for a while now, so Troy kept holding him up on his legs next to a chair and almost letting go, hoping he would stand by himself for a few seconds. But Matt just dropped down on his bottom and laughed uproariously. It was a good joke.

After the baby had his dinner and flicked some food around the kitchen, Troy gave him a bath and got him ready for bed. They had one last go at standing, and suddenly it happened: Matt was standing by himself, arms slightly out from his sides. He looked puzzled, stared at Troy, and burst into tears. But he stood there, wobbling, for at least five seconds before sitting down.

A few minutes later he was sound asleep. Troy, feeling like an early night himself, sat down to write Anna a note describing their son's great achievement. He felt happy. Kids, they fill up our days, stop us thinking about ourselves, he thought. This is all good.

SATURDAY

Thirty

The first video file came on Saturday morning. Troy got up before Anna and Matt, and went for a run along the beach. McIver had given most of the team the weekend off while he read through all the material gathered by the investigation. He shared Troy's view that it had reached a dead end, and wanted to give people the chance to clear their heads before starting again on Monday.

As Troy moved along the sand, he watched the orange sun rise over the line of ocean in the distance. There were a few squat container ships out there this morning, one of them breaking the far line. Some people claimed to be able to detect the curve of the earth's surface along the horizon, a triumph of imagination over eyesight he sometimes thought of when considering witness statements.

When he got home, Anna was awake in Matt's room and he made her a cup of coffee. Then he went to the computer that sat on a small table in a corner of the main bedroom, and logged on to his personal email. In the inbox there was a message with the subject *Detective Troy at Mornington Apartments*.

It took a while for the attachment to download. Then he opened it. The quality was good. It showed Troy standing next to a bed, the woman who'd said her name was Tanya kneeling before him. They were both naked. For a moment he was stunned.

'Honey,' Anna called from the doorway, 'can you put on the griller?'

As quickly as he could, he turned off his email program, a finger on the on/off button of the computer, ready to kill it if Anna came into the room. His heart's blood was roaring in his ears and he just sat there staring at the screen while his fingers automatically logged him off. An enemy hath done this. But who? He was so stunned he could hardly think.

He heard the toilet flush, then Anna came into the room behind him and said, 'Did you hear what I said?'

He didn't look at her, his eyes still on the blank screen. There had been no message accompanying the video file. He wondered how they'd got his email address. But it was not hard, he knew that.

'I have to go in for a few hours,' he said hoarsely. 'Something's come up.'

'Not today—we're going to the Matarazzos'.' She sounded disappointed.

He said, still staring at the screen, 'It's something important. The computer's broken too, it won't boot up.'

This seemed to worry her more than the news that he had to go in to work. She told him she'd been going to download some information on asthma for Liz, whose daughter also had the condition.

He shrugged. 'You turn it on and just get the screen, but nothing else happens.' He needed to get the computer out of the house, in case they sent the video to her as well. He stood up. 'I'd better have my shower.'

Really he ought to disconnect the computer now. But it might look suspicious. What he had to do was act as normally as he could, not do anything unusual or in a hurry. And even if he did do something to the computer, even if he smashed the bloody thing, it would only be a temporary solution. Anna took her email seriously. She would go to a friend's place or an internet cafe.

As the hot water ran over his body he continued to feel stunned. Doing what he'd done at the Mornington had been one thing—he'd

assumed that coping with any guilt he felt would be the big problem—
but this was something else entirely. He realised what a fool he'd been,
just how big a risk he'd taken. This intrusion into his home, the way it
had been achieved so easily, the threat it posed to things that mattered
to him so much. He assumed there would be a blackmail demand. He
knew Anna wouldn't be able to handle it if she found out. Apart from
her fragility at the moment, her view of the world was pretty black and
white, and this might put him in the black forever. The thought that
it could destroy his marriage, that he'd see Matt so rarely if she moved
back to Brisbane, made him feel physically weak, and he leaned against
the tiled wall of the shower for a moment.

As he dried himself, he wondered how the thing had been done.
Tanya had kissed him on the sofa in the lounge room. He'd heard that
prostitutes didn't kiss, but it hadn't seemed to be a problem for her.
Maybe it was part of the extra service Randall had boasted about. After
a bit she'd started to unbutton his shirt and he'd been playing with the
knickers she had on, things had progressed quickly and by the time
they'd reached the bedroom they had both been naked. Which meant,
he realised, that his wallet with his ID would have lain on the floor of
the lounge room for the next thirty or forty minutes.

Maybe someone had been there, in another room. They'd come out
while he was with Tanya, and gone through his things. Soon they'd ask
for money, although as he was a police officer they could hardly expect
to get much from him. Probably they'd ask for regular payments of
small amounts. He'd have to tell Vella. Kelly would find out. Christ, he
thought. But still, they'd sort it out. Anna need never know.

He wondered where Randall fitted in. Presumably Randall wasn't
being blackmailed himself, or he wouldn't have given Troy the number,
potentially putting him in the same position. Or was the opposite just as
likely? Was Randall being blackmailed himself, had he been told to get
other men involved? But how could they blackmail Randall? He was a
single man, an engineer with no public position. He probably wouldn't
care at all if people saw pictures of him having sex. But you never knew.
It all depended what sort of photos they had.

Troy tried to picture the layout of the flat but couldn't get it straight in his mind. He hadn't been paying attention. There could easily have been another bedroom with a closed door, someone else could have been in the place all along. He hadn't thought about it at the time; having dropped his defences in order to make the visit, he hadn't been thinking as he normally would. And he'd been drunk.

He remembered the mirror. It was floor-to-ceiling, attached to one of the big sliding doors on the built-in wardrobe lining one side of the room. The mirror had been part of the experience, he'd enjoyed seeing some of the things the woman was doing to him. The memory of it was still exciting, despite the danger he sensed all around him now. The mirror must have been two-way, with a camera behind it.

He went back to the bedroom and found Matt lying on the bed, playing with a wooden rattle. Anna was seated before the computer, her email program on the screen. Troy's heart seemed to stop. He couldn't believe he'd allowed this to happen. He stepped across the room and looked over her shoulder. She must have gone through her mail already, because none of the messages in the inbox was highlighted. He scanned the list of subjects and saw no reference to the Mornington Apartments.

'Your computer skills haven't improved much,' she said. 'When I switched it on, I had no problems.'

He listened as she continued speaking, telling him about some of the research on asthma that she'd found and wanted to share with Liz Matarazzo. Normally her focus on asthma annoyed him, but today he was glad she was talking so much, and listened closely, trying to detect if she was upset. Her voice ran through his head like the green line on one of the screens he'd seen when he'd visited McIver in the ICU. If Anna tried to hide anything from him, her tone would be different and the line would change direction, there would be a blip, and he would know. But she kept talking, and the line ran straight.

'I've been supposed to do a computer course,' he said, sitting on the bed and picking up Matt, holding him upright while he tickled his tummy. 'But it never seems to fit in with the jobs I get.' He paused. 'You know, there's no need to lock the door at night.'

'I don't like you standing there, looking at me,' she said, still staring at the screen.

'I just come in to kiss Matt when I get home.'

'The other night you were just standing there, staring at me, breathing heavily. It scared me, Nick.'

'I like to come in to say goodnight to him.'

And you. I still love you, even if the relationship exists only in my head.

'I opened my eyes and you walked out. I checked the clock later and it was after midnight.'

She was still staring at the screen but her voice had risen and the knuckles of the hand gripping the computer's mouse were white.

This was all new. The green line had changed, but not for the reason he'd feared.

'Don't lock the door,' he said. 'I have a right to kiss Matt goodnight. I won't look at you.'

There was no response. She was printing something now and he stood up, wandering around the room with Matt, glancing at the printer as casually as he could, checking that it was printing text and not pictures of himself screwing a Malaysian prostitute.

'Any chance you'll be able to make the barbeque?' she said, logging off. 'Mark wants to talk to you about putting Billy in Nippers this year.'

He told Anna he'd do his best, and got dressed. He thought twice about putting on his gun, which he'd got back after the stress shoot last week. In the end, habit prevailed and he strapped it on.

Twenty minutes later he was out of the house and driving towards the city. He glanced at himself in the rear-view mirror, feeling that he was handling it okay, checking to see that his face looked normal. He saw that he'd forgotten to shave. It was the first time he'd ever gone to work like this.

He parked at the station but didn't go in. Instead, he walked to the Mornington Apartments, up in Sussex Street. On the drive in, he'd been wondering if he should call Randall, find out what he knew. But the engineer might know nothing, and he didn't want to give him any idea of what had happened if it wasn't necessary. The fact there'd been no message with the video file was worrying him. He guessed that was the point, to fill his head with vague fears. At the moment he should do as little as possible, just wait. But it was hard.

He called Randall, got his voicemail.

'Something's happened,' Troy said. 'Call me now. It's urgent.'

The building was up ahead. Now he was outside it, looking in.

The concierge was the same young Chinese man who'd been there three days ago. Troy stood outside the glass door for a moment, watching him, wondering whether he was involved. The man was sitting behind a white counter looking at something on the desk. He ignored Troy until he pressed the button on the small speaker next to the door. The concierge looked up and leaned down to talk into a microphone.

'What you want?'

Troy identified himself as a police officer and held up his badge.

The speaker crackled again. 'Manager not here. Come back Monday.'

The response made Troy pause. He didn't want to do anything that would bring in the locals from City Central. What a mess.

He was still undecided when a couple turned off the footpath and came up to the door. Troy stepped back and the man approached the speaker and said something in Mandarin. Troy could see the concierge still hesitating, and then there was a buzzing noise and the glass door opened. Troy followed the couple inside.

He waited until the concierge gave them their key and they'd gone around behind the counter to the lifts. He kept waiting until the lift doors opened and the couple disappeared. The concierge was watching him uneasily. Occasionally he'd glance down. Troy walked around to the side and looked down at his desk, where there was a small DVD player. The man was watching the last *Batman* movie.

'How you going, mate?' Troy said, walking back to the front of the counter and leaning on it. 'You good?'

'Manager come on Monday. I have no authority—'

'Who's the tenant in number forty-two?'

'Forty-two empty. Moved out now.'

'Give me the key.'

'Don't have keys. Come back Monday.'

Without really thinking, Troy went over to the lift and took it up to the fourth floor. When he got there he went down the corridor and knocked on number forty-two, just as he had the first time he'd come here. For a moment he had a fantasy that she would open the door and he could change the past, it would be Wednesday night again and he would tell her he had the wrong address, turn around and walk away.

Come on, he prayed, as he waited there. Ask, and it shall be given to you; seek, and ye shall find; knock, and it shall be opened unto you.

But there was no answer, not even after he'd knocked again. He tried the handle, but of course the door was locked.

There were three other flats on the floor and he knocked on all of them. There was no answer from the first two. It was like one of those stupid game shows, if you picked the door of the right box your whole life might change. As he waited in the anonymous corridor, he wondered about the private worlds on the other sides of the doors, lives connected to other lives throughout the city and beyond. The third door opened and he forced himself to concentrate.

It was a young Chinese man wearing glasses. Behind him another young man was looking from the end of the flat's short corridor, as though they didn't get many callers. Music was coming from inside and he could see stacks of textbooks on a table in the lounge room. The door was on a security chain and the men looked anxious, so Troy showed them his badge. It did nothing to relax them.

When he asked about the occupants of the other flats, the man at the door said, 'Don't know,' speaking English with apparent difficulty. 'Students like us there,' he said, pointing to one of the doors Troy had just knocked on. He said the other was empty. As for forty-two, 'People come and go. Maybe tourists.'

'Have you seen a young Malaysian woman lately?'

The young man blushed faintly. 'Seen her twice in lift.'

'When was the last time?'

'Maybe last week?'

'What about your friend?'

'That my cousin. He only come from Taipei yesterday.'

After a few more questions, Troy thanked them for their assistance and the door banged shut. Again he was alone in the brightly lit corridor. He walked back towards the lift, looking at the three doors. After knocking on all of them once more, he took the lift downstairs.

He approached the concierge again, letting his coat flap open to show his gun.

The man said he had no idea who owned apartment forty-two, and gave Troy a card with the name of the managing agent. Some people came out of the lift with a lot of luggage, and the concierge left his desk to help them out to a taxi. While this was happening, four young people squeezed their way from the street into the lobby, talking loudly. Like the others, they were Chinese. One of them held a water bottle, and a map in a plastic holder hung from her neck.

'Short-term leasing,' the concierge said to Troy when he got back. He shrugged and returned to the small screen on the desk. Maybe he really did know nothing.

Troy called the number on the card, and received another number to call for weekend emergencies. He rang it and talked to a tradesman who claimed not to have a mobile for anyone at the agency, and hung up when Troy identified himself as a policeman. He wondered what to do next. Running a finger down his cheek he felt the bristles, and decided to buy a razor and have a shave back at the station.

He walked back around the counter and looked in the flat box on the wall from which the concierge had taken the keys he'd just given the group who'd come in. Inside were pegs, with the number of an apartment next to each one. There was at least one key on most of the pegs, presumably a spare. In some cases there were two, but there were no keys at all on the peg for number forty-two. Troy looked at the man.

'Manager has keys to clean flat.'

'Why's he cleaning it?' Troy said.

'Don't know. Come back Monday.'

On the desk was a plastic DVD case with a photocopied cover showing Heath Ledger. Troy hit the eject button on the player and took out the DVD. The disc was blank, except for some Chinese characters written in marker pen. He put the DVD in the case and waved it before the man's face.

'The courts are taking DVD piracy very seriously at the moment,' he said. 'I'm going to arrest you unless you give me the key to number forty-two now.'

He didn't think it would work. But he couldn't think of anything else to do.

It didn't work. The man just stared at him. Troy thought about his next step. He could pull out his gun and push it into the man's mouth, blow his head off, but it would probably be a mistake. The whole thing was like a nightmare, not just the content of the day but how it was progressing, in fits and starts. He seemed to have lost his sense of time, and there was even something askew in his feeling for distance, so that he wasn't sure if he was standing close enough to the man he was talking to.

There was a ping from around the corner and he looked at the lift. An old man emerged and walked slowly, calling out to the concierge in Mandarin. Then he saw Troy.

'Can I help you, detective?'

It was another dreamlike moment, for Troy didn't recognise the man, who was looking at him like they were old friends. Then it came to him: it was the guy he'd saved from being mugged the last time he was here. He even remembered the bloke's name, Mr Foo. They shook hands. The old fellow had thin, papery skin, and for a second Troy thought of Jenny Finch, but he pushed that away. The man seemed weak, and leaned against the counter, with the concierge up now and hovering next to him anxiously.

Troy explained his need to get into the flat upstairs, wanting to move on. Maybe he ought to try something completely different. He was wondering if he should talk to Inspector Harmer; she seemed a decent sort of person. Explain what had happened, throw himself on her mercy and see if she knew what was going on in this building. But then Siegert would find out. And Little.

He realised Foo, who'd been speaking to the concierge, was now talking in English again. 'Mr Chan has language problems sometimes. He will be happy to help you, but would be grateful if his assistance went unacknowledged.'

The concierge had gone back behind the counter and was rustling in a drawer. A moment later, he placed a ring with two keys on it on the counter and stood back, not looking at Troy. He seemed to be experiencing some sort of inner turmoil.

'You're very kind,' Troy said, looking at each of them. It was clear that as far as Chan was concerned, he still didn't exist. He added, 'So the place is empty?'

They just smiled at him, until finally he walked away.

On level four there was still no one about. He unlocked the door and went inside, breathing in the aroma of recently used cleaning products. For a moment he stood in the middle of the bare lounge room, recalling the other night. The dog returning to his own vomit. The apartment was empty of furniture, like a movie set from which all the props have been removed. In the bedroom he slid back the mirrored door of the wardrobe and awkwardly stepped inside. A large hole had been cut into the door. The mirror was an ordinary one, so the two-way they'd used to film him had been replaced. The hole behind it was the only evidence of what had happened. Apart from the footage itself. Methodically he searched the whole place but there was nothing: no phone, no scrap of paper in any of the cupboards.

Back in the lounge room he looked out the window at another residential block across the road. It was a modern place with huge windows that ran from floor to ceiling. Some of the flats looked neat; others were messy, with sheets and clothes piled up against the bottom of the glass. He thought of single men living carelessly in small apartments. That could be him, soon. For a moment he was struck by a sense of despair, and wondered how he could have been so reckless as to put his marriage at risk. He told himself Anna deserved it. Other men would have walked out by now. He realised it was foolish to have regrets, they would only weaken him, hamper his thinking about how to respond.

His phone rang. It was Randall, who said, 'Mate, what's going on?'

'That number you gave me the other night, I did use it.'

Randall whistled. 'Nice one. Have a good time?'

'Who told you to give it to me?'

'No one. What are you talking about?'

'Something's come up about that. I need to meet you now.'

'Can't do that. I'm out of Sydney.'

'When are you back?'

'Not until Monday. What's happened?'

Troy said nothing.

'I'm sorry, I had to get away, needed a break.'

'You could be hearing from some of my colleagues.'

There was a tiny pause. 'Mate, tell me what this is about.'

'This is the last chance to sort this out now. I know someone told you to give me the number. I want to know who that person was.'

'I got it over a year ago, from an architect I met in Shanghai. I've used it myself heaps of times. It's perfectly legit. Has something happened?'

'You'll be hearing from someone on Monday,' Troy said. 'It'll be out of my hands by then. You need to understand that, what it means.'

'Mate—'

Troy hung up. He didn't have a clue what he was going to do next. But he knew one thing: Randall had never called him *mate* before.

As he shaved in the bathroom at the station, Troy thought about Randall's involvement. He wondered if this could be about more than money, if someone wanted to influence his work, but that didn't make any kind of sense. He was only second in command of Tailwind, and had no knowledge that would help anyone. In any case, the investigation had been going only a few days, and he didn't see how anyone could have set up something like this so quickly. He thought about other investigations he'd worked on, court matters he had coming up. It didn't seem to fit;

it wasn't as though he dealt with crimes involving career criminals or large sums of money. Most murders were committed by people with no criminal background. He couldn't see anyone he'd caught recently organising something like this.

Troy dried his face and picked up the disposable razor. He was looking around for the bin when the door opened and Ron Siegert came in. Troy hadn't spoken to him since the early days of the investigation.

Siegert nodded and started to wash his hands. He looked at Troy in the mirror. 'How's Tailwind?'

'I've never been in anything like it,' Troy said.

Siegert turned off the tap. 'It's good you're back on it.' He seemed less aggressive than before. 'Your father was a good cop too. Do you know why he left the job?'

He was looking at his hands now, not at Troy.

'No. Do you?'

'It surprised me. He was a friendly bloke but suddenly he was gone. I never saw him again.'

'He went out bush a lot with his new job.'

Siegert looked as if he had something to say about that, but finally just nodded and banged on the hand-dryer. Over its roar he said, 'He was a fine detective. Good instincts.'

Thirty-one

When Troy got home it was one o'clock and Anna had already left. There was a note on the kitchen table with the Matarazzos' phone number and address. His wife, like himself, was well organised. She was constantly arranging their family and social life, cooking and cleaning up. Already she'd planned the next five years, was reading for the law course she planned to do. This suited him just fine. At a distance he could enjoy chaos—it was one reason he liked McIver—but home was different. Home, at least for him, was for security, not challenges. He wondered if that was where he and Anna had gone wrong, if they were just too similar.

Did he really know how she would react to the video footage? Maybe he was wrong to think she'd leave him. She might have depths of understanding and forgiveness. Maybe she'd already received the video by email, or photos in the mail yesterday, and had decided to say nothing. It might even be her way of compensating for the state of their relationship.

Ha ha.

He was hit by a need to know if she'd been sent the file yet. He didn't have the password to her part of their computer system, but knew she kept it written in a small blue notebook somewhere. He looked around but couldn't see it. He went into their bedroom and opened her side of the wardrobe and began to go through the drawers, ashamed of what he was doing but determined. There was a need to act.

He didn't find the notebook, but at the back of the bottom drawer there was a paper bag. It contained a repeat prescription written by a Dr Istvan Malecki for a course of Prozac. There was a bottle of the tablets in the bag too. He took it out slowly and looked at it. The bottle was almost empty.

Carefully he replaced the bag and closed the drawer, and went over to the computer in a daze. He'd had no idea Anna had sought treatment. A Google search revealed that Malecki was a psychiatrist.

'I know you think I'm weak,' Anna had said to him in one of their tear-filled discussions some months ago. 'I try hard, though. I really do.'

Cradling her when she cried. She had let him hold her, but it wasn't as though he was really there. Why hadn't she told him about the psychiatrist, when she knew it was what he wanted?

'My wife, my mystery,' he said to the magnolia tree.

And my marriage. In your twenties you think life will just keep getting better. You're full of the optimism of ignorance. And then something like this comes along.

It was not as though the Prozac had done much good. He thought back to her locking her door the other night, the story this morning about him standing in her room after midnight. It was foolish to hope; if anything, she was getting worse. He realised that if this was the state she was still in, despite the psychiatrist and the medication, finding out about him and the prostitute might be the end. She must never see those pictures.

He spent the rest of the afternoon working in the garden. The lawn in the front and back had to be mowed, and a load of mulch had been delivered out front during the week, which he moved by barrow into the backyard. Anna was responsible for the flowers and went for what he called the Bollywood effect, large splashes of colour; clumps of blue hydrangeas, blazes of azaleas. He spread some of the rich mixture around the plants. It was satisfying work, hot and sweaty, and for a while he stopped thinking about things.

Anna and Matt got home at six, with Matt asleep in his seat in the back of her car. Troy lifted him out, breathing in a strong aroma of stale milk and vomit, and the unmistakable whiff of a nappy that needed attention. He took the boy inside, laid him gently on the change table and went to work. When he got the nappy off, Matt woke up suddenly and let out a yell, then saw his father and went straight back to sleep. For a moment Troy was awash with emotion.

'He's exhausted,' Anna said, coming in from where she'd been filling the baby bath next door. 'He had so much fun playing with their puppy. Maybe we should get a dog.'

'He's filthy,' Troy said, looking at the dirt in the creases behind the baby's knees and the stains on the outside of the disposable nappy he'd just wrapped up.

'He's a lovely little man,' she murmured, tickling the boy beneath his chubby chin.

Matt woke up, looking startled for a moment, and then began to gurgle with pleasure. Troy always enjoyed seeing the way she did that.

She removed Matt's top so he was naked, and lifted him and took him into the bathroom. She did it effortlessly. Matt was not heavy, and Anna was strong. She took him on long walks in his stroller each day, up and down the big hills of the district, often with friends. She'd done this from soon after he was born, and by the time he turned one her figure had returned pretty much to the way it had been before she became pregnant. Troy knew some mothers became depressed because they'd lost their shape, but Anna didn't have that problem. It was one reason her depression had surprised him, because she'd always seemed like a person who got on top of things.

He picked up the used nappy and took it out to the kitchen.

'Are you hungry?' she called from the bathroom. 'Let's get some takeaway.'

After washing his hands he changed his jeans, and put his keys and wallet in his pockets. He found Anna in Matt's room, bending over him as she prepared him for bed. She was wearing the same clothes she'd come home in: a bright pink T-shirt over a blue skirt that went almost to her knees. From behind he could see the two silver earrings in her right ear. She'd once told him Indians had invented body piercing.

'What do you feel like?' he said.

She stood up and turned around, keeping a hand on Matt's leg as he lay there yelling gibberish and shaking a toy lamb.

'I'll have some of whatever you get. Aleisha has agreed to babysit on Monday.'

'Monday?'

'So we can go out.'

He wondered what was happening. Hoped it wasn't another ChristLife event. 'That'll be good.'

She smiled almost shyly. 'Our anniversary.'

I've completely forgotten, he thought. But then that's normal, and maybe normal is good right now. He hadn't bought a present for her yet, of course. What a present it would be on Monday, if she saw the video footage then. It came back to him now, the horror of his situation. He was overreacting, of course. No he wasn't. He didn't know what was happening to him.

He said, 'I'll get a pizza.'

SUNDAY

Thirty-two

Randall woke up slowly, staring at a wall that he gradually realised was unfamiliar. After a bit he turned onto his back and contemplated the ceiling, working out where he was. A resort near Pokolbin, expensive, nice restaurant and sauna. He turned his head and saw Kristin wasn't there; she must have gone to the bathroom. Checking his watch—just after midnight—he realised he'd been asleep for less than an hour. He turned back to the wall, willing himself to sleep again.

They'd hit the wineries in the afternoon, done some serious research. She'd got right into it, recovered from her grumpiness of the morning. But when they got to bed, he'd had problems again, had almost got there, tried to make it up to her in other ways. It hadn't helped that she'd forgotten to bring any coke with her; that had been the arrangement so he hadn't bothered bringing any himself, and they were dry. They'd argued about this, she'd told him coke was part of his problem, she'd done him a favour by forgetting it. She had no idea what his problems were.

Truth told, he'd got angry with her, started to swear, pushed her at one point. If efficiency was her thing, what she was proud of, if she wanted to be on a par with men in that area, she had to take the rough with the smooth. She shouldn't have forgotten to bring the coke: actions have consequences.

He'd promised himself not to bring his mobile away with him, but of course he had. If the blow was going to fall, you had to meet it. Couldn't spend the whole weekend wondering. As his ma liked to say, a coward dies a thousand deaths. He'd thought he'd be scared of Troy, but it hadn't turned out that way at all when he'd called the day before. The fellow was cracking up, you could hear it in every word he spoke, behind all the tough-guy threats. It was a sad business, really. Randall thought he'd handled the call all right. Pretended complete ignorance. The stuff about cops paying him a visit on Monday had been scary, but Troy was bluffing. Almost certainly. Still, Randall had made the most of the tastings afterwards, drinking to carry himself off to a more pleasant place. No risk involved, they'd been using a resort limo to ferry them around. Beautiful semillons, enough age on them, some superb plonk. He'd spent over a thousand dollars, even bought a case for Kristin too. Made her happy.

So where was she? Getting out of bed, he padded over to the bathroom and opened the door. Empty. Opening his bag, he looked for the headache tablets, saw a DVD in its case. It had *Iceland* written on the cover, it was Kristin and him. Henry had returned it a few days ago, said it was one of his best efforts. Randall had brought it along, thinking he might play it if necessary last night, get them going. But he'd forgotten all about it.

He straightened up and waited for his head to stop hurting. Surveying the bedroom, he realised all her things were gone. Opening the front door, he stared into the cold night at where her car had been. Jesus.

How was he going to get back home? Should never have let her drive. He'd arranged to pick her up from work but she'd called him Friday, said she was out at Villawood, some crisis, the Thai girl she was so excited about had disappeared. She would come straight into the city and collect him, they could go in her car. Randall didn't like women driving him, but it was not something to raise with Kristin. They'd spent hours in her Prius, crawling up the freeway in the heaviest traffic.

There was a note on hotel paper, telling him it was over, she was being transferred away from Sydney soon anyway and it was best to end their relationship now. What relationship? he thought. Earlier that night, when he couldn't do it, she'd been angry. Worse than the night before. How dare she! He couldn't remember what had been said, but he'd been furious. He could remember the fury. It was all her fault—if the stupid bitch had brought the coke like she'd said she would, everything would have been fine. He just needed to relax. She'd spoiled the whole weekend and been too proud to admit it.

What a stupid note, he thought, crumpling it and throwing it through the open door into the bathroom. Later he'd wipe his arse with it, tell her what he'd done on Monday. He got up and went over to the bar fridge, poured himself some juice. Took it back to bed.

He thought about the DVDs he provided for Henry, how he had watched Randall having sex with at least half a dozen women by now, and shivered. The man was one sick fuck. But still, it gave him a hold over Henry, the fact that he knew about his little peccadillo. You had to wonder what Henry wanted from Troy. Maybe if he knew he could work out another way, make them both happy and get the cop off the hook. But he didn't.

After Troy had called yesterday morning, he'd gone outside, had a smoke, rung Henry. Asked him what was going on.

'That's not an appropriate question,' Wu said.

'It's the mystery man, isn't it?' Randall said.

He had no idea where the thought came from, but it had been on the money, he could tell from the tone of Henry's denial. Something about the interest he'd shown when Randall had told him about the fellow the cops were calling Mr A.

Jesus, Randall had thought, dropping his butt on the gravel and stamping on it. Henry's right into the whole Teresi business. At some level.

'Troy's a decent fellow,' he said. 'If you let me know what this is all about, I can help you get what you want.'

He felt guilty. Scared. Excited.

'I don't know what you're talking about,' said Wu. 'And now I must go.'

'Don't—' Randall said, but it was too late.

He stared at the walls and drank the juice. Did the time calculation and reached for the phone on the table by the bed, dialled his mum. She was always delighted to hear from him; since his dad had moved out she had a lot of spare time. The old man's problems had filled her life for so long there was now a great emptiness. He knew from past experience that after ten minutes she'd start to talk about Mary Walsh, the daughter of one of her old friends. Randall had gone to school with her, and she'd been exactly what you'd expect of a girl named Mary. His mum would say how he should have married her, how she was still unwed, something big these days in the Cork Tourist Bureau. She'd always wanted him to stay in Ireland, marry someone local. Poor Ma, retreating into her own past, before the mess she'd made of her life when she'd briefly ventured from Ireland's shores all those years before.

And now it's my turn, Randall thought. To make a mess of things. Maybe it was time to go back. But let's not think of that yet. There was a click at the other end of the line and as she answered he realised he was crying.

'Ma?' he said.

Thirty-three

Anna took Matt to a service at ChristLife in Botany while Troy walked to Holy Family on Maroubra Road. At first he didn't pay much attention as the mass progressed, just thinking about his situation. When the sermon began, he tried to focus on what the priest was saying, in the faint hope it might contain some sort of message for him. But it didn't seem to; the priest was talking about evil but not with conviction, not as though he comprehended behaviour of the sort Troy was up against. Luke was different. When he spoke of evil you got the sense he knew its shape and feel. This was one of the reasons Troy had been drawn to him years ago.

Earlier that morning he'd checked his email, and there'd been nothing related to the other night. Anna hadn't looked at hers today, there was no reason to. Troy wondered when the next blow would fall, when he would be asked for money. He should inform his superiors of his situation now, but told himself it could wait until a demand was made. Telling what he'd done would be like giving a bit of himself away forever. He wondered how they'd react. Maybe he should talk to McIver first.

After mass he stood outside the church for a while, chatting to acquaintances about football, gardening, the weather. Nippers was due to start soon, and several parents wanted to check on the times. The ordinariness of the talk seeped into him, healthy as the warmth of the sun, and he was reluctant to leave, but he and Anna were expecting guests, so he made his way home.

While he walked he checked his phone and saw there was a message to call McIver. The sergeant had a string of queries about last week's work, and as Troy answered them he realised his memory was strangely fragmented. The pieces were there, but not always in the right place.

'We've found out something weird,' McIver said. 'The lab reckons Damon Blake's DNA doesn't match the skin we found under Margot's fingernails.'

Troy stopped walking. 'But he said she scratched him. I saw the marks.'

They'd examined Blake's back during the interview. The singer had said some of the marks were from his current girlfriend, but a few were from Margot. He looked at Conti while he said this, and Troy recalled her blushing.

'Something else, Conti's found out how the shooter got the key. One of the council admin workers sold it to someone who sounds like Bazzi, for a thousand dollars.'

'You've had a good weekend.'

'Conti's on the ball.'

Troy said, 'I'm coming in.'

'No you're not. If you do, I'll send you home. Siegert tells me you came in yesterday. What was that all about?'

'I had to pick up something.'

'He said you were shaving.'

'How many people have you got in there today?'

'I'm terminating this conversation,' McIver said. 'Try to relax, for Christ's sake.'

He hung up.

Ralph Dutton arrived at eleven o'clock with his wife Wendy and their two small boys. Troy had become friends with Dutton years ago, when they were both starting out as constables in Sutherland. Later they'd worked together for a while as detectives. Each had been best man at the other's wedding. They still kept in touch, even after Dutton left the force. Ralph was a big, naturally pale man, who wore a baseball cap whenever he was outdoors to protect his skull from the sun. He was wearing it today, the same faded Sea Eagles cap Troy recalled from years ago. Dutton used to wear it even with a suit, to the intense annoyance of an inspector they'd had at Chatswood.

The two families had arranged to do the long walk along the cliffs and beaches from Maroubra to Bondi. When they left the house, Troy noticed a Subaru Liberty standing outside, behind his own station wagon. Compared with the Camry, it was big and solid. Dutton saw him eyeing the vehicle and beamed.

'Had it for three months,' he said. 'We're very happy with it.'

'Four-wheel drive,' Troy said politely.

'The handling. You should take it for a run afterwards. Wendy feels a lot better driving it, the way the traffic is these days.'

Wendy said, 'We'd never go back to a Commodore.'

Troy nodded, thinking about what McIver and the others would be doing at The Tower. After a bit, he realised he was still nodding and forced himself to stop.

Once they got going, the wives moved ahead with their strollers and the men followed behind, Dutton carrying his elder boy on his broad shoulders.

'I see you've been in the papers again,' he said. 'Not like you.'

'I couldn't help it,' Troy said. 'Politics.'

'You don't want to get a reputation for that sort of thing. People start to notice you for the wrong reason.' Ever since they'd made Ralph a manager, it had become important to him to demonstrate his knowledge of how the world operated. He said, 'Don't worry, it'll pass.'

'It will indeed.'

One way or another.

Dutton told him about a family holiday they were taking next month to California.

'Bank balance healthy, then?' Troy said.

It was a subject Ralph liked to talk about. 'Over a hundred and fifty a year now. Not bad for a working-class boy.'

Troy grunted. A Homicide inspector might earn a hundred if he was lucky. And there weren't many inspectors.

As they walked along the edge of the dog park at the end of Coogee Beach, Dutton talked about the trip, how they were going to hire a car and drive to all the places he'd seen on television. Starting at Los Angeles and Disneyland, they'd go up the coast to Big Sur and San Francisco, then keep heading north to Seattle and the Boeing factory.

Dutton worked at the airport, and had gradually been acquiring an interest in aircraft. It was something Troy had noticed before. Intelligent men in boring jobs often took up hobbies, did courses or became wine bores.

'Airport okay?' he said.

It was what his conversations with Dutton consisted of these days, he realised—him providing openings so his friend could boast. There was little reciprocation. Dutton seemed to have almost no interest in police work anymore, except where it touched on his own professional concerns.

'Great,' Dutton said. 'There's a lot of technology involved, and liaison with government agencies. I tell you, Nick, with the scope of the terrorism threat, the private sector's become much more important in the wider security picture.'

'Is that so?'

'And we've got the budget to face the challenges.'

Unlike the police, Troy thought. Anything related to riots or terrorism had been well funded these past years, but often the money seemed to have been pulled from other areas of police work.

Dutton said, 'You still got the old Glocks?'

Troy smiled. 'This is where you're going to offer me a job, aren't you?'

Several times in the past year he'd received a call from a friend or acquaintance who'd moved out. Once he'd even been taken for a pleasant meal. But he'd never been tempted.

'No,' Dutton said. 'We're just about to expand and we've got some jobs going, good jobs. But I wouldn't offer one to you.'

Ridiculously, Troy felt almost offended, and asked Dutton why not.

The other man laughed. 'First, you don't need the money. You already have the home near the beach which half this city is working its butt off to achieve. So the normal incentive structure breaks down in your case. And second, you'd always regret it.'

'Why so?'

'Because you're a natural cop. The job matches your needs at a fundamental level.'

The insight displayed by Dutton's comment mildly surprised Troy. You should never underestimate people, he thought. Not even your friends.

He said, 'What about you? Do you regret leaving?'

'You think I just went for the money. It was partly that. But I hit a situation. I'm sorry I never told you. It's taken me a few years to see what happened.'

Dutton explained that he'd accepted a promotion into a section Troy regarded almost with contempt: the traffic branch. There'd been another promotion soon after, so Dutton had streaked ahead of him. Troy assumed the private sector had been the goal all along.

'There was a problem with the figures,' Dutton said. 'Up there, things become more blurry.'

'Up there in traffic?'

'In management,' Dutton said, 'I found I'd traded the satisfaction of operational policing for a lot of management bullshit. If that was going to be my life, why not get paid properly? So I walked.'

'Tell me about the figures.'

Dutton considered this and said, 'You don't want to know.'

'I do.'

'Believe me. One thing I've learned, ignorance really is bliss. A lot of the time.'

When they reached the Coogee shops the women stopped to let the men catch up. They were all feeling the heat. Wendy had turned a deep

321

shade of pink and Ralph was glistening with sweat. Troy looked him up and down, realised for the first time he was wearing boating shoes. Soon the Duttons would be moving to the North Shore. Anna was looking fine, apart from the perspiration marks on her T-shirt. She always said she hated the heat, and resented any suggestion she should be used to it because she'd been born in India. But she handled it well.

He said, 'Anyone for an ice cream?'

They crossed the road and walked beneath the awnings in front of the shops, found a gourmet place and bought expensive cones. Dutton insisted on paying. As they made their way back to the beach, he told the women the story of one of the city's classic crimes. In 1935 there'd been a saltwater pool here, and on Anzac Day a huge shark, recently caught along the coast and placed in the pool, disgorged a human arm. It belonged to Jim Smith, a police informant, and had been cut off with a knife.

'No,' said Wendy, waving her cone at her husband. 'No more.' She turned to Anna and said vehemently, 'I'm so glad he left that job.'

Troy saw the women exchange glances, and then Wendy looked at him defiantly. He could tell she was thinking about whether to say more. Then it came out: 'You ought to leave too. It saved our marriage.'

Troy smiled and shook his head. It was not the sort of thing he had any desire to even think about. He was enjoying the day, the past week on hold for the time being. The others were looking at him. When he said nothing, the moment passed. Dutton, looking a little embarrassed, bent down to say something to his son.

When they got going again, this time with the men in front and the little boy walking behind with his mother, Troy said, 'Do you regret leaving operations?'

They'd never discussed it before. They'd never had a conversation like this one before, but maybe they'd each grown up a bit.

Dutton said, 'At first you miss the stimulation, but then you realise that's actually a good thing, because the stimulation is unnatural, it's bad for you. You learn to live without it, and your life becomes better.'

'So people who need the stimulation are addicts?' Troy said.

'You realise that waking up every morning and feeling under pressure, maybe scared, isn't natural.'

Troy found this interesting: most mornings in the job, he'd never woken up feeling that way.

Fifteen minutes later, Dutton said, 'Can I ask you a favour?'

He spoke with an elaborate casualness, as though he'd been contemplating what he was about to say for a while. In general terms, Troy knew what was coming. He'd always thought this would happen.

'Will you mind if I say no?' he said.

'Of course not.' Dutton sounded offended. 'But you don't know what it is.'

'It was a joke.' Or maybe not, the way Dutton was looking.

'Look, I've never asked anything like this before, it's just—we go back, don't we? And this means a lot to me. I wouldn't ask, otherwise. You know that, don't you?' When Troy said nothing, he added, 'We'd be very grateful.'

'We?'

Dutton worked for an offshoot of a big merchant bank that had been buying infrastructure around the world. Freeways, airports, toll bridges.

'We've just taken over a stevedore company, Rice Turner. They're at Botany.'

Troy recalled the huge blue cranes and gantries he'd seen the last time he'd been down that way. 'I've been asked to review security there, all those containers. It's a massive project, a huge responsibility. Key question is whether to keep the manager, bloke named Chris Sutherland. There was some sort of police investigation six months ago, all the docks in Sydney and Port Kembla. Spare car parts, fakes, out of China. Nothing released yet.'

Jesus, Troy thought. This is not good. 'I'm sorry—'

'What they found, whether it's ongoing? This means a lot to me.'

'Look—'

'No. I'm sorry I asked. Happens all the time though, wouldn't hurt anyone.'

'I can't—'

'It's okay. You're not like that, are you? Sorry I asked.' Dutton looked out to sea. Then he said softly, 'You can be too pure, though.'

Troy wanted to ask why he didn't use one of his other police contacts, if this sort of thing was so common. If he was so respectful of Troy's feelings. But Dutton had rushed the end of the conversation, as though embarrassed by the whole thing and wanting to get it over as quickly as possible.

'I am who I am,' Troy said, but regretted the words immediately. He wanted to make some sort of stand, but it just sounded pompous.

'And we all love you for it,' Dutton said bleakly, slapping him on the back and turning to see where the others were.

Thirty-four

Randall paid off the taxi and stood outside the block of flats, his back to the building, admiring the darkening harbour. He'd just spent hours in a hire car, driving back from the Hunter Valley. No CDs, he couldn't get his iPod to work with the car's sound system. Just radio station crap.

That stupid bloody woman. He picked up a case of wine and hoisted the strap of his bag awkwardly onto his shoulder, made his way up the stairs. At least his stash was waiting for him in the cabinet in his apartment. He deserved a treat.

As he opened the building's security door, the door of one of the ground-floor flats also opened: Mrs Crawley, single mother of a rather attractive schoolgirl he'd never spoken with. Robin, the mother's name was, and she was holding some DVDs and a brown paper bag. She'd always been sour towards him, but today there was a glint of happiness in her eyes that he didn't like at all.

'These were on the stairs when we came in this afternoon,' she said, thrusting them at him. Wearily, he put the case down and took them. 'Your door was open. I was going to call the police, but Derek Taplin said he'd seen a woman here earlier he thought was a friend of yours. We weren't sure what to do.'

He looked at the top DVD case and saw the word *Mexico* written on it, in his own hand. Wondered what was inside the brown paper bag.

'Kristin and I broke up, and I'm afraid she's taken it badly,' he said, moving towards the stairs.

He'd come back later for the wine.

'So she has a key to this building?'

Randall smiled ruefully. 'I really thought she might be the one. On the stairs, you say?'

'Here and outside. Some had fallen out of the cases. I put them back in for you.'

He could see the daughter now, down the hall behind her mother, having a peek at him.

'Mrs Crawley,' he said, 'you're a saint.'

Inside his flat, he saw that the cabinet had been levered open. There was no sign of the tool that had been used, but he had no doubt Kristin had come well prepared. She was so competent at everything, she'd probably done a course in burglary. She must have been looking for the DVD of herself, but it was in his bag and he felt a twinge of triumph. And she would have seen the others, realised she was not alone, which served her right. All the DVDs from the cabinet were gone. He was holding four plus the one in his bag. That left three missing. Bloody hell.

He put down the DVDs and looked into the brown paper bag. A collection of assorted condoms he recognised from his own supply. He wondered where the other DVDs were. Someone might have lifted them from the steps out front. Or Taplin, a neighbour on his floor, might have grabbed some. Then there was Mrs Crawley and her daughter.

Jesus, he thought, reaching for the Mylanta. And then it struck him there was something else missing. Something important in his life. He lifted up the papers still in the cabinet, found his passport, birth certificate, plans of some of his past jobs. But no coke. The bitch had taken his supply. It seemed out of character. But this must be about revenge, not theft.

He had a swig of the Mylanta to try to dissipate the anxiety gathering in his stomach. Foul stuff. My consumption of white substances has come to this, he thought. How the mighty are fallen. He pulled out his phone and called Gregor, but there was no reply. Rang Kristin and got her voicemail. That was the problem, she wanted to play with the boys but she was a coward at heart. Testosterone, physique, they mattered. Or something like that.

He went into the kitchen and pulled a bottle of vodka from the freezer. Got a shot glass and returned to the lounge, where he turned on the sound system, cranked up some Coldplay. The music made him feel better, it seemed to slow down the traffic through his brain, he found he had more control over his thoughts. He turned the volume up higher, so high he wouldn't hear the knocking even if Derek-fucking-Taplin came to complain. Sat on the sofa for a long time looking at the final lights come on in the city across the water. The water that he knew was full of sharks, cruising around just below the surface, waiting for victims.

The thing about Kristin was he had her on film, and she must hate that; it was something he would always have. The more he thought about this, the happier it made him. Later he decided to watch the film and fetched the DVD from his bag and took it over to the player. He opened the case and saw the disc inside wasn't labelled. This was the one Henry had returned a few days ago. Must have been some muddle, he must still have the one with Kristin on it. Typical of Henry's general bloody sloppiness. Randall wondered if anything was on this one. Slipping it into the player, he returned to his chair.

There was a woman but it was not Kristin. It was a pretty young Chinese woman and she was naked. After a few moments Randall realised she was terrified. There were marks on her skin that made you want to adjust the colour, but the rest of the image was perfectly fine, technically. The woman was cowering on a bed and he recognised it as a room on Henry's boat. Now the camera was moving in and a man came into the picture from the side. You could only see his back but Randall could tell it was Henry, his sleeves rolled up and reaching for the woman. You could see his hands and there was a strand of wire

327

taut between them. She started to scream but there was no sound and then the man put his hands on either side of her throat and the camera went in closer, and the woman's eyes started to look strange. Randall hit the stop button on the remote and then turned his head away, unable to look at the close-up of the woman's face. He stumbled around until he found the other remote, the one that turned off the screen. Shakily, he ejected the disc and put it back in its case.

Sitting down again, looking out at the city, he wondered what had happened. Had Henry put the wrong DVD in the case by mistake or on purpose? He was a lazy, arrogant fucker, a mistake was quite possible. Henry wouldn't give a shit about the problems it might cause. Much later, after a lot more vodka, he saw that it didn't matter. Either way, he was in trouble. There was some rumour about Henry and a Chinese woman too, something Jamal had once mentioned. Randall thought about it, not sure if he really wanted to remember the details. But nothing came anyway.

What was there already was fear; it was everywhere and it was rising about him gradually. He took more vodka, far too much, but the fear was still there, like the water in the harbour. He could actually feel when it reached his chin.

MONDAY

Thirty-five

Many of those crowded into the room for the briefing had not worked with McIver before, and Troy sensed that interest was at a high pitch. The man had a reputation. As he went over the investigation, heads were nodding: what he said made sense, and implied things were now under control. It was all very different from Stone's lurching and incomplete performances. You could feel the increase in confidence.

One of McIver's announcements was that Bazzi had been tracked to Lebanon. He'd landed at Beirut on Thursday, using a different name. Over the weekend an account had been found in that name at the Commonwealth Bank. It had had a balance of just over a hundred thousand, until it was cleared out the previous week. In the year before that there had been large monthly deposits.

'We're assuming the money came from Sidorov,' McIver said.

There was a murmur of excited talk. Troy thought that, like so much in the case, it was interesting but it didn't take them forwards.

'The Lebanese authorities don't know where he is now,' McIver said. 'His escape was well planned. I doubt we'll see him again.' He waited for silence. 'Now, I know you're all wondering where we go next. I have some exciting news. We're going back to the beginning. We'll go over the whole investigation again. This time with feeling.'

There were groans but they were mixed with laughter. Troy saw two of the female detectives looking at McIver with open interest. He was wearing the dark blue shirt, beneath a tight black suit that emphasised his wiry body. The sling provided some lines of white across his chest. Occasionally the arm in it would lift out impatiently, to make a gesture or grab for a piece of paper, then fall back ineffectually.

'And on the home front, we've finally had a useful contribution from a member of the public.'

McIver looked at Conti, who explained that a woman in Darlinghurst had found a security pass behind a box on her front porch over the weekend. It belonged to The Tower and an electronic check showed it had been allocated to Sean Randall.

'In other words,' she said, 'it was discarded by the shooter after he left via the tunnel and crossed Hyde Park. We're hoping there'll be DNA on it from his sweat, and we'll compare that with the skin scrapings from Margot's fingernails.'

There was another murmur of excited conversation.

McIver called for quiet. 'Let's start with what we know about our victim.'

Troy looked at the photo of Margot Teresi on the board. Her attractive face, with a big smile full of white teeth, gave little suggestion of the obsessiveness that had taken her up The Tower at night to think about her father. Sometimes it took a while for a face to catch up with changes within. But then, maybe the obsession would have passed, had she lived. She might have become happy again, married. Had children.

McIver said, 'A publisher at Allen & Unwin says Margot approached them with a proposal for a biography of her dad. They were considering it at the time of her death.' He paused and pointed to another photograph, a grainy shot of Jenny Finch. 'Finch's parents are Margot's only surviving relatives; they've been on a walking tour in Spain and it took Foreign Affairs a few days to get hold of them.' He looked at Troy, who recalled

Jenny Finch nodding eagerly when he'd suggested she call her mum. Everyone lies. 'They returned yesterday, and I want Troy and Bergman to pay them a visit this morning.'

Before the briefing, McIver had asked Troy to take Bergman. Assuming there was no improvement in his work today, McIver would send the young detective back and demand a replacement. It was one of the routine tasks Stone should have done last week.

'What about Mr A?' someone called out.

McIver frowned and pointed at the board, to the smudgy photograph of the man about to enter The Tower off Norfolk Street. The man who looked like he was ducking into a brothel. Despite the request they'd put out through the media last week, they still had no idea who he was.

Ruth had been taking a call at her desk while McIver was speaking. Now she hung up and pushed her way over to him, and whispered something in his ear. The sergeant looked up with a smile. 'The Water Police recovered a body off Botany Bay this morning, it was spotted by some yachties. Nibbled by sharks and one foot missing. From the tattoos, they reckon it could be Andrew Asaad.'

More excitement in the room.

Troy said, 'And the sea gave up the dead which were in it.'

McIver beamed. 'How true. Sounds like our boy got a real Sydney Send-off.'

He assigned two detectives to visit Glebe to inspect the body, allocated some more tasks, and declared the briefing closed.

Ryan put up his hand. 'What's happened to Sergeant Stone?'

The room, which had been getting noisy, fell silent again. A few people chuckled at the question, and McIver frowned.

'Whatever occurred here,' he said, 'Brad Stone is a brave man who's done things few of us could do.' He turned and walked in the direction of the office at the end of the room.

Troy followed him. 'Do we know when Margot's funeral is?'

'They're planting Jenny today, Margot on Friday. Want to keep the events separate. They're expecting a crowd for Margot.'

'This is good, about finding Asaad.'

McIver shrugged. 'It's the people behind Bazzi and Asaad we want now, whoever was paying them and running the shooter and his mate.'

'Sidorov?' said Troy. The contractor was still saying nothing.

'I had a go at him on the weekend,' said McIver. 'He's too smart for us.' Talking to the police was the biggest mistake most criminals made when they were arrested.

'Not a word?'

'We need this bloke Jason. He provided the illegals and looked after them. My guess is our shooter and his mate worked for him.'

'Immigration can't help?'

'They think he's back in Jakarta. Apparently it's a big city.' He lifted a piece of paper from his desk, looked at it and let it fall. 'All these foreigners involved,' he said softly, 'but still, it looks like Asaad was thrown off a boat out at sea. Good to see the local traditions still being observed.'

Dan Bergman was ready to go and Troy led the way out to the car. Lucky with the parking this morning, it was only a hundred metres up the hill. He'd just unlocked the doors when his mobile rang. It was Randall, who said he was calling to say hello. Troy couldn't believe it. He took a few steps away from Bergman so he could talk in private.

'Have you decided to tell me what this is all about?' he said quietly.

'Mate, you tell me, for Christ's sake. I can't help you if I don't know anything.'

Troy put the phone against his chest and told Bergman he'd be a few minutes. He had to say something, to try to get Randall to open up.

'Someone's approached me about what I did the other night,' he said softly. 'I'm walking into my boss's office to tell him the whole story. If you want to tell me where you fit in, this is your last chance.'

'I have no idea—'

'Forget it. I'm going now. We won't speak again.'

There was silence, and Troy was about to hang up when Randall spoke.

'I was asked to give you the number,' he said. 'I believed the person involved just wanted to do you a favour. If anything else has happened, I'm very sorry.'

'Who asked you?'

'I can't tell you that.'

'Why not? Is it a criminal?'

'No way, mate. I wouldn't do that.'

For the second time that day, a line from the Bible came to Troy. A thorn in the flesh, the messenger of Satan to buffet me.

He said, 'Very soon, two angry detectives are going to come into your office. At that point it becomes official and your whole life changes, Sean. You'll be charged with blackmail. In the court case, my name will be suppressed. Yours won't be.'

Randall said nothing, and Troy could feel his own heart pounding. He said, 'Is this to do with The Tower?'

'No way, mate. No way.'

'What the fuck's going on?'

'Jesus. They'll kill me.'

'Who are they?'

Randall said, 'I am so sorry about this.'

His voice had changed. Partly it was because the usual energy had disappeared from it. There was also the resignation Troy was familiar with from the voices of criminals who'd been broken.

Troy said, 'Talk.'

'I was told to give you that number by someone I don't know. They have something on me. What have they done to you?'

'Who are they?'

'I have no idea. They contact me by email. They have something on me.'

'You mean they're blackmailing you?'

'That's right.'

'How could they? You're not married.'

'Believe me,' Randall sighed. 'They've got something.'

Troy felt as though he'd stumbled into another world, where

everyone knew more than he did. He sensed there were false notes in what Randall was saying, but there was a lot of truth there too.

'What do they want from me?' he said. 'Do you pay them money?'

Randall said reluctantly, 'I don't think it's money. You're a cop.'

'Is it to do with The Tower?'

'I have no idea. Honestly.'

Jesus, Troy thought. His mind raced to make sense of this but there was too much there. Too much that was unknown. But it was bad, much worse than before, when he'd hoped he'd just been caught at random. Then something occurred to him.

'Why would they think I'd use the number? If I wanted to blackmail someone it'd be a long shot, just to give them a bit of paper with a phone number on it. Unless I knew . . .' He thought about it. 'You told them about me and my marriage, didn't you?'

'I swear I did not do that, mate,' Randall said, his voice sounding distant. 'I have to go.' He hung up.

For a few minutes Troy just stood there, waiting for his heart rate to come down. It must be The Tower. And yet it had all happened so quickly. He still didn't understand how Randall could have detected his vulnerability so soon, wondered if he was missing something. But the man had some strange talents. Troy realised how much he must have opened up to Randall last week, how vulnerable he'd been. The shooting had affected him far more than he'd realised.

He looked around for Bergman, but the other detective had disappeared. Troy wrenched open the door of the car, got in, and started the engine. He pressed the horn. When Bergman didn't appear, he put the car into gear and drove off. He knew it was the wrong thing to do, but in the scale of things it wasn't that wrong. And he didn't know if he could cope with Bergman right now.

Thirty-six

Jenny Finch's parents lived in a brick and wood house on one side of a valley in Forestville. Dick Finch was in his late sixties, slightly stooped with white hair. He showed Troy into the lounge area of an open-plan layout. There were a few other people around, mainly women in the kitchen, and Troy realised he'd walked into some sort of gathering. Maureen Finch, a thin woman clasping a handkerchief, was waiting on a sofa and did not get up when Troy was shown to a seat.

'Jenny's funeral is this afternoon,' Dick said. 'We've asked our friends back to the house afterwards, and some of them have been helping Maur prepare the food.'

'I'm sorry to intrude on your grief,' Troy said, remembering that on Friday they'd be doing it all again for Margot. He knew there was nothing you could do at a time like this to make it any easier. You just had to be as respectful as you could and get on with the questions. He said, 'I wonder if you know anything about the interest Margot was taking in The Tower, before she died?'

Maureen broke into sobs and after a second stood up and staggered from the room, assisted by her husband. Troy sat there, staring out the large windows at the bush across the valley, distancing himself from

337

all the emotion in the house, the indignant murmurs of the helpers in the kitchen. He wondered if the house was ever in danger during the bushfire season.

Finch came back and sat down heavily. 'Do we really have to do this now?'

'I'm sorry.'

'Is there anything you can tell us about Jenny's death?' he said, running a hand through his hair. 'Have you talked to the officer involved?'

Troy looked at him for a moment, catching a glimpse of how it must be to be on the other side of all this. 'I was there when she took her life.'

Of course. He had something precious for the Finches. If Finch had not raised it, he might have left their house without mentioning he was the last person to talk to their daughter. He realised how distracted he was.

'I'm sorry,' Finch said.

'I beg your pardon?'

'It must be very distressing to have to deal with situations like this, with people such as me in a state of grief. You're so young.'

'I've been a detective for eight years,' Troy said, keeping his voice steady.

'And then, with all you've been through in the past week. Shooting that man, shouldn't they give you some sort of leave?'

Troy decided not to respond to this, not sure what he could say, and launched into the story. He explained how he'd gone to Margot's flat after her death for a routine check.

'Jenny was there and she let me in and we talked,' he said. 'She hadn't heard that Margot had died, so I told her. She was upset, and she started to cry.' He paused, remembering the pale, thin woman on the black leather couch. This man's child. 'I asked her if she was all right and she said she was, she just needed some time to herself.'

'Did you have a partner with you?' Finch said.

'No.'

'Don't detectives normally work in pairs? I imagine it's preferable to have a second opinion on things.' He didn't sound aggressive, but clearly it was something he'd been thinking about.

'Not always,' Troy said carefully. 'We prefer to, but in the early stages of an investigation there can be a lot of things that have to be done quickly with limited resources.' Finch nodded, as if he understood all about resource constraints, and Troy went on: 'I said I'd go and have a look at Margot's bedroom and her home office. At that point we were very keen to find her diary and her mobile phone.' They still hadn't found them. McIver had talked about that this morning. 'I asked Jenny if there was anyone she'd like me to call, and she said it was okay, she'd call her mother to come over.'

'But we weren't in Sydney.'

'I know that now. I didn't at the time, so I left her. She seemed upset, but in control of herself. I thought she was going to ring her mother.'

'They say people about to commit suicide often present like that. They can even appear happy.'

There wasn't much Troy could say to this, so he remained silent. Finch began to cry, holding his head at a strange angle as he burrowed into one of his trouser pockets for a handkerchief. He was tensing his upper lip in an attempt to stop the tears, but they were coming anyway.

'When I came back into the room she was gone,' Troy said, wanting to finish it.

He stood up and went over to the big windows, giving Finch time to gather himself. After a while, the other man began to speak. He told Troy about his daughter's upbringing, how everything had seemed normal until she had a breakdown in her early twenties.

'In retrospect there were a few things wrong before then, but we didn't pick up on them. Jenny was an only child; maybe if we'd had more we would have had something to compare her with. But she had friends, sailed through university. You think if your child makes it to that point, they're pretty stable. A doctor told us sometimes they can't explain these things.'

'Did you see a lot of Margot and her parents back then?'

'Almost nothing. They were in the States for all of Jenny's youth. Came back when Elena got the cancer—she wanted to be with her mum, who was still alive then, and Maur. The two girls started to see a lot of each other at family occasions, but I can't say they got on all that well. Margot was difficult, she resented having to leave California. And then, of course, her mother died.'

The talking had helped get the tears under control, and Finch blew his nose and put the handkerchief back in his pocket. 'We didn't see her for a while, but after Tony died, she started visiting a few times a year. Maur encouraged her, of course. Margot went to see Jenny when she was in the clinic, and the next we knew they were living together. It seemed to be going well.'

'Did Margot ever talk to you about The Tower?'

Finch nodded. 'I think that was one of the reasons she came here. I'm a structural engineer; before I retired I was an executive with Multiplex. It was a surprise the day Margot realised her boring old uncle in the suburbs was an expert on a subject that had come to mean a great deal to her.' He smiled and looked away. 'I think The Tower is a work of genius. I understand what Tony had to do to get it built. We ended up having a lot of long conversations about that. Maur and Jen would leave the room.'

He described some of these conversations, and Troy said, 'Do you think Margot could have committed suicide?'

Finch shook his head. 'Not a chance in the world. It wasn't in her. And anyway, she was determined to clear her father's name.'

'She'd been trying for a while. What if she'd realised it couldn't be done? What if she came to the conclusion he'd been a failure after all?'

'It's not possible. Morning Star treated Tony shamefully—they practically stole the building from him. Everyone in the business world knows that.' Finch's voice had sped up. 'I talked to Margot on the phone three weeks ago, just before we went to Spain. She was very positive, she had a new lead.'

'Do you know what it was?'

'Someone she'd met. She didn't say who.'

Troy pulled out a photo of the man known as Mr A and showed it to Finch, who shook his head. 'It's not very clear, is it?'

'You didn't put Margot on to anyone?'

'I suggested all sorts of people she could talk to, journalists and so on.'

'Anyone in particular? Anyone in the industry?'

'I'm out of touch these days. I gave her the number of Peter Wood, a friend at Multiplex. He used to be my deputy.'

'How old is he?'

'About fifty, but he has a full head of hair.' Finch smiled briefly. 'And you wouldn't get Peter skulking around someone else's building site on a Sunday night.'

Troy recalled that according to Margot's phone records, she had called Multiplex once. The police had got in touch with the switch there but they had no record of whom she'd been after. He asked for Wood's direct phone number and after Finch gave it to him, said, ' "Less is more". That's what Jenny said to me about the white walls of the block of flats.'

'Mies van der Rohe,' Finch said, his eyes tearing up again. 'A modernist architect.'

There was nothing more to say, so Troy stood up. One of the women in the kitchen called out to Dick, needing to talk to him about some arrangement, and Troy said he'd find his own way out. On the way he looked for Maureen Finch, but she was nowhere to be seen.

He took the steps down to his car, which was parked across the road. Another vehicle had just pulled up behind it and he recognised one of the cars from work. He stopped on the stairs, waiting to see who would get out, wondering if they had found out about the video and had come to take him in for questioning. A man stepped out of the car, looking around uncertainly. It was Bergman.

In the subsequent conversation, which took place next to the cars, Troy had to restrain himself from hitting the young man. Bergman explained at length how he'd been overcome on leaving the station by a desperate need to use the toilet. It was something to do with a goat curry he'd consumed in Newtown the previous evening. Seeing Troy's attention occupied by the long phone conversation with Randall, he'd ducked back inside. He'd been away for longer than he'd intended, but his mobile had been switched on throughout the ordeal—

'Forget it,' Troy said, pulling out his keys. 'The interview's over, I learned nothing. Let's go back to the station.'

Bergman started to talk again but Troy turned his back on him and walked over to his car. He opened the door but didn't get in, waiting there until eventually he heard Bergman drive away.

When the street was quiet again, he checked his mobile for messages. Anna had called, which was unusual. He rang back, his heart pounding. She answered straight away.

'You've had a strange call,' she said. 'A man asked me to tell you to meet him. I told him he should call your mobile, but he said he was calling from a public phone and didn't have any more money.'

'What was his name?'

'He wouldn't leave a name. He said to meet him at the Mornington Apartments. He said you'd know the time.'

It was as though a small explosion had gone off somewhere. So this is it, Troy thought.

'Thanks, honey.'

'How did he get our number?' she said loudly. 'He woke Matt, he was having a sleep. It took me an hour to get him off.'

She sounded almost hysterical. Troy wondered if he should have married someone with more experience of life. He'd wanted the serenity she seemed to offer, which came partly from innocence. He'd fallen deeply, hungrily, in love with it, as though it might counteract what he'd been through in his own life. But whatever peace he'd found, it had proved fragile.

'I have no idea. Maybe someone at the squad gave it out by mistake.'

'I have to go. Matt's crying again.'

Troy could hear that. 'I'll tell him not to call home again.'

She was gone.

He wondered how anyone could have got his home number, which was unlisted. Despite what he'd said to Anna, no one at work would give it out. Presumably the blackmailers had ways of obtaining it, would have someone they paid at a phone company. That didn't matter. What mattered was that they were playing with his mind, preparing him for some demand to come. It was important to remain steady.

Flipping open his notebook, he found the number Dick Finch had just given him and rang it. A secretary answered and said Peter Wood was in a meeting. Troy left his name and number and asked that Wood call him back as soon as possible.

He walked across the footpath and stood staring at the bush beyond. After a while he realised his mind had closed down, and he tried to focus on what he was looking at, to think about another subject. A strip a hundred metres wide had been cleared and covered with bark mulch, with the occasional native shrub or tuft of grass. It was well maintained. According to a small sign Troy found fifty metres down the way, it was cared for by local residents. There was even a rough, meandering path through it, and Troy imagined how pleasant it would be to bring your dog down here at the end of the day, chat with neighbours in the cool of the evening. There was nothing much to burn, so it would act as a break if a fire ever came up the valley. He turned and walked back to his car, looking up at the Finchs' house. A woman's white face was in one of the windows, staring down at him. He thought it might be Maureen Finch, although with the sun bouncing off the glass he couldn't be sure.

The phone rang and when he answered it there was an unfamiliar voice, distorted by some mechanical device.

'No need to visit the Mornington Apartments again, detective.'

Another distant explosion. In the silence that followed, Troy said nothing.

'The man you're looking for will visit you this afternoon at City Central at three. His evidence is perfectly acceptable if you don't push it too hard. If there are any problems, I'll send pictures of you and the lovely Tanya to your wife. The same if you talk to Mr Randall about this again.'

Troy said, 'I'm telling my wife tonight.'

'In my experience, it doesn't matter what a wife's been told, pictures will have a substantial impact. But we'll also send it to a large number of your colleagues and the media. And the internet. It will stay on the internet forever. The decision is yours.'

The speaker hung up.

The blow had fallen, and part of Troy's world changed. It was as though its component parts were separated, thrown up in the air, and as they came down they didn't fit together anymore. He got into his hot car and saw it was after midday. He thought about everything, and nothing. In the emptiness a line from the Bible came to him: It is a fearful thing to fall into the hands of the living God.

Not that this was God, but it felt like it.

At the office he logged on to his personal email account and there was another video clip waiting for him. Unlike the first one, this had some text: *A present for Anna?* It had been sent from an address he didn't recognise, just a string of letters and numbers that he recorded. Presumably it would be no good for a trace. Presumably the person who'd sent this knew what he was doing. He deleted the message without looking at the attachment, thinking about what the man on the phone had said, thinking about the images being on the internet. Forever. People he knew, his son when he grew older, could find them there.

He sat for a while, wondering what to do. Mr A must be important. Hugely important. Nothing else came to him and he realised his energy level was down, every decision was like lifting heavy weights. His mobile rang and he answered it reluctantly.

'Peter Wood,' the caller barked. 'You rang me.'

For a moment his mind was blank and then it came to him: the man whose number Dick Finch had given him. The man who just possibly might know something about the fellow Margot Teresi had met at The Tower. That was a piece of knowledge Troy should not have, if he was to follow the instructions of the man who'd called earlier. This was it, he thought: decision time.

'It's okay,' Troy said slowly. 'I thought you might be able to help with a query. But I think I've sorted it out.'

He stopped and waited. Now it all depended on whether Wood had seen the appeal for information about Mr A and connected it to Troy's call, in which case he might say something. And if he did this, Troy would have to act. But Wood just sighed loudly and hung up.

Troy wondered what he'd just done. He'd put a foot across the line, but he hadn't crossed it. He told himself there was still time to go back. Told himself he needed some time to think.

He typed a brief account of what Dick Finch had told him, leaving out the reference to Peter Wood. As he worked, he noticed the changed dynamic in the room, the organised energy as people came and went from McIver's office. Ruth called out that the corpse found off Botany Bay had been confirmed as Andrew Asaad, lots of sea water in his lungs, the leg chewed through by a shark. The people who'd disposed of the body had been unlucky: it should have sunk to the bottom forever. It was like the Shark Arm case Dutton had told them about, Troy thought. The Sydney Send-off was fallible.

After lunch, McIver yelled out and he went into his office. It seemed even smaller than when Stone had been the occupant. McIver was not as big, but he exuded more energy.

'You well?' he said to Troy.

'"Less is more." Know what that means?'

'Argument in favour of concrete boxes. If you make a building less attractive you can build it more cheaply. Look at this,' he said, pushing a large photograph across the desk. It showed a man's head, and looked like it had been taken on a street at night. Troy recognised the face. When he saw it he had to sit down. It was the shooter.

'You all right?' said McIver.

Troy nodded.

'CCTV from outside a school in Darlinghurst. Same street where the security pass was found.'

'Sunday night?'

'That smart Constable Conti tracked it down. She's not just a pretty face.'

Troy picked up the photograph and studied it. The quality of the picture was good. 'We're putting it out?'

'Immediately. What you been up to?'

After Troy had given a summary of his morning's activities, again neglecting to mention Peter Wood, McIver said, 'On Friday I rang a mate in the FBI, asked for a confidential briefing on Tony Teresi's time in the USA. Jack called me back yesterday. Says Tony Teresi was probably as honest as you could be in the casino business.'

'Meaning?'

'They've cleaned it up since the good old days. Organised crime is pretty much out of it. The main law enforcement issues now are the inducements offered to high rollers, basically sex and drugs. Teresi would have been involved in that on his way up the ladder. He would have hired people to do it for him when he got to the top. But in terms of his business dealings, his known associates, Tony was okay. There are lots of more corrupt industries these days.'

'What about Macau? Teresi had a casino there.'

'Jack says that's the new Wild West. Tony was one of the first outsiders to break in. He must have used political contacts, which means graft. That's all he knows.'

'You don't have a mate in Macau, I suppose?'

McIver shook his head. 'Asia's a young man's game. Maybe you should go up there, get yourself on a conference, make a few contacts.' He looked thoughtfully at Troy. 'But that sort of bonding involves a certain relaxation of normal standards. At least in my experience. Maybe not for the pure of heart, such as yourself.'

You'd be surprised, Troy thought.

Leaning back in his chair, McIver said, 'That was what finished my first marriage, the San Francisco conference.'

'Can't the pure of heart bond with each other?'

'Over cups of tea, you mean?'

Troy was tempted to tell Mac about the blackmail. But since the anonymous phone call, he knew it might set things in motion that would destroy his marriage. He'd lose his son. There had to be some other way.

He asked how the investigation was looking. In general.

'Basically, it's rooted,' McIver said cheerfully. 'I've got twenty people out there smelling their own farts, retracing steps, repeating interviews.'

Troy shrugged sympathetically and stood up.

McIver said, 'Feel like a drink later?'

'It's my wedding anniversary.'

'Don't forget to give her flowers. I always did.'

Troy was going to ask if this was the secret of his other two divorces, but he didn't have the heart for it. And anyway, McIver was already staring at his screen again.

Thirty-seven

When he got back to his desk there was a note saying a man was waiting for him in reception. He had information regarding the media appeal in relation to the unknown man who'd gone into The Tower. Picking up a pad, Troy gazed dully around the office. It was three o'clock.

'Bergman,' he called.

The detective was sitting with two others, going through some lists. Troy explained that he needed him for an interview and a sergeant asked if it could wait fifteen minutes.

'I want Bergman, and I want him now,' Troy said, and turned on his heel and left the room. In the corridor he said to Bergman, who came running after him, 'Let me do the talking. Just sit there, observe, and give me your impressions afterwards.'

'Is it true the sergeant is thinking of sending me back to my station?'

'Just concentrate on the job at hand.'

The man out front introduced himself as Geoff Rochford. He was in his late fifties, tall and balding, and Troy thought he could certainly pass as Mr A. When they shook hands, Rochford's was warm and slightly damp. Troy asked to see some ID and Rochford handed over a

348

driver's licence. They went into an interview room and Troy recorded the details on the licence before handing it back.

Opening a folder, he slid the still photo of Mr A across to Bergman, raising his eyebrows. Bergman scowled in concentration, looking from the photo to the man across the table and back again. Troy raised his eyebrows, and Bergman nodded vigorously.

Rochford told them he'd gone to The Tower to meet Margot Teresi on Sunday night. Troy asked why.

'Well you see,' Rochford said, 'I'm a grief counsellor.'

He reached into a pocket of his blue coat and handed over a business card. There was silence in the room for a while as Troy read it and recorded some more details. As he wrote, he shook his head in grudging appreciation. The person arranging all this was like someone putting on a show, and they were good at it. They'd probably done it before.

'A grief counsellor,' he said. 'Tough job?'

'I try to help people.'

'Society is grateful for the work you do.'

Rochford stared at him, said nothing.

Troy said, 'Why was a grief counsellor trespassing on a building site on Sunday night?'

'Margot had been seeing me for therapy for about six months,' Rochford said quickly, opening his briefcase and taking out a large diary and a receipt book. He pushed them across to Troy. 'You can see from my appointment book, she was on the first Monday of every month.'

Certain pages in both books had been tagged with yellow stickers. Troy flicked through each of them and then passed them to Bergman.

'Paid in cash, I suppose?'

'As it happens, she did. The receipts are all there.'

It was an impressive set-up, and Troy wondered how it had been done. Maybe Rochford wasn't a grief counsellor at all. Or maybe he was and the books had been cooked. The essential thing was not to query him or his story. That was the point of the phone call he'd received earlier in the day. The point, maybe the only point, of the blackmail. It seemed almost trivial, but of course it wasn't. Mr A, the real one, must be incredibly important to the investigation.

'Margot wanted closure,' Rochford said.

'You're sweating a lot, Mr Rochford,' Bergman said. 'Is anything wrong?'

Troy nudged Bergman with his knee. It was true Rochford was acquiring quite a shine. The last thing Troy wanted was for him to break down or walk out. 'Tell us about that night,' he said.

Looking eager, Rochford explained that Margot had visited The Tower about once a month, with the help of some of the security guards. The visits were of enormous emotional significance to her, but they were becoming increasingly risky as the building neared completion and became more busy. The guards wanted them to stop. Margot had formed the idea that a counselling session held in The Tower itself might help her finally deal with her grief.

'I was reluctant,' Rochford said, looking at Troy. 'But Margot was a very persistent woman, and she was in a state of desperation. She talked of killing herself several times.'

'Do you think—'

'I want to emphasise that. I thought Margot Teresi was suicidal.'

Bergman was breathing deeply and twitching, looking at Troy as though concerned he might have missed the significance of this.

Troy said to Rochford, 'You think she killed herself?'

'It's what I firmly believe.'

'And what you'll tell a court?'

'That's correct.'

Troy asked him to describe his visit to The Tower, and the grief counsellor led them through it, step by step. The way he spoke, it was like a child reciting a lesson learned by heart. He said they'd taken the lifts to level one hundred and ten.

'What was it like up there?'

'Cold. Windy. Dark. When we walked to the edge there was a sort of metal fence and you couldn't see anything. There was mist.'

Troy remembered that night, what it had been like on level thirty-one. It annoyed him that Rochford's lies could evoke the memory so powerfully. The man across the table was still sweating a lot, but apart from that he was doing well, consistent and assured. Troy asked him what Margot had been wearing, and received a detailed description. As the police had not released information about Margot's bag or coat, this meant Rochford had been briefed by someone who'd seen her that night.

'How did the counselling session go?'

'It was a disaster. Margot broke down and we returned to the ground floor with the man who'd brought us up.'

Troy pulled photos of Bazzi and Asaad from the file and Rochford identified Bazzi.

'I wanted to stay with her when we got downstairs, but this man insisted I leave. She told me to go, she said she would stay behind for a moment. She said she wanted to go up again, by herself. That was the last time I saw her.'

'And what time was that?'

'I was there about half an hour, maybe forty minutes. So it would have been something like ten to seven when I left. I didn't check my watch.'

Troy knew from the bank's CCTV that it had been 6.45 pm, so Rochford's estimate was close enough. This piece of information had not been released to the public either. Troy wondered where the real Mr A was. He stared at the man across the table, realising how close he was to the people who were pursuing him. It was one degree of separation; he could almost reach out and touch them.

'Mr Rochford, I have no further questions.'

As he said this he watched Rochford's face carefully. He could see it shutting down, as though the relief was almost too much to bear. The three men stood up and Troy opened the door.

'Why don't you go back to the office,' he said to Bergman, half pushing him out. 'I'll see Mr Rochford off the premises.'

When Bergman was gone, Troy shut the door and turned back to Rochford. He thanked him for his help and they shook hands.

Rochford's was almost wet now, and when Troy released it the other man took out a handkerchief and wiped his face.

'It's a nerve-racking business, isn't it?' Troy said.

'It's hot in here.'

'I mean lying to the police.'

'I don't know what you mean,' Rochford said, without any attempt at conviction.

'Can we help you in any way? My superiors know everything,' he lied. 'We can guarantee confidentiality.' For a moment he saw panic in Rochford's eyes. 'We can protect you.'

'No one can protect me,' Rochford muttered. Then, summoning energy from somewhere: 'I want to go now.'

Later in the afternoon, Troy ducked out and bought an anniversary present for Anna. It was an opal ring he'd seen in the window of a shop nearby. The opal was set in silver; he'd always liked the way silver looked against her brown skin. She did like jewellery, lots of it. One of their first arguments had been about the quantity of earrings and bracelets she'd been wearing when they went out to a film. He couldn't remember who'd won, but she still wore more jewellery than most women. He'd come to accept it. Sometimes people would stare, when they went out, but it didn't worry him anymore.

Soon after he got home that night, they drove down to a seafood place at Brighton-le-Sands. Anna had put a lot of effort into her hair and makeup, and was wearing a sari in rich shades of red and brown. She hadn't worn a sari in a long time, and it surprised him when she came out of their bedroom. He wondered what it meant.

They had oysters followed by grilled fish, and talked about the visit from the Duttons yesterday. After a bit he tried to change the subject, but she stuck with it.

Finally she said, 'Wendy says there's lots of jobs going at the airport.'

'Boring jobs.'

'Safe ones.'

She'd never talked about him leaving the job before this investigation. He wondered if it was just the events of last week, or if it had been on her mind for a while.

'Ralph said he wasn't going to offer me a job because he knows I wouldn't be happy there,' he said with a smile.

He looked around the room, desperate for something else to talk about, but it was too late. Anna's eyes filled with tears.

'I do want you to be happy, Nick,' she said. 'You know that.'

'Do you?'

She stood up and went to the bathroom.

Troy finished the wine in his glass and sat there, not sure how much more of this he could take. There was no pattern to their lives anymore. A waitress came by and filled his glass and flirted with him mildly. It was pleasant. When she left he picked up the glass, looked at its contents, and put it down. One day he might become an alcoholic, as a way of dealing with the way his life was going. He'd seen it happen to other men. But for now, he didn't have the time.

Anna assumed his patience was infinite, based on the belief he would keep coming back to her no matter how often she pushed him away. But one day he might not. Or was that the idea? Was she actually trying to push him away? If he left her, she would get half the house and could take Matt to Brisbane and live near her parents. Which, after all, was what she wanted. It was a shocking thought, and he felt guilty for even harbouring it. But as he sat there the guilt began to fade, while the thought remained.

When they got home he walked the babysitter to her place. He took his time on the way back, enjoying the stars and the spring night air, blowing in from the sea out of sight down the hill. Inside, he cleaned his teeth, turned off the lights, and went into the bedroom.

Anna was there, sitting up in bed in a red nightie he vaguely remembered. The lower part of her body was hidden by the bedclothes, but he could see most of her breasts, and even make out the nipples beneath the red silk. It had been a long time since he'd seen her like this.

'Well, are you coming to bed or do I have to get out and haul you in?' she said, her voice slightly hoarse.

Actually he felt like crying, an absurd feeling that passed quickly. He said he wouldn't mind being dragged in and she said it was time for him to show a bit of enthusiasm. 'I've been waiting here for hours, wondering what you've been getting up to with Aleisha.'

The words came out awkwardly but he appreciated the effort, and got out of his clothes. Pulling down the sheet, he climbed in next to her.

The thing was to take it as slowly and gently as he could. It would not be easy, the way he was feeling, but he told himself he could do it. She was still just sitting there, nervously, which helped calm him down. Twisting around, he kissed her softly on the side of her mouth. He kissed her some more and she turned slightly towards him, and responded for a moment, the feel of her skin and the smell of her almost overwhelming him with memories of what they'd had in the past.

But there was still no response, and presently he stopped. She just sat there and he put a hand on her shoulder. She flinched and he tried to rub her back. Then he saw her eyes were full of tears. Again.

'I'm sorry, Nick,' she whispered. 'I just can't.'

She started to get out of bed and he took hold of her wrist and said, 'Wait.'

With sudden energy she pulled her arm from his grip and moved to the side of the bed. He could have held her but he was so angry he didn't trust himself.

'Don't you dare,' she said.

'I'm not doing anything,' he said. 'I just want you to know we have to do something about this, we need some help.'

She slid out of bed, picking up her dressing-gown from the floor and slipping into it as she stood up, so he caught only a glimpse of her lower body.

'Let's not talk about this tonight, not on our anniversary,' she said. 'Please.'

'Won't you tell me what you're afraid of?'

'I'm not afraid of anything. You keep saying that, and it makes me really upset. I've just lost interest for a while, it's quite common.'

'This is destroying our marriage, Anna. I want us to go to counselling.'

As if that would automatically fix things. But you had to have some sort of plan. Plans implied hope.

'I just need more time.'

'You said that six months ago. There is no more time.'

Her face contorted in anguish. 'Don't say that.'

'I can't wait any longer.'

'My whole life depends on you. Don't you still love me?'

He said nothing.

'Have you found someone else?'

He was on the point of telling her about Wednesday night. But with a strange wailing sound, she turned and ran from the room.

The noise worried him. He stood up, all desire gone, and put on his pyjamas. The sound she'd made had been like an expression of pain. He went down the hall and found the door to Matt's room was locked. For five minutes he knocked on it gently and spoke to her, but there was no response. If the boy hadn't been in there he might have broken down the door, but having a child changed things. He went back to bed, thinking about the sound she'd made, her tears, all the emotion coursing through her body, her life. He realised he still loved her, and that this was the problem. If he didn't love her, everything would be much easier.

TUESDAY

Thirty-eight

A sound woke him, and he saw from the bedside clock it was early morning. Very early. He lay there for a few minutes, remembering what had happened last night with Anna, then thinking about work and Geoff Rochford. The man might be in the same situation as himself, lying awake somewhere in the city, thinking about the hold these people had over him. He wondered what had happened to the real Mr A. Perhaps he was dead. They would have to look at any murders of unidentified men his age in the past week. Suicides, too.

Troy got up and went out to the kitchen to get a glass of water. The door to Matt's room was open, which surprised him, and he looked in. Anna and the boy were gone. Matt's change bag was missing too. He raced to the front door and pulled it open. Anna's car was no longer out the front of the house. The faint odour of exhaust fumes lay in the cold night air. It must have been the sound of her driving away that had woken him.

In the kitchen he found a note on the table, almost two pages long. Anna wrote that she was going away for a while because of the guilt she felt at not being able to fulfil her duties as a wife. She was terrified something might happen to him at work, after the shootings in The Tower. She couldn't raise this with him because it would make him

359

angry, and she feared his anger. She also wrote she was scared he would no longer love Matt should anything happen to her. And she feared Troy might harm her physically; after the way he had behaved last night, she feared for her safety.

Troy couldn't follow the note, he couldn't follow her thoughts. This was not the way things were. He put the letter down, wondering about her state of mind, what she might do to herself and Matt. He did not think of himself as a particularly violent man, yet here she was, writing of fear and terror. If their normal life together could produce such a storm of emotion, he wondered what the sight of the video footage would do if she ever saw it.

'Jesus,' he said.

It was a prayer. A short one.

He wondered where she'd go. She had a lot of friends, but most of the really close ones were in Queensland, where she'd grown up. He couldn't think of anyone in Sydney she'd go to at this time of night, although it all depended on her state of mind, whether the letter marked her lowest ebb or was just a point on a descent into further chaos. He remembered a woman she'd been close to in her nursing days. Sara. But they hadn't seen her in a while. Maybe the Duttons. He hoped Matt would be all right, told himself that the boy liked sleeping in his capsule in the back of the car, he'd probably be fine. Troy wondered whether to call Anna's parents in Brisbane. There was a good chance she'd been in touch with them already, maybe even talked about all this. She rang her mother several times a week.

The question was whether to pursue Anna at all. That was his instinct, but he knew there were times when instinct should be resisted. Anna had said in the note she needed to be by herself. Maybe he should respect that. If he went after her, found her and brought her back, they'd only be where they'd been yesterday.

Unless she wanted him to come after her.

For hours these possibilities swirled around his mind, stimulating and exhausting him by turn. He couldn't help thinking about himself, how weak the blackmail made him, vulnerable because of what was being done to him when he should have been strong for her. Your adversary the devil, as a roaring lion, walketh about, seeking whom he may devour.

At some point, while it was still dark, he fell asleep again. But he awoke at dawn. There was no sign of Anna or Matt, and he thought about calling the Maroubra police. But it was too soon. Maybe later in the morning. It was too early to go to work, so he decided to have a run.

When he reached the beach, some young men were already out on their boards, wearing wetsuits and catching a nice break with a lot of power in it. He watched them for a while and recalled what he'd been doing at their age, in another part of the city, yellow fields and new houses mixed together, trees being cut down here, planted there, new roads and faces, everything always changing as the incoming tides of immigration pushed the population steadily out their way. He remembered the adjustment he'd had to make when he moved to Maroubra, a crowded older suburb next to the permanence of the ocean. All this he'd come to love, but it didn't seem so solid anymore.

He started to run, keeping to the firm sand between the waterline and the broad swathe of softer yellow to his left. As he ran he prayed that Anna and Matt would return to him, that they be returned. God shall wipe away all tears from their eyes. The sun, a vivid orange on account of the pollution sitting in the still sky, warmed the right side of his body as he passed other joggers, occasionally recognising someone from the surf club and grunting hello. His heart was bleak but the sound of the waves, the sunlight and the colour, soothed it a little. He ran on the beach for half an hour, then headed for home.

When he turned the corner of their street, Anna's car was in the driveway. As he got closer he saw that something was wrong with its side: there was a wide gouge running from the crumpled front left corner most of the way down to the back. There was no one else in the street as he stopped running and walked over the damp grass and looked in the windows. Matt was asleep in his seat, his little chest moving up and down. He seemed fine. Anna was in the front, also asleep, her head back against the seat and the side window. They both looked very much at peace.

He watched them for a long time, feeling helpless.

Driving to work later that morning, Troy agonised over what to do about the video. He and Anna had had a long conversation after she woke up. She told him she'd driven around for hours, not knowing where to go. At some point she'd fallen asleep at the wheel, down in Mascot, and sideswiped a concrete wall. She couldn't remember where. Then she'd driven home and fallen asleep. Crying a lot, she said she loved him very much and realised she needed to see someone, a counsellor. This was a huge breakthrough. After a bit she calmed down. Things were going to be all right, she could see that she had to change. They just needed time. He felt tremendously happy.

He told her he wanted her to call her parents that morning. A look of panic appeared on her face but he insisted. Either her parents or a doctor, that day.

'You should go up and have a holiday, stay with them,' he said.

'No,' she whispered, putting a hand on his arm. 'I want to be with you. I love you.'

The thought of her alone with Matt worried him. 'Ask them down here then,' he said. 'I'll buy the tickets.'

She agreed and he waited while she called them, listened while she set up the visit. After he'd sorted out the flights on the internet, he had a cup of tea with her in the kitchen and they talked some more. She was at peace, the way she used to be. Maybe last night was the low spot, he thought. Nothing lasts forever. We've come through something and now it's going to get better. Anna had made the decision to come back to him.

When Liz Matarazzo turned up with her children, he felt it was safe to go to work.

As he drove he found he was having trouble breathing. There was no way he could risk Anna finding out about his infidelity—not now especially, when everything had changed. And yet he had to do something. He reached the office at ten and asked McIver if he could have a word, still uncertain of what he wanted to say. The place was almost deserted, with only four officers at their desks. McIver was doing some stretching exercises with his left arm, and gazing out the open door behind Troy.

'Normally a pretty sight, an empty office,' he said. 'But we've hit the wall on this one. Bloody Geoff Rochford. He was our last hope.'

Troy shifted uneasily. McIver was staring at him, and he wondered if the sergeant could tell what was going on. But it was not possible.

McIver added: 'I've never felt like this before.' He looked tired, more dispirited than Troy could remember. It was unnatural.

'What would Jesus do?' Troy murmured.

'I'm sorry?'

Troy leaned back and pushed the door shut. Then, taking a deep breath, he told McIver everything. He had no idea where what he was now starting would end, but he could no longer keep it to himself.

As he spoke, McIver watched him seriously, stroking his jaw. Strangely, he didn't look surprised. Troy kept speaking and as he went on he felt a tremendous sense of relief. Deceit did not come naturally to him. There was no credit due for this: it was just the way he was.

When he finished, there was silence for a while. Then McIver said, 'You know you're a bloody idiot.'

'Things haven't been good between Anna and me—'

'I don't mean that. I mean for not telling me about this before.' He stood up and Troy wondered what was going to happen. The sergeant began to wave his left arm around in what seemed to be another exercise. As he moved it he said, 'This explains the leak to the *Herald* on Friday about the state of the investigation. The people with these pictures must have freaked out when you got tossed. All their hard work for nothing.' He stopped moving his arm and said, 'Did you tell Randall about Stone and his union investigation?'

'Randall knew already. He told me about it.'

McIver began to move his arm again, slowly. 'Which presumably means other people at Warton Constructions know about it.

Maybe even people at Morning Star.' He shook his head. 'Kelly. What a fool.'

'Randall reckons he doesn't know who's behind this. Says he's being jammed himself.'

McIver waved his good arm, dismissing Randall for the moment. 'The question is, who'd want to influence the investigation?' He rubbed his chin. 'You could say the Russian bloke, or his missing mate Jason. But the problem is, Stone's involvement complicates everything. It could be political, nothing to do with the illegals.'

'But Stone's out of it.'

'They might think someone else is carrying on his good work. We're right in the dark. I'll have to tell Kelly.'

'No.'

McIver looked at him. 'It's not a choice, mate. I have to tell her; she can get things moving. We don't like people trying to blackmail cops.'

'Anna might find out.'

He'd told McIver about the warning he'd been given by the man on the phone.

'That's a risk you'll have to take.'

'She can't find out. She couldn't handle it.'

McIver shrugged. 'Things can be done. We can get to her service provider, put a block on it. Even your mail, get the post office involved. We can put a ring around Anna.'

'It could be posted on the internet. Her friends would find out. You can't guarantee it will never get to her.'

He explained about Anna's state of mind and her medication. He could tell McIver was taking it in; he hadn't convinced him, but he was thinking again.

When Troy had finished, he said, 'Even so, maybe she'd react better than you think. These things are complicated.'

'They're not complicated for her. Believe me.'

'She's led a sheltered life, then.'

'It's not a crime. I'm asking you, as a friend, to help me here. Don't tell Kelly.'

McIver rubbed his jaw and looked away. His face was scowling, as it did when he was entirely serious. He said, 'I suppose you think I owe you for saving my life.'

'I don't—'

'I do. That's the way it is.' He shook his head slowly. 'So I'll do this. If you really want it.'

'Yes.'

'But there can be no pulling out. I don't want you thinking you can just jump back inside the system if this doesn't work out. Once you go out on your own, things are never the same again.' He looked at Troy almost fondly. 'Take my word for it.'

Troy nodded. He was already outside this system. And all others. 'It's what I want.'

'Why were you shaving in here on Saturday? Siegert told me.'

'I forgot to shave at home.' He'd already told McIver about his visit to the Mornington Apartments.

Now Mac looked at him and shook his head, as though this shaving business had some deep significance. 'You think you're in a condition to make this decision?'

'Yes. There isn't much time, is there? I'll stick to it, you know me well enough for that.'

McIver looked away for a moment and cleared his throat. 'We ought to get Randall in and bounce him around,' he said, 'but as you say, that would be dangerous. You've been warned off. The other lead we might have is Mr A. They want us to stop looking for him, so he must be important. And he must be findable. If he wasn't, they wouldn't have needed to go through all that bullshit with Geoff Rochford.'

'He might be dead.'

McIver shook his head slowly. 'In that case I don't know if they'd go to the trouble, the risk, of blackmailing you. Because it is a risk for them—cops don't appreciate this sort of thing. They couldn't be sure how you'd react.' McIver looked angry for a moment, but then he smiled. 'You feel better for talking about it, don't you?'

'I'm a Catholic. We like to confess things.'

'Everyone likes to confess things,' McIver said. 'It's what keeps us in business.' He drummed the fingers of his right hand on the desk for half a minute. Then he did the same with his left hand, more slowly and with effort. The result seemed to please him. 'It'd be nice to have allies, but Vella's about as much use as an ashtray on a motorbike. So we need to handle it ourselves.' His lips parted in a surprisingly gentle smile. 'Here's the deal. I'll do my best to sort this out without Kelly. And when I say sort it out, I mean so's Anna will never know.'

Troy felt a surge of relief. It was irrational, but overwhelming.

'But it might not work. You have to be ready for that. Okay?'

'Sure,' he lied.

'I'm going to have to use my own methods, might have to confide in one or two old mates. There'll be risk involved. Tell me now, are you up for that?'

'Yes.'

McIver looked at him dubiously, and seemed about to say something but changed his mind. 'It could go off quickly,' was what he did say. 'In the meantime, could you arrange a bust at home? I'm thinking we need to get the computer out of your house, in case they send the video to Anna.'

'Anna's on the edge of a nervous breakdown. She's always been worried about security, it wouldn't be good for her. And she'd just use one of her friend's computers, anyway.'

As he spoke, he realised it made his wife sound like an invalid.

'Well, it's your call, but I'd seriously consider it.' McIver seemed sick of the subject of Anna. He frowned and looked at his watch. 'Let me ring a few people. You think some more about Mr A, who he might be. And give me the number.'

'What number?'

'The one you called for your hour of indiscretion.'

Troy had thrown away the piece of paper Randall had given him, but he could remember the number. He recited it and stood up.

McIver said, 'Did you check it out?'

'Bought under a false name.'

McIver nodded. 'You know, you're probably right to fear Kelly. I've heard she tried to have both of us bounced after that Sunday night. It was Rogers said no, and not because he's fond of me. It's you. Any link there?'

'I've never met him,' said Troy. He was keen to get out of the small room and be alone.

McIver said, 'You've changed.'

'I'm the same. The world's changed.'

'They all say that.'

Troy wondered what he meant, but he didn't really care. He didn't want to know everything, not anymore.

McIver shrugged and picked up the phone. As Troy was about to leave the room the sergeant said, 'Was it worth it?'

'What?'

'You're being obtuse.'

Troy hadn't thought about it like that. He said slowly, 'Yes. It was.'

The answer seemed to please McIver. 'If you spread your kisses around,' he said, 'who's going to know, a hundred years from today?'

It sounded like something from a song.

'It's not a hundred years from today I'm worried about.'

McIver began to push buttons on the phone and said, 'I wouldn't make any plans for the next few days. As soon as we get an opportunity we'll have to move.' He paused and looked at Troy again. 'You really should have come to me about this before. Honesty's the best policy, in my experience. At least when all else fails.'

Thirty-nine

Just after ten, a young woman came to the office and asked for Conti. Her hair was almost silver and she was unusually pale. As they spoke at Conti's desk, other detectives looked at the woman from the corners of their eyes.

When she'd left, Conti went in to see McIver. Shortly, the two of them came out and stopped by Troy's desk.

'Come on,' said McIver. 'We're going out.'

'Where?'

'To a brothel.'

Troy stood up slowly, feeling the attention of the room upon them.

'Don't worry,' McIver said, 'Susan's coming to look after us.'

In the car, Conti explained that the woman was Kristin Otto, who worked for an NGO that investigated the trafficking of women. Conti had met her last week, when she'd interviewed staff at the brothel where one of the illegals had been on the night Margot Teresi died. Otto was assisting the Immigration investigation.

'I'm amazed the media haven't got on to this,' McIver said as they drove up Goulburn Street. 'A bit of sex to add to everything else they've managed to get into the story.'

Media coverage of the investigation was still relentless, fuelled over the weekend by a baseless story claiming one of the Triads was involved in providing illegal labour in Sydney. Troy had been rung several times by the two journalists he'd supplied with information on the night of the shootings, but he'd refused to talk with them further.

Conti said, 'Last night, Kristin saw the photo of the shooter we put out.'

'That was last week.'

'Well, she only saw it yesterday. You remember that Thai girl from the brothel I told you about? Turns out Kristin was visiting her last week at Villawood, and the guy was there.'

'The shooter?'

'He was talking to Sally when Kristin arrived, saw Kristin and left. He had someone with him, waiting in a car outside.'

'Why would he show his face at a place like that?'

'It was before we released his picture to the media. There was a delay, remember.'

Troy remembered. 'What did this Sally have to say?'

'She said it was a friend. Kristin didn't push it, the woman wasn't a suspect.'

'What about now? Has she talked to this Sally again?'

McIver murmured, 'Thereby hangs a tale,' as they turned into Reilly Street.

'Sally's not there anymore,' said Conti. 'She disappeared over the weekend.'

The Golden Arms was in a narrow street in Surry Hills, inside a neat-looking terrace with no sign outside. The men waited in the car while Conti went inside. She'd explained the local workers didn't like illegals because they attracted the attention of the authorities, which was bad for business. She thought they'd do what they could to help find the shooter, but the presence of male detectives would only delay things.

McIver was whistling, gazing around the street.

'Conti's going back to the Cross in a few days,' he said. 'Her boss only gave her to us for a fortnight. Stone agreed.'

Troy was disappointed. 'Can't we do something?'

'I tried and failed. Everyone wants the good ones.'

He whistled some more, looking at the entrance to the Golden Arms.

Troy said, 'You ever been in a place like this?'

Mac laughed. 'To be a good detective you need to be a man of experience. You know that.'

'Like Conti's father?'

'You can go too far.'

They waited some more. It was hot in the car; the mist and cold of the night Margot Teresi had died seemed long ago. McIver sung a slow blues about a levee breaking, and tapped out the beat on the dashboard with his fingers. Troy noticed he wasn't wearing his sling.

Eventually Conti came out and slipped back into the car. She had two possible addresses, places where Sally had lived in the few months she'd been in the country.

The first was only five minutes away, a Housing Commission block in Waterloo. The Joseph Banks was a vast place, about sixteen storeys high and very wide. It was approached by broad steps from the road, and as they climbed them McIver paused to loosen his tie and look at the sun. A thin man and a fat woman coming down stared at the detectives openly and with rancour, as though indignation were the only public emotion left in their lives. Conti bridled but McIver looked away from the tattooed couple and recommenced his ascent.

You could see through glass into the building's lobby on the ground floor. One wall was covered in small tiles, reflecting the fashion of the decade long ago when the place had been built. There were black metal security doors, and Troy wondered how they'd get in, but a tenant on his way out stopped and held the door open. They passed through into the confined space, and it was like going into a jail.

As they took a small lift up to the fourth floor, McIver wondered aloud how an illegal immigrant came to be living in public housing.

'I thought they reserved it for people with complex needs,' he said.

Conti frowned. 'Maybe Sally did have complex needs.'

'But were they legal?'

She stared at the sergeant, and Troy could see she was still trying to work him out. Suddenly Mac looked down and smiled at her, and she grinned back. Troy figured she'd be working in Homicide within a year.

On the way over, he'd put in a call to the government agency that ran the block. As they stepped out of the lift they rang him back and gave him a name. 'The tenant's Bronwyn Davies,' he said. 'The local office hasn't seen her in over a year, but apparently that's not unusual.'

'The advantages of electronic banking,' McIver murmured.

Up here it was warmer and the air was stuffier. They walked down the long corridor, looking for the number they'd been given. The style of the place was old, and the walls were peeling here and there and needed a new coat of paint. Troy felt as though he was slipping back in time.

'There's definitely a smell,' Conti said.

They stood outside the door at the end of the corridor, staring at it. There was a strong odour now, one Troy had smelled before. McIver drew out his gun and looked at him. 'Not that I think we'll be needing it.'

Troy took out his own weapon and banged on the door.

'Police!'

He called again and looked at McIver, who said, 'We should call the office.'

As Conti pulled out her phone, Troy kicked the door in.

The dead man was lying in a bedroom, visible from the front door. The detectives were immersed in the hot stench that rolled out of the apartment. Troy put his gun away and pulled out his handkerchief, which he pressed to his nose, although he knew it was largely a waste of time. When he got to the bedroom he saw the man had been strangled. There was no sign of the rope or wire that had been used. The man's face was swollen but recognisable.

'It's the shooter,' McIver said through clenched teeth.

He didn't want to open his mouth. There were a lot of flies.

Forty

Turn the noise down, buddy,' yelled Jamal.

Randall fumbled with the volume control of the boom box he'd bought yesterday, when he'd moved into the big hotel room. The music became louder.

'The other way. The other way.'

Jamal and the girls were laughing at him and he joined them. Good, healing laughter that went on for a long time. Laughter to keep the cold away.

He sat up, bumping the head of one of the girls but not too hard, and she fell back in mock distress, setting off the laughter again. He sat on the side of the bed, glancing down at himself proudly. A hard-on you could crack bricks with. He leaned over the magazine lying on the bedside table. There was a pile of white powder there.

'Careful, buddy,' Jamal called. 'You haven't paid me for that yet.'

It had come to this: Randall was buying from Jamal because Gregor wasn't returning his calls. He opened the drawer and put most of the coke inside, spilling only a small amount. The way the party was going, things getting active, it would be foolish to leave it lying around. The girl was against his back, nibbling his ear, laughing and asking for some more.

'More?' he cried, trying to remember the scene from *Oliver!* 'You want more!'

They were all laughing again now, the four of them. He doubted they had *Oliver!* in the Ukraine but it was funny anyway. Everything was funny.

'Buddy,' Jamal said from the other bed, tears in his eyes. 'Let's just keep the noise down, okay?'

But Randall liked the noise. It was an essential part of the way he was feeling now, which was all good. He didn't want to have to think of the world outside the noise.

This afternoon was Jamal's way of saying he was sorry, and as far as Randall was concerned, the apology was accepted. Well and truly. 'Apology accepted,' he cried as he made way for the big girl, who tried to keep her hair and breasts out of the coke as she bent over and hoovered up a healthy quantity.

'You don't need to say it again, buddy,' Jamal said above the noise. 'We're good, man, and that's what counts. You just enjoy yourself.'

Randall was having the time of his life, and after the past week he deserved it. Final straw had been Gregor going dead on him, but Jamal had come through, proposed lunch and turned up with the baggie of coke and two Ukrainian lovelies. Apologised for what he'd done with Henry, giving him Asaad's address. Explained he'd had no choice, it was the only way to keep his contract. Henry was the rock that everyone else revolved around.

'You dropped me in it,' Randall had said on the phone, allowing himself a moment of self-pity.

Jamal had blathered on, enough to get Randall to come to lunch.

Then, much later, when they were well gone, still at the restaurant at this point, Jamal had put his head next to Randall's.

'You've got to understand, buddy, Wu despises everyone, all of us. The only thing that matters is that he's got a need for you. Not just you, I mean, but all of us. Me.'

'I know that.'

'He still needs me and he still needs you. That's all that matters. You're sweet.'

Randall's heart had surged. 'What does he need me for?'

'Stuff he's got going on at The Tower, essential to have someone he can trust in your position. The wrong character could shut the whole thing down.'

'What? What's he up to?'

Jamal had reared back, put a finger next to his nose. 'Everything.'

Randall had no idea what he was talking about. 'The illegals?'

'Other stuff too.'

'I gave him some copies of invoices once. Big figures.'

He told Jamal what they were, details of various goods and services. Jamal nodded, went into a long explanation Randall couldn't quite follow, setting out how the invoice details could have been used for a certain type of scam. The words just rolled off his tongue, Jamal seemed to know a lot about finance. Good friend for a man to have.

The girls had been getting restless. Jamal paid the bill and they went to Randall's hotel. He'd moved in yesterday after one of his neighbours had called—not Mrs Crawley but another one—said she wanted to talk to him about a DVD she'd found on the front steps. And then there was the matter of personal security. On Sunday night he'd kept waking up, thinking Nicholas Troy was in the room. He wasn't, of course, but Randall's mind went on playing tricks on him. You put a fellow's marriage under threat, he might get very warm in the first few days. Until he sees it's the way things have to be.

So Randall had decided a hotel would provide him with some peace of mind for a week or two. And it had all worked out. He was in control again. The security management course he'd gone to in KL, the Brit who ran it said security started with controlling the situation; if you do that you can control how people think and feel. Temperature, light, sound, mood. Get all that right and everything else follows. Randall realised you could do that to yourself too, make yourself feel good by controlling inputs like music, drugs, where you were. It seemed the most brilliant insight.

And so. He'd already come once, was ready to roll again, the girl was lying back on the pillows now, playing with herself, calling him to her. What bullshit Kristin had spoken about coke and his dick.

'Just a minute,' he said, standing up uncertainly and fumbling in his trouser pockets for his wallet. Jamal was up on the other side of the room, getting dressed. He'd said earlier he had to go back to work. Means I get both, Randall thought, looking at the girl sprawled on the other bed. Big rubbery teats on her like you saw on a baby's bottle. Lucky me.

'How much do I owe you?' he said.

He only had a few hundred in the wallet, and started to pull out one of his cards. Jamal was laughing.

'Pay me later, okay, buddy? I don't take cards.'

'Okay. It's just—'

'The girls are good. Everything's taken care of, buddy. Sorry I have to go, but like I told you, crisis needs to be sorted.'

He was strapping on his gun. As a security manager, he had a licence for a firearm, although he had no need of one. The girls liked the gun, they'd been playing with it before. Randall had felt jealous, wondered if he could get a licence too because of his job. Have to ask his old mate Troy. He turned up the music.

'Don't do that, buddy, someone will call the front desk.'

Jamal had one hand on Randall's back, the other down at the boom box, firmly pushing his fingers off the control knob and turning the volume down. 'You just have fun. I can see you got a lot to give.' He turned to the other girl. 'Nina, you come over here and help your friend. Mr Randall's a good man, but he needs a lot of loving.' He was at the door now, opening it. 'You take care,' he said, and then he was gone.

Randall was safe, alone in a hotel room with two girls and more coke than he knew what to do with. It was funny how things usually turned out all right. Often better than all right. He breathed deep, wagged a finger at the girls. Let's get imaginative here.

'This,' he said with a big grin, 'is what we're going to do.'

Forty-one

Mclver and Troy left Conti in the flat where the dead man was and walked out of the Joseph Banks apartment block. The crime scene officers had already arrived, and Vella, who was back from Bourke, was on the way.

They'd have to go back soon, but McIver wanted some fresh air. There was a pub just down the road, the Duke of Wellington, and he led the way in, ordered two middies. They needed to get the taste of death out of their mouths.

'We still don't know anything about them,' Troy said.

'Them?'

'The two of them.' Where all this had started. 'The friend at Villawood, the man Kristin saw waiting in the car. He must have realised Kristin might recognise the shooter at some point.'

'That's it,' McIver said slowly. He emptied his glass and placed it carefully on the bar, looking at it with sorrow. 'Lucky they didn't kill Ms Otto herself. But then, this is neater.'

There'd been no sign of ID in the flat where the man had died.

McIver said, 'I'm sure the DNA will confirm we've just found the second killer of Margot Teresi. It'll be his skin under her fingernails.'

God rest her soul, Troy thought. Getting sentimental in his old age. And anyway, she could not be at peace yet because her killers were anonymous, and one of them had died an anonymous death.

McIver said slowly, 'We could stop here.'

Troy nodded. 'It's what they want, isn't it? I'd say it's Sidorov.'

The contractor had been released on bail of a quarter of a million dollars, after providing a written statement to the police that had admitted no guilt and told them nothing they didn't know.

'And the elusive Jason.' Immigration had found no trace of the people smuggler. McIver said, 'Still, after today, people are going to be happy.' He put some emphasis on the last word. 'We know who killed Margot Teresi. We're pretty sure we know why she died—she stumbled on evidence of the illegals and was killed to keep her quiet. People are going to like all that.' He smiled at Troy. 'It's pleasant to be popular.'

'We still have to investigate who killed the killer.'

'Of course. But the way things are, resources will be limited, unless we push for them. I think maybe this is a good place for this to stop. There'd be no more reason to blackmail you.'

He was staring at Troy, who looked away and thought about the offer that had just been made. At last he said, 'No. We need to do this properly. It's not finished.'

'Even though it could destroy your marriage?'

Troy thought about it and said, 'Yes.'

'You don't think you're being offered a choice here?'

'I do,' said Troy. He'd stepped over the line, but now that McIver was offering to help him stay there, he realised it wasn't where he wanted to be. 'I do.' He pushed himself off the bar. 'Let's get back to work.'

When he was back in the office, Ralph Dutton called. They talked about The Tower for a minute or two. The media had got wind of the discovery of the body at Waterloo straight away; someone in the block must have tipped them off. There'd been reporters and photographers waiting when they'd got back from the pub. Lots of locals had turned up too, some bringing folding chairs and eskies so they could enjoy the show.

'Anyway, congratulations,' said Dutton. 'I guess this is case closed. You'll be a sergeant before too long. Look, I know you're busy, but I just wanted to know if you'd had a chance to think about that matter we discussed Sunday.'

For a moment, Troy couldn't think of what he meant. The family walk in the sun. Eating ice creams. Talk of the Duttons' American trip. Then it came back to him, slowly: information about the docks, fake car parts.

He wanted to say he didn't realise he'd been supposed to think about it, but it would sound offensive. Although, with this phone call, Dutton had gone too far, and maybe he needed to be offended. This was all new, it was a big change.

'I've never asked you for anything like this before,' Dutton said into the silence. 'It's very important to me.'

'I'll call you back.'

Troy went out for a walk. After a bit he found a public phone and called his friend's mobile.

'Your phone off?' said Dutton.

'Who knows? Look, you know how I feel about this sort of thing. Why don't you ask someone else?'

'I have. I wouldn't put this on you if it wasn't absolutely necessary. My job, mate. My job's on the line.'

'Ralph—'

'I feel terrible, take that as a given. To be honest, I've slipped up a few times here, need to pull something out of the hat. The name's Chris Sutherland, bloke runs the dock. If you could just tell me yes or no about him, one word's all I need. I heard the Gangs Squad were part of it.'

'Ralph—'

'If there's anything you want. I mean a lot—this is worth a great deal. Don't make me beg, mate—'

The words ran on with fluency, as though they'd been road-tested before on other people.

Troy hung up. It was a hard thing to do, but it was the right thing. Now, though, the right thing didn't seem as natural as it had, because he'd lost his bearings. It was odd, but not as odd as it ought to be. He'd felt like this before, in the years after his parents died, and for a while there before he met Anna. Maybe this confusion was really his natural state.

During the afternoon he called home twice, and Anna sounded better each time. Liz was still with her, and they were preparing an early dinner for the kids. Anna's parents were coming down in two days. There was a playgroup at ChristLife the next morning, and she'd arranged to go to a friend's place afterwards.

'I love you,' Troy whispered into the phone.

She told him she loved him too.

The office was full of noise. People were making arrangements to go out after work to celebrate the discovery of the shooter. They still needed to find out who'd killed him, though. It had to be done. Troy picked up his phone and rang Peter Wood at Multiplex.

The executive was out visiting a site, and eventually returned Troy's call from his car. When Troy explained what he wanted, the other man grunted. 'I heard it on the radio, you've caught the other bloke who killed Teresi's daughter. Congratulations.'

'Well, we're not sure—'

'You seemed in a hurry last time, so I figured you had what you needed,' he said. 'But I was thinking of ringing you anyway. Margot did give me a call, and I gave her the name of a quantity surveyor who used to work for us. Retired guy, name of Des Ferguson.'

'Does he look anything like the man in the pictures we gave to the media?'

'I wouldn't know. We've been at our place near Orange, no television there.'

'Tall, balding, late fifties?'

'Yeah, but older.'

'Did Margot say why she wanted to speak to him?'

'She thought her father had been ripped off when he sold The Tower. The issue was what materials had been delivered and paid for before the date of the contract. She wanted someone who could make an informed judgement about certain costs. Ferguson's an expert at that sort of thing.'

'Do you think Tony Teresi was ripped off?'

'How long's a piece of string?' Wood laughed sourly. 'Do you want Ferguson's number?'

Troy rang it immediately and got an answering machine. He used his computer to get the address that matched Ferguson's phone number: a house in Turramurra. Then he called the locals and asked them to have someone drop by as soon as possible. He was worried about Ferguson.

Half an hour later, a uniformed officer rang. Des Ferguson and his wife had left for Europe suddenly, last Monday. The day after Margot died.

'Does the neighbour know where in Europe?' Troy said.

'No.'

'Any children?'

'An adult daughter, Cheryl. Lives in New York.'

'Got an address?'

'No. But the neighbour has two phone numbers, in case of an emergency.'

'I don't suppose you took them down?'

'Have you got a pen?'

Again using his computer, Troy submitted an IASK request for Ferguson's flight details. He marked it urgent and sat thinking until the answer came back. Ferguson and his wife had indeed flown out the previous Monday, but not to Europe. They'd gone to Los Angeles, and there was no onward flight. No return one, either. Troy thought for a moment, and clicked on the program that gave foreign times. It was very early morning on the east coast of the United States. Good, he thought: Cheryl Ferguson should be asleep.

As he was dialling, Troy saw Ron Siegert come into the office with Bruce Little. He could tell from their expressions that something was up. They seemed happy—everyone in the office was happy this afternoon—but it was more than that. They went into McIver's office and Troy's attention was distracted by the voicemail message he'd just got. It sounded like he'd called her work number, and she was employed by some sort of bank. Troy left a message and called the other number. While waiting he saw Siegert come out of McIver's office and walk out of the room. He was still smiling, in a grim kind of way.

Cheryl Ferguson answered the phone, sounding sleepy. Troy explained who he was and what he wanted, and she said her parents were in Europe on holiday. She asked him which police station he was calling from, and he told her and hung up. Five minutes later a call came to him from the switch.

'I'm sorry,' Cheryl said, 'but Dad made me promise to be careful. A stranger rang yesterday at work, said he was a cop too.'

He wondered how long she'd been in New York. She had a soft American accent.

'I need to talk to your father urgently,' he said.

'He'll be calling me tomorrow. Today. I'll ask him to call you. He might not.'

'Tell him things have developed over here,' Troy said, giving her his home number and his email address. 'And you take care.'

'Should I be worried?'

'Not if he talks to us soon.'

He hung up just as McIver and Little came out of the office. They were laughing. As they approached his desk, McIver dropped back and shook his head gently at Troy, preparing him for a surprise.

'You are not going to believe this,' Little said. 'Sean Randall, the bloke who runs security in The Tower?'

Troy nodded; he knew who Sean Randall was.

'Our uniforms have just arrested him in a hotel room with two Ukrainian hookers and a bag of coke.'

Troy felt his eyes opening wide. He looked at McIver, who was shrugging. Even he couldn't have organised something like this so soon.

'We were talking about Randall only a while ago,' he said to Little.

'They were having a party,' said McIver. 'The music got too loud and the guests in the next room complained. Hotel security went up and one of the ladies threw an ashtray at him. One thing led to another.'

'A party,' Troy said. 'At four in the afternoon.'

'The girls aren't saying anything,' said Little. 'We're holding them until we get some ID. Good-looking women.'

'Superintendent Siegert has kindly agreed we can deal with Mr Randall,' McIver told Troy. 'I've explained we'd be grateful for a bit of leverage, that we're not entirely happy with what he's been telling us.' He looked at Little. 'Why don't you deal with the Ukrainian lasses?'

Little grinned and went off to his desk. They could hear him whistling.

McIver said, 'I like to see a man enjoying his work.'

'This is quite a coincidence,' Troy said.

'Maybe not. First the shooter and now this. You believe in God, don't you?'

Troy hadn't prayed at all about the blackmail, because it hadn't seemed right. But maybe Randall's arrest was some sort of sign. He told McIver about Des Ferguson and the sergeant's eyes gleamed.

'Not a word to a soul until you've found out what he knows. Now, Siegert says Randall wants to speak to you. I'm thinking we'll let him stew.'

Troy nodded, reluctantly.

McIver said, 'How you holding up?'

'Better than I should be, most of the time. Sometimes worse. It's hard to take in.'

McIver looked around and lowered his voice. 'You want to change your mind?'

'No.'

'Look on the bright side. We found the bad guy today. It doesn't happen very often.'

'But someone else found him first.'

'One step at a time. We'll sort out your problem. Hang tough. What you're going through, it's like punctuated equilibrium.'

'I was thinking the same.'

'It's a theory about evolution. Says nothing much happens most of the time, then bang—there's a big change. In my experience, life's like that. Calm or storms, but not often much in the middle.'

McIver walked away and Troy stared after him. The difference between McIver and him was McIver liked the storms.

Later, they went to the cells to interview Randall about his cocaine party.

Troy said, 'I still think it's a coincidence, Sean falling into our lap like this.'

'Coincidences happen,' McIver said, 'don't knock it. Prostitutes, drugs—strike you as extreme behaviour from him?'

It was not a question that required any reflection.

'No.'

'Well then.'

'How are we going to do this?'

'I go in alone,' McIver said, 'ask him the name of his dealer. He doesn't tell me, I say we're going to charge him with supply, intend to give it maximum publicity because there's some sort of government push on. Then bang, change direction, tell him if he explains what happened to you, he walks free now.'

They reached the cells.

Troy said, 'He wants to talk to me.'

'I bet he does, but he can't,' said McIver. 'That's how all this started. Remember?'

While he waited, Troy called home. Anna sounded tired and he said he'd get some takeaway for dinner. They discussed the preparations for her parents' visit, and then Matt started to cry in the background. Anna kept talking, about bed linen.

'Isn't that Matt?' Troy said, interrupting her.

'Oh yes,' she said slowly. 'Yes, it is.'

'Is he okay?'

'He's fine. He's just tired.'

'Do you think you'd better go to him?'

There was a pause.

'I'd better go, Nick. See you soon.'

Troy waited some more but there was no sign of McIver. Eventually he returned to the office, deserted by now, and sat down to do some paperwork. It was a while before McIver came back from the cells.

'Pub,' he said to Troy.

'I have to get home—'

'Pub,' McIver said, leading the way.

As soon as they had their drinks and were seated, he began to talk. 'The bloke's terrified. It didn't take much to get him to open up.'

'You told him honesty's the best policy?'

'Something like that.'

'Did he know anything about the shooter or Bazzi?'

'He says not, and I think I believe him. But he does know a lot about your own little problem.' McIver explained that before working at The Tower, Randall had been with Warton Constructions based in Hong Kong. He'd been manager for a project in Shanghai where some men had died. 'It was Randall's fault, he overlooked something he was supposed to check. That job was for Morning Star too, and their local manager got the authorities to cover it up. I gather that sort of thing is not hard to do in the People's Republic. He saved Randall from being prosecuted.'

'Saved the company's reputation too.'

'Sure. But the key point is, he saved Sean Randall's career.'

'Ah,' said Troy.

McIver nodded. 'Bloke by the name of Henry Wu. I believe you've met?'

One of those that have turned the world upside down. 'So it's Wu?'

'Brought him here. Randall calls Sydney his second coming. So he's in Wu's pocket, and the bloke was calling him every day about the investigation. It was Wu told him to give the number to you on the night you went to the restaurant.'

'But Wu's a major executive,' Troy protested. 'Why would he do stuff like this? I saw him with Kelly and Siegert. They were treating him with respect.'

'Randall was very interesting on the subject,' McIver said, savouring what he was about to say. He liked this sort of thing, learning how the city worked. 'Wu's one of the most influential Chinese businessmen in town, because of Morning Star and The Tower. But that's not enough for him. He's used that status to build up personal business interests that have nothing to do with the insurance company. And some of them are extremely dodgy.'

'Risky. Unnecessary.' Wu already had so much. Why would he want more?

'According to Randall, the bloke's crazy, a big gambler, as well as a psychopath. Volatile combination, and apparently he likes taking it to the edge. There's some personally destructive behaviour Randall didn't want to talk about. Someone like that might have trouble in the corporate world here in the West. But where he comes from, it doesn't seem to have held him back.'

Troy thought over the investigation, wondering where else Wu might fit in. 'He's into people smuggling?'

'Randall doesn't know. But he said he's got a finger in so many things it's possible. He talked a bit about an insurance scam on some factory, drugs, smuggling through the docks. With the sort of people Wu deals with in his spare time, I'd be guessing there'd be no trouble arranging the sting on you.'

Troy drained his glass and placed it carefully on the table. 'You think he had Margot killed?'

'Who knows? Maybe she was getting close to something, with the help of Des Ferguson.' McIver frowned. 'But I doubt it. Despite what Randall says, the bloke's not stupid. Why would he have had her killed at The Tower and draw attention to the place? If she'd died in a motor accident, or in a fire in her house up the river, we'd never have gone near The Tower.'

Troy shrugged, said, 'Or she saw something that night which someone wanted hidden. Maybe Ferguson saw it too.'

McIver nodded. 'Such as the illegals. Possibly someone connected with them killed her on the spur of the moment when she saw something she shouldn't have. Like two men coming out of a tunnel. They panicked. So Henry Wu had nothing to do with her murder, but he sure wanted it covered up.'

'And being a criminal anyway, he knew what to do about it,' said Troy. 'Feel like another drink?'

McIver shook his head slowly. 'We need to get back to your own little problem. Last night I thought some more and decided the thing to do was throw you off the investigation—that would have finished the blackmail. But if Wu's as vicious as Randall says, it mightn't help. Could still send the video to Anna.' He paused and rubbed his cheek. 'Now we have a name, there's things we can do. I know a bloke this sort of thing happened to once before, Special Ops helped him out. Few fellows in an unmarked van, ballied up, they pull the blackmailer into the back, shotgun to the head. A few words of warning. Chuck him back onto the street. He got the message.'

Troy nodded. That sounded good.

'You'd incur some debts if we go down that road. You understand that?'

Life, Troy thought. He nodded again.

'You coming to the celebration?'

'I need to get home to Anna.'

'Well I have to put in an appearance. It's a big day, you know. Kelly's over the moon.' He looked at Troy and smiled. 'Then I've got some people to see.'

They stood up.

'What about Randall?' Troy said.

'You stay right away from him. I charged him with a small quantity, personal use only. He squealed but I explained that Wu'd hear about the bust anyway. He'd smell a rat if we didn't charge Randall with something.'

They walked down the stairs. On the footpath, Troy shook McIver's hand.

'Thanks for all this,' he said awkwardly.

'That's all right, I'm enjoying it.'

'I'm not.'

McIver smiled. 'I used to think you were a good bloke, but a little boring.' He grew serious. 'The next twenty-four hours could be pretty rough, now we're closing in on Ferguson. We need to get to Wu before he finds out about that.'

'How could he?'

'Randall says he's got a good contact in the job. I don't think we've got much time left.' He looked at Troy. 'I'm talking about the blackmail,' he said gently.

Troy nodded. He knew.

WEDNESDAY

Forty-two

The phone woke him at twelve minutes past four. It was Des Ferguson, calling from Chicago. Troy was alone in the bedroom, but even so he got up and went out to the lounge room, so the conversation wouldn't disturb Anna or Matt. Closing the door quietly, he thanked Ferguson for calling him.

'I'm very nervous about this, officer,' said the voice at the other end of the line. He sounded nervous. 'But I was going to call the police anyway.'

'Why don't you tell me what happened that night?' Troy said, as calmly as he could.

The way Ferguson sounded, he might hang up at any moment.

'It's not just me, it's my family.'

Troy turned on a lamp and sat down in an armchair. A pad and two pens were on the small table next to it. He said, 'I propose keeping anything you tell me confidential between ourselves and my senior officer until we can guarantee your safety. You have my word on that. Does that make things better?'

There was silence and Troy prayed the line had not dropped out. He should have asked for Ferguson's number.

'Yes,' said the other man at last. 'I'm basically a decent middle-class citizen. Keeping things from the police hasn't been easy for me. I'm just scared.'

'You'll feel better afterwards.'

'You think so?'

Troy wondered if he was a religious man. Let us therefore cast off the works of darkness and let us put on the armour of light.

He said, 'In case the line drops out, would you give me your number?'

Ignoring this, Ferguson began to tell his story.

The first part Troy knew: how Ferguson had been contacted by Margot, who believed Morning Star had robbed her father and then destroyed his reputation. The company had even hired a public relations firm to plant derogatory stories about Tony Teresi in the media after he died.

Troy frowned. 'What was the point of all this?'

'I can't explain it on the phone, it's very complicated, but basically when I went into it I found it's all about money laundering. Morning Star have used the purchase and now the construction of The Tower to produce a lot of fake invoices and receipts for goods and services that either don't exist or are worth a fraction of what's being claimed.'

Troy had still been a little sleepy, but not anymore.

'That's an extraordinary claim,' he said. 'Morning Star are a major corporation, in Hong Kong anyway.'

'I know,' said Ferguson unhappily.

'How much are you talking about?'

'I've found evidence of three million but it could be more. I don't know why Morning Star are bothering. They're making a lot of money as it is, quite legitimately. And the benefit here is going to the contractors they're using, in any case.'

Ferguson must be unaware of Wu's personal business interests. The CEO would have links with the contracting companies.

Troy said, 'Wouldn't Warton Constructions know about this?'

'There's an unusual accounting arrangement,' Ferguson said. 'Morning Star is handling all the financials. Apparently, Warton went along with it because it was the price of getting the work, even though it's a right pain in the bum. Morning Star has a tame quantity surveyor who approves the payment of the dodgy invoices, says the goods or services have been provided in full when often they haven't been. From a fraud point of view, he's the key man. Margot was pretty sharp; she suspected this and hired me to prove it.'

'Why were you there the night she died?'

'One of the timbers they're using around the lifts on each floor, and through the sky lobbies, is called New Guinea Rosewood. It's a beautiful wood and the shipment was valued at three and a half million dollars. Margot took me down to where it was stacked in one of the car parks—I have particular expertise in fine timbers. It was the real thing, had stickers on it from an NGO called East Green. They're an environmental group which certifies that the timber has been sustainably logged, so the Australian government allows it to be imported. But next month the United Nations is going to proscribe East Green, because it's really a front for Asian timber interests. The rosewood I saw was cut in forests in West Irian that are controlled by the Indonesian military; it was logged illegally by Malaysian companies. Once the proscription comes in, countries like Australia will refuse to accept any timber certified by East Green.'

'But Morning Star have already got theirs.'

'The industry has known for months what the UN was going to do. There's a huge glut of New Guinea Rosewood. The unofficial price has plunged as they try to offload it before the bans come in. The point is that, according to documents Margot obtained, Morning Star says it paid the old price, even though it didn't have to.'

Troy, who was trying to record all this in his notebook, said, 'It's very complicated.'

'This is all about the receipts,' said Ferguson. 'It means the company that sold the timber to Morning Star, a broker based in Australia, ended up with a receipt for over a million dollars they hadn't actually received. That receipt could be used to justify the equivalent amount of income from illegal activities.'

'Who owns the broker?'

'I don't know.'

Troy could guess. 'And there were other examples?'

'Suppliers here and in Asia. Margot had some documents and she was getting more. I think she knew someone who was providing her with information. The money involved must be enormous.' He paused. 'It's actually a brilliant concept in a perverse way. The Tower is like a giant washing machine for illegal money.'

'Where does Tony Teresi come into this?' Troy said. 'Why was it necessary to smear his reputation?'

'That's completely separate, mainly to do with taxation. The sale of The Tower was rushed. For various reasons, it became important later to know just what the state of the project was at the time of the sale, if certain major deliveries and transactions occurred before or after. Basically, Morning Star argue that Tony Teresi did a lot of foolish things, some of them fraudulent, before the sale. Some of those who used to work for him don't accept that, they say these transactions occurred after the sale.'

'Surely accountants can sort that kind of thing out objectively?'

'There's more subjectivity than you'd imagine, once you get to a certain level. It comes down to preparedness to grapple with an immensely complicated situation, sometimes going back years. Reputation becomes important, it can shape decisions on whether to pursue stories in the financial press, major tax audits, investigations by government watchdogs. Morning Star had a lot to gain by getting people to see things their way.'

Ferguson said he needed a glass of water. While he was away from the phone, Troy shook his hand, which was sore from all the writing. He hoped his notes would make sense when he reread them later in the morning. When Ferguson came back on the line, he asked him to describe what had happened on the night Margot died, after they had inspected the timber in the car park.

'I said I had to go. I had a dinner engagement that evening, and to be honest I was nervous about being on the site.'

Margot had said she wanted to go to an upper floor to check on something, but would show Ferguson back up to the ground floor first.

'We were by ourselves down there on the retail level, and we were going towards a stairwell when there was a noise from the end of this corridor, quite a long way from where we were, and two men appeared. We stopped and looked back. Margot wanted to talk to them.'

Troy was tempted to stop taking notes and just listen. At last they had a witness to the events of that night. At last.

'What did they look like?' he said.

'There wasn't a lot of light down there, but I could see two men, maybe Pakistani. I suppose they were the ones you and your sergeant encountered later on. They were carrying big bags but they put them down when they saw us, and I could hear them talking to each other in some other language.'

A memory of that night came back to Troy, the memory of his cold hand clasping the gun. He rubbed his forehead until it went away.

'Did they sound surprised?'

'More upset, but their voices were low.'

'Could you see their faces?'

After a pause, Ferguson said quickly, 'They were the men whose pictures you gave out. I saw them on the internet. So, Margot started to walk back towards them, they would have been about a hundred metres away.'

'Why'd she do that? Did she know them?'

'I don't know. She seemed surprised at first, then interested, something about them engaged her interest.'

'But she didn't tell you what?'

'No. I got nervous, we weren't supposed to be there, we were almost at the stairs. I told Margot I was going and she said, 'That's fine.' Then I thought maybe she knew them, maybe they had something to do with the security guards. She seemed completely confident about going over to talk to them. And being found there would have had different implications for her and me. So I just opened the door and left.'

'What happened when you got to the ground floor?'

'The security guard who'd shown us down was there, but no one else was about. I told him Margot had stopped to talk to some men, and then I left.'

'How did he react to what you told him?'

'I can't say. He was a very impassive person.'

Troy asked Ferguson if he'd seen Margot Teresi again.

After a pause, he said, 'I did, actually.' His voice changed. Suddenly it was hoarse. 'I walked down to the intersection of Norfolk and Castlereagh streets and crossed over. Then I stood for a bit under an awning, just thinking about the timber and the invoices she'd shown me, working through the implications. They were pretty heavy. After a while I realised I had to go. I remember seeing a police car coming up the street slowly, and a female police officer looking out at me through the rain. She probably wondered what I was doing just standing there. I took once last look up at The Tower and . . . I saw a body falling. It was Margot.'

My God, Troy thought. 'How could you be sure?'

'I just knew. Those men . . . I'd put them out of my mind. But there was something about them. I think I was really worried about her, and that was why I'd stopped on the corner. That sounds stupid. But it was one of those things you realise only after something happens.'

'Do you know where she fell from?'

'I saw her for only a few seconds. Then she, ah . . . she hit the police car.'

After the conversation with Ferguson finished, Troy couldn't get to sleep. He stood in the lounge room with the lights out, remembering the shooting, staring at the front yard. It was pitch-black but he watched it for so long that finally dawn came.

Ferguson had said he'd assumed the men he and Margot had seen were associated with Morning Star, and Margot had been killed because of her inquiries into the money laundering. As he'd seen the timber too, he feared for his own life, which was why he'd left the country with his wife the next day. They'd been planning a holiday anyway; they usually visited their daughter in New York once a year.

But he'd had a change of heart. Following the story on the internet, he'd realised that Margot's death probably had nothing to do with the money laundering: it was about the illegal workers. He'd agreed to give a formal interview to a member of the Australian Federal Police as soon as Troy could arrange for one to fly from the embassy in Washington to Chicago. Later that day, they'd have a copy of his formal signed statement. Like so much else the investigation had uncovered, it might do nothing to help identify the men who'd killed Margot. But it would end Henry Wu's career. He saw that it was after six and called McIver, arranging to meet him for breakfast.

They ate at a cafe around the corner from the station. McIver liked the big breakfast they served, and there were tables down the back where the two men could talk without being overheard. There was music playing and Troy recognised 'Water and Wine'. In the past few days he'd heard it several times.

'Would you turn it down, love?' McIver said to the waitress. 'I admire your taste, but I've got a bit of a head. Mr Bailey would understand.'

She smiled and went away to adjust the music.

'Mr Bailey?' said Troy.

McIver winced. 'I really need to lend you some CDs, don't I?'

Troy thought the sergeant seemed a little wired, his eyes bright and one foot tapping the floor as he looked around for another waitress. There was a slight smell of sour alcohol about him, but he was lively.

'Have you seen the papers?' he said. Coverage of yesterday's find at Waterloo had been extensive. 'Shocking picture of you. Lucky they didn't catch us coming out of the Iron Duke.'

'Good celebration last night?'

'You bet. Went on for a bit.'

While they waited for their food, Troy described his conversation with Des Ferguson. Their breakfast came and McIver began to eat his eggs, speaking between mouthfuls.

'We'd be thinking the two men were carrying something for the illegals—food, clean washing, whatever?'

'Yes.'

'Margot sees them, suspects something's wrong, thinks this might be a chance to get some dirt on Morning Star. She's a feisty girl so she approaches them for a chat, they panic and kill her. Apart from being involved in the labour racket, they might be illegal immigrants themselves. Then they panic some more and think it's really clever to make it look like a suicide. Maybe they talk to Bazzi about disposing of the body some other way and he tells them it's not on. Margot lands on a cop car, Bazzi shoots through, and they're stuck up there without a pass to the lift. So they start to walk down, blunder into us, and the rest is history. The shooter got out of the building through the tunnel.'

'So Wu had nothing to do with it,' said Troy.

'No, though he'd be glad Margot was dead. But the big thing is, from what Des told you, we know Wu would have been desperate to avoid any sort of inquiry at The Tower. So he wanted to get a hold over someone in the investigation, to get any influence he could, and you fell into his lap. You can see the thing had become toxic as far as he was concerned.'

'What about killing Asaad? And the bloke we found yesterday?'

'Someone is covering his trail. Maybe Sidorov—he's still a man of mystery.'

'Perhaps Wu and Sidorov are connected.'

'This is true.'

McIver called out to the waitress and ordered another mug of black coffee. He went on: 'Last night I talked to some mates and found something interesting. Wu has protection because someone tried to top him last year. Chinese bloke whose girlfriend disappeared, reckons she was having an affair with Wu.'

'Did we look into it?'

'The girl's gone, but there's absolutely no evidence. The complainant's very upset, made threats. Wu's had his own guard since then, at least one big bloke with him everywhere he goes. So any idea of pulling him off the street's a no-go.'

'We can't get to him?'

McIver scratched his chin. 'You still don't want to go to Kelly?'

'No.'

'Then we have to get creative. And it has to be soon.'

Troy nodded.

'I've got a mate.' McIver looked around the empty cafe and lowered his voice. 'He's going to send Wu a present by courier. Wu works on his boat most mornings, so it'll be delivered to the marina. It's a small inactive bomb, in a sort of shoebox.'

Troy stared at him.

'I stress the inactive part of that.'

'No.'

He couldn't believe it. A bomb.

McIver's eyes were gleaming. 'Three reasons this is a brilliant idea. One, it's easy to arrange the courier pickup so no one gets seen. Two, Wu'll get to see it, even if someone else opens it. And three, once he's seen it, he'll start thinking about bombs, under his car, on his boat. I defy any man not to.' He paused and smiled. 'I'd be pretty scared myself.'

'We can't do this.'

'The thing is to get inside his mind,' McIver said, as though he hadn't heard. 'The bloke might be a nutter, but he's still human.'

Troy leaned back in his chair. He was going to protest again, but realised the impulse came from habit only. He re-examined his feelings. A flash of anger shot through his head, and when it cleared he thought of his family. Why shouldn't Wu get a shock? You put together all the things the man had done, to himself and others, and something unusual was needed. Something extreme.

And so, he nodded. Couldn't quite believe he was agreeing with what McIver had proposed, but he was. He said, 'And then I get in touch somehow, let him know.'

'I wouldn't think that'll be necessary,' McIver said as the coffee came. 'By all accounts, he's an intelligent man.'

Troy said, 'What happens if he ignores it?'

'You're thinking too much—a great danger in your situation, if you don't mind me saying so. He will get the message. At the moment he's waiting to see how you react. With this, he'll know you're going to make trouble. Good chance he'll back off.'

Troy licked his lips and thought about it. Much could go wrong. But even if it did, he didn't see what he had to lose. He was desperate. The need to act, to do something, was intense. If this didn't happen, something else might. He had to manage his emotions here.

McIver stood up. 'When will you have Ferguson's statement from the feds?'

'Midday.'

He'd talked to someone in Washington and they'd sounded excited, happy to hop on a plane and work through the night.

'I'll arrange for us to meet Kelly at one, and brief her on the money laundering. It'll be out of our hands from there, over to the Fraud Squad. They might pick Wu up then, but I suspect they'll watch him for a few weeks, listen to his phones.' He put his good arm on the table and leaned forward, his eyes burning into Troy's. 'Which means we lose any chance of access, so it's got to be done now. Agree?'

There were no choices, not anymore. Troy nodded.

'Good,' McIver said, looking at his watch. 'The courier pickup was five minutes ago.'

Forty-three

Randall came down the last flight of stairs tentatively. On the whole he was feeling better than he should, at least in the physical sense, despite what he'd drunk yesterday, but he was beset by a familiar melancholy he knew would not lift until later in the day. He'd decided to walk up to Military Road to get some of the toxins out of his system. He'd catch a bus from there into the city. In his bag he had the DVD he'd started to watch on Sunday night, the one with Henry and the girl. He didn't know what to do with it, but he didn't want Kristin finding it if she made another raid on his apartment.

He looked around the corner, making sure the lobby was empty. The hotel had kicked him out, of course, and by the time the cops had released him the previous evening all he'd wanted to do was lie down and sleep for a long time in a familiar bed. A taxi had brought him home and he'd made it to the flat without seeing any of his neighbours.

The police charge was minor and with luck no one would hear about it. His email and mobile showed no messages from Taylor, so the excuse he'd given for being away yesterday afternoon seemed to have held. Have to give Angela a little something for her trouble. Things, he thought, were going all right. Another chapter in the saga of an interesting life. He opened the glass door and slipped outside, into the sunlight. As he paused the alcohol hit him, as though the hangover had been hiding in wait. Christ Almighty, he thought, as his mind clouded over and the pain went to work inside his skull.

At the bottom of the stairs he found himself face to face with two Chinese guys in suits standing in the sunshine. They must have been behind the sandstone wall, both of them had cigarettes in their hands. He'd seen one of them before, the one with the blue mac over his suit, fellow with the unlikely name.

'Mr Wu would like to see you now.'

The other one opened the door of a Lexus standing at the kerb. Randall tried to think about things but it was no good. No thoughts came.

'I've got to go to work,' he mumbled. 'I'll call him. Mr Smith, isn't it?'

'He say you not return his calls. Has urgent business.'

The fellows were on either side of him now, hustling him towards the car. But they hadn't actually touched him, it was possible he could just walk away. Of course he could, here on the street in Cremorne Point. People all around. He looked more carefully and there weren't any people, not right now.

Randall gazed up the street undecidedly. There was risk here, but to panic and walk away from Wu if there was no need would be the foolish end of everything. He needed to control his cowardice, and behave rationally. The men were standing still, watching him. They didn't seem to care what he did. Maybe . . . he was about to make a move when he heard the noise of the front door up the stairs opening. Mrs Crawley and her daughter were coming out. He so much did not want to talk to them. Bending his head, he slid into the back of the car. The door closed after him and he raised his hand to cover the side of his face, breathed in the nice smell of leather. Another lucky escape.

It was the thing about life, you had to keep moving. Otherwise you'd fall over.

It was not a long drive, and it took place entirely in silence. As they cruised through the familiar streets down to Mosman Bay, passing queues of schoolchildren and adults waiting at bus stops, Randall relaxed. Henry might have heard something, be annoyed at him for getting busted, but so what? The detective McIver, man who looked like an extra from a 1970s cop movie, had handled the whole thing nicely. Randall had been bad, and he'd been punished. He'd do the normal confession with Henry if necessary, have some coffee, maybe get a lift into town. The only problem was if Henry had something for him to do. He'd need to think about that. Henry's requests were starting to affect him emotionally. Which wasn't good for anyone.

At the marina he felt his mood improving from the smell of the sea and the warmth of the sunshine on his back. Life was good. Beneath the morning-after effects of the coke and the vodka, the fundamentals were sound. As he passed the sailing boats he remembered an offer to crew a boat in the next Sydney to Hobart, something he would surely do. Icing on the cake, really, just the thing before The Tower opened and he returned to Houston.

Henry was in the main cabin as usual, peering at the day's papers. The cops had caught the shooter, the second fellow involved in Teresi's murder. Sensational stuff. The man was dead, although they weren't saying how. Nothing there about him, Randall knew: he'd checked the online editions earlier. Wu smiled as he came on board, nodded to the two guys, who turned around and walked back towards the car park. Everything was sweet.

'You could have just called,' Randall said.

'I did.'

'Little problem at a party yesterday,' he said. Might as well come clean, Henry had his police contact after all. 'I was charged by the cops with possession of a very small amount, less than one gram, personal use only.'

'That's not going to do your future in security much good,' Wu said, fiddling with coffee cups. He didn't seem too fussed.

'No one will know,' Randall said. 'And after this job's finished, I don't plan to work in security again. I'm a builder.'

'Coffee?'

'Thanks.'

Wu handed over the cup and looked at the photos on the front page of both newspapers. Even the national daily, the *Australian*, had a picture of Troy and his sergeant, fighting their way through a crowd outside some awful big block of flats.

'A stupid man,' Wu said, stabbing Troy's face with a finger. 'Not emotionally intelligent. I don't see how he can be a policeman.' Reaching beneath the paper he pulled out a DVD case. The cover showed the city skyline and the words *Tower of Babel*. It must be an advance copy of the documentary on The Tower. Wu looked at it in disgust and threw it to the floor. The case cracked and the disc rolled away into a corner. He said, 'Your own problem is insignificant right now, wouldn't you say?'

Randall nodded, dumb with relief.

The intercom buzzed and Wu picked up the handset, listened intently for a moment. 'An unexpected guest,' he said. 'Could I ask you?' He pointed through the open door that led to the rest of the boat. 'Please take your coffee.'

'Sure.'

The fellow hadn't asked about the other DVD, the one of him and the woman, that was the main thing. Mustn't even know Randall had it. Nothing else really mattered. Randall saw a box sitting in opened wrapping paper on a side bench. 'Someone sent you a present?'

'A strange gift.' Wu smiled. 'Came by courier. It's a bomb.'

Randall laughed and ducked down the stairs into the main cabin. Not sure he'd heard correctly.

Wu closed the door behind him, and Randall looked around. He sat down in a leather armchair, the sun coming through one of the windows that ran along the side of the room. He found a copy of the *Spectator* and flicked through it, feeling the slight give of the boat as someone came aboard, the distant murmur of voices.

He must have fallen asleep, because suddenly he was awake and the engines were thrumming softly. The boat was moving. Randall got up and went to open the door, but it was locked.

'Henry?' he called. 'What's going on?'

Forty-four

Troy got to the office at 8.45 am. Gradually, other detectives arrived, some nursing heads from the night before. There was talk of a new strike force to handle the investigation into the shooter's death, and McIver was off arguing with Vella that it should stay part of Tailwind. A decision was due later in the day, maybe when they met Kelly.

By mid-morning, Troy estimated that Wu must have the parcel. You had to wonder how he'd respond. Everything depended on it, but of course they had no idea. Really they had little sense of the man at all, apart from what Randall had told McIver yesterday: a vicious psychotic gambler. Not quite the picture of Wu he'd painted for Troy.

Feeling jumpy, he checked his email every ten minutes, but there was nothing of interest. No more video footage of him being pleasured by a young Malaysian woman. At eleven he called Anna, who sounded like she was enjoying herself at playgroup. He wanted to dash home and check her email too, but he needed to be here all morning to establish an alibi of sorts. And anyway, he still didn't know her password. He should have kept looking when he'd found the Prozac that day, but he hadn't. The discovery of the drug had completely thrown him.

Later, he went out to walk around the block and buy a cup of coffee. As he came back, he saw Susan Conti and David Johnson, the big detective. They were standing in a doorway, kissing. He paused and then kept walking, and they disengaged and went towards the station, Conti saying something to Johnson and letting him go on ahead, slowing down to wait for Troy.

'I'm leaving tomorrow,' she said.

'You're a good detective.'

'I'd like to work in Homicide one day. If anything comes up.'

'I thought you weren't impressed with us.'

'That was before McIver came along. You've changed, too.'

He was being played, but it was pleasant. Conti was going places, you could tell. He wondered how Kelly and McIver felt about her father, if his reputation would hold her back.

'Call me if I can help,' he said.

'Thanks.'

Her eyes held his, disengaged with a smile, then she turned and went into the station.

After a moment he followed. Wu must have received the parcel by now.

Forty-five

The big boat was moving slowly, much more slowly than Randall's imagination, which was feverish, racing despite the fog from the alcohol. He wondered where Henry was taking him. Maybe it was out to sea, maybe he knew Randall had the DVD and had to be disposed of.

He wanted to let Henry know he had nothing to fear and got up and banged on the door, calling out to him, asking him to come and talk.

'Sean?'

It was Wu's voice, suddenly, on the other side of the door.

'Open up please,' he cried. 'Henry?'

'We're just going to the other side. I'm sorry to inconvenience you but there's someone you don't need to see. I'll unlock the door when he's off the boat. It's good to keep things separate that aren't meant to be together. You do understand that, Sean?'

Randall was damp with relief. 'I'll do anything,' he said, 'anything you want.'

'I do apologise, Sean. It's a busy day. Just relax.'

Randall walked back to the chair, the perspiration continuing in his armpits and on his brow because he knew from the man's voice something wasn't quite right. He pulled out his mobile and looked at it, and told himself he must be in no danger, because otherwise Henry would have taken it from him. Maybe there was nothing to fear.

No longer able to resist the tension of not knowing, he wrenched the DVD case from his backpack and slipped the disc into the player next to the big screen. CNN had been on all the time he'd been in the room, with the sound turned off. He found the remote and got the DVD on the screen, pushed fast-forward. He hoped it might not be as he remembered, but it was worse, you could see the Chinese woman on the bed was scared for her life, flinched back in horror, briefly her eyes met his, and then the hands with the wire went to her throat and Randall was stabbing at the remote with his thumb as though the button was some bug he had to kill. But the film didn't stop until he'd seen what happened to the woman's eyes, until she'd stopped writhing and had gone still.

He heard a noise and jumped around, but there was no one there. It would almost have been better if there had been, if someone had come through the door. Anyone. He desperately needed the company of another human being, the sound of a living voice. With fumbling fingers he extracted the DVD and dropped it down behind the bench running along one side of the room. Henry need never know he'd seen it. He turned the screen back on to CNN and sat down again, waiting for the shaking to stop, telling himself he'd never seen the DVD at all.

Looking out the window he saw the Harbour Bridge, and this gave him a boost of confidence. They weren't taking him out through the Heads at all. The shock was starting to fade now. Henry did not know he had the DVD, and here he was safe in the middle of the harbour, surrounded by the city. He could see several groups of people in grey overalls, climbing the big bridge's arch, and if he could see them, they could see him. Everything was sweet. But still, he needed the sound of a voice. He pulled out his phone and dialled Kristin, not knowing what he'd say when she answered.

Forty-six

The morning dragged on. Troy checked his email for something from the feds, read some more witness statements, trying to concentrate. People kept calling to talk about the stories in the media. Every fifteen minutes he used the internet to check his private email account. There was nothing there, nothing anywhere. He thought about Wu a lot. The faces of Anna and Matt kept coming into his mind, reminding him of why he was doing this. You have to keep your nerve, he told himself every few minutes. You have to stay strong. Finally, at midday, McIver came out of his office, jingling his keys in his left hand and looking cheerful.

'You got Ferguson's statement?'

'Not yet.'

He'd emailed the feds who were in Chicago, received no response. McIver said they'd keep their meeting with Kelly anyway. The information was too important to withhold any longer. 'Shall we dance?' he said.

'You heard anything?' said Troy, thinking about Wu.

'Not a word. Lunch is on me.'

They stopped at McDonalds on Victoria Road.

While they were eating, McIver said, 'I didn't tell Kelly what this was about. I think she'll be pleasantly surprised, it might persuade her to let us handle the shooter's death too.'

'Good.'

'It is good. This whole thing is good, it'll help you. I'm told she took that business with Stone very poorly. Reckons you talked to the media, thinks you've done it before.'

McIver chewed his burger.

'It was Randall,' Troy said.

'We know that. Can't tell her.'

Troy guessed Kelly was used to people lying to her. She must know there were all sorts of reasons people lied. He finished his orange juice, which was very sweet. On the whole he liked McDonalds, especially since they'd introduced their more substantial burgers. But their juice was too sweet.

They reached Parramatta at one o'clock. Kelly's door was closed and her staff officer explained she was taking an urgent call and had asked them to wait. A few minutes later, the officer's phone beeped, and he told them they could go in.

Kelly was wearing a pinstripe suit over a cream top and pearls. She didn't stand up when they came in, and told Troy to shut the door.

'Sorry to keep you waiting,' she said, not even trying to sound sincere. 'It looks like we'll be getting four positions filled next week.' Her eyes were gleaming.

'That's wonderful,' McIver said. 'Despite the staff freeze!'

The superintendent touched her hair girlishly. 'I think at the end of the day they had to concede we had some pretty good arguments.'

Taking a seat, McIver said, 'It'll make a big difference.'

'I hope so. Congratulations on the Teresi investigation.'

'Ma'am.'

'You have something else? A new witness?'

McIver ran through the state of the investigation. Kelly interrupted frequently with an unnecessary observation or question. Troy realised it was her way of asserting herself. One of his colleagues had once said Kelly would die if she had to remain silent for more than a few minutes.

'But now, a new witness,' McIver said. 'He doesn't identify the killer, but he's given us an amazing amount of stuff about The Tower. Turns out it's Sydney crime central.'

He looked at Troy, who began to speak. He talked for five minutes, and this time Kelly did not interrupt. She opened her mouth once but said nothing, as Troy's revelations overtook whatever it was she'd meant to say. Her reaction made him realise just how big this was. Ferguson's image came back to him: The Tower as a gigantic washing machine for dirty money. Millions of it.

When he had finished, Kelly took a deep breath, a huge gulp of air, and then grabbed her phone and talked rapidly to someone named Andrew. When she'd finished she said, 'Superintendent Stavros will join us in a moment.' The head of the Fraud Squad, where Stone had once allegedly worked.

While Kelly rang someone else, Troy wondered what had happened to Stone. He doubted the sergeant was involved in anything to do with fraud, which was kind of funny, now it was turning out to be right through The Tower. Kelly picked up the phone again, listened while she stared at the door. Troy looked at McIver but the sergeant ignored him. He was staring at Kelly with fascination.

She put the phone down and it rang immediately, causing Kelly to start. She grabbed it and said hello, listened again for a minute, her eyes moving from the door to McIver and then to Troy. You could tell something had happened, her composure was under stress. When the call ended, she put the phone down, slowly this time.

'There's been a development. Have you heard about the explosion on the harbour this morning?'

Troy wondered what she was talking about. The harbour was a long way from The Tower.

'Ma'am?' said McIver.

'That was Jim Collister, from the Wateries. Your man Henry Wu had a boat, a big boat. It blew up in the middle of the harbour a bit after nine this morning. It appears he was on it.'

For a moment no one spoke.

'Blew up?' Troy said, feeling numb.

'Exploded,' Kelly said a little impatiently. 'They don't know what happened, but it tore the thing apart, above the waterline. The hull's still floating. Someone at the marina saw Wu sailing out half an hour earlier.'

Troy didn't believe it. He wondered if it was some sort of trick, maybe a dream. The thing could not be true.

McIver asked if there were any bodies.

'Two dead, by the look of it. Only one body so far. They have Wu's coat with his wallet in it. Presumably he took it off while he was sailing. His briefcase too. They're searching, but Collister said it could be a while, maybe a few days. The tide's very strong there.' Sometimes the bodies of people who died in the harbour turned up kilometres away. Kelly was staring at them. 'The body they found . . . it's not Henry Wu.'

'Yes?'

'There's an ID pass. Sean Randall.'

'No!'

At first Troy thought he'd said it himself. But he was incapable of speech for the moment. It was McIver who had spoken, almost cried the word in protest, resolutely not looking at Troy. Kelly's eyes flicked from one to another as she registered this.

'Wu and Randall?' she said. No one said anything. Troy realised Kelly didn't know anything about Randall. Officially, he'd never been a major part of the investigation. She said, 'Speak to me.'

McIver looked at Troy, then turned to Kelly. He explained who Randall was, leaving the relationship with Wu out of it. He described Randall's arrest the day before, presenting it as just a normal drug bust, humorous even.

Kelly wasn't all that interested in Randall. 'Accidents do happen on boats,' she said. 'But the timing here . . .'

'Tailwind should look into it,' said McIver.

'Who would want to kill Wu?'

McIver spoke quickly: 'If Ferguson's right, and Wu was using The Tower for major scams, he must have been in business with some very unpleasant people. If they knew he was about to go down, maybe they wanted to sever the link to The Tower. Killing the shooter was part of that too.'

Troy nodded. He still felt dazed. But what McIver was saying made sense. At least, it would in some parallel universe where he hadn't been involved in sending a bomb to Henry Wu that morning.

An inactive bomb.

Kelly looked at him. 'You're not saying much, detective?'

'I'm . . . ah . . . trying to think how anyone could have known Wu was about to go down,' Troy said. 'How many people knew I was going to talk to Ferguson.'

McIver said, 'There's another possibility. Last year a Chinese national claimed his girlfriend had disappeared after going to see Wu at the casino. He told North Sydney detectives that Wu had killed her, but there was no evidence.'

Kelly looked interested. 'The complainant wasn't happy?'

'There were threats. Wu took to travelling with a security guard.'

Kelly thought about what he'd said and announced her decision. Other officers would look into Wu's death. McIver tried to argue with her. Troy could see it was useless. She was jotting down notes while she spoke, hardly listening to the sergeant at all. After a few minutes she looked up. 'The media on this,' she said, 'is going to be phenomenal.'

As McIver and Troy stood up to go, Stavros arrived and Kelly's phone rang at the same time. Troy just wanted to get out, go away and think about Randall's death. None of it made sense. Kelly put the phone down. 'Sean Randall's at the morgue,' she said. 'He has family here?'

Troy shook his head. 'There would be colleagues,' he said. 'At Warton.'

'Will you go? The body's not intact.'

Troy nodded and left the room. Behind him, Kelly was already talking to Stavros, telling McIver to stay, launching into the new and expanded story of The Tower.

*

In the morgue again. He did not want to be here, felt his body trying to twist and leave, and had to restrain his muscles as though they belonged to someone else. Soon the attendant was showing him a big screen with a picture of Randall's upper body on it. He could have asked to go into the other room and see the actual corpse, but there was no need. In his job he saw enough bodies.

Sean had never been quite right, he thought as he stared at his face on the screen. You could make out the features quite well. He stared at the half of his face not hidden by the sheet. The mouth and chin were intact, the silly little beard beneath the lower lip perfectly preserved. Troy had once read that sensualists had thick lips. Randall had been a sensualist, but his mouth looked about average. The nose and one of the eyes were visible, one side of the shaved skull. Looking at what was there, he thought there were few clues to the character of the man he'd known. It was all gone.

He left the room and worked his way through corridors that became warmer until he rejoined the living. It was the smell that got to you more than the temperature, though, and when he arrived back on the street he breathed deep, sucking in the city's tainted air gratefully. He thought about the bomb: everything came back to it, and it still made no sense at all. Logically he should accept the coincidence, that on the same day Henry Wu had received Troy's package, he'd been blown up by someone else entirely. But in his heart he couldn't accept it, because of his guilt, which was impossible to dismiss. Something must have gone wrong with the device. Mistakes happen. Terrible mistakes. Criminals tell you all the time: I was just trying to defend myself, I took the gun along just to scare them, I had no intention of using it.

But we don't accept these excuses from criminals, and Troy knew he couldn't accept it from himself. It had reached the point where he needed to tell someone what had happened; make a clean breast of things to Kelly, lift the load. The problem was McIver, there was no way he could implicate the sergeant. The man had tried to help him and now he must be protected. The secret would have to be kept forever.

THURSDAY

Forty-seven

Kelly's staff officer had called just after eleven, demanding his immediate presence. No reason had been given. McIver had been out and Troy rang him as soon as he got Kelly's message, but his phone was off. And then, when he reached Parramatta, McIver was waiting outside the office. Before they could talk, the staff officer called them straight in.

Kelly's eyes were alight with emotion. She looked tired compared with yesterday, and indicated for them to sit down while she walked up and down behind her desk. The newspapers were there, pictures of the hull of Wu's big boat on the front pages. Occasionally she looked at the two men, but for a while she said nothing, as though too agitated for speech. But finally the words came.

'I don't know where to start,' she said. 'You need to know police have been watching Henry Wu for some time. I'd guess you didn't know that. In fact, there's been an investigation in progress regarding some of the matters you told me about yes—'

'So—'

She put a hand up. 'Don't,' she yelled at McIver.

Surprised, Troy felt his back pushing against the chair. He struggled to keep his posture, the energy draining from him as he took in the implications of what she had just said. At the least, she must know about the delivery of the parcel to Wu's boat. A wave of shock hit him.

Kelly was staring at them both a little wildly, as though for a second she didn't know who they were. She grasped the top of her chair with both hands and looked down at the carpet for a moment. Then she said, 'Actually, let's start again. I need to talk to Nicholas alone. I have to be very careful about who knows what in all this. Sergeant, it's better for you not to be part of this conversation. So get out.'

'Just one thing,' McIver said quickly. 'I know you haven't suggested this, but I swear to you neither of us had anything to do with these deaths.'

McIver looked around the room and Troy knew what he was thinking. The place might be bugged. Kelly might be about to try to entrap Troy with some offer. These days, you could never tell what was going on with complete confidence. Not if you didn't trust the other people involved.

But Kelly was nodding, looking at him and nodding. 'It doesn't look good for you,' she said. 'But there is a reason to believe what you're saying. I can't go into the reason now, but for what it's worth I believe you.'

'Thank you, ma'am.'

'It's not worth much. Don't get your hopes up.'

Wearily the sergeant stood up, looking pale and drawn. Without a word he left the room, moving slowly. As he went out, he shut the door.

The sudden draining of all energy from McIver struck Troy, who was already confused by what had just been said.

Kelly said, 'You don't understand how close you are, how close to being thrown out of the police.' She held up a thumb and forefinger and examined the gap between them. It was necessary to stop her hand from trembling, and the effort seemed to calm her a little. 'We have to be very careful in this conversation, because it's important I don't learn some of the things you know, and vice versa. You understand?'

Troy shook his head. He had no idea what she was talking about.

Ignoring this, Kelly went on, 'I know what happened, on the boat. I know it was an accident but I also know about your involvement. There are other investigations going on.'

She looked at the door, and Troy knew she was talking about McIver. The realisation hit him hard, and for a while he resisted it, almost physically. He wondered if Mac knew, if that was why he'd gone so quietly. 'But—'

'I am not going to talk about it except to say this. Someone has to go from Homicide as a result of it. Do you understand? I'm not talking about a public scapegoat—for the good of the force we do not want that. But internally, I have to show certain powerful colleagues that action has been taken. For the good of the squad, after what you idiots have done.'

Troy sort of followed what she was saying. It didn't make perfect sense, but it was getting there.

Kelly said, 'That's been made clear to me. And I'm afraid it can't be McIver, not at this point in time.' He must have looked puzzled, because she repeated: 'Not at this point in time. I can't go into details.'

He shrugged; the last thing he wanted was to argue against Mac.

Then she completed her speech. 'So, it's going to be you.'

'Me?' he said.

Of course, after what she'd just said, he shouldn't be so surprised. But he was. It was a day for surprises.

'Why?' he said, and she just looked at him while his mind churned.

Maybe the investigation into McIver was responsible for Kelly's decision: they wanted to get more evidence on him. Or maybe it was just that Mac was more powerful. He'd been involved in stuff with others over the years, he knew things about too many people. Perhaps he had to be treated gently, whereas Troy was clean, he'd been a good officer. Which meant they could do what they liked with him. Troy looked at Kelly and noticed just how drawn she looked.

'I'm sorry,' he said. 'About all this.'

'If you go quietly, no one else will be hurt.'

He nodded, and this seemed to calm her. He saw then that she was not a bad person, just someone trying to do a good job of something that was not possible to do well.

She looked at one of the newspapers on her desk and said, 'Nicholas, this is a terrible thing. Can't you see what you've done?' She was genuinely upset. 'Why?' she said.

He told her about the prostitute. And the blackmail. She grew impatient as he spoke, as though none of this, the threat to his marriage, mattered. When he'd finished she shook her head.

'Why didn't you come to me? We could have sorted this out. These things happen.'

'I couldn't see what you could do to stop my wife receiving the video. Wu was crazy, it would have got out there.'

'Wu was under surveillance. We could have contained it.'

'I didn't know that.' He stood up and said, 'I'll apply for a transfer.'

She said nothing, still hoping for something more from him, but he had nothing more to give. After a while she understood this.

She said, 'Until then, you're on leave.'

'If you find the video, will you destroy it?'

She nodded. 'I'll do my best. That's a deal, Nick, a personal thing, between you and me. If you go quietly. Do you understand?'

He understood.

In a daze he walked down the corridor and into the large squad room, collecting a cardboard box as he went. When he reached his desk he sat down heavily. There was a small pile of phone messages in front of him. They'd been there yesterday but he hadn't had time to visit his desk. Now he picked them up and dropped them in the bin.

''S'up?' It was McIver.

'They had Wu under surveillance. She knows everything.'

'Rubbish.'

He told McIver what Kelly had said, how he was being ejected from the squad.

When he'd finished, the sergeant sat down and groaned. 'That means they know about my mate. They would have seen the courier, traced it back by now.'

Troy said, 'You're staying, though.'

'That's not right. Is something up?'

'I'd say so. But I don't know.'

McIver looked confused now, and Troy turned away so he didn't have to watch. He said, 'If I go quietly, she'll make sure if they find the film on Wu's computer, it'll be removed. My marriage is safe, which right now is all I want.' He'd do anything to achieve this. At least this business had clarified that.

'You deserve more.' McIver stood up. 'Don't go away.'

'No,' said Troy, grabbing his left shoulder and pushing him back down into his chair. 'She's very upset about the bomb. I really wouldn't push it.'

The sergeant was squirming in pain. 'Let go of my arm.'

'It's finished.'

Quit you like men, as the Bible put it. Be strong.

'This is stupid.'

Troy saw Kelly walk past the door of the squad room, hurrying down the corridor holding a briefcase. McIver tried to pull away again, but Troy held him down. He could tell that this was what McIver really wanted. Half a minute later they heard the sound of the lift arriving. Troy gave it a moment and then he let the sergeant go.

Once on the road, he headed west, his mind hardly functioning. He rolled down the car windows, as though this might relieve the pressure he was feeling, but of course nothing changed. At the Light Horse interchange he turned left, heading down the broad ribbon of the M7 to Campbelltown.

St Joseph's was cream brick and glass, a 1960s building from the days when the south-west had been identified as the city's new frontier. The presbytery, a standard bungalow made from the same bricks as the church, had bars on all its windows. Troy pressed the buzzer and waited in the bright sunlight.

It was a while before Luke answered the door. He was clean and shaved, wearing a T-shirt tucked into track pants. Blinking in the light, he seemed confused by Troy's arrival.

'No, come in,' he said, shaking hands. 'Lucky to catch me, I was taking a quick nap before the Mertons arrive. My three o'clock.' He closed the door behind Troy, locking it carefully. 'Pre-marriage counselling. They come, but they don't listen.'

Troy walked down the hall into the familiar lounge room, with its impersonal selection of furniture. It was neat and well-maintained—Luke had a part-time housekeeper—but sometimes it made Troy sad. The sort of room that needed to be filled with people. Right now it was dim, the blinds drawn, the red light of the answering machine blinking in a corner.

'Have a seat,' Luke said. 'I see you've sorted out the Teresi case. What can I do for you?'

Troy sat down on the sofa, and watched as Luke eased himself slowly into an armchair, as though sitting down was an effort. He was only sixty-six. Maybe sixty-seven. These days, that was nothing. But with the painkillers he was dopey, the edges of his character all blurred.

'Do for me?' Troy said, and laughed, the sound loud in the stillness of the room. 'I just felt like a chat.'

Luke nodded, and a moment later smiled.

'It's always good to talk, Nick,' he said. 'What do you want to talk about?'

Troy felt like standing up and leaving. But he'd come all this way, and the man was sick, he deserved some patience. So he began to talk, and as he went on it gathered force and he told Luke everything, about the photos and the blackmail and the attempt to frighten off Henry Wu with a fake bomb. A long shot, he said, but the only shot he had. And how it had all gone wrong and he'd been kicked out of the squad.

'Expelled from Eden,' he murmured at the end, because he was in a presbytery and that was about how it felt.

Luke had his eyes closed but opened them when Troy finished speaking. He said, in a low voice, 'Are you sorry for what you did with that whore?'

Troy winced. 'I wish I hadn't done it.'

Not the same thing, he knew, but Luke had already moved on, was shaking his head.

'Anna is everything, you understand that? I married you. Remember the day, the church here—'

He went on, gesturing in the direction of the church outside, but Troy wasn't listening anymore. It was the wrong church, they had been married in Maroubra.

'This bomb,' Troy said, interrupting him. 'My intention, it was quite different.'

Thinking of Randall. Thinking of all the men who'd used this argument to him in interview rooms: I didn't mean to do it. And now here he was, trying it out himself on God's representative on earth. God was merciful. But did he deserve mercy? That was why he was here.

'What I need to know—'

'Are you sorry for what you did with this woman?' Luke said, his eyes still closed. 'I won't call her a whore—who can see into her heart? And we all need God's mercy.'

'That's it—'

'You must repent in your heart. You're still a young man, and the temptations of the flesh—'

What is it about these guys and sex? Troy thought. It had always been a big deal with Luke. Maybe younger priests were different, less obsessive. But Luke was all he had. All he wanted.

He wondered how he could change the subject from sex, and said, 'I wanted to ask you about a situation involving a friend of mine.'

'Another cop?'

Troy nodded. He told Luke about the Perry case, leaving McIver's name out of it, explaining how a biker had been set up to be sent to jail. He kept it simple; Luke's eyelids were growing heavy, although he was obviously interested in the story.

When it was finished, the priest said, 'It was a sin. But a, sin committed for a reason like that, I would say there were extenuating circumstances. I don't know what the law would say, but that's what I would say, if I was hearing the man's confession. It was you, was it?'

'No. It wasn't me.'

Not long ago, he would have said with certainty he could never do a thing like that. But not anymore.

The priest had stopped talking and was just sitting there, his eyes still closed, very still. Troy waited patiently. After a while he looked at Luke more closely. He couldn't be dead, not just like that. Anxiously he stood up and took a step towards him. Then the old man's head tilted back and his mouth dropped half-open. Softly, he began to snore.

Back at City Central, he logged on and went straight to his email, hoping Ferguson's scanned statement would have come through from Chicago. There was nothing there, and he leaned back in his chair, looking around the busy room for McIver. He was in his office, talking to several detectives. They were taking notes.

A few people came up to Troy and told him they were sorry he was going. He could see they were confused that he was leaving, after such a week of triumph, but they seemed to accept the story about stress leave. Perhaps he should go with it too, see how he handled two weeks' compulsory holiday. Find out what else he had in his life. There was the new room on the back Anna had wanted for a long time, maybe he would look into what was required to become an owner-builder. Buy himself a good hammer.

Little came up and said a few words. He seemed to have some idea that things were not as they seemed, but Troy brushed aside his questions.

'You'll come out tonight?' Little said. 'We'll give you a send-off.'

'Tomorrow.'

Tonight he had to be with Anna. The way she'd been behaving lately, he knew he had to look after her.

His mobile rang. It was Sergeant Sally Offner, AFP Washington, calling from the Chicago Omni. Her portable scanner had broken and she was about to go to the hotel's business centre to send Ferguson's signed statement. 'There's something I thought you'd want to know as soon as.'

'Yes?' He should hand the call over to someone else, but he wanted to hear what she had to tell.

'We heard about the death of Henry Wu, so I told Ferguson. He hadn't heard. I thought it might help him open up, given he'd been so scared . . .'

'Did it?'

Offner paused. Then: 'He saw Wu at The Tower. That night.'

Troy sat up straight. 'Go on.'

'There were two other men there, as Ferguson told you. But Wu was with them. Margot Teresi had never been able to get to see him before, and she started to swear and told Ferguson to leave, she was going to grab the chance to talk to the man who'd destroyed her father.'

Troy stood up. He turned around and ran a hand through his hair, feeling the need to move. 'He's sure it was Wu?'

'They both recognised him, from photos. Margot said words to the effect, "That bastard, I'm going to have it out with him."'

'And then Ferguson left?'

'Gone before Margot reached the three men. He didn't think there was any chance of danger. Not with a man like that, a big executive. He just didn't want any part of it himself.'

Troy said nothing.

After half a minute, Offner said, 'You still there?'

'Yes.'

'But when Margot died, he knew Wu was involved and might come after him too, because he was there. From what he knew about the man, he didn't think the police could protect him. Seems a nervous type of bloke, said to say sorry.'

'What?'

'For not telling you. But now that Wu's dead, everything's changed.'

425

Troy thanked her and put down the phone. Feeling like he was sleepwalking, he stood up and went across the big room, bumping his leg against a desk as he went. The pain cleared his head, a little.

He leaned against the doorframe of McIver's office and said to the detectives inside, 'Give us a few minutes.'

McIver said, 'We're almost finished.'

'Whatever you're doing,' Troy said, 'this is more important.'

The detectives filed out and Troy closed the door after them. The room was stuffy. He told McIver what he'd just learned from Offner. When he finished, McIver let out a yell of joy. Everyone outside was looking at them, Troy could see them through the glass. He smiled, wishing he could share the full extent of McIver's emotion. But he did feel some happiness; after this news, Wu's death was even less difficult to regret.

'There you go,' McIver said. 'Explains why Ferguson left Margot with a couple of dodgy strangers.'

'That's been worrying you?'

'Gent of the old school, abandoning a young lass not much older than his daughter? You bet.'

Troy knew what he meant. 'I can't believe Wu would kill her. On the site.'

McIver looked around his desk, which was covered in papers and files. He gave up the search and waved a hand over the pile. 'I've just got some stuff from our embassy in Beijing. Henry Wu was seriously cracked. Saw his father beaten to death by a mob during the Cultural Revolution. When he swam across to Hong Kong, two of his group didn't make it. Sharks. Then there was what he had to do to succeed over there. He was involved with some very dodgy characters, still is. The bloke's lived more lives than most of us, and they've all been bad.'

Troy thought about it, how his life had crossed that of a man like Wu, who'd escaped the sharks and become one himself.

McIver said, 'Lots of business execs are violent men, it's why they're good at it. But they keep it under control. Wu's used to getting away with things, and that's not good for the soul.'

'And then he came here.'

To this city.

'Easy pickings.'

'It helps explain why he didn't want us talking to Ferguson,' Troy said. He shook his head, still taking it in. 'He knew he'd been seen there. He knew but still went ahead and had Margot killed. Imagine a man in his position, taking such a risk.'

'The risk was the whole point. The bloke was a nutter and a serious gambler.'

And now it's over, Troy told himself. He didn't say this to McIver, because he didn't feel like he deserved to be off the hook. But he was. You couldn't help being happy.

McIver was staring at the wall. Someone knocked at the door, looked through the glass panel next to it, and the sergeant shook his head at them, almost angrily. One of the things about being a cop was you found out things before others did. McIver wanted to relish their new knowledge a little longer.

But as well as the pleasure of secrecy, there's the pleasure of disclosure. After a minute's silence, he sighed and smiled at Troy. 'Let's go tell the troops. It's going to be another big night.'

That night, Anna came to him. When he arrived home and gave her the news about leaving the squad, she was delighted. Of course he couldn't tell her the real reason for what had happened, so he told her it was time for a change. She came over and kissed him, told him anyone who'd been through what he had deserved a break. He saw how other people would automatically see it this way too. It fitted in with the times, a familiar response to trouble. Fall to pieces. Walk away.

Maybe he had fallen to pieces. Maybe he should have walked away.

'Actually,' he said, stroking her hair, 'that's the official version but it's not the real one. I made a mistake. I did something to try to put pressure on a witness, and a man we're investigating found out and used it against me. Helen Kelly told me I had to go.'

She wasn't interested, put a hand on his cheek and told him he was a good man and she was sure he'd done the right thing. She said she was sorry he had to leave the squad, but he knew she wasn't.

Mary and Charles were arriving the next morning, and Anna was busy preparing an elaborate range of food. He looked after Matt for the next few hours, giving him a bath and feeding him amid the smells of curry and other spices. As he played with Matt he wondered if he could bear being another sort of cop now, or if it might be better to leave the job completely. Follow Ralph Dutton into the private sector. But of course he wouldn't.

Once Matt was in bed and they'd eaten, Anna kept working in the kitchen. Troy watched television for a while, not taking it in, and eventually turned the thing off. He went into the kitchen where Anna was washing up, put his hands on her shoulder and kissed her neck to say goodnight.

There was no acknowledgement of his presence; her arms were still working away on the pots in the water.

'Good night,' she said without turning.

He was almost asleep when she came into the room and slipped into the bed and cuddled up next to him. He put out a hand and realised with surprise she was naked, and then she pulled him to her and they began kissing. It was difficult at first, even after he realised this was going to be different from the other night, that this time she was not going to leave him. It was like making love to a stranger, but gradually he began to recognise the curves of her body, the once-familiar mounds and hollows. They made love and it went on and on. For a long time he forgot about everything that had happened.

It came to him as he lay next to her when it was finally over, holding her tightly: he had had to lose one part of himself in order to regain another. His job for his wife. The trade-off was cruel, he thought, running a finger down her back so that she giggled. You had to wonder if other people's lives were this complicated. But he had his family back, and the threat was gone. It was a good deal.

FRIDAY

Forty-eight

Troy bought a copy of the *Herald* and read it as he walked home from his run. The story about Henry Wu's boat was on page three today. There was a photo of Kelly and two homicide detectives at the Water Police premises, inspecting the hull. The paper said it now looked like the explosion had been deliberate. There were no suspects, and Wu's body had not yet been found. The journalist repeated the information about strong harbour tides. Adjacent to the main story was a box headlined TOWER OF DEATH, with some photos and descriptions: Margot Teresi, whose funeral was to be held today; the two men from level thirty-one; Andrew Asaad; Sean Randall; and Henry Wu. At least they hadn't found out about Jenny Finch.

Troy thought about Randall as he walked. Although he dealt in death every day, it was a long time since anyone he knew had died. It was absurd, but he felt a tiny sense of gratitude to Randall, despite all that had happened. Having sex with the prostitute had been a terrible mistake, but it had shaken things loose and this did not feel completely wrong.

His phone rang. It was Susan Conti, now back at Kings Cross station, saying she'd just had a call from Kristin Otto. Turned out the United Nations woman had had a fling with Randall.

'That's a coincidence.'

'Not really. He learned about the brothel where one of our illegals went that night and told her, so she muscled in on the Immigration investigation.'

'Making work for herself.'

'Probably. Anyway, Randall rang her the morning he died. Called her at home and left a message. She thinks he called her mobile but it was off, so he called her place and left a message there.'

'Which was?'

'Cryptic. If anything happens to me, to tell you a name: the *Ocean Pearl*.'

'Me?'

'"Detective Troy, The Tower fellow", is what he said. It's a freight ship—I checked.'

'That all?'

'Yes. She's been away, got back this morning and found the message. Called me because she had my number.'

'Thanks,' he said. He should tell her to call McIver, but that would mean explaining he was off the investigation. She mustn't have heard. 'I'll pass it on,' he said, and realised it was a poor choice of words.

She sounded a little puzzled as she said goodbye but he didn't care. He was thinking about last night, and Anna. It was what he had to do now, focus on the things that mattered, rebuild his life. He called McIver to give him Conti's piece of information, and got the voicemail. He asked Mac to call back.

When he got home, Anna was up and dressed, and kissed him on the mouth as he sat down for breakfast. He held her hand for a moment, but sensed her impatience to get away and continue with the preparations. Her parents' plane was landing in just over an hour.

'I thought we could take both cars to the airport,' he said as he ate. 'Then I can go to the building centre.'

When Anna met up with her parents, they always had a lot of family stuff to discuss. He'd found it was easier if he gave them some time. It would be a good chance to ask an expert about the extension project for the house.

They drove to the airport and met Charles and Mary at the Jetstar terminal. Charles was above average height, thin, balding and wore glasses. A retired accountant, he was a quick and eager man who'd always seemed to disapprove of Troy's choice of profession. Troy thought it must be something to do with the police Charles had known back in India, but he'd never been able to discuss it with him. The man was so polite it was difficult to tell what he really thought a lot of the time. Still, the two of them had come to enjoy each other's company. They spent a lot of their time together talking about cricket.

Mary was like Anna, a cheerful woman devoted to her three children. The others still lived in Brisbane, and it was her aim in life to get Anna to return. She and Troy usually argued about this once a day when they were together, but even so he got on with her well enough.

Troy walked slowly along the broad corridor at the terminal, carrying Matt and listening to the others chatting about Anna's brothers and their families. He rubbed noses with his boy, admiring his light brown skin. In this country, with all the sun, it was good skin to have. He told himself that despite the problems at work he had turned his life into something good. After all the bad times of his youth, it was something to be thankful for. You needed to remind yourself of these things. He remembered the feeling of Anna's body against his last night, and wondered if she would move back into their bed now. Of course she would. She'd have to, while her parents were staying. Maybe they'd make love again tonight.

He handed Matt over to Anna, and he and Charles recovered the bags and made their way to the cars, where Troy loaded the luggage into the back of Anna's station wagon. When they said goodbye she kissed him. It was a quick kiss, but not as quick as the ones he'd got used to; this was softer and longer. Just a bit, but enough. She got into the driver's seat and he waved them off. He watched her drive away and told himself he was going to make this work.

Forty-nine

When he got home at lunchtime, the driveway was empty. Maybe they'd all gone down to the beach, although Charles might have stayed behind, he wasn't exactly a beach person. He got out of the car slowly, still thinking about what he'd learned at the building centre. The front door was open and he went inside. There was no one there. He looked into Matt's room and couldn't see Charles and Mary's bags, which was strange. In the bathroom, he saw that Anna's toiletries were missing. Quickly he went to the bedroom where he saw a note in front of the computer.

Goodbye Nicholas, it read. *I know we've had our problems and I'm sorry about that, but this is not something I can live with. I can never trust you again. Anna.*

The screen of the computer was dark, but a flashing light told him it was on standby. He stabbed a key to reveal what was there, and winced as the image appeared.

It seemed much later but maybe it wasn't. He was standing outside, in the backyard, looking at the wall he would have to remove to add on the extra room. Realising this was stupid, he shook his head to try to clear it. Nothing changed.

He had to do something, talk to Anna. He tried to imagine what she must be feeling now, and knew he had to get in there, be part of it, before she shut him out forever. She was like that, one for decisions, final choices. For a brief moment it occurred to him that maybe it was for the best, that the marriage had not been working out, despite last night. But he pushed that away, almost panicking at the thought.

If only he'd told her himself, he'd have had more of a chance. Or maybe not. Last night was affecting the way he was seeing things now; it was necessary to remember the long drought before, the barrenness. It got to you, wore you down, you started to die early. He needed to remember these things or else this might drive him mad.

Inside, he found his phone and turned it on. There was a message from McIver but not from Anna. He called her and got her voicemail, begged her to call him. Then he left the house and got into the car, hardly aware of what he was doing. He put it into gear, surprised he was able to function—he didn't know if he'd closed the door of the house—and started to drive. He just drove, he had no idea where he was heading, except that he did, of course. When he came out of it after a while, he saw he was almost at the airport. Somewhere overhead, planes were moving across the sky. He almost missed the turnoff but made it, and realised he was more alert now but this was not a good thing. Everything had become more difficult; for a few seconds he even forgot how to operate the car and felt a sense of panic—was he driving on the right side of the road? It was as though he was drunk, but another part of him wasn't, and he reached the car park entrance telling himself he could do this, go inside the airport, find Anna, talk to her, about her, then Matt. She couldn't take his son away.

He parked carefully and sat in the car, watched a group of people walk by, a boy pushing the luggage trolley awkwardly while a man and woman tried to hug and kiss and walk at the same time, a teenage girl with them looking embarrassed but happy. Suddenly Troy wanted to weep, it seemed like the thing that needed to be done, but no tears came. He looked up at a plane that had just taken off and wondered if it was the one, or if they were still in the terminal. Realised it was the wrong time to talk to Anna. If he'd told her what was going on himself, he'd be owed something. But now, looking at it from her point of view . . . he was going in circles.

The terrifying thing was how quickly it all collapsed on you. You think there's a man, Nicholas Troy, who has a job and a family that are important to him, you could even say they're part of him. But who would have thought that if you took them away you'd find they were *all* of him, there was nothing left. Almost nothing, just a shell that looks like a man but is barely able to function. All of a sudden everything is questionable, even the past. Why had he married someone from another culture? For some reason Little's comments about Indians came to him, now of all times. And what he felt was ambiguity, followed by a wave of anguish. Maybe if he'd married someone more like himself? It was foolish, of course, but it was there and you had to wonder where it had come from. Troy clasped the steering wheel, wondered if he was capable of driving home.

And everything goes at once. His parents. No, they'd gone a long time ago. But their absence was pressing in on him now, when he could least deal with it, and this was strange. Everything was strange. Then there was Luke, who'd been one of his compass points. Now he was gone, too. With the sickness, Luke was definitely gone.

He wondered what was left inside him, what he still felt. If he was going to rebuild himself, he needed a place from which to start. He searched the emptiness, hoping to find an emotion. Henry Wu flashed through his mind a few times, and after a while he decided to think about Henry Wu. Good old Henry. The fact Anna had received the film, what did it mean? Troy thought about this for what seemed like a long time.

It could have been sent by an employee, or accomplice. But why would they? Troy sat there, thinking about what had happened, the strangeness of the explosion on the boat, the fact Wu's body had not been found. He took the pieces of what had happened apart and put them back together in different combinations, added the sending of the film this morning, and finally it came to him. 'You bastard,' he said, seeing it now. He looked out the window, angry that he'd missed it before. Wu was still alive.

It took a while to accept, but he saw that it was true, the man was out there somewhere, living and breathing. And he found the realisation invigorating, it gave him something to cling to. A tiny rock in the ocean where he had been drowning.

Troy turned on the engine and carefully drove out of the car park. He paid the fee, functioning well enough now he was thinking about Wu. The possibility of revenge was running hot inside, giving him strength. Wu was smart, he'd looked at the bomb and turned it from a threat into an opportunity. Get rid of Randall, who knew too much, fake his own death. Get away.

Troy realised he was the only one who knew this. The knowledge made him feel better, the pain inside him receded a little. He had to find the man who had destroyed his marriage, his family and his life. There was no one else to turn to. It was between the two of them now; the police structure he'd relied on for so long had let him down. Anyway, by sending the film to Anna when it was no longer necessary, Wu had made it personal, in the way things had been personal once upon a time, before Troy had become a cop. He could do this. Wu thought he was a fool, lacking in ingenuity and imagination. But Wu did not know him.

The man needed to be stopped, and Troy had the right to do this, he'd been given that right by what had been done to him. It came to him that he'd also been given the opportunity to right this wrong with Conti's phone call this morning, the divine accident of it, her not knowing he was off the investigation. And McIver being busy when he'd called to pass on the information. The name of the ship was a gift from fate. The ship on which Wu would leave Australia. Henry Wu had been given to him, to deal with. After only a few minutes, he saw how it could be done.

He stopped in Maroubra Junction and walked around, looking for a public phone. When he found one he rang Dutton and asked if he still needed the piece of information about the docks investigation. At first

Ralph said nothing, perhaps too surprised to speak, and then it poured out of him.

'Mate, oh mate, that is lovely. Oh I am extremely grateful. I don't want to rush things but any chance you could find out today?'

Troy had already found out. 'It has to be today,' he said.

'Okay. Good. Excellent.'

'You said you'd give me something in return. Anything.'

'Mate, of course, anything. Within reason of course.'

'I don't want much.'

'Well, have something, mate. That's how these things should work, you're doing me a big favour here. Take something for yourself.'

Troy waited for him to run down but he just ran on, almost babbling. Maybe he was in mild shock from the call.

'What I want,' Troy said, 'is a gun.'

There was silence.

'You've already got a gun. Mate?' Said in a pleading tone.

'Pistol, untraceable, at least twelve rounds.'

'Jesus—'

'And access to Rice Turner's. Tonight.'

More silence. Dutton had thought he was in charge, just a matter of building the emotional pressure on his old mate, whose conscience, at the end of the day, was expendable. Troy felt a surge of anger but pushed it down. Now he was in charge.

'Mate—'

'It has to be tonight.'

Troy knew Dutton was just making noises while he assimilated the offer.

'This dock thing, I got to tell you,' Dutton said. 'The gun's a possibility, but—jeez, you're not going to use it, are you?'

'No, but it has to be untraceable.'

'It's just—access to the wharf, their security's tight as.'

Troy looked at his watch. 'You haven't got much time.'

'What about we give you a car?' Dutton said. 'Something nice but not too flashy. Time you upgraded the Camry.'

Again the anger inside Troy, and he shifted on his feet. The anger was there but he was managing it. Just before he hung up he said, 'I'll come by your office at seven.'

Later he rang Anna's parents in Brisbane, figuring they'd be home by now. He rang them on their landline, wanting to confirm Anna was there. If she was unsure about things, she might have stayed in Sydney. But if she'd gone home to Brisbane, he knew it was over between them. Brisbane for her represented something apart from himself, an alternative.

Mary answered the phone and he asked to talk to his wife. She said Anna didn't want to speak to him.

'She's there?' he said.

He heard Mary saying something to someone else in the room; there was an emotional response. 'She says no. You should go away now, Nicholas.'

The phone went dead. Like his marriage.

Fifty

Margot Teresi's funeral was being held at the Northern Suburbs Crematorium and Troy got there quickly, taking the Harbour Tunnel and then the Lane Cove one. He'd been here several times before for work. This was not work, though. He wasn't sure what it was, but going to Margot's funeral felt like the right thing to be doing on this day.

When he arrived, the ceremony had begun and the car park was full. Troy parked along the driveway and walked up the red road, thinking he'd stand up the back for a few minutes, say a prayer for Margot, and leave before it was over. Up ahead another late arrival was walking along the road, a man in a black suit. He turned a corner and Troy couldn't see him anymore, but he thought he'd recognised the man. It was Damon Blake. As he approached the corner himself, he sensed a commotion.

It was a media scrum, surrounding the singer. Through the trees, Troy saw the Spanish-style crematorium building, and a large crowd outside one of the chapels. This must be Margot's service, and there was no way he was going to get inside. Speakers had been set up and he could just make out Dick Finch's voice, sounding tired but defiant.

A reporter in the pack surrounding Blake looked around and saw Troy. She grabbed the arm of one of the cameramen and they detached themselves and came towards him. He turned and walked away, ignoring her urgent cries as he rounded the corner and sped up. As he went, he passed more people in dark clothes. It was as though all of Sydney was coming to the funeral, like flies to the bloated face of the dead man they'd found on Tuesday.

Most of the people looked and some nodded as though they knew him. He realised they had recognised his face, despite the poor quality of the photographs in the newspapers. The human face is so distinctive that each of us is recognisable, even if caught crudely on CCTV. He thought of the grainy image of Mr A, and it struck him that however many more billions there will be, each of us will still be unique. This will be so even as new pairings, new diets, new circumstances and the whole wonder of DNA provide unlimited identities. There was something precious about this process, but it could throw up horrors too. And they had to be dealt with.

The people in their dark clothes were still coming towards him. He felt like telling them to go away. The chapel was full and there was no more room. Margot was dead. No one could ever know her now. It was too late.

'Detective?'

A man and a woman, late fifties, pausing in their haste. The man held his hand out. 'Peter Wood from Multiplex, we spoke on the phone.'

He looked like a good man, a normal sort of person. His face was open and smiling, and you could see that at heart he just wanted to be happy, and for you to be happy too. The thing about being a detective was that you could end up outside of things. Troy shook Wood's hand warmly and smiled at his wife. Someone had to protect these people, what they had.

Fifty-one

Dutton's office was in a prefabricated building on the edge of the airport. The corporation that ran the place these days was privately owned, and Troy had expected something grander: his own office at the squad had been in a solid modern building, and he'd always assumed the private sector did better in these matters. This place seemed strangely temporary, although it was all new and clean, and there were shrubs on the lawn outside the windows, just starting to come into flower. The door was locked, so Troy pushed the buzzer on the wall.

Dutton appeared quickly. 'Come through to my office,' he said, standing just inside the door in his shirtsleeves, looking Troy up and down. 'You okay?'

'Why wouldn't I be?'

Troy almost had to push him aside to get in. He looked around for a CCTV camera in the reception area, but realised he didn't care about that. He didn't care about anything anymore, except seeing this thing through.

'It's just,' Dutton said, closing the door behind him, 'this is a very unusual request. Two of them.'

'There is no explanation.'

'You don't want to talk? I was your best man, for Christ's sake.'

He turned and began to walk, as though he'd thought better of the idea the moment the words were out. Troy followed him down a corridor. The offices on either side were empty, this must be some sort of admin block. It looked like a sterile place to work, and Dutton receded even further in his mind. Some old friends, the time comes when you need to move on. But he needed to say something, Dutton was too nervous. One of the old stories should calm him down. 'Remember that guy who'd been shot? At Silverwater?'

He and Ralph had been young constables called to a report of shots being fired in a house. They'd found a man sitting against a wall with a bullet hole through his chest. He must have lived for a while after he'd been shot, because he'd placed a schooner glass against his stomach beneath the wound, to catch the blood coming out of his chest. When the constables had arrived, the man's hand was wrapped tightly around the glass.

They had often talked of it, but not today. Ralph nodded in acknow-ledgement of the memory and said, 'Sure you don't want to talk about why you want a gun?'

'Best you don't know. Believe me.'

He sounded like Kelly, but why not? Maybe this was how the world ran, on secrets and lies.

'I heard they've kicked you off the squad.'

'These things happen.'

'You'll be back. With your record.'

Funny, Troy thought. I can read this guy, yet Sean Randall fooled me completely. He came in by another door. One I left open.

'Don't worry,' he said as they turned into Dutton's office. 'I'm not going to gun down Kelly.'

It was a pleasant room, view of saplings through the window, art photos of airport terminals on the walls. Dutton went to the other side of the desk and stood in front of the chair there, staring at Troy again. Then he reached down and opened the top drawer, removed a paper bag with something inside it and passed it across to Troy.

'Should be familiar,' he said.

Troy took out the gun, a Glock, and checked it, opened the box of ammunition to make sure the contents matched. My weapon of choice, he thought: whenever I shoot someone.

He put the gun and the ammunition back in the bag and said thanks, asked about access to the dock.

Dutton sat down heavily, still staring at Troy. 'The war on terror,' he said slowly. 'Docks are difficult. I haven't worked out how to do this.'

Troy had.

'I'm here, right?' he said.

Dutton nodded reluctantly.

'I dropped by to talk about job opportunities in the security industry. Nothing definite, just a general discussion after recent events. Blowing off steam.'

'I see.'

'Now we're finished, I say I need to make a call, my battery's flat, so can I use the phone. You say sure, you're going to the toilet, give me some privacy for the call. When you get back, I'm gone.'

Dutton's eyes were still searching Troy's face for a clue. 'So that's it?'

'You work late tonight, until eleven. Maybe then, maybe later, you discover the pass you left in the pocket of your blazer over there—' he nodded at the blue jacket hanging on the wall, 'is gone.'

Dutton looked at the blazer. He sighed and said, 'Right.'

'Your pass is good for the dock?' Troy stood up. 'Let's do it.'

Dutton shrugged. 'One last thing.'

Troy came alert, wondering what it was. Dutton was staring at him, looking tense. Then he got it: he still had to fulfil his own part of the deal.

'Your man is clear,' he said. 'So's your wharf.'

Dutton smiled, more widely than Troy had ever seen him smile before. How what pleases us changes, he thought.

'No sign of any fake parts coming in through Rice Turner?' Dutton said, unnecessarily.

Troy shook his head and took the pass Dutton slid across the desk. The truth was, something illegal must be coming through the dock, if Henry Wu was linked to the *Ocean Pearl*, given the sort of man Wu was. But probably not spare parts.

Fifty-two

It was eight o'clock when Troy reached Botany. He parked at the end of the line of workers' vehicles outside the fence, and walked towards the main security entrance. He was wearing Dutton's baseball cap and, a hundred metres before the vehicle entrance, waved at the security office and turned to the pedestrian turnstile. Using the pass, he let himself in and strode confidently towards the first big pile of containers. It was all normal; Dutton had explained he'd been coming here at odd hours ever since his company had bought the business, checking things out. Ralph was probably very good at his job, Troy thought, as he walked around the corner of the five-container stack and stopped.

Even though it was dark, the place was alive. An enormous blue gantry was moving rapidly past, a thirty-metre-high steel frame that ran on rails and carried containers from one end of the dock to the other. A truck sped by on the far side of the gantry, moving even faster. The enormous corridor between stacks of containers was illuminated by powerful lamps and the place was as busy as daytime, a group of men crouched around a hole in the ground in the distance, more moving trucks visible in the gaps in the huge walls of containers. One day he would buy toy trucks like this for Matt, toy containers too. They would play with them on the lounge-room floor. Ha ha.

Troy oriented himself and headed towards the water, looking for the ships. He found two, being worked on by massive cranes, and he stood watching them for a while, getting a sense of what was going on, before he stepped out from the last row of containers and walked across the final expanse of tarmac. The ships were like gigantic cut-out shoe boxes, and the containers were stacked so high the vessels looked unstable. Their bridges, on top of the superstructure right up the back of the ships, were wide, on one ship even wider than the hull below, and were perched on top of what must look from the front like flat steel cliffs, against which the containers were piled to within a metre or so. Troy was slightly disturbed by the functionality of the vessels' design, so different to his idea of the shape of a boat or ship. He rubbed his eyes, dismissing the thought. He had to concentrate.

The cranes were much higher than the gantry he'd seen earlier, even taller than the ship's funnels. But it was the speed at which they worked that caught his attention, picking up a container with magnetic clamps at the end of steel cables, lifting, moving and placing the enormous box precisely and with no pause for thought. Again and again. Doing in a few minutes what had once taken fifty men half a day.

The hot liquid of revenge was in his brain, spurring him on. He walked along the side of the closest ship until he could see the name on the bow. *Perimbula IV*. Turning back, he went behind the row of containers and worked his way up to the other end of the dock, emerging at the second vessel. It was the *Ocean Pearl*.

This is for you, Sean, he said as he walked down to the point where the gangway led from the wharf up to an opening in the ship's side. And for Anna too. Some people had died and others lived on, with their worlds shattered. He climbed the gangway, seeing no one about. The monstrous crane was working only ten metres away from him, but the ship's crew must have been asleep or ashore. He reached the top and looked around, briefly casting a glance over the dock. All the activity went on, gigantic machines hummed and moved, the big steel boxes passed through the air, hovering briefly high above the ground. Troy looked straight down and saw glints of light on the narrow strip of water between the dock and the side of the ship.

He stepped inside, into an enclosed steel space, and walked down a corridor of painted steel. As he penetrated the ship's interior it started to look more like a building on land, with carpet and lined walls. He climbed a stairway, wondering when he'd meet someone. The place didn't seem as big as it had looked from the outside.

Coming to a short dead-end corridor lined with doors, he began to open them. They were bedrooms, bigger than he'd expected, most empty. A man was sleeping in one, a Chinese guy, but in the light from the corridor Troy could see he wasn't Henry Wu.

Returning to the beginning of the corridor, Troy wondered where to go next. Someone appeared at the end of the next corridor and came towards him, an old Chinese man in a blue work shirt and trousers, wearing sandals. He smiled vaguely at Troy, and went to walk by.

'Mr Wu?' Troy said.

The man pointed behind him and upwards, and kept walking. Troy looked in the direction he'd come from and turned back to the man, but he'd disappeared.

'Sent by God,' Troy said into the silence.

But he hadn't been of course. The man had just been going to one of the bedrooms.

Matt would be asleep in his cot by now, up in Brisbane. Anna would be hunched over a cup of tea in her parents' kitchen. He tried to imagine her pain, but on top of his own it was unbearable. Best to concentrate on the job at hand. He went to the end of the main corridor, turned right and found another stairway. A murmur of sound was coming from somewhere. When he reached the top he found a large room, with a big plasma screen and lounge chairs scattered around. There was one man there, watching some sort of game show on the television. When the man heard Troy he turned around and an expression of surprise flickered across his face. It was Henry Wu.

Too easy, Troy thought. They've made it easy for you so you'll be confused. But it won't work because I have the anger, and it is just too strong. He took the gun out from his holster and pointed it.

Wu's attention had gone back to the screen. Apparently.

'They don't see that boxes three and five have a twenty per cent better chance of being the right one,' he said. He picked up the remote control and clicked off the television.

'My wife got the film,' Troy said. 'She's left me.'

Wu nodded. 'I'm sorry,' he said, his voice warm with concern, but not too warm. 'I programmed my computer to send it if anything happened to me, if I didn't check in after twenty-four hours. In the event, I had to leave in a hurry, there was no time to reprogram.'

He didn't seem at all anxious. There was even a certain dignity to him. He's a fine-looking man, Troy thought, and a fine-speaking one. You have to remember what lies behind that face. The misery he's caused.

'I was just a cop, doing my job.'

Get on with it, he told himself. Wu looked at the gun, then into Troy's eyes. 'You still are, I hope. Anna will come back to you.'

He exuded willpower, charisma. Even now.

'Why Randall?'

'An accident. He shouldn't have been on the boat. Your present scared me. Sean was a friend of mine.'

Troy steadied his gun.

Wu said, 'Think of Matt.'

Troy felt a stab of anger. This man, this creature, did not know him. Wondering how Wu knew the name of his son, he said, 'I am.'

'If you do this, one day he'll know about it. What you've done.'

Troy breathed deeply, telling himself Wu could not take this away from him. Not now. Important not to allow the man to play with his mind. He lifted the gun to eye level. It was not the best way to shoot, but it blocked the sight of Wu's face.

'You're clever,' he said.

Once before, things had frozen for him, but that was after he'd killed a man, not before. For half a minute he stood there, thinking to

449

relish the feeling, but he waited too long. He found he was no longer in the moment but able to look in on it, in on himself. There was a great stillness, and then the moment had passed.

He lowered the gun. The meaning of the action still hung in the balance.

'You haven't won,' he said. Then, really seeing it now, thank God: 'You've lost.'

He turned around, needing to get away, and someone punched him in the face.

It was a big man, lots of muscles and tattoos, and as Troy went down the man wrenched the gun from his grip and threw it over to Wu. The man stomped on his groin and Troy jerked away just before the blow landed, so it hit his inner thigh instead. He pushed up from the floor and the man went to kick him in the head, but the blow missed and struck his shoulder. Troy spun awkwardly, and went down again.

'Quickly,' he heard Wu say.

The man had him up now, and everything was moving fast, he was dragging him down the stairs. At the bottom, he threw Troy against a wall and roughly ran his hands over him, searching for a weapon. When he'd finished, he grunted to Wu and pushed Troy to the floor.

Looking up, Troy saw Wu was holding a piece of wire between his hands, excited like a young kid. He pulled it tight: the wire must be attached to small handles at either end.

'The hold,' Wu said, 'we'll do it there.'

Troy tried to get up but the man pushed him down easily now. The guy was not all that quick, but he was strong, and Troy was winded and sore. He thought of Margot Teresi.

Looking up at Wu, he said, 'Did you kill her yourself?'

Ignoring him, Wu said, 'Let's go,' and the big man reached down for him. Troy struggled but he was too dizzy from the blow to the side of his head when he'd hit the wall. He was recovering his wits, but not quickly enough. The man got him up, his arms wrapped around Troy's own arms and chest. Now he was on his feet again, Troy saw Wu was watching the fight with intense interest.

'Move aside,' a voice said.

Who'd spoken? Troy realised it was Wu, but his voice had changed. It seemed to be in a higher pitch than before, definitely more excited.

'Get away,' Wu cried to the big man, impatiently waving his hands with the wire in Troy's direction. As though he couldn't wait.

Troy wrenched himself sideways and the big man spun backwards, slammed into the wall. Then he let go and Troy, disoriented again, began to fall to the floor. The man stepped away and as Troy hit the ground he saw Wu move towards him.

Then someone yelled out, the voice loud in the enclosed space. Troy didn't hear what was said, but it was new voice, one he recognised. There was a scream from someone else, a high-pitched yell of rage that went beyond the physical and into some other realm of frustration and anger. Halfway to his feet now, Troy saw that Wu was grappling with a man, and a moment later he saw it was McIver. He had no idea where he'd come from. Another man was behind them, trying to get around the entwined bodies in the narrow corridor. It was Dutton.

'Police,' McIver rasped out, sounding breathless.

The big man stopped, turned, and ran back past Troy. Dutton came over and leaned down to help Troy up. Beyond him, Troy saw Wu shake himself free of McIver. Troy called out and Dutton turned to see what was happening. He started to move towards Wu, who produced Troy's Glock and fired. Dutton bent over and fell to the floor, clutching his leg. McIver grabbed for Wu's arm and wrestled the gun off him, doing most of the work with his right arm. Wu looked at the gun in McIver's hand for a split second, then turned and ran. Troy went after him, past McIver, who was panting heavily, around the corner and up some stairs.

He came out onto the ship's bridge, a long room lined with large windows along one side. At either end, steel doors with large glass panes opened onto balconies that jutted out over the side of the ship. As Troy cleared the top step he was disoriented for a moment by what he saw through the windows. There was a red container there, an enormous box over ten metres long, just outside the glass, blocking the view entirely. How could they operate the ship if the containers were stacked so high?

But then it began to move to the right, and Troy realised it was in the process of being lifted out of the hold by the crane, and was dangling in space as it was pulled horizontally towards the dock.

At the far right of the bridge, Wu was pulling at the heavy door, getting it open, stepping over the little wall at its foot designed to keep the water out, moving onto the balcony. McIver came banging up the stairs, his face red, and Troy went after Wu, the sergeant close behind. He started to pull open the door and saw Wu checking out the small white deck, which was surrounded by a steel wall about chest-high, realising there was no other exit.

Troy got one foot through the door and turned to let McIver through.

'No!' the sergeant yelled, looking past Troy at Wu.

Troy turned.

The lights up here were almost as bright as below, and he could see every detail of what happened. Wu had already got up onto the wall and was standing on its flat top, his arms half-extended to balance himself. His attention was focused on the big red container moving past him, a little below his level and now only a few metres away, maybe less. As McIver came through the doorway, Wu jumped, his arms outstretched and high.

If he'd had a run-up he might have made it, but as it was, he didn't even touch the container, which continued to move on its way while Wu fell through the air, his hands clutching at emptiness. Then he was out of Troy's line of sight. Troy took a few steps forward, but stopped before he reached the wall.

McIver came past and peered over. Troy saw his shoulders jerk, and a few seconds later he turned around.

'Long way down,' he said.

Troy walked over and looked at the tarmac far below. The way the body had landed, it was as though Wu had been slammed sideways into a wall while running. You could see the blood on the concrete from up here.

A man came walking quickly towards the body, a worker in a hard hat and a jacket with reflective patches on. When he was about ten metres away he slowed down and paused. Then he turned and walked back in the direction he'd come from, more slowly now.

Troy went over to McIver, who was leaning against the door, still getting his breath back. There was a roaring in his ears.

McIver said, 'We need to get back to Ralph.'

'Ralph?'

'He called me,' said McIver.

'We had a deal.'

'He broke the deal. He was concerned about you.'

Troy felt like he was waking up, waking up from a sleep of anger. He didn't think you could compare anger with sleep, but that was how it had been. Thick and heavy.

'I didn't shoot Wu,' he said.

'No,' said McIver. 'He fell.'

'I mean, I could have shot him before. But I didn't.'

'You made the right choice.'

Troy wasn't so sure: it felt more like some force had stepped in and saved him. But the important thing was how it had turned out.

'What happened to your arm?' he said, noticing that the sleeve on McIver's forearm was ripped and bloody.

'He had a garrotte,' said McIver. 'Tried to get it over my head and I used the arm to protect myself. Quite a scrape.'

Troy thought back to the man lying on the bed with his swollen face among the flies at Waterloo. The man who'd been strangled. He took a deep breath and nodded.

'There's something else,' McIver said, as Troy wrenched open the heavy door and they went inside. 'The Wateries took some DNA from Wu's house to match with any body parts they recovered from the harbour. When the lab processed it, they ran the results though the computer, and got a match.'

Troy shook his head, seeing what was coming.

'Margot Teresi,' he said.

McIver nodded. 'The skin scrapings beneath her fingernails.'

So, Troy thought, it is finished. This, at least.

They could hear a siren, somewhere outside the docks.

McIver said, 'We'd better go see if Ralph's okay. He got shot in the leg.' He paused at the top of the stairs. 'By the way, he told me on the way over that Anna's staying at his place. He didn't want me to tell you.'

Troy felt a stab of joy. 'They're not in Brisbane?'

'Apparently not.'

'I'll go and see them.'

He wondered what would happen. He had no idea.

McIver looked at him and nodded. 'I would,' he said.

THANKS

It takes more people to write a novel than I ever would have imagined. Among those I want to thank are: Robert Alison, John Baffsky, Trevor Bailey, Margaret Connolly, Frank Devine, Lauren Finger, Carl Harrison-Ford, Dave Higgon, Ali Lavau, Gail MacCallum, Graham McCarter, Jane Palfreyman, Alex Snellgrove and Carla Tomadini.

The song 'Water and Wine' mentioned in the novel was written by Paul Comrie-Thomson and recorded, but never released, by The Saints. I am grateful to them for permission to use it as the book's theme song, and they retain the relevant copyrights. To hear the song, and to learn more about Nicholas Troy and Jon McIver, visit www.cityofsharks.com